PREDATOR

RUSSELL C. CONNOR

PRAISE FOR RUSSELL C. CONNOR'S WORK:

GOOD NEIGHBORS

"Connor's ability to richly develop each character and plot thread is fascinating even when the horror is reserved... the constricting pressure as the dread piles on makes this book hard to put down and even harder to go to sleep after reading. This is a great novel..."
-David J. Sharp, *Horror Underground*

SECOND UNIT

"Intricately plotted and vividly layered with suspense, emotional intensity and strategic violence."
-Michael Price, *Fort Worth Business Press*

"Drips with eeriness...an enjoyable book by a promising author."
-Kyle White, *The Harrow Fantasy and Horror Journal*

FINDING MISERY

"Major-league action, car chases, subterfuge, plot twists, with a smear of rough sex on top. Sublime."
-Arianne "Tex" Thompson, author of *Medicine for the Dead* and *One Night in Sixes*

THE JACKAL MAN

"Connor delivers a brisk, action-packed tale that explores the dark forests of the human--and inhuman--heart. Sure to thrill creature fans everywhere."
-Scott Nicholson, author of *They Hunger* and *The Red Church*

Also by Russell C. Connor

Novels
Race the Night*
The Jackal Man
Whitney
Finding Misery*
Sargasso*
Good Neighbors
Between
Predator

Collections
Howling Days*
Killing Time*

The Box Office of Terror Trilogy
Second Unit*
Director's Cut

The Dark Filament Ephemeris
Volume I: Through the Deep Forest
Volume II: On the Shores of Tay-ho
Volume III: Sands of the Prophet
Volume IV: The Halls of Moambati

eBook Format
Outside the Lines*
Dark World
Talent Scout
Endless
Mr. Buggins

*Indicates Dark Filament Ephemeris supplementary connection

When the key rattles in the lock, Kerry doesn't even bother moving. It's easy for your ears to play tricks on you in here. Once he could've sworn the whoosh of the air-conditioner through the ceiling vent was speaking to him for an entire day, a ghost who murmured about all the unfulfilled promises of his youth. But when the heavy steel door finally squalls open, he closes his book, sits up on the bunk, and blinks at the stark daylight that floods into his cell from the corridor.

Pedernales stands in the doorway, his guard uniform so starched and crisp it's a wonder the collar doesn't slice his throat. One side of his lips stretches into a smirk beneath his wiry mustache.

"Wakey wakey, Denton. Get your shoes on and let's go."

Kerry opens his mouth to speak, but all that comes out is a rusted squawk from the depths of his throat. Not surprising; he has no way to tell the date in here, but, if he counted his meals accurately, this is the first time he's conversed with another human being in three months. Or even used his voice, for that matter. Kerry has noticed that the cons who talk to themselves while in solitary tend not to lose the habit when they come back out. He swallows and tries again. "Is it…is it April 14th?"

"Ha, you wish!" Pedernales walks into the four-by-ten cell and snatches the worn canvas slippers from the top of the piss-stained toilet in the corner. He throws them on the floor at Kerry's feet. "You got another four days before you're a free man. Now c'mon, I ain't got all day to jack around with your sorry ass."

Kerry swings his legs off the bunk, resting his feet on top of the shoes. Everything is happening too fast, like a sped-up recording. "Where are we going?"

Pedernales' smile grows even wider. The anticipation in it is unmistakable. "You got a visitor."

"Since when does solitary get visitation?"

And just like, the grin vanishes. The guard is silent for a handful of seconds, long enough for Kerry to realize he's probably asked one question too many. Then he lunges across the cell, grabs Kerry by the scruff of the neck, and forces his head down until his nose is between his knees.

"I don't give a flying fuck what you think about it, pervert," he snarls in Kerry's ear. *Pervert*; an oldie but a goodie. Kerry has been called a lot worse during his stay in Wayne Clifford State Penitentiary, but this one never stops stinging. "Just because you're outta here next week don't mean you can get an attitude. Until you walk through those big metal gates, I still own your sick ass. You got that, pervert?"

The hand on Kerry's neck squeezes. Tears spring to his eyes. "Yes sir, yes sir, I got it."

"Good. Cause I can march down to the warden right now, tell him you attacked me. Get your stay extended another month. Or hell, I'll have you transferred back to gen pop, let them close that smart mouth. You developed quite a little fan club while you hid in here. I'm sure they'd *love* another chance to put you outta your misery." After one final squeeze, he releases Kerry and steps away. "Now get your fucking shoes on. I'm not gonna tell you again."

Kerry gets the fucking shoes on. His mind is slowly cycling up, shaking off the lethargy. The sensation is like breaching the surface of the water after a long time submerged. He keeps trying to figure who would be important enough to get him pulled out of solitary for a visit. The most likely candidate is his lawyer, with more details about his release.

Except there was that smile. That devious, I've-got-a-surprise-for-you smirk on Pedernales' face. It lights an uneasy fire in Kerry's stomach.

He stands. The guard slaps a pair of handcuffs onto his wrists—closing them tight enough to pinch—then gives him a shove through the doorway and out into the long corridor lined with solitary confinement cells. The same cells where Kerry Denton has spent the majority of the last four years of his life, from age 20 to age 24, staring at the same plain white walls, taking his food through a slot in the door, reading whatever books he can get his hands on, and wondering how the fuck his life took such a nosedive.

More sunlight pours through dingy skylights in the hallway outside solitary. After three months in his drafty cell, it almost blinds Kerry. But god, is it beautiful. Each individual ray seems like a miracle. As a teenager, he used to put heavy black curtains over his windows to keep the sun out so he could sleep all day, like some sort of vampire. Jesus, what a stupid, naïve kid that person had been. He would give anything to stand in that sunlight, drink it in, feel the warmth on his skin, but Pedernales forces him to keep moving along the concourse toward A Block.

They could keep going through these clean, bright hallways, detouring around the main prison complex to the administration wing. Might take a few extra minutes, but at least it would be a peaceful stroll. Kerry isn't surprised, however, when Pedernales unlocks the outer gate into the Block instead.

It appears they will be taking the short cut through gen pop.

The air in the Block is muggy, thick with the stench of sweat and old food. And semen. Two hundred men fucking one another or masturbating into their filthy sheets every night amasses a sweet, cloying funk that always reminds Kerry of copper pennies and overly ripe pears. These hallways are not bright and antiseptic, like those that the prison executives get to traverse; they are gray and dim covered in a layer of grime that those on janitorial duty can never quite scrub away.

His and Pedernales' footsteps echo in the dank corridor. Kerry hopes they might slip through unnoticed, but the catcalls begin before they even reach the first run of cells. No doubt his fellow convicts have been tipped off in advance by his escort.

"Lookin pretty there, Denton!"

"You ain't never gonna see the outside of these walls, you twisted piece a shit!"

"C'mon in here and let me show you how it feels to get raped, boy!"

"You're a *dead* man, motherfucker!"

The hoots and shouts all blend together into one unintelligible roar of noise, like the cheers at his basketball games back in high school, except nowhere near as pleasant. They are lined up at the wall of the common area too, pounding on the glass, thrusting their hips at the barrier, shouting more threats. Some of the faces are familiar, many are new, all of them united in their hatred. He keeps his head up and walks, careful not to make eye contact. Behind him, Pedernales snickers.

Kerry has been in and out of general population throughout his entire sentence. Each time he tried to remain as unobtrusive as possible, to quietly serve his time. But when someone came looking for trouble—which was often—he went for blood. It was either that or invite far worse, as he'd witnessed several other men with similar convictions do. He got slapped back into solitary for a couple of weeks after each of these scuffles (for his own protection, of course), where the seconds dragged but at least he didn't have to look over his shoulder. For a guy that had never been in a fight before and weighed 170 pounds on a six foot frame, these brawls went surprisingly well, resulting in bruises, crushed knuckles, and one broken bone, but they were never deadly.

That is, until his parole got approved, and those who'd contented themselves with making his life hell saw their last chance to dole out prison punishment. The very next day, two Latin Kings tried to shiv him in the common room, one of them screaming about how Kerry would never touch *his* kids, the declaration especially strange since Kerry didn't even know the guy's name, much less who his children were. He only managed to survive by holding them off with a chair long enough for the guards to get there. Thank god Pedernales hadn't been on duty, or he probably would've let them do it.

Both of Kerry's assailants were handed two weeks of extra bathroom duty for the attempted murder, while the warden decided it would be safer for him to serve out the remainder of his sentence in solitary, his longest stretch by far.

At last they reach the end of the Block, and the shame parade ends. The corridor beyond goes through two security checkpoints and then into the administration wing, where visitations take place. Pedernales leads him to the check-in desk, where another guard shoves a clipboard with a sign-in sheet at him.

Kerry picks up the pen with his shackled left hand. He puts it to paper, but the tube instantly squirts through the space that used to be occupied by the upper half of his fourth finger and tumbles down the other side of the desk.

"Sorry," Kerry says with a grimace.

The guard grunts in annoyance, then bends over, retrieves the pen, and slaps it back down on the counter. Kerry picks it up and holds it pinched between his thumb and first two fingers. The awkward grip makes his writing illegible, but this is the only way he can compensate for the shortened digit. He scribbles his name, then Pedernales yanks him away from the desk by his collar and drags him through the doorway to the visitation stalls.

They head down the row, passing behind other cons and their visitors. The eyes of the latter follow Kerry from the opposite side of the plexiglass partition as he walks by, a weary, dull glimmer reflected in each of them. They're the eyes of people forced to be here because of obligation, but would rather be anywhere else. He remembers his mother and father having that same look, the few times they came to see him.

Then they reach the sixth stall and Pedernales forces him down onto the stool, then claps him on the shoulder and whispers, "Have fun, scumbag," before retreating.

Kerry looks at the man sitting across from him. A shaky gasp escapes his lips.

He hasn't seen the face on the other side of the glass since his sentencing, when it fixed him with a baleful, triumphant glare as he walked out of the courtroom to begin his new life as a guest of the Texas penal system. Except in his dreams, that is; this face has a prominent, recurring role in those.

Though their last encounter was only four years ago, the man sitting across from him appears to have aged at least thirty. The powerful mane of brown hair has thinned and taken on a drab shade of gray at the temples, his skin looks pale and rough and crowded with wrinkles, and heavy pockets of dark flesh drag at his lower eyelids.

But his eyes...they're still the same. Blazing with hatred and fixed on Kerry with unflinching intensity.

Kerry reaches out with his cuffed hands—the maimed left one curled into a tight ball, the stump of his finger suddenly throbbing—and flips the switch on his side of the partition that turns on the two-way speakers.

"Mr. MacCallum," he says, his voice barely above a whisper. That name opens a deep wellspring of memory inside him, full of emotions so vivid they make his whole body go frigid. The man says nothing, just continues to stare at him. Words come out in a stumbling rush from Kerry's mouth. "I-I heard about...what happened. Please...please tell me, did she say anything before...? Please, I have to know."

Still the man doesn't speak, but his hands turn white at the knuckles where they grip the edge of the table on his side of the glass.

Black, crushing grief washes over Kerry, grief that could never be expressed behind these cold, concrete walls in front of his fellow inmates, grief that grew in its neglect and now threatens to swallow him whole. "I'm sorry," he chokes out. "I'm so sorry. I never wanted this. Tell me you at least believe that much."

On the other side of the plexiglass partition, Robert Mac-Callum—'Rob Mac' to his many friends and business associates in the construction industry—finally opens his mouth to speak.

"Four years isn't enough for what you did to my daughter," he says through clenched teeth. His eyes never move from Kerry's, never so much as jitter. "That's why I'm going to make it my mission to ruin you when you get out of this place. And then, after I've made your life as miserable as you've made mine…I'm going to kill you. I *promise* you that."

He pushes back from the glass, stands, and walks away.

STATUTORY

ONE

The day Kerry exits the front gate of Wayne Clifford—with nothing more than fifty dollars in his pocket, handed to him in an envelope by the exit clerk—is clear and blue, the few clouds in the sky like soap scum on a freshly washed windowpane. He can't stop staring outside at it as he's processed through administration, made to sign an endless series of forms, and then brought his clothes. After four years of loose orange jumpsuits, the dress shirt and khakis he wore to court feel much smaller and itchier than he remembers.

Pedernales waits with him while the chain link trundles open. As Kerry walks through, the guard mutters, "Keep your dick to yourself, asshole. You come back here, you'll regret it." Kerry shoots him the finger with his good hand, but waits until the other man is facing away before he does so.

And just like that, he's free.

Kerry stands outside the gate and tries to decide if that fact thrills or terrifies him.

The land around the prison is all open prairie. Murket, Texas is home to nothing but the state pen, and the services that support it. He's never seen the facility from the outside before; he was too busy trying to control a raging panic attack while the transport bus dropped him off. From out here, the place looks small and insignificant in the middle of so much empty space.

The thought of spending a lifetime here, as many of its residents will, is depressing beyond words.

Outside the gate sits the visitor parking lot, with an automated bus stop kiosk at the far end, where he can catch a ride that will take him on the forty-five minute trip to Dallas. From there, he'll have to figure out a way to his destination, depending on how much gate money he has left.

Kerry walks across the asphalt toward the bus stop. This early, the parking lot is mostly empty except for a few vehicles up near the building and one white Honda parked away from the others, in the middle of the lot. Kerry can see someone sitting behind the wheel. The person appears to be watching him.

A lead weight drops into the pit of his stomach. It gets even heavier as the driver's door opens and a man gets out, then crosses the parking lot to cut him off.

He can't be much older than Kerry. Maybe early thirties, at most. He has short, neatly groomed black hair and a matching soul patch under his lip, and wears a bright yellow t-shirt emblazoned with a frowning smiley face and the supremely douchey phrase, 'Have a Good Day Somewhere Else.' If street clothes were allowed in prison, Kerry figures a shirt that obnoxious would get your ass stomped in an hour.

The man halts a few feet away and removes a pair of sunglasses. "Kerry Denton?"

"Yeah?"

He sticks out a hand. "Brad Sanders. I'm your parole officer."

"Oh." Kerry shakes the offered hand. He recognizes the name from somewhere in his release paperwork.

"They didn't tell you I was coming." Sanders rolls his eyes. "Ask me if I'm surprised."

"Nope. I thought we were supposed to meet next week."

"Well, technically, that's right. This is more of a social call."

Kerry gives a halfhearted laugh. "Social call, huh?"

"Something funny about that?"

"Nah, it's just, the only 'social calls' I've gotten lately involved someone trying to put their fist down my throat. Or their dick in my ass."

To his surprise, the parole officer cracks an amused smile. "I noticed you put on your release plan that you wanted to take the bus into the city. Thought I'd swing by and see if you wanted a lift."

The offer catches Kerry off guard. He figured the guy is here to hassle him, maybe even administer a surprise drug test here in the parking lot. Just to let him know, right off the bat, who's in charge in this relationship. His lawyer—a harried man who wore threadbare suits and introduced himself as Gerry Stevens, Esquire—cautioned him that some POs like to lord their power as much as the prison guards, and that it should be accepted every bit as meekly. "Is chauffeuring a normal service offered by the courts?"

"Not at all. Most of my colleagues would just as soon spit in your face as speak to you. But I find my job gets much easier if I make sure my charges get settled. Especially when they're staying at a group home. You'd be surprised how many guys walk through that gate and go straight back to doing the thing that landed them in there in the first place." He lifts a shoulder. "Or maybe you wouldn't, what the fuck do I know? So anyway, how 'bout it?"

"Thanks," Kerry says. "I mean, I appreciate it, but that's cool, you don't have to."

"And yet, here I am. So if you turn me down, I guess I drove all the way out here for nothing."

Kerry glances at the bus stop. The sudden decency from this stranger makes him as wary as a dog that's been kicked too many times.

"C'mooooon," Sanders prods. "Don't spend your government-bequeathed cash on bus fare. You'll need it, trust me."

"I don't know, man..."

"Plus I got some breakfast burritos in the car with your name on them."

Kerry can feel a smile creeping onto his face, the expression so rare it makes the muscles in his cheeks hurt. He vaguely remembers this sensation, being treated like a human being. "Okay. Yeah, sure."

Sanders claps his hands one time in excitement. "Excellent! Saddle up then, my friend." He gets behind the wheel and starts the car while Kerry goes around to the passenger side.

The interior of the vehicle is small and the back seat is host to a veritable mountain of paperwork stacks and file folders. As they pull out of the parking lot, Sanders points to a greasy paper bag on the dashboard, from which wafts a glorious smell. "Help yourself, man. Anything in there is bound to be better than prison food. There's coffee too, if you want it."

"Thanks." Kerry digs in while studying Sanders from the corner of his eye. The man puts back on his sunglasses and whistles a Foo Fighters tune as they drive down the winding road to the freeway onramp, passing signs that say, DO NOT PICK UP HITCHHIKERS. He certainly doesn't act—or dress—like a court official. Kerry thinks of his visitor a few days ago and an awful certainty strikes him, one that he wishes had come much sooner. "Do you have, like, an ID or anything?"

Sanders glances at him with a cocked eyebrow and quizzical grin, then nods at the glove box. "Take a look in there."

Kerry opens the small door and reaches inside. Nestled amid auto service receipts and more fast food wrappers, he finds a gleaming silver parole officer's badge and a Dallas County Penal System ID card on a lanyard with Sanders' picture, as well as a holstered nine-millimeter pistol. Relief warms him.

"Who'd you think I was? A kidnapper that waits around outside the prison for ex-cons? Because I gotta say, that's probably not the most lucrative business model."

"No one. It's nothing." Still though, the paranoia remains. Getting into cars with strangers; that's Kindergarten 101. Kerry puts the badge back, closes the door, and busies his mouth with food. They're on the freeway now, speeding along with the sparse mid-morning traffic.

He gets a few bites into a tortilla-wrapped conglomeration of egg and potato—which does taste much better than the grub in prison, but probably doesn't have the state-mandated nutritional value—before Sanders speaks again. "To tell you the truth, I was a little surprised you applied for a spot in a home."

"How come?"

"For starters, it wasn't a condition of your release. And not that this place is bad—you actually lucked out on getting a spot there—but, you know…a lot of my charges say they prefer prison to a halfway house."

Kerry shrugs. "I didn't have anywhere else to go."

"No friends, no family?"

"No." He has no siblings, and hasn't heard from a single one of his friends since the night before his arrest. Even the ones that knew about his new relationship—including the *very* few that condoned it—turned their backs as soon as the law got involved. Being associated with Kerry Denton became social suicide overnight.

"What about your parents?"

Kerry shifts in his seat. "Not to be rude, man, but I'm rethinking that bus ride about now."

Sanders holds up a hand. "Sorry. You've been out fifteen minutes and you can't even enjoy your first meal, huh? We'll have time to talk later."

"No, it's...it's fine." Kerry takes his time chewing a bite of the burrito and then says, "My parents moved away. About a year after the trial. Said they loved me and didn't blame me, but they couldn't take the... attention."

Sanders nods solemnly. "How bad did it get?"

"People they'd known for years stopped talking to them. Their cars were vandalized. My mom even got death threats on Facebook."

"Pssh, death threats. That's a valentine on the internet these days."

"Yeah, well, paying for my defense bankrupted them, so they had to move in with my aunt in Wisconsin." Kerry continues staring at the food in his lap, which suddenly doesn't look so appetizing. "That makes it kind of hard for me to live with them seeing as how I can't leave the state. They offered to come back and try to find an apartment, but I don't want them uprooting their lives again because of me. They've gone through enough already."

The conversation lapses into silence, and Kerry forces himself to finish eating. A few minutes later, the first signs for

Dallas flash by overhead, the city itself and the bubble of Reunion Tower visible on the horizon. Kerry's heart lurches at the sight. He lived in Irving his entire life, and went into the city to party every weekend once he got old enough to drive.

Home, he thinks in amazement. *I'm going home*. For a moment, it's all too easy to dismiss the last four years as a terrible dream.

Then he remembers that someone else owns the home he grew up in, and everyone he knew either left to start their lives or hates his guts now. Or a combination of the two.

"I want to be honest with you about your situation," Sanders says. "That's important to me, that we keep an open, truthful dialogue."

"Oh god, here we go," Kerry groans.

The parole officer laughs again. "If you think I'm bad, wait till you get into the therapy sessions at the home. Which are mandatory, by the way, as a condition of you living there. But seriously, honesty is the only way we'll ever be able to trust one another. And the only way you'll ever get better."

"I don't need to get *better*," Kerry snaps.

"Poor choice of words. I meant, get you back on your feet." He takes his gaze from the road for a moment to study Kerry behind his sunglasses. "I've read your file. I've reviewed your case. In my opinion, you got a raw deal. Four years on a first time statutory at your age, with no priors of any kind, is, pardon my French, some fucking bullshit."

Statutory. That's how Kerry's lawyer insisted on phrasing it also, during the trial. Which was probably one of the man's smarter tactics. It makes the crime sound mechanical and boring without that ugly word 'rape' tacked on to the end.

When he doesn't respond, Sanders says, "I'm guessing you either hired the worst attorney in the world, or someone on the prosecution had some serious sway in the court. Any of that on the nose?"

Kerry flexes his four-fingered left hand, the action almost subconscious. "Yeah. You could say that."

"And, to make matters even stupider, the parole board classifies you as a level two offender, when there's nothing in your background that indicates you will ever be a danger to anyone else." Sanders shakes his head in disgust. "Well, we can bemoan the state of the American justice system all we want, but that's the situation, and those're the boundaries we have to work within. My job is to help you through it and get all of this behind you, *capisce*?"

"Okay."

"Okay. So again, in the name of brutal honesty, I know things were probably bad in prison, but your life on the outside ain't gonna be a picnic either. A normal parolee has it rough, but for someone with your particular conviction, it's ten times worse. It won't matter that it was statutory, all anybody will see is that big red SEX OFFENDER label. Housing—when you get to that point—will be difficult. Finding a job will be next to impossible. And the courts will use any excuse to send someone like you right back to prison." Sanders pauses his spiel to suck in a breath. "Now, that being said, do you understand all the release mandates?"

Kerry begins listing the numerous restrictions he can remember on the fingers of his good hand. "Must live 2,000 yards away from any school or playground, cannot come within 500 yards of any school or playground, no leaving the state, must check in with a court provided parole officer once per week, no drinking or drugs, no owning a computer, smartphone, tablet, or any other device that accesses the internet." He drops his hands, then adds, "Oh, and, of course, enrollment on the fucking sex offender registry for a period of no less than ten years."

"If you were level three, it would be for life," Sanders tells him, as if that fact somehow makes his sentence any easier. "And that's an important one, too. I've already got your initial listing set up, but if you decide to leave the home, you make damn sure you keep your address with the SOR current. That's the quickest way to end up back behind bars." Sanders flips on his turn signal to move toward the exit lane. "Maybe you're smart enough that I don't have to tell you this, but stay away from children altogether. That way no one has any reason to file a complaint against you, false or otherwise. And for Christ's sake, whatever you do, do NOT have any further contact with the girl that got you arrested. I know she's older now, but I don't care if she's got 'legal' tattooed on her vagina and God Himself is waving you in for a landing, she is off limits. Understand?"

Kerry looks away, out the window, as the rolling plains give way to the first sprawling buildings of the city. "That won't be a problem," he says.

TWO

Fifteen minutes later, they're winding through the heart of Dallas and into a trendy, gentrified neighborhood, where dive bars and hip pizzerias intermingle with warehouses renovated into condos. Kerry can't help wondering if his old neighborhood far to the west became something similar and decides he doesn't want to know. Sanders babbles on while Kerry watches people jogging along the sidewalk, dining on the tiny patios of narrow cafes, walking out of an all-natural grocery store called Caulfield's with bags—recyclable canvas, of course—in hand, their freedom intrinsic and irrefutable. None of them have any idea how quickly life can pull the rug out from under you. He knows he was one of them once, but that state of mind is all but impossible to recapture. His only contact with this world during his incarceration was the few times he ventured into the common area to watch television, and that's how this feels now, like a picture on a screen that he can change by flipping the channel. The idea that he can get out of this car and walk right into it is about as plausible as climbing into a TV.

"Reentry shock?" Sanders asks suddenly, as though reading Kerry's mind. The man obviously possesses good instincts when it comes to people. An important fact to keep in mind.

Kerry picks up his coffee from the armrest and fiddles with the lid. "I guess. Seems kind of weird to feel this way though. I mean, I was only in for four years."

"Yeah, but that's what? A full sixth of your life spent behind bars? Institutionalization sets in fast, but it does fade. So long as you don't break any laws and get yourself jugged again. And that's not gonna happen, *right?*"

"Definitely."

"That's what I like to hear."

They roll through another block, where the shops and apartment buildings open up on the right into a long green lawn of immaculately kept grass. A large fountain stands in the middle, topped by a bronze sculpture of running horses. A young couple lays stretched out on a blanket in front of it, with a picnic breakfast between them. On the far side of this public park sits a two-story red brick building that can only be a school. An adjacent, fenced-in playground full of cavorting children confirms this theory.

Sanders pulls the car to a stop at the curb and nods at the building in the distance. "For the record, this is 500 yards. Memorize it. You cross this line around any school, playground, day care, water park or Chuck E. Cheese, and I won't be able to help you."

"So you're saying I'll have to put off my trip to Disney World?"

The parole officer pulls down his sunglasses. "I'm serious as a heart attack, pal."

"I got it," Kerry says. This mystical barrier was drilled into him by his attorney also, except Mr. Gerry Stevens, Esq.

called it 'the Parole-a Triangle.' Because going into it would make your parole vanish forever.

Sanders drives on. Two minutes later they're on a much older street, where the houses are big and stately, with huge, full-grown oak trees in every yard. Sanders stops in front of a two-story colonial in desperate need of a paint job, with dormered windows on the upper floor whose decorative shutters are cracked and peeling, and a line of tall, shaggy bushes along the front. It looks like a dilapidated mini-mansion from a horror movie, especially compared with the immaculate properties to either side. A wooden sign on poles at the curb reads, 'Hopeful Sunshine Group Home' with an anthropomorphic cartoon sun peeking over the horizon. The expression on its orange face is surely meant to convey cautious optimism, but comes off like they've caught him in the middle of a powerful orgasm.

It's not exactly the kind of sunshine he longed for during those endless days in solitary, but beggars can't be choosers.

Two cars are parked in the house's driveway, one of them a tiny, rust-eaten Subaru, the other a huge navy blue Econoline van with blacked out windows and an elaborate, painted mural on the side of what appears to be a pickle zooming through outer space like the Starship Enterprise. As he pulls in behind it, Sanders mutters, "Damn it. I *told* him not to buy that thing."

He kills the engine and reaches for the door, but pauses when he notices Kerry is still sitting inside, staring up at the property. "What's wrong?"

"It's an actual *house*," Kerry says in amazement. "I thought it would be, like, a dorm or a barracks or something."

"Most of them are," Sanders confirms. "But they're filling up, so the state is experimenting with residential facilities like this. For a…how did they put it at the last budget meeting?…a 'smoother societal reintegration.'" He rolls his eyes. "What that really means is that those dorms can develop a severe prison mentality with so many ex-cons packed inside. And if they become another place where you can get shanked over Benadryl speed, then what's the point of getting paroled?" Sanders smiles and drums his hands on the steering wheel. "Like I said, be glad you got a spot here."

He steps out, and this time Kerry follows, clutching his manila folder. They walk up the long driveway, passing the painted van—the parole officer runs a finger through the dust caked along its side panel—and then head toward the front door. Two houses down, an elderly man in a guayabera and Crocs stands in his front yard, spraying his flower bed with a garden hose. He cranes his neck to watch their every step as they approach the house.

Kerry raises a hand to wave. The old man scowls, throws down his hose with water still gushing from the end, and turns to go inside.

"This place ain't exactly popular with the neighbors," Sanders remarks over his shoulder. "They've tried several times to get us kicked out, but they can't quite scrape together the dough for the legal fees. This neighborhood is nice, but all the real money moved toward the outer 'burbs or the inner city condos." He pushes open the wide door of Hopeful Sunshine without knocking and allows Kerry to step through first.

The entrance opens onto a cheery vestibule with checkered black and white tile, mopped to a gloss so high Kerry thinks his shoes might slide out from under him. A wide archway to the left grants him a brief view of a cavernous kitchen with an industrial chrome oven and a matching stove big enough for a restaurant, all polished and gleaming. It's far cleaner and homier than he imagined after seeing the exterior. To the right is a closed door with some sort of sign-in sheet tacked to it, next to the bottom of a staircase that curves around the periphery of the room to reach the second floor. But Sanders walks straight ahead, to a set of open double doors from which arguing voices drift.

They step into a high-ceilinged living room with champagne-colored carpet, lit by a long bank of windows along the left wall. The opposite side holds a mounted flat screen television, currently muted and playing a reality show of the rich housewife variety. Cheesy motivational posters decorate the rest of the space, the kind with pictures of leaping killer whales and kittens dangling from clotheslines, and a banner runs above the windows which reads, WE STRIVE TO BE HAPPY, HEALTHY HUMANS! It sounds like the name of the world's least offensive punk band to Kerry. A beaten leather L-shaped couch takes up most of the floor space, along with a glass coffee table.

The arguers stand in the middle of the room and resemble polar opposites from some comedy personality chart: one of them a white, short, middle-aged bald man in a yellow dress shirt and a pair of glasses with thick frames, the other a curvy younger black woman decked out in hip-hugging jeans and a midriff top. Her hair—pulled back in a greasy, rat's nest of a ponytail—has a streak of blazing purple squiggling through it.

"Just because we all livin together don't mean you our daddy!" the woman rants. She towers over the other guy, and jabs a finger with a chipped green nail in his face to punctuate every sentence. "You don't control who I'm friends with!"

Frustration flashes across the bald man's face. He takes the time to smooth it out before saying, in a subdued, patient tone, "No, I do not approve of your free time associations, but this isn't about them. It's about the fact that you violated curfew for the third time this month."

The woman sweeps her pointing hand violently to the side, as though backhanding the words away. "That's some bullshit, Les! Everybody else up in here gets to stay out as late as they want! You a racist! You *know* you a racist!"

"I assume by 'everybody' you mean Mark, Lorie, and Scott." The man—Les—adjusts his glasses, then puts his hands on his hips in a gesture more pathetic than imposing. "Let me remind you, they get extended curfews because *they* have full time jobs."

"Yeah, well, it's a lot easier for they lily white asses to find work, ain't it?"

"D'libra, let's take it down a notch." Sanders says, moving across the room toward them.

"Oh, so now you all gangin up on me." 'D'libra' takes a step back from Les as Sanders comes to stand beside him. The shorter man looks relieved to have some backup, but the woman clenches her fists at her sides and stamps one foot in frustration, like an angry toddler. "This shit ain't fair!"

"What's not fair about it? You broke the rules and now you have to face the consequences."

"Don't be talkin to me about consequences, Brad! That's all this place is, consequences! You wanna be down on a nigga fo' *ev-ry-thing!* And who the hell is this skinny cracker eyeballin me?"

Kerry, still lurking in the doorway, freezes in place.

"That's Kerry Denton. Your new housemate," Sanders tells her. "Kerry, this is D'libra Barnes."

"Hey," Kerry ventures.

She eyes him like a dead bug at the end of a microscope. "Whatchoo in for, boy?"

"Uh…" Even though it's the first question anyone asks you in prison, the starkness flusters him. "I was…you see—"

"Statutory sex offense," Sanders answers for him. Even though he sounds nothing but diplomatic, Kerry feels his cheeks flush.

D'libra groans. "Fuckin great, another goddamn creeper! I swear to Christ, I'm suin every one of ya'll the first time I get raped up in here!" This time she points in Kerry's direction, and he sees the puckered scar tissue running up and down her brown arm. "I'll tell you what I told that tubby skeez upstairs: keep yo' dick in yo' pants, or I'll chop that chicken nugget right off!"

"All right, enough!" Sanders barks.

D'libra swings back to him. "I do everything around here! Buy the groceries, cook the meals. Hell, I clean this whole place every damn day, top to bottom! All I want is a li'l fun!"

"No job means extra chores," Les says quietly. Sweat beads on his bald pate. "And violating curfew means you're going to get even more."

"Go fuck yo'self, you dick-lookin muthafuckah!"

Kerry clamps his mouth shut against a flood of laughter.

"Stop." Sanders doesn't find this insult as hilarious as Kerry does. His words have a razor-sharp edge. "You say anything else, I will contact your PO and have you transferred out of here."

D'libra looks back and forth between the two men. Her face makes Kerry think of a volcano well on the way to blowing its top, but she wisely keeps her mouth shut. Then she stomps away, coming around the couch and heading toward the door of the living room. Kerry scoots out of her way before she can bowl him over.

"Welcome to Sunshine, Chester," she spits as she passes by.

THREE

"Didn't mean to embarrass you," Sanders says. Now that the heat of the moment is over, he seems sheepish. "If I didn't tell her, she would've looked it up on her own. But we try to be open about residents' conviction records. By the same token, I guess I should tell you D'libra served three years for—"

"Drugs," Kerry interjects. The parole officer raises an eyebrow at him, and Kerry gestures along the inside of his own elbow. "The scars."

"Oh, right. 'Narcotics possession and distribution' is the official logline, but yeah, drugs." He puts a hand on the bald man's shoulder. "And this is Lester Norris, the live-in psychologist slash social worker slash residential advisor for Hopeful Sunshine. He runs the therapy sessions and basically keeps all you yahoos in line."

"Please, call me Les." The psychologist uses a forearm to wipe the sweat from his brow. "Sorry you had to get involved in that on your first day. D'libra has been a challenge for all of us, to say the least. A word of advice: don't eat her ice cream sandwiches in the freezer or the wrath you face will be much worse than what you just witnessed."

Sanders grins and tells Les, "Denton here shouldn't give you as much trouble as Barnes. He's a little more even-tempered."

"Wonderful. Then let's take a tour and get you settled in your room."

The three of them walk back through the living room, heading toward the staircase, as Les launches into a rehearsed speech. "The purpose of the Hopeful Sunshine Group Home is to provide newly-released convicts with a safe haven from which they can attempt to reenter society, one step at a time. We help with rehabilitation, housing, and even financial education assistance for those who qualify. Our goal is to give each resident the opportunity to become a productive citizen and reduce the chance for a repeat offense." He stops at the foot of the stairs and faces Kerry. "We do, however, maintain a strict code of ethics that all residents are expected to follow. They're all listed in the welcome packet in your room, but the major ones are no drugs, no alcohol, group therapy sessions every Tuesday, Thursday and Saturday, and all residents without full time employment must be present between the hours of 9 PM and 6 AM. You'll also be expected to seek such employment in the interest of eventually being able to support yourself. Good so far?"

"Sure." Kerry's life has become nothing but an endless series of restrictions and regulations since getting out of prison; what difference does a few more make?

"Great." Les continues up the stairs. "With you, we have six residents at the moment, although we're zoned for up to ten. And this house is a collective. We all work together to keep it running smoothly. Everyone takes on chores and responsibilities, and everyone respects the rights and property of other residents. We've never had a problem with theft, so let's not start now. And if you have an issue with another resident, come to me and I will be happy to mediate." Witnessing the argument with D'libra makes Kerry wonder how effective that mediation would be.

Les comes to a halt and looks back at Kerry. "Oh, and while we're on the subject of other residents, there is to be absolutely no fraternizing, in or outside of the house."

"Fraternizing. Is that, like, going out to dinner, or—"

"No fucking," Sanders translates. "No hand jobs, blowjobs, anal, felching, Dirty Sanchezes, et cetera. Avoid swapping bodily fluids and you'll be fine."

"Gotcha."

The landing at the top of the stairs opens up into a wide space that runs the width of the house, surely meant as a game room or play area. The space is taken up by a small entertainment center with a dusty, outdated video game console, a scuffed pool table, a shelf full of books—most of which appear to be self-help tomes of the *Dummy's Guide* sort—and, in one corner, a desk with a computer and printer. Two parallel hallways take up the rest of the second floor, lined with closed doors. Professionally-made metal signs on the wall label the left passage for FEMALES and the right for MALES.

"We call this our media center," Les tells him. "You're welcome to any of the amenities or to reserve time if you want, but there shouldn't be any problems with usage. Half of our residents are employed full-time at the moment, so they're not here all that often."

"Question." Kerry hikes a thumb at the desk. "I thought I wasn't allowed to own a computer."

"You don't own one," Sanders says. "*We* do. You just use it."

"That's…kind of a loose interpretation, don't you think? I mean, what about all that 'follow the mandates' talk?"

Sanders steeples his fingers in front of the frowny face on his t-shirt, the pose like some wise Buddha monk. "Listen, it's all well and good to keep sex offenders away from any possible avenue they could use to target another victim. I'm all for that. But you can't very well expect someone to reintegrate in the modern world, search for a job, or have any sort of marketable skills without letting them have access to a computer. What the courts want is someone to *monitor* that usage. In most cases, that's not feasible. But we have the means."

"You'll have a login name that blocks all social media and pornography sites," Les adds. "And every key stroke is logged for all accounts."

"I don't know," Kerry says. "Feels like a trick or something. Like Chris Hansen is gonna pop out of a closet the second I touch the keyboard."

Sanders shrugs. "It's a rule bend, not a break. I'm your PO, and I say it's hunky dory."

The tour continues, through the large communal bathroom that adjoins the two upstairs hallways and then down to the bedrooms on the male side. Les stays in the master suite downstairs, but everyone else lives on the second floor. As they pass the first room, Les tells him, "No locks allowed on any of the doors. Rooms are subject to a search at any time. And you can't have any decoration in the hallway, but the interior is all yours as long as you can revert it to how you found it when you move out. Before I forget, we had a package sitting on the doorstep for you yesterday. I left it on your bed."

"Probably my clothes," Kerry says. "I asked my parents to ship some here."

"Les, you mind if I take him the rest of the way?" Sanders asks. "I want to have a word with his roommate."

"Not a problem." To Kerry, the psychologist says, "It's great to have you here. Read through your packet and let me know if you have any questions. The meeting room for the therapy session tomorrow morning is that door right at the foot of the stairs. Let's see, what else? Oh, you're welcome to any unclaimed food in the fridge for lunch, and we take turns getting dinner ready every day around 6." Les gives him a fatherly pat on the back and then starts back down the hall.

"Roommate?" Kerry asks Sanders, once the other man is gone.

The parole officer is already heading to the last door on the left. "You didn't think you'd get a private suite, did you?" He raps on the door with the back of his knuckles and calls, "Ray! Raymond, you big lunk, are you decent? Or as decent as you ever get?"

Kerry doesn't hear an answer, but Sanders opens the door anyway.

The square room beyond can't be more than twelve feet to a side; smaller than most college dorm rooms, but far bigger than any of the cells at Wayne Clifford. Still, since Kerry was in and out of solitary so much and always shuffled to a new cell, he rarely had to share that space with anyone else on a consistent basis. The left side of the room is bare and empty except for a narrow wooden frame bed with a cardboard box and a set of folded sheets and blankets on top. But to the right, a series of shelves are bracketed to the walls around a matching bed, upon which hundreds—perhaps thousands—of tiny, colorful figurines are displayed. It takes Kerry several seconds to realize they're all made from paper, each one incredibly intricate, three dimensional origami folded and painted to exhausting detail. He can see miniature representations of all sorts of animals, enough to fill a zoo, mythical monsters, horror movie creatures, superheroes, historical figures, and even a few buildings like the Tower of Pisa and a replica of the Sydney Opera House that both look like something you would see in a Ripley's museum. The largest of these stands no more than five inches tall, while the majority are quite a bit under that.

In the middle of it all, sitting hunched over a small table with a pile of paper scraps on the floor big enough to bury his legs up to the calves, is a chunky, mid-forty-ish guy in running shorts and a green t-shirt, with a curly shelf of shockingly orange hair pushed up off his forehead by a sweatband. A pair of huge, ancient headphones are clamped around his wide head as he peers through a magnifying glass mounted to the table, at another piece of paper he's using tweezers to fold. On the other side of the lens, his grotesquely magnified eye swivels up to them, then he straightens and pushes the headphones back. A wide, dopey grin splits his freckled face.

"Hey Brad! What's shakin, bacon?"

Sanders sighs loudly. "You had to buy that van, didn't you?"

That grin gets even bigger, revealing an uneven row of yellowed teeth. "My money for the last batch came in! It's awesome, huh?"

"No, it isn't. I told you so when you showed it to me on Craigslist."

The smile falters. "You and Les said I needed a vehicle if I ever wanted to be independent."

Sanders bangs his forehead softly on the doorframe. "Yeah, a *vehicle*. Not a broken down, mobile pedophile dispenser. Jesus Ray, the windows are even blacked out. You know I trust you, but...have some tact."

The chubby man slumps in the chair, defeated. "I thought it was, you know, kinda kitschy."

"We'll see how kitschy it is when you have to replace the engine in six months. But it's your money, do what you want." Sanders moves aside to reveal Kerry. "I have your new roommate, by the way. This is Kerry Denton. Kerry, this is another one of my charges, Raymond Leary."

Ray leaps up from his seat, his melancholia disappearing in a heartbeat. He has to kick through the dense mountain of paper on the floor around him. His bare feet come into view, revealing a thick, black band around his right ankle, to which clings a rectangular box with a glowing red light. But Kerry doesn't get the chance to look at it for long, because the other man flies across the room and enfolds him in two doughy arms.

"It's so *grrrrreat* to meet you!" he exclaims, and Kerry can't tell if the Tony the Tiger imitation is intentional or not. "We're gonna be like brothers! Just like brothers! I've never had a brother, but I figure that's how we'll be!"

Kerry can find no suitable reply. He stands stiff and awkward until the embrace mercifully ends and Ray steps away from him, beaming that idiot's grin.

"You'll have to excuse Ray," Sanders tells him. "His people skills are a little rusty."

Ray gives a donkey's bray of laughter and pats the parole officer's cheek. "No they're not, shut up!"

Now that there's sufficient space between them, Kerry's eyes stray down to the device strapped to the other man's leg. "Is that...an ankle monitor?"

Ray lifts his foot off the floor—almost losing his balance in the process—and taps the red light. "Yep, this is my little buddy for life! But don't worry, we can still go out and parrrr-tay! I'm not on house arrest or anything, it just keeps a record of where I go."

Kerry, who never felt less like parrrr-taying in his life, asks, "A record for...for what? I mean, what did you...why are you...?"

"Oh, uuuuh..." Ray squeezes his eyes shut so hard Kerry thinks he must be in pain. His mouth twists into a grimace. Then he grinds the heel of one hand into his forehead, as though trying to massage the answer out of his skull. When it comes, it's spoken in a flat monotone, completely devoid of his previous exuberance. "I w-was convicted of t-t-two counts of sexual abuse of a m-minor."

"But that was a long time ago," Sanders adds quickly, "and Ray is turning his whole life around, aren't you?"

"Yes, I sure am!" The brief storm cloud lifts from his face. "I served my time and I got all better and Les says I'm ready to be a happy, healthy human!"

Bitter revulsion uncoils in Kerry's guts, a disgust so deep he tastes it in the back of his throat, like a squirming insect. He turns to Sanders and says, "Can I talk to you in private?"

The parole officer glances at Ray, takes a deep breath and nods.

They step into the hallway, then head toward the media center, out of earshot.

Sanders speaks first. "I know what you're gonna say."

"Good. Then I don't have to."

"Granted, he's a little strange—"

"He's a goddamn child molester!"

Sanders favors him with a tight, wry smile. "Isn't that the pot calling the kettle a sex offender?"

"It's not the same thing," Kerry says through gritted teeth, but so many images from the last four years elbow into his thoughts, chief among them that day in the common room, when the two Latin Kings rushed at him with a shiv made from a ballpoint pen and the blade from a disposable razor, one of them screaming that Kerry would never touch *his* kids.

For that reason, Sanders' next words come as no surprise.

"To a lot of folks, it very much is. I would hope that after everything you and your parents went through, you would understand that." The parole officer's gaze is heavy and unflinching. That friendly, hip persona has vanished, and now Kerry can easily see him as an extension of the court. "Fine, I'll put it like this: it was a mistake he made at about the same age you made yours. Except he received a 20 year conviction, spent in a state psychiatric hospital where he got some much needed help."

"Jesus Christ! Is that supposed to make me feel better while I'm sleeping across the room from him?"

"No, it's supposed to make you see that he's a person trying to get a second chance, the same as you. And he's also one of the few people on earth that might understand what you're going through. I recommend you take advantage of that. Besides, I can guarantee you, he's absolutely harmless now."

Kerry runs a hand across the short mop of his dark hair. "How can you be sure of that? What'd he do, anyway?"

"You'll have to ask him that. You're privy to each other's convictions, not life histories. As you saw though, he's not too keen on talking about it."

"But they have *empty rooms!* Can't I stay in another one?"

"No, you can't, because that's not how things are done at Hopeful Sunshine. And keep in mind, unlike everybody else, you're not required to be here. You don't like the conditions, the street is thataway. But once you leave, you don't come back." Sanders walks away, ending the conversation. He returns to the open door of Kerry's new room and tells the other occupant, "Show Denton the ropes around here, okay? And do me a favor, take him on his meet-and-greet Saturday, just to get it over with."

Sanders strides back toward him, digging in his pocket along the way. He produces a business card and hands it to Kerry. "You can give me a call about anything, night or day. Especially if it concerns your parole. Keep your nose clean, cause you never know if I'm going to pop by. Other than that, I'll see you next week."

He leaves Kerry on the landing and heads down the stairs.

FOUR

Kerry waits until he hears the front door close before slinking back down the hall. He pauses beyond the threshold. Takes a breath. Thinks about what Sanders said, about his new roommate understanding what he's going through, a claim that Kerry highly doubts. And even if it's true, he doesn't want such commiseration from *this* guy. In prison, a guilt-by-association factor kept the sex offenders isolated, even from one another, which was fine with him. The crimes of most of the men serving time for such violations repulsed him as much as they did everyone else.

For a moment, he really does consider walking right out of this house. It isn't like he's helpless. He had his own apartment before prison, and a job as a night manager at a Whataburger to help him pay for the portion of classes that his scholarships didn't cover. That life can be rebuilt, perhaps even picked right back up where he left off, as though the world paused while it waited for him to return.

He doesn't need to be coddled or told to go to bed.

Or 'rehabilitated.'

Oh yeah? And is that fifty bucks in your pocket gonna get you by long enough to find a job and a place to live? You think there's an apartment complex that will take your parole paperwork as a deposit? Jesus, you'll be panhandling in front of a 7-11 before the end of the week.

"Fine," he mutters. "But as soon as I find a job, I'm gone."

Kerry walks through the door.

Raymond Leary stands right where they left him, as though he only exists in the presence of other people. His orange hair and matching freckles are so bright, they catch fire when the morning sunlight hits them. It occurs to Kerry that this is what Archie Andrews might look like in his middle age, after Veronica Lodge bleeds the life out of him. His face brightens as soon as he sees his new roommate. "Hey buddy! I missed you! Did you bring me back a present?"

"Uhhh…"

"I'm just joshing." He gives another wet chortle, a noise that brings to mind creatures who live in mud at the bottom of scummy ponds. "You don't have to give it to me now. My birthday's in three months. No, I'm kidding again. But it is."

"Okay. Sure." Kerry moves toward his side of the room, takes in the bare bed and the big cardboard box on top of it.

"You need help moving in?" Ray asks eagerly behind him.

"Nope." Kerry taps the box. "This is it."

"All right. I saved the left side of the closet for you. Unless you want the right. We can swap. Or mix all our clothes up and share everything."

"The…the left is fine."

"Okay, that's good. I don't think I could fit in yours anyways. That was a dumb idea, huh? I don't know why I said that. I guess I'm nervous. I talk when I'm nervous. Well, and also when I'm not."

Kerry doesn't answer, just moves the cardboard box to the floor and busies himself making the bed, hoping it will discourage conversation. After a few seconds, he realizes Ray is watching over his shoulder, close enough that he can feel the heat of the man's breath on his neck. "Fuck man, do you mind?"

"Sorry." Ray hurriedly shuffles a few steps back. "At the hospital, they diagnosed me with social interaction disorder and boundary issues, so—"

"I don't care. Look, not to provide the basis for a sitcom episode or anything, but why don't you stay on your half of the room, and I'll stay on mine?"

A twinge of guilt worms through Kerry's chest at the crestfallen look on the man's face. "Yeah. Okay. Ten-four. No problem. *Ándale ándale arriba.*" He sits back down at the small table and, after one last forlorn glance, resumes work on his paper creations.

Kerry ignores him while he finishes tucking in the sheets and spreading the blanket, then sits down on the bed and tries to figure out what he should do next. He doesn't want to unpack whatever his parents sent with the weirdo around.

This room in the middle of suburbia is suddenly tinier than any cell. In prison, all he thought about were the things he would do when he got out, as every convict does, but now that he's free, his mind is blank. Hell, he doesn't even have a book, and reading is how he kept from going insane in solitary.

He finds himself watching his roommate instead, hunched over and peering through his magnifying glass at the tiny bits of folded paper in front of him. Shit, if he's stuck here for a while, might as well try to keep things friendly. Or, at the very least, not awkward, although that's going to be hard with this guy. Knowing he'll regret it (and, for some reason, hearing Pedernales' awful laughter in his head), Kerry asks, "Is that, like, a hobby or what?"

"No no no! I mean, it used to be, but now it's *way* more than that!" Ray bounces up and down in his seat, so eager to talk about the subject he looks ready to ejaculate. "I'm making so much money, it's pretty much my job!"

"Wait. You mean people actually buy these things?" Kerry hops off the bed and moves toward the shelf on the opposite side of the door, careful not to cross over what he is already thinking of as a line of demarcation up the middle of the room. He bends to take a closer look at the paper figurines.

"Oh yeah, tons of people! Les helped me get a website set up and everything! I've got orders from all over the country and even one in China. I make them in bulk for things like weddings or birthdays, or I even take special orders from people who want something one of a kind."

"Weird." Kerry catches sight of a miniature Cthulhu, three inches tall, painted in such exquisite detail that he can see the suckers along the underside of the tentacles reaching in all directions from its face. It's amazingly lifelike, but the damn thing looks like a gentle breeze would disintegrate it. "How much does somebody pay for something like that?"

"Depends. I usually let them set the price. The last batch of superheroes I did for this one kid's bar mitzvah came in at five hundred."

"*Dollars?* For a bunch of folder paper and paint?"

"Sometimes I cheat and use glue."

Kerry can't help wondering what the spoiled little *chutzpah's* parents would've paid if they knew their goodie bag giveaways were being crafted by a convicted pedophile. "Shit man, where'd you learn to do this anyway? You get a book or something?"

"No, I learned it in the…the hospital." His face screws up like it did before when talking about his conviction, one hand rising to knuckle against his temple. "The d-doctors wanted me to keep b-b-busy with a hobby. If my mind stays busy, then the v-voices can't tell me bad th-things." Ray bites his lower lip with his eyes still closed. "I don't lll-l-like the voices."

"Ooookay." The way the other man's voice deadens as he states this turns the hair on Kerry's neck into porcupine quills. Here it comes, the guy is going to flip out and stab him with his miniature paper-folding tweezers, he just knows it. The only thing keeping Kerry from bolting out of the room is Sanders' assurance that his roommate is harmless. "By all means, keep busy then. Go, fold."

The hand lowers, Ray opens his eyes, and goes right on talking in his normal, cheerful tone. "It stinks though, cause Les says this doesn't count as a full time job cause I'm not technically 'employed,' so I can't stay out past nine. That means we probably can't go to the disco clubs together. Sorry."

"We'll manage." Kerry looks around at the other shelves. "Well, what do you have to do to be cleared to move out of this place then? If you're making that much scratch off these things, surely you'd be able to find a semi-decent place to live."

Ray shakes his head emphatically, eyes wide and horrified. "Oh no, I'm not ready for that yet. Les promised no one would make me move out if I don't want to." A high-pitched beeping noise fills the room. Ray looks at his plastic wristwatch and presses a button that cuts it off, then leaps to his feet. "Yay, *Adventure Time* in ten minutes! I watch it every day! Except on Mondays, because it's Mark's day off and he gets the TV to watch *700 Club*." He wrinkles his nose. "You wanna come watch with me?"

Kerry, who remembers some of his friends liking that cartoon—mostly while high—says, "Nah, I might catch a nap. Didn't sleep too well last night. You know, excited about getting out and all."

Ray nods, then suddenly slings an arm around Kerry's neck and yanks him forward, smothering his face in the blubbery chest of his t-shirt. "Love you, buddy!" he cries. Then he lets go and bounces out of the room, the whole thing happening so fast Kerry doesn't even have time to protest.

He closes the door behind his roommate instead, wipes his face vigorously, and then spends the next few minutes exploring his new digs. The closet is small, the right side overflowing with Ray's clothes and some plastic storage bins, but it should be plenty of space considering Kerry owns nothing. The windows on the male side of the house look out on the front lawn and the wide avenue leading back toward the freeway, giving a sweeping view of several blocks. Over the rooftops of the large houses across the road, he can catch a glimpse of Caulfield's, that neo-Bohemian grocery store he and Sanders passed on the way here, now far in the distance. An old billboard looms over it, closer to the freeway, its advertisement a scratched and faded mess.

He retrieves the cardboard box and sits down on the bed to open it. Seeing his parents' names on the return address causes a sorrowful pang behind his ribcage.

The package is filled to the brim with clothes, at least enough to get him through a week without having to do laundry. On top of them is a letter in his mother's scratchy handwriting, telling him they will send him more when he gets settled, but that they got rid of a lot from his apartment. She says they love him and will come for a visit as soon as he tells them it's all right.

Which won't be anytime soon. He doesn't want them to see him in this place any more than he did prison. His mother cried the first time she saw him in an orange jumpsuit; his father looked pale and ill and beyond disappointed.

All of this came as a complete shock to them. They had no idea who he was seeing until the night they came to bail him out of jail after his initial arrest, his finger freshly amputated and still oozing blood through the bandages. Kerry often wonders what they would've said if they'd known, if they would've encouraged him to put a stop to the relationship before things reached the point of no return.

He also wonders if he would've listened.

Underneath the clothes are a few other personal belongings. His old watch and wallet, with his driver's license still inside, the damn thing even still valid for another four months. Some pictures of family and friends. His favorite DVD's. He removes them all one at a time until he uncovers the last item and stiffens.

At the bottom of the box lies a miniature replica of the Alamo, not too different from Ray's creations, except this one is made of plastic, and crushed on one side. A note from his mother is taped to the front: *We thought you might want this.* Kerry lifts the model out of the box and flips it upside down in his lap to look at what he knows is inscribed there, the words carved into the plastic base.

For my clumsy fuckface! Love you always,
Kayla.

The day trip to San Antonio. He'd thought about it so many times. She'd skipped school so they could go without anyone knowing. In the Alamo gift shop, he'd stumbled and stepped on the replica, but only because they were making out while they walked. They couldn't stop laughing afterward, both of them seized by a fit of giggles so hysterical the manager accused them of being stoned. Kerry was flat broke from a tuition payment, so she'd paid for it to keep the store from calling the cops.

Pain whipcracks through his left hand, an electric jolt that stiffens his entire body on the bed. It's quickly followed by another and another, the new blasts coming quicker than the old ones can fade. His entire palm is soon crawling with an unpleasant burning, tingling sensation. The origin for these lightning bolts feels like a spot about two inches above the severed end of his ring finger. Kerry curls the remaining digits into a tight fist several times, clenching and unclenching methodically, then grips the puckered stump and begins to rub and squeeze the flesh, even though it never helps.

Ghost finger. AKA, phantom limb. That was the diagnosis from the prison doc, after the strange attacks became so severe that Kerry would wake up weeping in the middle of the night. Pedernales and the other guards called him a faker. The prison doc at least acknowledged that *Kerry* thought the pain was genuine—told him that it was most likely randomly misfiring receptors in his hand reaching out to the digit and, upon finding it gone, concluding that it must be damaged— but refused to dole out any pain medication, since he believed the attacks themselves to be psychosomatic in nature.

Kerry doesn't care if the man thinks he's imagining it, or if his nerves are scrambled, or if his hand has become a haunted house with a screaming banshee inside. The sensation is real, and it hurts, but it's also frustrating. It feels like he could stop these attacks if he could grab hold of that ethereal digit, scratch that impossible spot the electricity seems to emanate from.

As he sits there in his new bedroom at the Hopeful Sunshine Group Home, the pain is his hand is washed away by a sudden surge of anger, at chances lost, at lives ruined. He picks the Alamo model up from his lap and throws it across the room as hard as he can. It hits the wall and shatters into a million pieces, leaving behind a sizeable gouge in the plaster. This destruction isn't enough to sate his anger, but all he has left is the empty cardboard box, which he bats away. It tumbles into the floor, landing on its side.

Which is the reason he notices the envelope stuck to the bottom.

It's plain and white, a full size document mailer, hanging from the box by an errant piece of packing tape. Kerry pulls it away—being careful not to disturb his shortened finger, which is finally beginning to cycle down—and looks at both sides. His name is written on the front in neat, blocky script, but there is no address, no postage. If it was delivered to the doorstep, then it didn't come through the mail.

He breaks the seal and lets the object inside slide out onto his lap: a glossy 8 x 10 photograph carefully mounted on cardstock. Kerry stares down at it, trying to make sense of what he's seeing.

It's a class picture, the kind the schools always take at the end of the year. There are no adults in it, and nothing at all to indicate where it was taken, but, judging by the picture quality and the style of dress, it must be from the seventies. The kids in it look small enough to be first or second graders, maybe even kindergarten. They stand in rows on a tiered grandstand, dressed in their finest polyester jackets and flared jeans, but Kerry's gaze is drawn to their faces before he can notice any of this.

All of their eyes are torn out of the photograph, the edges

of the tiny holes rimmed with red ink to make them look bloody. Maroon drips down their cheeks like tears.

The effect turns their camera-ready smiles into grimaces of unutterable pain.

HAPPY,
HEALTHY
HUMANS

FIVE

Kerry leaves the house before lunch on his first day at Hopeful Sunshine, then walks all the way down to Caulfield's and uses some of his gate money to buy a cheap alarm clock and a few paperback books. At first, he's just anxious to get away before Ray's cartoons end, but once outside and moving, Kerry realizes how much he needs to see that he *truly* is free, that he won't be shot in the back for setting foot off the property, that Pedernales isn't going to leap out of the shaggy bushes in front of the house and yell, *Ah ha, gotcha, pervert! We were just joshing the whole time!*

The walk takes a half hour each way. Kerry spends the remaining afternoon reading through his welcome packet and most of a thriller on the back patio, where wicker furniture sits around a barbecue pit and the lawn rolls down to a wooden fence that separates the property from a wide dirt alleyway running between the house rows. Even though the air and sunshine are wonderful, the photo of the eyeless schoolchildren creeps into his thoughts and derails his concentration. The awful picture is currently under his mattress until he can decide what to do with it.

As for where it might've come from…all he has are suspicions.

It was easy to put MacCallum's threat out of his head while still in prison; why worry about someone outside the walls when plenty of people *inside* wanted to hurt him? But that promise—delivered through clenched teeth from the other side of the scratched visitor booth partition—comes back to him as he watches the sun sink behind the dwellings of the happy, healthy humans that live around them. Even now, Kerry wants to believe it was just words. Lingering anger stirred up by news of his parole that will fade, given time.

But he knows all too well what the man is capable of, how far his fury can take him.

And besides, he's got a lot better reason to hate you now…doesn't he?

Kerry can't stand that smug, jeering voice from the depths of his subconscious. Its snide jabs usually cause his ghost finger to rattle its chains. But, even if it does have a point about Rob Mac, sending an anonymous photo as a threat—especially one that disturbing—isn't exactly the man's style.

So maybe the voices in your new roommate's head told him to make you a little housewarming present.

That thought touches off a deep, inward shudder.

By the time Kerry ventures back inside from the patio—long after he can no longer see the words on the pages of his book anymore—the house is quiet, the occupants either out or holed up in their rooms. He finds a tray of leftover meatloaf in the fridge with a note from Les inviting him to it, and eats by himself at a tiny table in the gleaming kitchen. Then he turns on the TV in the living room, flips through channels, but recognizes none of the shows. It seems the world didn't pause in the least while he was away. When he finally goes up to his bedroom, Ray is already snoring from across the room.

How is he supposed to sleep around this nut job? Even if he didn't send the gruesome photo, there's always the possibility that his 'boundary issues' could give him the grand idea to crawl under the covers with his roommate, and fraternizing policy be damned.

Because of these thoughts and so many more, Kerry Denton's first night as a free man is not too different than many of his nights as an inmate.

He stares at the ceiling and forces himself to stay awake as long as possible.

SIX

Kerry's fitful slumber is broken the next morning by his new alarm clock. He's dismayed to see the opposite bed is already empty. Stealth is not an attribute someone as big as Ray should possess.

He set the alarm early enough that he could jump in the shower and get dressed before his first group therapy session at 8. The welcome packet stresses he should not be late for these. Kerry crawls out of bed, wearing a t-shirt and flannel pajama bottoms that his mother sent, grabs a pair of jeans from the closet, and slips out of the room.

The house is much more active than last night. He can hear country music playing from one of the other male rooms, and catches the heavenly aroma of cooking bacon from downstairs. Kerry walks to the bathroom down the hall and pushes open the door.

At the same time, the entrance door from the female side of the house swings into the room. A slim blonde wearing nothing but a towel steps inside and flips the light switch. She jumps when she sees him, but recovers quickly with a theatrically relieved swoon against the door. "Oh fuck! Jesus, you scared me! You the new guy?"

"Yeah, that's me." He politely averts his eyes, but they land on the long mirror above the double sinks, where he can see all of her anyway. She's older than him, probably late 20's, and a bit on the scrawny side—delicate bones jut around her slender neck in a way that makes him think more of cadavers than supermodels—but so tall that the towel wrapped around her torso barely has enough length to cover the area from breast to crotch. "Sorry, I probably should've knocked."

"No biggee." Her eyes flick up and down him. One corner of her mouth hooks upward. "I'm Lorie."

"Kerry." He clears his throat. "Do we need to reserve bathroom time or something? I didn't see anything in the packet."

"Nope. First come, first served." She sidles closer, leaning sideways on the counter beside him and tilting her head in a gesture that's half-inquisitive, half-seductive. The position causes the towel to ride up a few more inches on her thighs. "You mind if I go? I have to get to work right after group."

"Sure," he says, trying—and failing—to be unaware of the smooth mound visible between her legs, peeking out from beneath the hem of the towel. "No problem."

One hand rises from her side. Long fingers brush up the front of his pajama leg, sending a pleasant spark through his groin. She stops at his waist and toys with the knot on the drawstring. "You're welcome to get in with me if you want. Water conservation and all that."

Kerry manages to stop the surprise from showing on his face. "I think that would probably violate the whole 'No Fraternizing' rule."

"What they don't know won't hurt them."

"Still…I'll take a raincheck. But thanks for the offer."

"Your loss. I can do things with a loofa that will blow your mind." She turns around, undoes the towel, throws it over the shower rod, then steps into the tub and closes the curtain behind her nude backside. The water is already running by the time Kerry retreats into the hallway and closes the door.

"Is everybody in this place insane?" he mutters.

And is quickly reminded of the answer to this question as he ventures further down the hall, into the media center, and hears, "What's new, Mr. Magoo?"

Ray sits at the computer, snickering at his own nonsense. Today he wears a different jogging outfit and headband, although it's hard to imagine that he's ever moved faster than walking speed in his life. Kerry sighs, throws his jeans over his shoulder, and walks over. "Absolutely nothing, Ray. What're you doing?"

"Checking my website! That bar mitzvah lady must've told some of her friends, cause I got orders for three more batches! I don't even think I can produce them fast enough. I'll probably have to take the one that pays the most."

"How difficult your life must be." Kerry perches on the edge of the desk and glances at the man's website, which sports garish colors and lots of pictures of Ray's creations. "So…give me the lowdown on the group sessions. What do we do, just talk about our feelings and shit?"

"Kind of, I guess. We're supposed to visualize our past, present, and future to correct the course of our lives."

"*Past, present, and future?* God, is it therapy or time travel?"

Ray lifts a shoulder and lets it fall. "Les says it's how we become happy, healthy humans." He swivels his chair around to face the computer screen. "And guess what? I checked this morning and your picture is on the house with me now! Yay!"

"Huh?" Kerry looks around the room, thinking that maybe he's missed some kind of wall with photos of the residents. "What picture?"

"On the computer, dumb dumb." Ray types on the keyboard, laboriously hunting for each letter. As a new page loads, a hard fist of anxiety punches Kerry in the stomach.

At the top, in big, bold, not-messing-around letters is the header, **STATE OF TEXAS SEX OFFENDER REGISTRY**. Below that stretches a map of the state, divided into counties. Ray moves the arrow over to a link on the side that invites users to *Check My Address for Nearby Offenders*.

"I don't know if I wanna see this..." Kerry mumbles.

"Hold on a sec, it's really cool!"

"Ray...a lot of things in life can be classified as 'cool,' but I'm going out on a limb here to say that finding your own listing on the sex offender registry probably ain't one of 'em."

But Ray is already typing in the address for Hopeful Sunshine and hitting ENTER. A Google Map replaces the registry, displaying a swath of Dallas County from so far above that individual streets and residences are indistinguishable amid the shades of gray and white. A legend below this states, *Displaying Offenders Within a 3 Mile Range*. Two red dots burn in the middle of the graphic, a fact that makes Kerry feel as lonely and isolated as being on the moon. Ray spins the wheel on the mouse to zoom in on them until their neighborhood and the very house where they now sit take up a good chunk of the screen. The red dots vanish, replaced by photos of both men which float above the gray outline of Hopeful Sunshine.

"Neat, huh?" Ray asks. "Like a government satellite tracking spies or something!" And then, in an accent that sounds suspiciously French, "My name is James. Bond. James Bond. Wait, that's not it…"

"You mind if I take a look?" Without waiting for a reply, Kerry squats beside the computer chair and slides the mouse over to him. His stomach is still churning, but he forces himself to study the screen.

The picture is from his booking four years ago. It still resembles him closely enough to be recognizable, although he looks pale and haggard from his trip to the emergency room a few hours before, with deep circles under his eyes that make him appear absolutely ghoulish. Ray's photo, however, is just the opposite: a slimmed down, healthy version of the ginger beams happily into the camera like he's having a glamour shot made instead of being put away for half his life.

Again, Kerry thinks of the schoolchildren with the bleeding holes in their heads and suppresses a shiver.

He uses the mouse to hover over his own face and clicks.

A stat sheet comes up, like something compiled on a pro sports player. But in place of touchdowns and RBIs are complete details on his physical description, arrest, charges, sentencing, prison record and release. Everything but his jumpsuit size, and even that might be buried somewhere in the volumes of personal information the website offers.

Deep shame steals over him, a humiliation that makes his entire body too warm. He understands the purpose of such a database is to warn the world of the evil that could be stalking them at any given moment, but Kerry would rather be forced out onto a stage in front of a crowded auditorium completely naked than to have his sins put on display like this.

Of course, if you did that, then you'd be on this stupid blacklist for life instead of just the next decade.

Beside him, Ray says happily, "I used to be all alone on there, but now I got you, buddy! See, I told you we'd be like brothers!"

"Yeah," Kerry agrees. "Brothers."

SEVEN

Kerry has no time to shower after Lorie vacates the bathroom. Rather than attend his first group therapy session in his pajamas, he goes back to his room, throws on a change of clothes and hurries downstairs. The door of the meeting room to the left of the staircase is open now, and he can see a circle of chairs set up within, one of them already occupied by his roommate. Since he doesn't want to endure more bizarre small talk, Kerry goes the opposite way and enters into the kitchen, following the smell of bacon.

The kitchen has definitely been in use, but whoever did the cooking is long gone. A pot of scrambled eggs and a plate of biscuits sit on the counter. Kerry scoops some of the former into one of the latter, takes a bite, then turns around to find a tall Hispanic man in a dark blue suit standing at the coffee machine beside the fridge, pouring himself a mug from the pot.

"'Ey bro, you the new guy?" He's around Sanders' age, fit and good-looking, with jet black hair that lays flat along his skull and a threadbare mustache. He puts the coffee pot down and sticks out a hand with a small tattoo of snake-eyed dice above the thumb. "Les mentioned we were gettin somebody else. I'm Scott Ramirez."

Kerry introduces himself while the other man crushes his fingers to the point of discomfort.

"So how you likin the place so far, man?"

"It's okay. Way more rules than prison."

"Right? 'Cept here they're always threatenin to throw you *out* if you break 'em." Scott takes a sip of his coffee, winces at either the taste or the temperature, then says, "Seriously though, livin here can change your life, if you work at it. I'm proof, bro. I did seven years for grand theft auto down in Huntsville, and now Les got me set up at a car dealership. You believe that shit? Used to steal Corvettes from fat suburban dads and now I sell them to 'em. Yo, I never coulda got a job like that before I went in. I'm 'onna petition to move outta here when my mandatory period is up in three months."

"Scuse me, boys." Lorie breezes into the kitchen, now dressed in tight yellow capri pants and a black camisole, blond hair piled on her head in a neat bun. She squeezes between Kerry and Scott to pull open the fridge door, grabs a peach, then leaves the same way she entered, running a finger lightly along Kerry's arm and tossing him a smile over her shoulder. Kerry watches her leave.

"I know that prob'ly looks like a million bucks after prison," Scott says, lowering his voice, "but I would steer clear, bro. She's been in and out of jail for prostitution since she was, like, fifteen. Mommy didn't love her enough, daddy loved her too much, all that shit. Now she claims she's just a sex addict, gets with a different guy every few days." He sips from his mug. "Ask me, she's better off as a ho. Least then she's gettin paid to collect diseases."

"Romance is the last thing on my mind," Kerry assures him. But at least the encounter in the bathroom makes sense now.

Scott grunts. "Ain't gonna be no romance with that *chica*. Just a good ol' pump and dump. Few times, when I was desperate, I thought about saddlin up myself, but, you know, I got a girlfriend now." He slaps Kerry's chest with the back of his hand. "Yo, they got you roomin with that freak, huh? Jesus Christo, I can't even stand bein under the same roof with that fuckin molester, don't know what I would do if they told me I had to sleep next to him. That fat shit gives me the creeps, shut up in his room all day, makin his stupid paper animals. Prob'ly jerkin it to kiddie porn. I fuckin *hate* sex offenders, man. 'Ey, what were you in for anyway? Les never said."

"Uh...well...actually, it was...statutory," Kerry mumbles, using Sanders' word like a shield.

The other man freezes with his coffee mug halfway to his lips. "We, uh...we better get to group." He walks away, leaving Kerry with burning cheeks and a brick in his stomach.

After piecing back together his self-esteem, Kerry leaves the kitchen and walks across to the meeting room. He stops at the door to sign his name to the list posted there, under today's date, then looks around.

This room is more colorful than the rest of the house, painted in pleasant tones of light green and gold. More motivational posters hang on the walls, along with a list of Group Therapy Commandments that includes, 'No Cursing,' 'No Disrespect,' and 'Constructive Criticism Only.' Another sign proclaims, 'Three Strikes = Demerit, Five Demerits in a Month = Expulsion.' Great; more rules to keep track of. The circle of chairs is filled up, except one empty seat between Les and Ray. Kerry works his way along the periphery toward it, passing behind D'libra—sitting with arms and legs crossed over an ensemble of pajama bottoms and a top that rides the line between immodest and indecent—and another white man in his fifties that he assumes must be Mark.

As Kerry slips into the seat, Les says, "Excellent, we're all here on time!"

"Whoop-dee-do," D'libra mutters.

"Even the small victories are worth celebrating," Les tells her cheerfully, but turns away before she rolls her wide eyes toward the ceiling. Today the psychologist wears a plaid sweater vest over his short sleeve dress shirt, but perspiration is already soaking through the armpits. Kerry thinks he must have to drink gallons of water every day to replace all that lost moisture. "As you can see, we got a new housemate yesterday. For those that haven't met him, this is Kerry Denton. Please make him feel welcome."

There is a smattering of polite applause. Except for D'libra, who leaves her arms firmly folded across that shiny scar tissue in the crooks of her elbows, and Ray, who smashes his hands together so hard Kerry is afraid his wrists will snap. He tips them all a quick salute.

"Because he's new—and because some of you need a reminder—I'd like to go over the way we structure these sessions." Les holds a hand up with fingers splayed, like a movie director setting a scene. "You see Kerry, our lives are a ship, and the rudder is the choices that we make. And sometimes, when we go astray, we can correct our course by examining where we've been, where we are, and where we're going. We do this by visualizing our—"

"Past, present, and future," Kerry interrupts. "Yeah, Ray sorta filled me in."

"That's great," Les says, although his annoyed tone suggests otherwise. "In each session, I decide which segment we'll be discussing, and each member is invited to share something—a story, a memory, a feeling, or just a hope— that fits within the framework and illustrates a decision they made which did—or *is*, or *will*—shape their own personal life course. Does that make sense?"

"Um...I'm sure I'll catch on."

"Of course!" Les beams. "Now, you must share *something* to receive credit for the session, but, keep in mind, the point of this is to help you, so the more you tell us, the more tools we have to work with. After you speak, everyone else is invited to give their respectful thoughts on your contribution."

"Yeah, yeah, okay, let's get this started, bro," Scott says from his seat between D'libra and Lorie. "Some of us gotta get to work, know what I mean?"

"So what are we telling today?" Lorie asks. "Oh, please let's do past, I remembered something that I really wanna get off my chest."

"Ugh, girl, I can't listen to no more of yo' skank-ass sex-capades," D'libra groans.

"Language," Les cautions.

"'Ass' ain't no curse word. They say it on TV."

"Well, it is in here." Les straightens in his seat and mops at his glistening brow with the back of one wrist. "I thought today, since this is Kerry's first session, we might do dealer's choice. Anything you want to talk about is fine."

"Then wouldn't that be *players'* choice?" Mark asks. He wears gray slacks and a crisp white dress shirt. A huge gold cross is visible through the fabric, dangling from his neck. "Not that I gamble, because that's not part of the good Lord's plan for me, but—"

"Yes, players' choice, whatever," Les cuts in. "Who wants to go first?"

Lorie volunteers, and proceeds to tell an overly embellished story about accepting a Home Depot gift card to sleep with her half-brother at the age of nineteen. "I've never even been inside a Home Depot," she says, sounding as utterly bewildered by her actions as the rest of them. Scott talks about his plans for the future, finding a place to live in three months and asking his girlfriend to marry him. D'libra refuses to say anything until Les threatens her with a withheld session credit—"Your *third* this month," he cautions—after which she relents and mumbles a few sentences about the first time she tried heroin. Then comes Mark, who, Kerry learns, spent eight years in prison for a DWI manslaughter, during which he found Jesus. He sobs as he tells a story about the last time he had supervised visitation with his children, and asks the group to pray with him that he will get to see them again. Throughout all of this, each story and the lively group debates that follow, Kerry remains silent.

"I wanna talk about the present!" Ray exclaims, when his turn comes. They have been in the session for close to an hour by this point.

"What a surprise," D'libra says. Scott grunt laughter.

"Go ahead Ray," Les encourages.

"I got some more orders this morning! And a new room-mate!" He grabs Kerry's shoulder, but doesn't notice that Kerry shies away from the contact. "I'm so thankful that my business is doing well and that I have some money for the first time ever and that I'm making people happy!"

"Okay, that's good news! Does anyone else want to respond to that?"

"How can we?" Scott asks. "He says the same thing like every time."

"I told you, I refuse to respond to anything that man says," Mark proclaims.

D'libra uncrosses her legs and leans forward in her seat, granting an unhampered view of her cleavage. The purple streak in her hair falls across her forehead. She stares at Ray with brown eyes as hard as flint. "You know what else makes people happy? Not raping they damn kids."

"Hey!" Les barks. "That's not constructive!"

"Ask any parent and I bet they say it is."

Ray's exuberant face darkens, the joy falling away. He slouches in his seat and stares at the floor. Lorie pats him lightly on the forearm. "I think it's great. I wish I had a talent that people paid me for."

Scott grins so big his cheeks nearly touch his eyeballs. "Yo *chica*, I think you did." Lorie gives him the finger, for which she receives a first warning from Les.

"This conversation doesn't seem to be going anywhere," the psychologist says. "Kerry, you've been quiet all morning."

"I guess I'm trying to figure out what to say. I get the concept and all, but…I don't have anything prepared."

"Then just speak from the heart. Start out by telling us why you think you're here. Your side of the story."

"There is no 'side,'" Kerry says quickly. He hated those people in prison who came up with endless reasons for their innocence. The other offenders that tried to lie or hide their crimes from the inmate community received brutal beatings, so he got used to honesty. "I know why I'm here. I committed a felony statutory sex offense."

"Another one of these people?" Mark groans, placing a hand over the outline of the cross on his chest. "Lord give me strength in the lion's den."

A snort comes from the other side of the circle. "Yeah, that's some way to pretty it up, Chester," D'libra says. She directs the laser beam of her gaze from Ray to him. "What you mean is you raped a li'l kid, right? But at least you own up to it, unlike your friend over there."

Kerry holds up a hand. "Look, I committed a crime, I know that, I admit it, but...I think it's important to distinguish that I'm not a child molester. Okay? And I didn't rape anybody. I had sex—*consensual* sex—with a sixteen-year-old. That's all."

"So? Even if that's true, the law say she a kid, and that makes you a sick fuck." She sits up straight and smirks at Kerry, daring him to argue.

"That's two, D'libra. One more curse and you're out of here," Les cautions. He turns to Kerry, sweat coursing down his temples, and says, "But I *do* think it's important for you to respond. With the stigma placed on such relationships, it's likely you'll face that sort of accusation a lot."

Kerry's teeth grind together. His face is reddening, from a potent brew of frustration and humiliation. There are words inside him, words that he wants to use to make them understand, to make them see what he and Kayla had, maybe even to remind himself that their short time together meant something in his otherwise miserable existence, but those words won't come, and he suspects that it would make no difference to these people even if they did. He looks down, sees that he's rubbing at the shiny knob of scar tissue at the end of his amputated finger, and forces himself to stop. "There's a difference, okay? There *is*." The same thing he said to Sanders, and it sounds even more pathetic this time.

D'libra's smirk widens. This is obviously fun for her, getting a free pass to belittle someone. For a moment, he wonders if she might not be the mystery photo-defacer. "The only difference is that *your* playmate had a li'l more grass on the field for you to play ball in."

This time, Scott bursts out laughing and offers the black girl a high five. The sound of their palms smacking together makes Kerry wince.

Lorie speaks up from the other side of Ray. "But doesn't that kinda...I don't know...take away someone's accountability?"

"Elaborate on that," Les says, rubbing his chin thoughtfully.

"Well, I mean...he got in trouble, but this girl that he slept with...she's just as much to blame, right? She still had free will. I mean, if it, you know...happened the way he says."

Kerry is about to ask what she means, but D'ibra shakes her head. "Don't matter how it happened. If a person under 18, they don't got no free will."

"That's not true! I mean, when I was sixteen I knew if I wanted to fu—uh, have sex with a guy or not. And some of them were a *lot* older than me."

"That just means you a ho, and they shoulda gone to prison too."

"Oh, okay. I'm so glad you're the queen of morality and know what everyone else is thinking and feeling all the time."

"I know what you thinkin, cause it's the same thing you *always* thinkin." D'libra forms a circle with the thumb and index finger of her right hand, extends the index finger of her left, and begins jamming it vigorously in and out of the circle.

"Yeah, so what?" Lorie fumes. "I like sex. At least I'm not too repressed to admit it."

"I think what Lorie meant," Les cuts in, "is that, from a wider perspective, eighteen is an arbitrary age assigned by the law. It doesn't speak to a person's emotional maturity. That's why the Romeo and Juliet laws are in place, to protect people that are suddenly told they can't continue to see someone just because they crossed a legal boundary."

D'libra's lips purse in disgust. "Whatevah, Les. Defend him all you want. But I think Chester over there and everybody like him should have they balls cut off...just like his fatso roommate."

Les sighs heavily and checks his watch. "I think that's a good place to stop for the day."

EIGHT

The end of the meeting triggers a mass exodus out of the house. Mark and Scott carpool to work, Lorie has something called an 'Uber' waiting for her, and D'libra jumps into the back of a dark blue sedan with gold rims that pulls to the curb and lets out a belch of sweet-smelling smoke as she opens the door. Kerry lets them all leave before slinking out himself. As he crosses the entry, Les shouts from the kitchen, "We need to talk about your chore schedule tonight!" All the sentence needs is a 'young man' to make him feel like he's back in high school.

He stomps down the driveway, seething and embarrassed, but jumps when he hears, "Where you going?"

Ray sits in the driver's seat of the van with the bizarre space pickle on its side, the dark tinted window rolled down. The engine is off but he rests both hands on the steering wheel anyway, like a five-year-old pretending to drive.

"To look for a job," Kerry tells him. "I have to find another place to live as fast as fucking possible."

"How come?"

"*How come?* Did...did you not hear any of that? They crucified both of us. I can't listen to that bullshit every day."

"Oh." Ray's hands slip off the wheel and fall into his lap. "Where do you wanna work?"

"I don't care. Fast food. Construction. Fucking grave digging. Hell, I'll work in raw sewage if it means some cash coming in. I'm gonna apply at every store in the goddamn mall, then go from there."

Hope lights up Ray's face. "I can give you a ride."

"No thanks, I'll grab a bus."

"Okay. Bye."

Kerry walks away, gets as far as the sidewalk, then returns. "Do you even have a driver's license?"

Ray nods eagerly, his orange curls falling in his face. "Les helped me practice for the test! I did real good, except with parallel parking. I sorta tore one of the poles out of the ground."

"Fine, whatever. Jesus, why does everyone guilt me into taking a ride?"

He goes around to the passenger side and examines the artwork on this panel—a potato chip standing on a diving board over a pool filled with some white substance that he takes to be dip—while Ray leans across the center console to unlock the door. A heavy fog of fried food and old grease smacks Kerry in the nostrils as soon as he pulls it open. He pushes through the stench to sit down on the cracked vinyl seat, but rolls down his window before closing the door.

Ray produces a key and starts the van. Something beneath the hood gives a cat-in-heat squall. A puff of smoke squirts from one side. He puts the vehicle in gear, slams the brakes before crashing through the garage door of the house, then switches to reverse and backs down the driveway. Kerry grabs for his seatbelt only to find that the clasp is broken.

"You're gonna have a hard time getting this thing to pass inspection, you know."

Ray spews laughter that sounds like a goose honking as he swerves onto the street too fast, switches gears with a horrible grinding noise, and drives on. Kerry takes the opportunity to check out the rest of the van. A heavy fabric curtain hangs behind the seats, now pushed to the side to allow a view of the rear. The vehicle's cargo space is lined with steel cabinets and wire shelves, along with several cooking workstations. Kerry spots a microwave, a mini-fridge, a grill, and even what appears to be a tiny deep fryer. "Where did you buy this thing anyway?"

"From a deli! They took delivery orders and made the food in the back while they drove, so it stayed warm!"

"Ah, now I get the paint job. And what happened to this brilliant venture?"

"They went out of business."

"You mean people didn't want to eat French fries cooked in the back of a disgusting minivan? Shocking."

They roll on, through the endless reel of residential streets, and once Kerry gets used to Ray's herky-jerky driving, he sits back and enjoys the wind in his face through the open windows. The other man babbles on for a few blocks, then stops in the middle of a detailed recounting of yesterday's cartoons and says, "Uh oh."

Before Kerry can ask him what's wrong, Ray hits the brakes in the middle of an intersection hard enough to send them into a skid. Kerry throws out a hand to keep from flying into the dash. The maneuver elicits an angry honk from the car behind them. Ray twists the wheel and takes an abrupt right.

"What are you doing, the freeway's straight ahead!"

"Nope, nope. Can't go that way." His hands jitter on the steering wheel like gigantic spiders. "We have to go around. Boy, was that close."

Kerry twists around to peer through the van's rear windows and catches sight of the school Sanders pointed out receding behind them. If they'd kept going, the van would've passed by the long, rolling park that lies in front of it. "It's okay to drive by, man. Sanders said the street is far enough away for us."

Ray reaches down and feels for the black band around his ankle. The light on the monitor glows an angry red in the floorboard. He raps his knuckles on the plastic casing and says loudly, "I'm sorry, okay? I didn't mean to. I wasn't gonna go there."

"I don't think they can hear you through that, Ray."

"I know. But just in case." His freckled face is dour and serious as he sits back up. "I don't like to get close to...to places like that. If they think I'm going there, they...they might m-make me go back to the hospital. But I'm g-g-good now. The doctors made me good."

"Ray," Kerry says gently, "back at the meeting, what did D'libra mean? They didn't really chop off your...you know...did they?"

The other man's Adam's apple dips and bobs as he swallows several times. "I have to go to the doctor every three months. Les takes me. If I don't go, the police will come and get me. The doctor gives me a shot, and...and I don't hear the voices anymore."

"Are you...?" Kerry swallows a cold lump in his throat. "Are you talking about chemical castration?"

Ray stares dead ahead through the windshield. "They wouldn't let me out of the hospital unless I agreed."

"How do you...I mean...what does that feel like?"

Ray raises a shoulder and then lets it slump. "Doesn't feel like anything."

Kerry supposes that makes sense. It wouldn't necessarily be a sensation, but rather a *lack* thereof. As in, no sexual urges whatsoever. He knew of some offenders that plea bargained for a lesser sentence in exchange for the hormone therapy, and all of them were terrified. When the tide started to turn in Kerry's trial, Gerry Stevens, Esq, brought it up as an option to throw out, but Kerry shot him down without a second thought. Even the side effects—weight gain, depression, mood swings—sounded like a nightmare.

A bud of genuine sympathy for this man begins to grow inside him. Kerry squashes it before it can blossom. It doesn't matter if they found a way to leash him; the man is still a child-molesting monster, no ifs, ands, or statutories about it. It does, however, make him a feel a bit better about sharing a room with Raymond Leary. "But are you numb down there or what?"

"Uh...well..."

"Can you still, like...get it up?"

Ray's face begins to scrunch.

"Okay, never mind, let's talk about something else." Ray, of course, obliges by immediately launching into a new topic with his usual cheeriness, but Kerry's mind doesn't follow. He can't stop wondering what that would be like, to never have sex, to never get horny, to never feel that warmth in your belly when you see a woman that you just *want*, in that same mysterious way that you want food or air. Kerry thinks a lot of guys in that situation would probably feel like lesser men, but really, if they're being honest with themselves, do they even miss it? Most of the time, a dick does nothing but get you into trouble. Kerry can attest to that.

Don't cheapen it, he scolds himself. *Don't pretend that you and Kayla were just about the sex. Otherwise, you're no better than him.*

Still, as he watches Ray talk, a phrase floats through Kerry's head, one his mother used to say often: *there but for the grace of God.*

He's still thinking about this when Ray asks a question that cuts through his daydreaming. "So what happened to *you?*"

"Huh?"

"Your finger." Ray reaches toward Kerry's hand where it lays on the seat between them. He jerks the appendage away before the other man can touch it and crosses his arms, hiding the missing digit in his armpit.

Ray's faux pas doesn't register. "Did it get cut off?" he asks in awe. "When I was a kid, this boy at my school brought a little guillotine from a magic kit to show and tell. He could cut carrots in half but when he stuck his finger in, it didn't even bleed! Then at lunch, this other kid took it out of his locker and tried to do it to himself, and sliced off the end of his pinkie! Did that happen to you, did it accidentally get cut off in a magic trick?"

"Not quite," Kerry says, and offers nothing more on the subject.

The closest mall sprawls across multiple blocks of prime Dallas real estate. Kerry came to the movies here a few times in high school, and had a girlfriend that worked at the Auntie Anne's Pretzel stand. On a Thursday morning like this, the parking lot is as vacant as the prison's was yesterday. But, when Ray slows down to turn onto one of the empty aisles, the angry blare of a horn sounds behind them, unexpected and close enough to make them both jump.

"What the hell is this guy's problem?" Kerry looks in the side mirror hanging outside his door, but can't see the person behind them until they pull around the van. A beaten, scratched-up red pickup roars past him. The driver—a man in a green trucker hat—hangs from the window, glaring at Kerry, as does a passenger on the other side of him. Then they're gone, speeding across the parking lot. The bed of the truck is filled with tarps and cans of plaster, and a huge, attached toolbox stretches the width of the vehicle below the rear window.

It looks like the kind of truck that would be very much at home on a construction site.

Sudden paranoia strikes him, the same as in Sanders' car after the parole officer picked him up outside the prison. It's a cringing desire to crawl into a hole somewhere and hide.

"I guess they were in a hurry," Ray says.

"Yeah," Kerry agrees numbly, then tells himself, *You have to stop, or you'll be seeing Rob Mac's hand at work every time the damn weather changes.*

Ray pulls forward and parks the van in a spot up next to the entrance to Sears. He opens his door to get out, but Kerry says, "Hold on, man. Thanks for the ride and everything, but…you know…I can't have you tagging along while I'm trying to find a job. You understand, right?"

"Yeah. Oh yeah, sure. You gotta be free in case they wanna take you out for cocktails. *Mad Men* and all. That's how business is done."

"Something like that."

"You want me to wait for you?"

"Nope, go home. I'll catch the bus back."

Kerry gets out before the man can sucker him in with more pity and walks away from the van.

The next three hours are an endless drudgery of disappointment and embarrassment as he goes from store to store, inquiring about employment opportunities. Very few places are even hiring (all of them cite 'THE ECONOMY' for this, in the same tones that one uses when talking about the boogeyman in the closet), but he finds a few vacant positions for part time work. At every one, he's invited to fill out an application, and, as he attempts to do so with his crippled writing hand, he's stopped time and time again by the same question.

Have you ever been convicted of a felony?

His answers to these are light on details but entirely truthful; he's not sure if lying on an employment application could land him back in prison, but he sure isn't about to find out. He leaves them by the register and hustles out of the store with his cheeks on fire before they can be read. Except at the electronic boutique, where they sell video games that all look like the same military first-person shooter to Kerry. The manager is eager to interview him on the spot until he scans through the paperwork. Then he abruptly states that he'll give Kerry a call to set something up. Outside the boutique, Kerry hangs around and watches through the glass storefront long enough to see the man point out something on the app to another employee. The other guy makes the sort of face one pulls at the smell of rancid milk, then the manager tosses the paper into a trash can next to the checkout counter.

Just as Sanders said, no one is going to hire him. Why would they, when there are so many candidates seeking work these days with clean records? Except Kerry can't help wondering if Scott—with his gang tattoo and felony record full of theft—would ever receive the same treatment that he did.

He leaves the mall defeated and weary and heads to the bus stop down the street. On the next corner is a Chase bank location. Kerry decides he can at least do something to get himself back on the path toward legitimacy.

Thirty minutes later, he has reactivated his bank account, which was frozen due to inactivity. There's even still close to a hundred bucks in his checking, and he adds the last of his gate money to it. In time, he's confident there will be steady paychecks to deposit. The clerk—a perky blond with a slim waist and alluring green eyes—gives him a friendly smile and touches his forearm as he leaves.

It's not much, but, as Les said, even the small victories are worth celebrating. It makes him feel a little more like a human being. Maybe not a happy, healthy one, but still a human being. It gives him hope that he might be able to climb out of the black hole his life has become with a little effort and positivity. His mood lifted, Kerry pushes open the glass front door of the bank to step out into that sunlight he loves so much.

And immediately has it flung back in his face.

The thick glass smashes into his nose and forehead hard enough to cause a burst of stars across his vision. He stumbles to the side, the world wavering, and puts a hand on the brick exterior of the building to steady himself. Two tall, burly men come around from behind the door and walk past him into the bank. Kerry stares at them as something wet trickles out of his right nostril. Both are chuckling, the first sporting shaggy blond locks down to his neck, but the second guy's hair is covered.

By a green trucker's hat.

"Better watch where yer goin, pervert," he whispers, "or you might get hurt even worse."

He keeps his eyes on Kerry, walking backwards as he enters the bank. The gleeful sneer on his lips is so wide, it shows every nicotine-stained tooth in his head.

NINE

"You want me to do *what?*" Kerry asks.

"Just knock on the door, read the script to whoever answers, and then move on to the next house," Les tells him. "Think of it like trick-or-treating."

"Yeah, except absolutely no one is going to give me a handful of candy for this."

It's Saturday morning, and they stand in the overgrown front yard of Hopeful Sunshine after another rousing group therapy session. The focus of this one was the future, which, Lorie assured him, is always the easiest, the one that Les chooses when he wants the meeting to be short. Each of them took their turn to share with little commentary, although D'libra did mutter, "Good luck," after Kerry expressed his goal to find a job and go back to school. Then Les brought him outside and handed him the piece of paper he now holds, on which is written one paragraph that begins with, 'Hello, my name is ______________ and I am a registered sex offender who recently moved into your neighborhood.'

Kerry reads through the script and says, "This doesn't

make any sense. I'm a level two offender. The state requires residency notification at level three, and even then, don't they just mail something out? I thought this door-to-door thing only happened in the movies."

"It's not for the state, it's for the house. I agree, it doesn't make sense, but unfortunately, it's one of the provisions we agreed on to get the city to zone the property for us. Their views are a bit more…reactionary when it comes to these matters." He chuckles uncomfortably. "I wouldn't be surprised if they got the idea from a movie."

"Fine, then I'm not doing it. If it won't get me sent back to jail, then the city can go fuck itself."

Les bristles, a good sheen of sweat already making his bald head glisten. "Then you'll have to leave the home. We can't risk getting our license pulled."

"Good god, you guys love to pull out that threat for everything, don't you? *Make your bed or we'll kick you out. Don't leave the toilet seat up or we'll kick you out. Don't snore too loud or we'll kick you out.*"

The psychologist places his hands on his hips, a gesture that instantly ages him a good decade or so. "Somehow, I don't think the threat of withholding dessert would have the same effect on a bunch of ex-cons."

Kerry's shoulders slump as he looks both ways up and down the street. The old man is outside again two doors down, staring daggers at them. Kerry tries to imagine giving his impromptu recital to that bundle of joy. "How many houses do I have to do this at?"

"Every one within a thousand yard radius. Three blocks in each direction should cover it. All you have to do is attempt to read it and then move on. If anyone cuts you off or refuses to listen, count them as complete. Same with anyone that gets a little…"

"Homicidal?"

"I was going to say 'belligerent.'"

Kerry glowers at him. "Goddamn it, this is fucking dangerous, Les. Nobody wants a sex offender showing up on their doorstep. You're sending me off with a 'Kick My Ass' sign around my neck."

Les makes a pooh-poohing gesture. "No one is going to kick anything. And even if they did, that's why Brad insisted you have backup."

They turn. On the driveway, Ray is using Windex and paper towels to clean the ridiculous mural on the side of his van. He waves when he see them watching. "Ready to go, G.I. Joe?"

Kerry ignores him and looks at Les. "That is not comforting in the least. Are you telling me *he* did this, too? Mr. Bash My Own Brains Out If Anyone Even Mentions My History?"

"Well…no." Les squirms a bit. "His doctors at the institute wrote a dispensation stating that it could be damaging to his mental health."

"That's wonderful. So I'm also the guinea pig for this fantastic community outreach effort." Before Les can say anything further, Kerry beckons Ray like an impatient parent. "C'mon if you're coming. But you stay in the street the entire time, understand? The last thing I need is you trying to tweak their nipples or some shit while I'm reading this."

They begin next door, where no one answers, then head toward the old man, who immediately shoos them off his property like stray cats before they can get a word out. Only at the third house does Kerry ring the doorbell and get a response. A hefty, middle-aged woman in a housecoat smiles at him while three children ranging in age from toddler to kindergarten crowd around her ankles and stare up at him with wide, curious eyes.

"Um, hello," Kerry says, reading directly from the script, which now shakes in his hands hard enough to make the paper rattle. After seeing himself on the registry, he felt like everyone for miles around must know him on sight, but there is no recognition on this kind lady's face. "My name is Kerry and I'm a registered sex offender who just moved into your neighborhood. I am introducing myself to everyone so that—"

He gets no further than this. The woman's jaw drops. She urges her children away frantically, swatting the toddler's behind to get him to move faster. They scurry to the end of the foyer and peek around the corner when their mother's back is turned.

She closes the door until she's looking at Kerry through a two-inch wide crack and demands shrilly, "You...y-you live in that house down the street?"

"Yes ma'am. Hopeful Sunshine. I'm sorry, I just meant to—"

"Go! Get off my property!" she screeches. "If you ever come back, I'll call the police!"

The door slams shut. Kerry can hear the sound of several deadbolts engaging.

"That went well," he murmurs.

When he gets back to the sidewalk where his roommate waits, Ray slings a doughy arm around his shoulders and says, "You would've made a great Girl Scout, pal."

A reluctant smile inches across Kerry's face.

The treatment is repeated at every house he visits for the next hour. Doors are slammed, names are called. One man lifts up his shirttail to show Kerry the butt of a pistol jutting from his waistband to encourage his speedy departure, but otherwise, it's nowhere near the orgy of violence he envisioned. He gets all the way through the script twice, once to an old woman who seems confused about what Kerry is selling, and once to a waifish, wide-eyed guy whose heavy breathing and request for details about Kerry's crime imply that the residents of this neighborhood should be far more worried about him.

The police do show up as he walks the second block, a cruiser that drifts slowly up to them and flashes its lights to get his attention. Ray moves behind Kerry as the cop at the wheel rolls down his window and studies them through mirrored sunglasses, his face expressionless. "Boys, I had a report of a pervert roaming the neighborhood and bothering people in their homes. You two know anything about that?"

Kerry holds the script in front of him like a shield. "I'm sorry, sir. We're from the Hopeful Sunshine group home on the next street over."

"Halfway house?"

"Yes sir. This is part of my requirement for staying there. Door to door notice of my residency. We didn't mean to cause any trouble."

The cop nods thoughtfully. Kerry sees the name 'Prentiss' on his nametag. He has a sharp, angular face, and a bristly mustache that creeps across his upper lip like fungus. "All right. No problem. I'll let dispatch know to ignore any further calls." He pauses for a second, then leans further out the window and asks, in a much friendlier, more conversational tone. "Say…I bet this is humiliating, huh?"

Kerry nods. "Yes sir. Very."

A small, mean-spirited smile wipes the friendliness from Officer Prentiss' face. "Good." He pulls away from the curb and rolls up the street away from them.

The day heats up as noon approaches, and Kerry quickly works up a sweat. By eleven, Ray's orange hairs hangs around his face in limp corkscrews. He begins to lag further and further behind, plopping down on the curb and waiting for Kerry to get several houses ahead before he catches up. Eventually they reach a one-story home like something from a fairy tale, with a white picket fence and a brilliantly green lawn mowed to military precision and stained glass wind chimes hanging from the trim around the porch. Kerry rings the doorbell, no longer nervous, just anxious to get this ordeal over with.

The woman who answers the door is as prim and neat as her house: mid-fifties, dumpy but well-kept, strawberry blond hair perfectly coiffed in a side-swept wave, and dressed in a business casual outfit of khaki slacks and red blouse. Despite her suburban conventionality, there's a hardness about her; the steel in her eyes as they narrow at Kerry isn't too different from that of the toughest inmates of Wayne Clifford.

"I'm sorry, we don't allow solicitors here." She uses a manicured fingernail to tap a small metal plate above her doorbell inscribed with this eleventh commandment.

Kerry doesn't bother to correct her, just starts into his script. When he reaches the first 'sex offender,'—the point in the script where most people begin backing away in utter terror—a smug, amused look comes over her. Instead of retreating, she crosses her arms and waits patiently for him to finish. The reaction, poised and somehow battle-ready, gets him so nervous he begins to stutter toward the end. Something about this woman makes him feel like a rabbit in the shadow of a circling hawk.

"You're from Hopeful Sunshine," she states once he stops speaking. "I can't help wondering, how many of you child-raping monsters are they going to cram into that place?"

Kerry turns to leave without a word, but her hand flashes out and clamps onto his upper arm, halting him in his tracks.

"You introduced yourself, now it's my turn," she tells him. Her voice is stern, but that delighted grin stays in place. "My name is Regina Velder, and I'm the head of the neighborhood committee created to get your little convict hostel shut down."

"I-I'm sorry, I didn't know," Kerry mumbles. And then thinks, *Could've used a warning, Les.*

"No, why would you? You and your fellow degenerates don't care about anything but yourselves. The fact that you make the rest of us stare at that eyesore of a house is proof of that." Velder seems to notice that her hand is still gripping his arm. She releases him and steps back, wiping the palm on her tan pant leg as though she crushed a bug with it. "We haven't forgotten about you, though. Oh no. We are still very much committed to having you all removed from this neighborhood and sent back to whatever garbage pile you crawled out from under. We're confident that we can have an injunction filed very soon."

Kerry knows he should go, but anger keeps him rooted to this officious woman's porch. "We're just people, all right? We're trying to get back on our feet. Make decent lives for ourselves."

"'Decent?'" She turns from the door, and he hears the rustle of paper as she reaches for something beside her. At first, Kerry thinks she might be going for a weapon and tenses to run, but when she comes back, she's clutching a folded section of the Dallas Morning News that she thrusts at his chest. "This person did the *decent* thing, young man. Maybe you should follow his example. Good day to you."

TEN

Velder steps back inside and closes the door. Kerry shuffles away, off the porch and down the concrete path back to the sidewalk, as he scans the paper to figure out what she meant. She's given him the Metro section, and halfway down the middle page is a single column whose headline reads, **Paroled Sex Offender Commits Suicide.**

An uncomfortable coldness slips over Kerry despite the day's warmth. He comes to a halt at the sidewalk. His stomach churns and, for a moment, he's back in prison, reliving the worst day of his life, holding the payphone in the common room to his ear as his mother speaks rapidly to him, but her voice is dampened by an acidic combination of regret and anger that pumps deeper into his veins with every squeeze of his heart.

Then the memory is gone, leaving behind an aching hollow in his chest and a brief shock of electric fire in his maimed hand.

He scans the article. The offender in question, one Dominic Zabawski, was released from prison two months before.

There is no mention of his past crimes or, thankfully, his method of self-termination, only that he took his life in his sister's house. There are a few other details that might prove why this is so newsworthy, but Kerry's perusal of the article is interrupted by mocking laughter.

Up the street, three junior-high-age boys on bicycles are riding around Ray where he sits on the curb, going past on the street, then coming back on the sidewalk, like sharks circling a meal. They shout something in between peals of malicious cackling, but Kerry only catches the creatively bankrupt epithets 'homo,' and 'ass-bandit.' Ray is hunched over with his arms wrapped around his head, rocking back and forth like a man in the throes of severe constipation.

"Hey!" Kerry breaks into a run, dropping the paper on Velder's perfect lawn, glad to be rid of it. The boys scatter and ride away, still screeching laughter. Kerry wonders if they were sent out on this harassment errand by their parents, after said parents got a visit from the pedophile fairies.

He reaches his roommate a moment later. Ray keeps his eyes closed as he grinds the heels of his hands into both temples, massaging so hard that his skull might cave in. He's moaning something under his breath, a quick stream of words, and, as Kerry kneels down in front him, he's able to make it out.

"Not my fault, not my fault, not my fault. The voices told me. It was bad, I *know* it was bad, I'll never do it again..."

"Ray, stop. They're gone. Snap out of it."

The man continues to mutter and squeeze his forehead. Kerry grabs his wrists and forces them away from his face, wincing as the stump of his finger makes contact. He can't stand the feel of it touching someone else's flesh. Ray's eyes flutter open. A film of tears covers them. He looks around in dazed confusion and then says simply, "They were mean."

"Yeah, I know, but who gives a shit?" Kerry lets go of his hands and falls backward, plopping down on the asphalt of the street. "Jesus, people are always going to be *mean* to you, Ray. Wasn't anybody *mean* while you sat in the looney bin for twenty fucking years?"

Ray lifts his shoulders one time, more a spasm than a shrug. He reaches down to touch the red light on his ankle monitor. "S-sometimes."

"Then why does it cause you to blow a gasket every time?"

"It's just...when I think about...about t-those things..." His face goes sour-lemon. "I g-get scared, and then I can't b-breathe..."

"So man up and get over it. Sticking your head in the sand doesn't erase the past." Kerry swallows a hot lump that rises into his throat. "And ignoring the choices you made doesn't change them."

"But the v-voices—"

Kerry shakes his head. "There are no voices, okay? It was *you*. You did...whatever you did. You don't have to be proud of it, but you do have to face it. And the next time you have a meltdown, just...I don't know, just pinch the shit out of your arm, like this." He grabs the meat of Ray's forearm between thumb and index finger—using his right hand for this operation, of course—and clamps down. Ray yelps and jerks the appendage away, then rubs the spot that Kerry pinched with a reproachful frown. "Hurts, right? Hard to be scared when you're suffering though. Believe me, pain always trumps fear. So if you start getting panicked, you do that, focus on the pain, take a deep breath, and you'll be able to think."

Ray's eyes fill up with watery hope. "You...you think that will work?"

"Gotta be better than trying to give yourself a lobotomy." Kerry stands and offers his right hand to Ray. "Why don't you head back to the house? I'm sure you've got some paper giraffes or something to make."

"Naw, I already did the giraffes. I do have an order to finish…but I can stay if you need me! I don't mind!"

"It's only another couple of blocks. I can finish up on my own."

Ray nods gratefully and shambles down the sidewalk toward home, head ducked and shoulders hunched. Kerry watches him turn the next corner and then goes back to work.

It's now one in the afternoon, and the sun is blazing. Kerry's stomach sounds like a muted chainsaw, and his shirt is more sweat than cloth. At least the excessive perspiration keeps him from needing to urinate. He continues going through the motions, but suspects some of his neighbors were warned about him, because fewer and fewer doors are even answered. Yet he can still feel eyes on him, and sees faces peeking out from behind curtains, like the scared townspeople in a western.

On the last block, the house on the corner is a tall but narrow colonial with dark siding and a weedy lawn, more like the type of house you would see on the crowded streets of San Francisco. A sign on the edge of the threadbare grass proclaims it to be a foreclosure, with the name and number of a real estate company. Kerry figures it must be empty, but walks up onto the porch anyway. The dilapidated front of Hopeful Sunshine is visible from the steps, three streets down and a few houses over, his bedroom window under the eaves. He rings the doorbell twice, leans forward to squint through the glass in the front door, and then jumps back as it swings open.

Standing on the other side is a light-complected, raw-boned man, with black hair carefully combed over his skull. His cheekbones strain at the skin, creating a sloping concavity down to a grim mouth and sharp chin. The gauntness and fair skin lend his face a regal quality, like some elf from a fantasy novel, but the eyes cause Kerry to freeze. They're a deep, rich brown, the color of fertile earth, so dark they blend in with the pupils, creating huge ebony craters.

"Sorry, I didn't know if..." Kerry trails, still put off by those unnatural eyes, then recites his script. "Hello, my name is—"

"I know who you are," the man interrupts. There's no contempt, no malice, just a simple statement of fact. So the neighbors really have been calling ahead. "You look ready to fall over from heatstroke. Come in and I'll get you some water." He walks away, leaving the door open, and starts down a long hallway that runs straight through the house.

Kerry hesitates. Les never told him what to do if someone invited him in, but he can more or less figure that one out for himself. It's possible this guy is like the other one, whose interest in Kerry seemed unhealthy, to say the least.

He glances around, finds the street empty and quiet. The sides of the porch even hide him from anyone who might be watching from the other houses. The thought occurs to him that no one would know if he went in.

Or if he never came back out.

In the house, the man with the strange eyes disappears through a doorway without looking back. His calm voice drifts back to Kerry: "Either come inside or leave."

Maybe it's boredom, maybe it's curiosity, maybe it's just that he could use some water, but Kerry steps into the house. The cool air within is heavenly, chilling his damp skin. He pulls the door shut and rushes to catch up with his host, passing several closed doors. The hallway itself is dim, but a glow comes from ahead. Kerry steps through the doorway where the man disappeared and finds himself in a quaint breakfast nook connected to a rectangular kitchen that runs along the side of the house.

The man stands at the sink, taking a glass down from a cabinet above. He fills it with water from the sink and holds it out. His hand is as slender as his face, the flesh pale. Kerry accepts gratefully. The water is room temperature, but he drinks most of the glass in one go, then comes up panting for breath.

"My name is Solomon," the man says, not specifying if this is first or last. His timbre is deep and even, the pace measured so that each syllable is distinct. It's like listening to those cellphone apps with the robotic assistant that can find restaurant addresses or order shit off Amazon.

"Nice to meet you. Thanks for the water."

Solomon says nothing. His dark gaze is so direct that Kerry has trouble meeting it. He looks away instead, taking in the kitchen. It's sparsely decorated, nothing personal on the walls or sitting out on the counters. There's not even a refrigerator, just a shallow indentation in the wall where the power and water hookups are visible. And the house is silent, not a TV or radio playing, no other voices in a residence that must have at least three bedrooms.

"Did you just move in?" he asks, thinking of the foreclosure sign in the yard.

Solomon gives a distracted, breathy affirmation, an 'mmm' sort of noise. The silence in the kitchen spins into a sticky web. He continues to study Kerry, like a painter debating the best way to capture a model. A vague unease swells in Kerry's chest, the feeling that he made a mistake coming inside this man's house. He glances around the room again, formulating an excuse to leave.

Then his host says something that causes Kerry's head to whip back toward those two black pits in the middle of his eyes.

"She was sixteen, correct?"

"*What?* Who?"

"The girl you raped."

A sledgehammer of shock smashes into Kerry's lower stomach. "How...h-how did you..."

"Your entry on the sex offender registry." Again, it seems as though this is something that should be said with disgust or, at the very least, taunting glee, but there is no such emotion on Solomon's face. Or any emotion at all, for that matter; his expression is as passive as the corpse at a wake. "I pay attention to what happens in this neighborhood."

Kerry regains his composure enough to deliver his standard defense. "I didn't rape anyone."

"Then you and the state of Texas have different definitions."

"I'll be going now." Kerry sets the glass on the counter and heads for the door.

"That wasn't meant as an insult," Solomon tells him somberly.

Kerry halts in the hall beyond the doorway. "Then you and I have different definitions."

For the first time, Solomon smiles. It's a mirthless, perfunctory affair, but it keeps Kerry from following through with his exit. "I was speaking of technicalities. The nature of the crime of which you were convicted, and so forth."

"My crime isn't any of your business."

"Then why is it listed on the registry, for anyone to find? Why are you informing us all about it?"

"I didn't have much say in that."

One of Solomon's eyebrows makes a ponderous climb up his forehead. "Would you not agree those who reside close to you have a right to know they're in possible danger?"

"Okay, stop. Nobody's in any danger. Being on the registry doesn't mean anything. You can get on there for public urination, for Christ's sake."

"But I don't think anyone ever served four years in prison for it first," Solomon purrs. His knowledge of Kerry's history is as unnerving as his eyes. Their black depths go on forever. It's a relief when he breaks contact this time, long enough to grab the glass from the counter and put it in the sink beside him. "And what about your housemate? Mr. Raymond Leary. Once upon a time, he fondled two eight-year-old boys. Did you know that?"

Kerry lets out a heavy exhalation. "No, I didn't." *Because I don't curl up with the sex offender registry for kicks.*

"Do you believe our *neighbors* have a right to know about that?" Solomon presses. His inquiries are coming harder and faster but still with that same aloofness, that same calculated, leisurely tone. Now it reminds Kerry of the prosecuting attorney in his trial, grilling him on the stand.

"Yes, probably."

"So what you're saying is that your own punishment is unsuited to the crime."

"What I'm saying is, where does it stop?" Kerry can feel heat rising from his chest, climbing his neck and settling in his cheeks. He can't quite figure out how he got here, how he came to be standing in a stranger's kitchen having a legal debate, but he means to say his piece. "We also have a former car thief living down there. You don't see him going door-to-door to warn people to lock up their vehicles. Hell, we have a prostitute too, but she's not even on the registry. Why do you think that is?"

Solomon's measured answer comes without a moment's hesitation. "Because they committed crimes. But corruption of the innocent...that's a *taboo*."

This time, Kerry is stunned to silence. After a few befuddled moments, he walks out again. This time he makes it back down the hallway and has the front door open when Solomon calls out from behind him, "Tell me, what do you think *is* a suitable punishment for offenses such as yours and Mr. Leary's?"

Kerry answers without turning back to meet those horrible eyes. "I don't know. I guess that all depends on whether the person is truly sorry."

"And what about you? Are you sorry?"

This question was asked at Kerry's parole hearing. He answered those grim-faced bureaucrats immediately and unequivocally, told them exactly what they wanted to hear so he could escape that hell, but this time he takes a moment to consider. As he said at his first therapy session, he acknowledges that he committed a crime, but admission is not the same thing as regret.

"Depends on the day," he says over his shoulder, and pushes through the door.

Kerry heads straight back to Hopeful Sunshine. If they want to kick him out for not ringing the last few doorbells, so be it. The walk gives him time to build up a head of angry steam. He stands in the yard for a minute, taking in the chipped paint and sagging rain gutters. Velder is right; they haven't given themselves any reason to hold their heads high in the community.

Struck with sudden inspiration, he marches into the house, finds Les on the couch in the living room, and says, "So about those chores I'm supposed to do…"

ELEVEN

For Kerry's first parole meeting, Sanders picks him up at Hopeful Sunshine and drives to one of the hip little coffee shops up the street called Grindhouse. Today the court representative is wearing jeans and a brown blazer over an Offspring t-shirt from the *Smash* tour—a piece of clothing that is nearly as old as Kerry himself—and carrying a beaten leather satchel. As they wait in the line to order, Sanders tells him, "You look good."

The note of slight surprise in the compliment makes Kerry examine his own jeans and collared black shirt in bewilderment. "Is there a reason I shouldn't?"

"After that first week of freedom, you never know. But since you don't have hollows under your eyes, itchy skin, or a nose Rudolph would envy, I'm guessing there's no need to make you take a drug test?"

Kerry rolls his eyes and nods. "Not that I wouldn't kill for some good weed."

"I'm going to pretend you didn't say that. This is on me, by the way." He orders a large decaf, Kerry asks for a vanilla bean concoction that sounds more like a milkshake, and Sanders hands him ten bucks before going to search for a table in the crowded shop.

The woman at the counter—a late fifties looker with frizzy brown hair—puts a hand to her cheek and says, "Sheesh, I'm so sorry for the wait, our register went down. Give me a sec to total this up for you." She begins punching numbers into a calculator app on her phone.

Kerry finds the prices for their drinks on the overhead board. "Should be somewhere around $8.32, with tax. Tell you what, just give me a buck fifty back and we'll call it even."

She flashes him a bemused grin. "You sure about that?"

"Pretty sure." Numbers have always come easy for him. He hadn't declared a major before he traded school for prison, but it would've been either business or education in mathematics.

"I don't know, sounds a little high," she teases. "I wouldn't wanna cheat you."

"You can mail me the rest. I live right up the street."

She laughs and gives him the change, and Kerry goes to find Sanders. The PO has somehow secured them a couple of heavily padded leather chairs in a secluded corner. He puts the satchel on his lap and, as Kerry sits down, he digs through the contents and pulls out a manila folder like the ones piled in the back seat of his car. Kerry spies his name on the tab as the man places it on the small table between them and clicks a ballpoint pen. "Les told me about your restoration project at the house. I gotta say, I'm impressed. That, my friend, is exactly the kind of initiative and positive attitude you need to get through this transition."

"I just thought the place could use a makeover." In reality, the 'restoration project' hasn't made much headway, as

Les tries to get budget approval from the state for the materials they need. But the psychologist was equally excited when Kerry suggested he could make repairs to the exterior of the group home in his free time.

Of which he has an abundance.

Their coffee arrives, brought to them by the older barista, who tips Kerry a wink as she puts them down. Sanders hunches over the table to stir in creamer. "So tell me, and be brutally honest: how are you adjusting? How's rooming with Ray?"

"Turns out, he's the least of my worries."

"Whew!" Sanders drags a hand across his forehead as though mopping imaginary sweat. "I got a little worried with the way we left things, so that's fantastic news. See, I told you he was all right!"

Kerry grunts and holds up a hand. "Woah, hold on, nobody said anything about 'all right.' The guy's got serious issues. Are we sure he didn't *escape* from that mental hospital?"

"Nope. They slapped a CURED sticker on him and booted him through the door." He makes a flicking motion to illustrate this. "You've probably spent more time with him than anyone by now. You think he's a danger?"

"Maybe to himself, if he pops his head like a zit from all that squeezing. But at long as you leave him alone to watch his cartoons and fold his paper crap, he's fine." Kerry uses a straw to stir the drink he ordered, then realizes that a man at the next table is surreptitiously staring at his four-fingered hand. He hides it beneath the table. "Guy got another huge local order for those things. It was all he talked about this morning. I can't find a job cleaning toilets with my tongue, meanwhile he's making money hand over fist selling origami for children's parties. Which, if you ask me, is in extremely poor taste."

"Is that jealousy I detect?"

"Can we call it resentment instead?"

"I'll make some inquiries. There are plenty of organizations that help ex-cons get employment. We'll find you work, but like I said, it's gonna take time." Sanders settles into the deep-backed chair with the folder open on his lap. "So if it's not Ray, then what's the problem?"

"Gee, let's see, maybe fucking *everything else?* The other residents all hate me, that D'libra chick is on my case constantly, and now, thanks to that idiotic game of Meet the Pervert, the whole neighborhood wants to shoot me on sight."

Sanders' lips scrunch over to one side of his face. "I take it that didn't go well."

"Duh. Christ, did you expect them to thank me for my honesty and put me on their Christmas card list? I think this one old dude forked the sign of the evil eye at me. And don't even get me started on Regina Velder..."

"Who?"

"The head of the official neighborhood Kick Out the Parolees Committee."

"Ah yes, her. I'm truly sorry you had to do all that, Denton. It's an overreaction on the city's part, but we have to play by their rules."

Kerry thinks about the assortment of terrible and angry characters he encountered during the ordeal, all the humiliation heaped upon him. Even with the endless parade of animosity, one image stands out most vividly: Solomon and those two black holes in the middle of his face, drinking in every inch of Kerry. "Yeah, but I'm already on the registry. Which, by the way, gives an incredible amount of information about me. My date of birth? Why would the public need to know that? I mean, god forbid someone wants to steal my identity, cause here's an itemized list."

Sanders chuckles. "Nobody wants to steal a sex offender's identity."

"You know what I mean. It seems like it would be, I don't know, an invasion of privacy or something."

"As long as you're on that list, you don't have any privacy."

"Fine, fair enough. But my point is, I'm there. Anybody can look me up at any time. Yet they still wanna parade me out in front of the neighborhood. Why? What more do they want?"

The parole officer considers this for a moment, pen tapping on the surface of the folder in his lap, then says thoughtfully, "To put a giant 'P' on you."

"Why would they wanna take a giant pee on me?"

"You ever read *The Scarlet Letter*? It's this novel about—"

"Yeah, yeah, Hawthorne, I took freshmen lit. Maybe you should make your references a little more clear, ass."

Sanders laughs. "Okay, good, then you understand. In my experience, people have an innate need to ostracize sex offenders. It's not enough for you to be sentenced and pay your debt to society. They want to make an example of you, a spectacle, all under the guise of public safety. You know, there's a lot of research that says the registry doesn't do jack. That it's the equivalent of putting you guys in the stocks in town square so folks can huck tomatoes. If the public could find a way to make it legal, they'd just brand all your foreheads and be done with it."

"Then...how do they ever expect us to move on with our lives?"

"They don't. They don't ever want you to forget what you did. The most bleeding-heart of liberals will fight for the rights of every mass murderer, but they're more than happy to watch a sex offender fry. Face it, Denton. You're now part of a demographic that's universally hated across all social strata. It's just you guys and the atheists." He takes a long swallow of his coffee while letting his eyes roam the crowd. "I think it's because, deep down, if we're being *truly* honest, everyone can see themselves stealing if the circumstances are right, or maybe even murdering someone they hate. But nobody wants to think they have the capacity to violate another human being like that. Especially a child."

Corruption of the innocent…that's a taboo, Solomon whispers into Kerry's ear, the voice real enough to make his mind flinch away. "I guess the scarlet P stands for 'Pedophile?'"

"Don't be so self-centered. The 'pedophile' label excludes all the regular rapists."

"So…'Pervert?'"

"Too ambiguous. Everyone has their fetishes. You label people perverts, then you have to take a good hard look at yourself."

"Then what? 'Pariah?'"

The parole officer gives him a disapproving scowl, his brow knitting together. "The P," he says, "is for Predator."

The interview continues for the next half hour, Sanders asking questions and scribbling the answers on whatever forms reside in Kerry's folder. Most of them revolve around his future goals, a topic of interest to everyone apparently, but, as the parole officer closes the paperwork and drops it back into his briefcase, he leans forward, fixes his gaze on the table in an uncharacteristic show of discomfort, and says, "In all seriousness, I want you to be able to talk to me about anything, okay? *Anything.* Understand?"

"Uh, yeeeah," Kerry answers, drawing the word out. "You expecting me to head for the border or shoot up a mall or something?"

"No, nothing like that." He takes a breath, raises his gaze, and Kerry is surprised to see how haunted his eyes are. "One of my other charges…another sex offender…he killed himself last week."

"Was it…Zabawski?" Kerry recalls the name from the article not because of its strangeness, but rather the uncomfortable circumstances under which he obtained it. "Dominic Zabawski?"

Sanders' brow rises in surprise. "You knew him?"

"No, just saw something in the paper."

The parole officer wets his lips and slides his fingertips back and forth across the coffee table, as though searching for imperfections in the lacquered wood. "Don't get me wrong, he was a first class scumbag. The world ain't gonna miss him. Drugs, spousal abuse. Molested half his son's first grade class at an overnight lock-in. But he tried to keep his nose clean after a decade behind bars. And he sure didn't seem like the type to tie an electric cord around his neck…" He winces at his own words.

Kerry looks away quickly, out the front window of Grindhouse, mostly so the other man won't see the pain that tightens his jaw. "You can't tell what's going on in a person's head," he murmurs.

"True. And I might be willing to chalk it up to that, except… well, between you and me, this isn't the first time it's happened."

Kerry's head whips back to him. "What do you mean?"

Sanders glances around the coffee shop, then leans in closer and lowers his voice. "Over the last year or so, a lot of paroled offenders around the Metroplex have committed suicide."

Kerry gives a small shrug. "Don't mean to be insensitive, but doesn't that just, like, happen? I would think the shame drives a lot of 'em to it."

"Of course it does, that happens with every kind of ex-con, but we're talking about an unusually high and focused statistic all of a sudden. Like it's in the water or something. And I've talked to some of the POs for these other suicides. Like my guy, there was no sign, no cry for help, nothing. Now the courts are on all of our asses, wanting us to make sure that our charges' emotional needs are being met."

"So they wanna brand us and shame us, but they don't want us offing ourselves?" Kerry's hand closes around his coffee cup hard enough to crease the thin plastic.

"Not if it makes them look bad," Sanders confirms. "That's why I'm telling you, if you feel depressed or frustrated or angry…hell, if you get a goddamn hangnail, you call me. And if you can't get me, you go straight to Les."

"I'm *not* going to kill myself," Kerry says, the words coming out harsher than he intends.

"A week ago I'd've said the same thing about Zabawski." There's a buzzing from his pocket. Sanders pulls out his cell and checks the screen, then scrambles to his feet. "Shiiit, one of my guys got himself pinched for narcotics distribution. I have to get you back."

"It's cool, I can walk."

"You sure?"

"Yeah, I like the time alone."

Sanders leans down and gives him a fist bump. "All right, keep up the good work, my man. You're on your way up and out."

Kerry stays in the chair as the parole officer gathers up his briefcase and rushes through the door of Grindhouse. He watches the traffic through the window. A few moments later, the barista who took their orders wanders over and begins cleaning the table beside him.

"I promise I'm leaving in a minute," he tells her.

"Take your time, we don't need the space anymore." She sweeps a hand around the coffee house. The place emptied out while he and Sanders talked, only a few college-age kids left, studying at one of the big tables. She comments, "That sure looked like a serious conversation you were having."

Kerry catches a pin on her black shirt that says MAN-AGER. "He's…helping me look for a job."

"I see." Her brow furrows. "Is he with a temp agency or something?"

"Sort of." Kerry shifts in the chair. "You don't have anything open here, do you?"

"No, sorry." She collects some empty cups and carries them to the trash. Kerry sees her deliberate before circling back to him. "Listen…the owner won't let me hire anyone else, but the truth is, we could use someone to help out with the morning rushes." At the hope on his face, she adds, "I'd have to pay you off the books and I couldn't guarantee you any sort of regular hours…"

"That's fine," Kerry says quickly. "Whatever you need, I can be here at a moment's notice."

"As long as you bring that calculator in your head, it's a deal." She sticks out a hand. "I'm Barb."

TWELVE

The day is bright and already warm by the time Kerry steps outside, another Texas scorcher in the making. By the end of the summer, his desire for sunshine will probably have waned a bit. Traffic on the main thoroughfare is at a lull between breakfast and lunch, the sidewalks of this urban paradise all but deserted. Caulfield's stands a few blocks down, its parking lot empty and lorded over by that billboard covered in ripped and peeling layers of faded banners from the companies who rented this space over the years, advertisements for law offices and radio stations and movies that finished their box office runs years ago. Kerry realizes this billboard is like a window into the past. If he peers long enough, maybe he'll be able to see a time when he was happy, when life was taken for granted and 'pervert' was what you called your friends when they teabagged your corpse in Halo. He trudges toward home.

Barb's offer should make him happy, but instead, he actually feels worse. An under-the-table job making coffee a few hours a week, and he jumped at it like a starving dog after a bone. Is this what he's been reduced to? Undocumented labor, like an illegal immigrant fresh over the border?

Ten years he's going to be on that goddamn registry. He'll be in his mid-thirties by the time he can slip back into anonymity, an age that feels bafflingly old to him. And even after he's off, the felony charge will follow him around to every job he goes after.

How will he ever build a life? Jesus, how will he ever have a relationship? The thought of having to explain his current status to a potential girlfriend makes him queasy.

Sanders is right. The world is never going to let him forget this one mistake.

Is that what it is now? A 'mistake'? Because I distinctly remember you telling Kayla you would die for her. Die to protect her from him.

Yeah…but I didn't. All I did was lose one lousy finger. So maybe I deserve everything that's happening.

He's careful to stay beyond the boundaries of the Parolea Triangle as he passes the school, but still experiences a moment of nervous, queasy guilt. Scarlet P or not, the world has labeled him a Predator, a dangerous wolf among the sheep, and everything he does from now on—every conversation with a woman, every friendly smile at a child—must be monitored and scrutinized and second-guessed so as not to give them any reason to bring out the wolf-skinning knives.

That's why, at the block where Solomon's house sits, Kerry hurries by, afraid that the man will come out and try to talk to him in his maddeningly calm voice. He can't help glancing through the uncovered windows along the side though. The rooms he can see appear to be empty also, and again he wonders if the unpleasant man is moving in or moving out. Hopefully the latter.

By the time Kerry reaches Hopeful Sunshine, he feels moody and distant and unfit for human interaction. Having Ray blab at him and Les question him and D'libra make snide comments is more than he can handle. Instead of going through the front door, he circles the block and walks down the alley that runs between backyards. Maybe he can sneak through the back gate and have some time alone on the patio before anyone knows he's there.

Kayla, he thinks, as he walks down the packed dirt lane, conjuring her face in his mind. When was the last time he even said her name out loud? *It wasn't supposed to be this way, goddamn it.*

Kerry is so intent on railing about the unfairness of life that he almost doesn't hear the growl of the engine behind him until it's too late.

He spins in time to see the gleaming grill of a familiar red pickup bearing down on him from the end of the alley. The vehicle's speed is still increasing, a pall of dust rising in its wake. Through the windshield, Kerry catches a glimpse of a figure in a trucker hat behind the wheel before he flees.

The alley is five or six yards wide, and lined with high wooden fence planks on either side, leaving no escape. He can see the back gate of Hopeful Sunshine ahead to his left, but a quick glance over his shoulder tells him he will never make it there before the vehicle runs him down. The pickup's engine rumbles like a tornado as it closes in, doing at least forty miles an hour in the narrow confines.

A dumpster sits against the fence to his right. Kerry dives on the far side of it as the truck roars by. Its front bumper catches the corner of the metal container, shoving it into Kerry hard enough to toss him to the pavement on his side. He rolls over, ribs screaming, and looks down the alley.

The pickup screeches to a halt and begins to reverse, the tires kicking up spumes of dirt.

Kerry clambers to his feet and runs back the way he came, one arm wrapped around his sore torso. The pickup is coming, but it can't get the same speed in reverse. He checks the latches of the gates letting onto the other properties, finds one that's unlocked. Kerry slips inside a backyard with a sparkling blue pool and pulls the entrance closed.

In the alley, the truck pulls abreast of the gate and stops with its engine idling. Kerry slips a few yards further down, then holds his gasping breath and peers between the fence boards at the vehicle. He can see both men in the cab clearly now, and there is no doubt they are the same ones who slammed the door into him at the bank.

The passenger window rolls down. Raucous laughter drifts from the cab. The one with the greasy mullet leans out and shouts, "Whassamatter boy? We play too rough for you?" Beside him, Trucker Hat cackles and pounds the steering wheel.

Mullet's eyes move across the fence until they zero in on where Kerry cowers. He grins and points a callused finger. "*I see youuuu,*" he croons softly. Then the grin falls away, and he whispers, "Rob Mac sends his regards, shitheel. We'll be seein ya again. Real soon."

The pickup drives away, toward the opposite end of the alley, its pace leisurely and unafraid. Kerry lets the sound of its engine fade before stepping out and heading home.

THIRTEEN

"Today we're talking about the past," Les tells the group. A discontent grumble runs around the circle of chairs. Scott groans the loudest and slumps in his seat.

The beginning of every meeting is fraught with tension as they await the verdict. The next step in their path to becoming happy, healthy humans. And this topic is hands-down the least favorite among the housemates. Probably because talking about their sins and transgressions leaves them vulnerable, yet results in the most arguments, as though they can't wait to attack each other's weaknesses.

Kerry has lived at Hopeful Sunshine a little over two weeks now. After the fiasco in his first session, he tried to stay on the periphery of these discussions, offering little about himself that can be latched upon and staying positive while discussing everyone else. So he's caught completely off guard when the psychologist turns to him where he sits between Ray and Lorie and says, "I'd like to start with you, Kerry."

"*Me?* Um, I don't have anything yet. Can we maybe circle back?"

"No, we can't." The sternness in his voice jolts Kerry even further. "I hate to say it, but you've been skimping in these sessions since you moved in. The honeymoon is over. It's time we delve deeper into what brought you here."

An uncomfortable rush of warmth spreads up Kerry's neck and into his cheeks. He is very aware of everyone's eyes on him, senses D'libra's smirk from the far side of the circle. His whole life, Kerry has always frozen under the spotlight. Suddenly he's ten years old, called to the front of the class to deliver a book report that he didn't write. As he tries to speak, his brain drops a dam across the river of his thoughts, much like when Pedernales came for him after his three-month stay in solitary. "I...I don't know what you want me to say."

Les adjusts his glasses and purses his lips thoughtfully. "I've been thinking about when I asked you to tell your side of the story, and you said you didn't have one. That you fully admitted what you did was wrong. Do you remember that?"

Kerry nods, thinking of his conversation with Solomon.

"Now, taking responsibility for your actions is healthy, yet, when D'libra challenged you, you readily defended yourself. To me, that sounds like a man who doesn't completely accept his guilt. Wouldn't you agree?"

"I was just trying to clarify what I was guilty *of*," Kerry says quickly, but he can see the trap he's falling into.

"Okay, by all means, let's clarify." Like Sanders with his endless folders, the psychologist keeps a leather-bound notebook that he sometimes writes in during the sessions. He opens it now, flips through pages, and glances at something inside. "Why don't you tells us about this girl?"

The heat spreads to Kerry's forehead. He imagines his face is lit up like a stoplight. His ghost finger gives a single flare of pain that fades in his palm like a smoldering ember. "What if I say no?"

Les shrugs. "Then you get no credit for the session. That's not meant as a threat, just a consequence of your decision. Past affects the present affects the future. But know that I will continue to press this. It's not fair for everyone else in the group to bare themselves while you stay withdrawn."

Kerry throws up his hands in surrender and immediately regrets it. The motion sets off a chain reaction along his bruised ribs. A week has passed since his encounter with the two men in the alley, but his entire side is still a ruddy yellowish-green color. "What do you wanna know?"

"Just start at the beginning. Explain the circumstances that you feel brought you to this point in your life."

He sighs. Looks at the tile floor between his feet. "Her name was Kayla." Something heavy presses on his chest as he says this, tension or fear or anger, he can't tell which. He's never told this story to anyone, not his parents, not even his attorney. The trial—which lasted three days—was based entirely on the strength of his character and lack of prior criminal record, what Gerry Stevens, Esq called a 'not-guilty-because-you're-a-really-good-person plea.' Explaining the details, he said, would only hurt Kerry's case. Now, Kerry doesn't even know where to start. "I met her at a friend's party. I mean, I guess he was more of an acquaintance. I knew him from high school, but he was a few years younger than me. It was his senior year and he threw this rager. Sounded like fun, so I went."

"A high school party then," Les says. "So you knew there was the possibility that underage females would be there."

"Well, yeah, but I didn't go with the intention of hooking up or anything."

From across the circle, D'libra blows air through her lips.

Kerry ignores her and continues. "I hung out. Caught up with some people I hadn't talked to since graduation. When I first saw her…she was dancing with a group of her friends. That girl loved to dance." For a moment, he's no longer in this room painted as brightly as a day care, but in that house, the smell of smoke and beer heavy in the air, watching Kayla as she moves to a bass-heavy beat, as unselfconscious as if she were the only one in the room, wearing a short, frilly black skirt that would become one of his favorites. "She looked amazing," he murmurs.

"Jesus H, bro, wipe away the drool," Scott says. "Of course she looked amazing, that's why they call it 'jailbait.'"

"Let's save discussion for the end," Les requests. "Go on, Kerry. How did the…" He rolls his hands in the air as he searches for the right word. "…*incident* transpire? Was she intoxicated when you approached her? Maybe even unconscious?"

"What? *No!*" Kerry's skin is itchy with disgust as he realizes what Les is implying, that he forced himself on some passed out, underage drunk chick and called it consensual. "*I* was the one intoxicated! Look, I…I'd just broken up with this other girl, I failed a test in world history two days before, and I drank too much that night. Ended up face down in a toilet, puking my guts out. Embarrassing as hell. The guy throwing the party kicked me out. Kayla, she…volunteered to get me cleaned up, and drove me home." The words suddenly burst through the dam in his brain, and he speaks them quickly, eager to get this over with. "Then, out of nowhere, she calls me the next day. Got my number from someone at the party. Checking to see if I felt better. I wasn't, I was more hung over than I'd ever been in my life. So she came back to my place and fixed me dinner. Then we stayed up watching a *Friday the 13th* marathon."

He comes out of the pleasant memory long enough to see that the others are staring at him in disbelieving silence. "You all thought this was some sleazy, date rape type of thing, huh? Sorry to disappoint you, but we dated for *months*. Yes, we started having sex a few weeks later, and yes, we snuck around while we did it because we knew it could get me in trouble. But we had a relationship. A *real* one." He shakes his head, willing his eyes to stay dry. *P is for Predator*, he thinks, *and that's all you'll ever be.* "Then her father found out and…well, let's just say he didn't take an instant liking to me. He's the one that… got me arrested. There's not much more to it than that," he lies.

"And your finger?" Les asks, gesturing to Kerry's lap. "What about that?"

Kerry looks down and is both surprised and not surprised to see that he is methodically rubbing the stump of his left ring finger with his opposite hand. Those lightning-quick strobes of pain are cycling faster now, the confused nerves misfiring like a car engine with bad spark plugs. He forces himself to stop and hides the appendage away at his side. "That's a different story," he says softly.

"Well, I think it's sweet," Lorie says, laying a hand a bit too high up on Kerry's thigh, which he gently brushes off. "It really is like Romeo and Juliet. You know, star-crossed lovers and all that."

"Bitch, are you retarded?" D'libra demands, then holds up a finger with an orange nail to silence Les before he can admonish her. "This scummo warped some poor little girl's mind and then took advantage of her. They weren't in no damn love." She holds this last word out sarcastically, until it becomes a slurred 'luuuuve.'

"Okay, that's bullshit." Kerry grips the sides of his chair as Les gives him his first warning. The fire in his hand begins to blaze as a result, but he doesn't care; if anything, it's distracting from his anxiety so he can defend himself. Pain always trumps fear, after all. "You don't know anything about it. You think because I was twenty and she was sixteen, we couldn't be in love? What difference would four years make if we were in our thirties? Or fifties? Or *seventies*?"

D'libra crosses her arms, a pose both haughty and stubborn, but also, Kerry figures, designed to hide her arm decorations. "*That* would be love. They's a time for everything. If you was a real man and you really loved her, you woulda waited till she was old enough."

"So what, there's this magic line and love only exists on one side of it?"

"No. Just a line where it's right on one side and wrong on the other. And you wrong." A flash of real anger breaks the mold of superiority in her dark features. "'Sides, you wanna talk about lines, Chester? Then where would *you* draw one? If she was fifteen and said she wanted you, would you've stuck your dick in her then? It's all consensual, right, so why not? What about twelve, or ten, or five? I suppose if a toddler had danced around in some slutty dress you woulda been hot to trot." Her nostrils flare. "That's why they made the law, to keep freaks like you from havin sex with babies and callin it a *relationship*."

Kerry is so angry he can't speak, can't even think. He sits rigid in the uncomfortable plastic chair, hands fisted so hard the muscles ache, his ghost finger a ball of white-hot fire against his palm.

"While acknowledging that Kerry did, in fact, break the law," Les begins, speaking calmly and pulling up the back of his collar to wipe at the sweat trickling down his neck, "I do want to point out what a gray area this is, even within our own country. In Maine, for instance, the statutory rape minimum age is 16, with a differential of 5 years. So what Kerry did would be perfectly legal there."

D'libra tucks the streak of purple hair behind her ear, her foot tapping the floor angrily. "Then that state needs to get some Jesus up in there."

"Amen, sister," Mark says. He scoots to the edge of his chair and points across at Kerry. "Forget the law for a second. *I* have a daughter. She's not sixteen, but even if she was, I wouldn't want her seeing a guy like you either. Sounds to me like this man did what he had to do. Can you honestly blame him? Wouldn't you do the same, if it was your daughter? Tell the truth, now!"

No one speaks as they wait for Kerry's response. He takes slow breaths to quell his anger and says, "I don't know. I only know how I felt about her."

"Yeah, well, obviously she didn't feel the same," D'libra tells him. "She ain't here now, is she? You went to prison, but she grew up and moved on, cause you didn't mean shit to her."

Kerry's vision is awash with red. A vein beats somewhere in his temple. He can feel it, pumping him full of fury and bile. He wants to stand up and lunge at her, this woman who suddenly represents Pedernales and Solomon and Velder, the embodiment of everyone that knows so much about him and his life and thoughts, his intentions and emotions. For a moment, he's sure that he's going to, but then Les is speaking, thanking him for sharing, saying that it's time to move on to someone else.

"Who would like to go next?" Les asks. The psychologist looks a little rattled himself, the armpits of his shirt practically dripping. "Mark, you were discussing some possible motives last time for—"

"I touched them," a small voice interrupts. It's so soft, it takes Kerry a moment to realize that it's coming from right beside him. He turns to Ray, who has yet to speak a word in the session. Or even at all this morning, as far as Kerry can remember. When he rolled out of bed, Ray was already up and working on his origami in the corner with his oversized headphones on, something he's been doing more and more over the last few days. Now Kerry's roommate sits bolt upright in his chair, but drawn in on himself somehow, shoulders squeezed together and arms tucked into his doughy sides, like a turtle cowering in its shell. His eyes are fixed on the far wall somewhere near the ceiling.

Les glances at Kerry, his brow knitted in alarm. "Touched who, Ray?"

"There were two of them." His voice is somber and measured. Not like his creepy, inflectionless, robot voice, but distracted, almost cautious. It's far and away the most mature Kerry has ever heard him sound. "They lived in my neighborhood. I used to see them outside, playing with action figures or riding skateboards."

Everyone in the room grows still as they understand what Ray is talking about. Les begins to turn pages in his notebook. The psychologist's movements are painstakingly slow and careful, the motions of a man trying not to startle a bird into flight.

"I don't know why I called them over. At first I...I just wanted to talk to them about their skateboards...but then the v-voices started talking in my head..." Ray falters; his face begins to scrunch. For a moment it seems like this may be the end of the story until, to Kerry's amazement, one of his roommate's hands rises and floats over to his other arm, then proceeds to grab a quarter-sized chunk of flesh and gives it an abrupt tweak. The tension around his eyes and mouth smooths out. "I told them I had ice cream and got them to come into my garage…"

"This is sick," D'libra says. "I ain't listenin to this."

Les whirls on her, fire in his eyes behind the large spectacles, and points at the door. Her mouth falls open as she comprehends the message and, for the barest of moments, Kerry sees a flash of hurt on her dark face. Then she stands and stomps to the door, followed quickly by Mark and then Scott, half the room emptying in the less than fifteen seconds. The psychologist watches them leave and then begins furiously scribbling in the notebook on his lap. "What happened in the garage, Ray?" he asks without stopping.

Ray is still lost somewhere in his head. He struggles with the words for a moment, then pinches himself again to get back on course, hard enough to leave an angry red mark on the skin of his forearm. "They came in and I…I shut the door and told them they would have to w-work for their ice cream. I m-made them…take off their clothes. And then I g-got down and I…" His voice cracks. A single tears slides down one of his chubby cheeks. "I still don't understand *why* I did it. It didn't even f-feel like me. It was like someone else was controlling m-me…" All at once, his rigid bones melt. He collapses over in his chair, falling against Kerry, who stiffens as the other man clutches at him.

"*I'm sorry,*" Ray bawls, burying his face in Kerry's shoulder. "*I hate it, I hate myself, I wish I'd never, ever been born!*"

Bit by bit, Kerry relaxes. He puts a reluctant arm around his roommate's quaking shoulders. From beside him, Lorie reaches over and takes one of Ray's hands as Les continues to write. They sit like that for several minutes, three people whose lives have been ruined by the strange quirks of human desire and all the awful psychological trappings that come with it.

FOURTEEN

Kerry spends the rest of the day on a ladder, scraping paint from the siding as part of his restoration project. He already mowed the lawn and trimmed the hedges; now it's time to get to the big items on his list. The work is grueling, far more taxing than any job he's ever performed in his life, but there's something relaxing about it. It's also his turn to make dinner for the house, so he comes in early, showers, and changes into fresh clothes. Ray is sitting in the corner of their room, hunched over his magnifying glass, giant headphones over his ears. Kerry decides not to interrupt him.

He throws together spaghetti and meatballs, one of the few recipes he's comfortable with. The pasta comes out sticky and the meatballs are burned, but very little of it is eaten anyway; the house has been empty since group therapy ended, except for him, Les and Ray.

"He's never talked about it," the psychologist says, as the two of them prepare their plates. "Not once, not even in all those years at the hospital. I called his doctors there to check. They want to know all about my methods." A proud smile hovers at the edges of his mouth. "I could get my name in a medical journal. This is a major breakthrough."

"For him or you?"

"Him, of course! He's letting out emotions that were bottled up for decades. Did he say anything to you at all? Act any differently?"

Kerry decides not to burst the man's bubble. "Not really. Just been working on his paper dolls for that huge order."

Les strokes his chin and says, in a professorly voice, "Maybe all he needed was a little normalcy in his life. A purpose, a job."

"Capitalism heals all wounds," Kerry agrees, pouring sauce on his pasta.

The psychologist nods and wanders away with his food. Kerry hears him mutter, "And what was with that pinching thing?"

He takes his food to the back patio of the house and eats as the sun goes down. Darkness glides over the lawn, swallows him up. Now that he knows for sure that he isn't paranoid, that MacCallum really did sic a couple of goons on him, being outside like this make him feel exposed and jumpy. He can easily see Trucker Hat and Mullet as the masterminds behind the bizarre school picture that still resides under his mattress, and he is sure they told the truth about not being finished with him. But he refuses to be forced back into a box like the one he spent four years trying to get out of. Kerry reclines in the deck chair and enjoys the night, the sounds of distant traffic toward the freeway, the shouts of children from several blocks away.

At close to 9:15, the gate at the edge of the lawn creaks open. A shadow eases through from the alleyway beyond. Kerry tenses, ready to run, then glimpses dark, coffee-colored skin in the moonlight, and black hair with a blaze of purple through it.

D'libra Barnes slinks across Hopeful Sunshine's backyard like a cartoon burglar, low to the ground and moving in spurts. Kerry stays quiet, hoping she'll pass by without seeing him, but she scurries to the deck chair next to him and attempts to hide behind it while she studies the rear of the house. He stays still, trying to remain invisible. Her eyes finally cut over to him and she flails backward onto the lawn, bringing a fist to her mouth that barely stifles a high-pitched squeal of surprise. He can tell the exact moment when she recognizes him though; her brow collapses and her eyes squeeze into angry slits.

"What the fuck you doin out here in the dark, Chester?" she hisses, still crouched in the grass. "Crankin your meat?" In the wan light from the house, he can see what she's wearing: a pair of tight, threadbare jeans, and a green tube top under a short-sleeve black leather jacket that leaves her taut midriff exposed.

"Tell me something," he says, matching her hushed tone. "Why do you keep calling me 'Chester?'"

She rolls her eyes, which are huge and white in the darkness. "As in Chester the Molester? Jesus, you even dumber than you look, white boy."

Kerry waves her on. No way is he getting into this again. He can sense her anger gathering at the brush-off, but before she can respond, the back door of the house opens and Les barrels out onto the patio.

"I see you, D'libra!" he barks. "You broke curfew again! That is it, five demerits this month! You are gone, I'm calling your parole officer in the morning and—!"

"She's been out here with me." The lie is out of Kerry's mouth before he's even aware he means to tell it. "Got home about 8:30 and sat down to check out the stars."

Les' jaw continues working as he takes in this information, but no sound comes out. He's like a wind-up toy that's slowly running down. Kerry suspects he might have been *excited* about the prospect of kicking her out. He finds his voice and asks D'libra, "Is that true?"

She scowls, runs a hand through the grass, and shrugs. "I don't know. I ain't wearin no damn watch."

"Fine." Les pushes up his glasses and composes himself. "But you should know, Kerry, getting caught in a lie for someone else in this house will have consequences also." He turns on his heel and retreats inside.

D'libra and Kerry sit in strained silence for another handful of seconds. Then she stands up, brushes off the seat of her pants, and grumbles, "What, am I supposed to thank you or somethin?"

"I don't care what you do. I just didn't feel like listening to another screaming match between you two."

"Good. Cause I don't owe nobody nuthin," she declares. Yet she doesn't leave, just stands on the patio, nudging the table with the toe of her boot. Then, in one sudden, violent lurch, she comes around and plops down in the empty deck chair beside him with crossed arms. "So did your creepy friend manage to tell his disgustin story without stutterin hisself to death?"

"He's not my friend. I just room with the guy. Is Lorie *your* friend?"

"Heeeell, no. That skinny white girl ain't friends with nuthin that don't have two balls danglin under it." She grunts in amusement at her own wit, then grows still. "Seriously...is the fatso okay or what?"

"Do you care?"

"No." Kerry thinks the denial is tinged with too much shock and disgust to be the truth. "Just wanna know if I should be movin the dresser in front of my door at night. Don't wanna wake up with that Richard Simmons fuck jackin off in my mouth or some shit."

"He's gonna be all right." Kerry has no idea if it's the truth, but he's surprised to find that he wants it to be.

Silence descends on them. Despite what he told Les, there are no stars visible this deep into the city, just a blank, chalkboard-like expanse hanging over their heads. So the two of them sit and stare into the night, over the fence and across the alley, toward the back of the house opposite Hopeful Sunshine.

Finally, she says, "Look, I didn't mean to get on your case this mornin, all right?"

"You sure? Cause I kinda think you did."

"Yeah, okay, I did." She gives a long, rattling sigh. "I just...I hate that shit, okay? My gran'pa used to fuck me every chance he got. When I told my moms, she protected that muthafuckah. Said it was a *misunderstandin*. You believe that? Didn't feel like no *misunderstandin* when he was tearin open my cooch."

The confession is thrown out as casually as the plot of a movie, but her voice roughens towards the end. Kerry glances over, expecting the shimmer of tears, but D'libra's dark face is stony and inscrutable. Her hands, though, are tracing the pattern of knots and scars along her forearms. "Well... I'm not your grandpa," he says.

"Don't patronize me, Chester. I know who the fuck you are. You're a man who can't keep his dick in his pants, like every other man."

"And you're the mouthy black bitch who hates white people. A true original."

"Hey, gimme some credit! I hate everybody!"

"Sorry, I stand corrected."

She snorts. "Sides, with you and me, it sure ain't about skin color. I just can't stand people who make up excuses for they actions."

Kerry certainly shares that sentiment, but he dislikes hypocrites as much as excusers. "You mean like the ones you give for why you can't follow any of the rules around here?"

D'libra reaches over and grabs his bicep, digging her nails into the flesh. It reminds him of Regina Velder, standing on her front porch as she told him he would be better off dead. With her arm stretched out between the chairs in the moonlight, he has a very clear view of the old track marks that cluster around the inside of her elbow. The puckered circles could've been made by something the size and shape of his finger stub. "I do *not* make up excuses," she growls.

"Didn't you say you were late once because you got lost in the mall? And then because all the buses in the city broke down at the same time?"

D'libra holds on to him a moment longer, as though trying to decide between letting him go and tearing the appendage off. She ultimately lets go and settles back in her chair. "Ain't my fault Les don't make allowances for Black People Time," she says sulkily.

"See, *that* is an excuse!" Kerry laughs bitterly and throws his hands up. "Where do you go anyway?"

"Out with friends."

"The kind of friends that drive hotboxed pimpmobiles?"

She lets loose a long peal of surprisingly melodic laughter. The sound is so unexpected, it makes Kerry jump more than when she latched on to him. "You should definitely avoid the slang, Chester."

"Answer the question, Barnes."

"Not that it's any of yo business, but they my friends from back in the day. Might be a little shady, might not always be on the right side of the law, but they was there for me when no one else was."

"And yet I'm betting these fantastic friends taught you how to use your arms as a pincushion."

D'libra looks over at him, her eyes flashing. Then she holds up her arm as if displaying that chewed-up patch of skin inside her elbow. "I made my choices, same as you. And I make another one every single goddamn mornin: that I ain't *never* puttin that junk in my veins again." She climbs out of the chair and stands up to stretch, her bare, muscled torso inches from Kerry's face. "Nice talkin with you, Chester...but know that I *still* hate you."

She walks away, toward the back door of the house. Kerry twists in his chair to watch her go, and can't help noticing the way her back end swells and rolls in the skintight jeans.

NEW TRACKS

FIFTEEN

The days fall into droning routine for Kerry.

He wakes up. He goes to group therapy. He searches for jobs to no avail. He works on his house restoration project and ignores the stares—and, in a few cases, the angry shouts—of the neighbors. He meets with Sanders. He talks to his parents, assures them he's doing fine. He watches TV. He reads on the back patio. He goes to bed, and does it all over again the next day. About the only thing out of the ordinary is when he begins applying to colleges for the upcoming fall semester, a prospect that genuinely thrills him…until he finds that every school now asks about sex offenses, and all of them require background checks.

A slow, suffocating panic seeps into his head, like stagnant groundwater in the foundation of a house. The walls of Hopeful Sunshine are starting to look as cold and unforgiving as the cells of Wayne Clifford ever did.

Except there isn't a parole from his present situation coming anytime soon.

So, when Barb calls the house phone the following Thursday night and asks if he can come in to Grindhouse Friday morning, he can't say yes fast enough.

The shift is only five hours, from six in the morning to eleven, but utterly exhausting. The place is packed with hipster office drones wearing skinny Dockers and skinnier ties, women with multiple piercings and dark eye shadow, harried mothers on their way to drop off children at school, and none of them are in a good mood before receiving their daily injection of sugar-laden caffeine. Kerry mostly runs the register, taking on the task with minimal training, but Barb teaches him how to make a few specialty coffees whenever the line slows down. At the end of the day, she slips him sixty bucks and thanks him profusely for doing such a great job. He wonders if she's just being nice, until she calls him in four more times over the next week to fill in for a chronically sick employee.

The money is great, but not enough to account for the strange elation he experiences every time he reports for duty. The days that find him standing in front of a register, taking orders from rude millennials, are his happiest since leaving prison. At first, Kerry thinks this is because the job breaks the monotony, then realizes something more is afoot. He's always been a goal-oriented person, the type that stays focused on that point in the distance where the railroad tracks meet the horizon, which is probably the reason he survived Wayne Clifford with so much of his personality and sanity intact. And, even though his own train has gone off the rails indefinitely, this job at least gives him a few scraps of wood to lay a new set of tracks.

Near the end of the fourth shift, Barb approaches him as he goes around the room, cleaning tables and restocking sugar packets, and slides into a seat across from him.

"Sooooo, guess what," she says. Her eyes twinkle and she's trying very hard to keep her lips from stretching into a huge grin. Before he can even attempt to humor her, she blurts, "Cici's not sick at all, she apparently took another job and didn't want to tell me. She just called to quit."

"Then why are you giddy with happiness?"

"Because she's a worthless excuse for an employee, and now that she's gone, I can hire you on officially."

Kerry stops cleaning mid-wipe but doesn't look up from the table.

"It still won't be full time, but it'll definitely be more hours than I'm giving you now. I want you to fill out an app before you go today. Then I can send it to the owner for approval, get all the background checks out of the way, and have you in the system for next week." Barb bounces out of the chair without waiting for a reply. Her bubbly personality often makes her seem sixteen instead of nearly fifty. Kerry has come to like her a great deal over the last week. She pats him on the back and then starts toward the supply room.

"Barb," he calls after her. Uncomfortable heat blooms in both of his cheeks, twin furnaces of shame. "Um, before we do all that..."

"Oh, your college classes!" she exclaims. This is the lie he's told her about the days he leaves early to attend therapy back at the house. "That doesn't matter, we'll work around whatever we have to!"

"No, it's not that. It's just...my background check... something might come up..."

She slices her hands through the air as she comes back toward him. "Don't worry about any of that. Whatever it is, I'll vouch for you to the owner. You're too good of an employee to lose."

"Okay. Uh, thanks."

She grins at him. "One more thing, would you go down to Caulfield's and grab some creamer for us to get by on until I make the Costco run? Take some money from the till and I'll replace it with petty later."

"Sure. No problem."

Kerry's thoughts spin with the force of a tornado as he grabs a twenty from the register and walks next door to the organic grocery store. He should be happy about the prospect of a real job, but he doesn't want his past dragged out into the light to get it. This is far worse than an interview with some random employer. He *knows* Barb, and can't bear the idea of what her face will look like when she finds out the truth about him.

Inside Caulfield's, he stops to use the restroom, then makes his way back to the coffee section. As he squats to grab a jumbo creamer container from the bottom shelf, he glances up and catches the eye of an older couple further down the aisle. Except he doesn't exactly *catch* their eye, since they're both staring at him intensely already, with matching expressions of disgust and outrage. He recognizes such looks well; they're the same ones he gets within a three block radius of Hopeful Sunshine. But if these two are neighbors whose door he knocked on during his Meet and Greet, he doesn't remember them. Kerry checks his apron to see if maybe he's spilled something on himself, then frowns at the duo, confused. Both hurry up the aisle like they're fleeing from a rabid dog.

Do they *really* know him? Is the sudden paranoia that grips him unfounded?

P is always for Predator, my friend.

Kerry stands with his creamer and makes his way back toward the register kiosks to find two sackers huddled together between checkout lines and talking as they watch him. One of them points in his direction and smirks. He ignores them and keeps walking, out of the aisle and into the wide area at the front of the store.

Except now *everyone* is openly staring at him, with the same loathing as the old people, and they aren't as easy to ignore. Other shoppers come to a complete stop so they can shake their heads. Employees snicker. People in line shrink away from him with noses wrinkled and lips peeled back. The combined weight of their eyes makes him stumble back a step.

Kerry's stomach is like a lump of iron in the bottom of his guts.

This is every nightmare he's had since seeing his entry on the registry.

Except now, weeks later, it's actually happening for some reason.

He hurries forward, keeping his head down, and gets into the shortest line. The customer in front of him spins her cart around and pushes it away from him with a grimace. Kerry is thankful for the reaction this time; it means he'll get out of here faster. He reaches the front of the line, puts the creamer on the counter. The clerk, an acne-ridden young man with no chin, scowls at him, but makes no move to ring up the purchase.

Before Kerry can say anything, another employee in a dress shirt and slacks hurries over to stand beside the clerk. "Get out of my store," he says.

"What? I don't understand—"

"*Leave.* Or I will call the police."

Kerry considers arguing, considers telling him to go ahead and call the police, but it's the thought of what Sanders would say that stops him. Right or wrong, he can't afford any run-in's with the law. He leaves the creamer, exits the register kiosk, and hurries toward the door. Before he steps through, someone behind him yells out, "Sicko!"

He runs outside, baffled and embarrassed. "What the fuck is going…"

Kerry trails. In the busy parking lot of Caulfield's, people are standing beside their cars with their heads craned back, staring up into the sky in the direction of the freeway, theirs mouths hanging open in shock. He follows their gaze…

And a gasp of surprise escapes him.

The scratched and tattered billboard that stands behind the grocery store—his window into advertisements past—is no longer blank; in fact, there are two men in white overalls up there right now, tying down a huge tarp that stretches across its entire surface. If they were there as he walked into the store, he was too distracted with Barb's job offer to notice.

His own face stares out from the tarp, blown up to Godzilla-size proportions. The photo is his mugshot, the same one that graces the sex offender registry, but at such an outrageous size, his haggard features and the circles under his eyes make him resemble the three-day-old corpse of a demented hobo.

Beside his face, written in bold, three-foot high letters, are two sentences: THIS MAN RAPES CHILDREN. HE WORKS IN THIS SHOPPING CENTER.

The world spins slowly around Kerry, a queasy carousel. That beautiful morning sunshine grows bright enough to sear his eyeballs.

"Hey!" The shout cuts through his dizziness. He gazes around until he finds the shouter, a wide, beer-bellied guy in a checkered shirt getting out of a Hummer on the second row. "Izzat you up there? You rape kids?"

"I...I-I..." Kerry's tongue is glued to the roof of his mouth. Mr. Hummer is barreling toward him now, pushing through a crowd that's quickly gathering in the parking lot. The guy is big enough to toss him like a caber. Kerry tries to walk away and finds his path blocked by shoppers and employees that have crept out of Caulfield's behind him.

Hummer reaches the sidewalk and stands in front of him, glowering. "That's you up there, idn't it?"

"L-listen, you don't understand," Kerry sputters. The other people are forming a loose-knit circle around them, with more people drifting up all the time. "I didn't do anything wrong!"

"Um, then why are you on the sex offender registry?" a girl at the front of the crowd holds up her phone like a magician asking for card verification. She must have performed an area search to find him, but, even from here, Kerry can see that she's only navigated to the screen with his basic entry, hasn't bothered to click the box that explains his crime.

Do you think it would make any difference if she did?

"So you're just a fuckin child-molestin scumbag, ain't ya?" Hummer asks in a tone that's almost jovial. He reaches out and shoves Kerry's shoulder with a hand the size of a Christmas ham. "*Ain't* ya?"

"No, it's not like that!"

Hummer advances, gives Kerry another shove. "I think it is. And I don't want nasty pieces of shit like you in my grocery store."

Kerry can't quite fathom how fast the situation has spun out of control, that he's in very real danger of getting his ass kicked—or worse—on the sidewalk outside Caulfield's. Most of the people in the crowd—*though, let's be honest,, what you have here is a* mob, *the kind that traditionally loves pitchforks and bonfires*—are grumbling angrily, nodding their approval of Hummer's declaration, watching Kerry with malice and the revulsion one usually reserves for moldy food in the back of the fridge. He lets his eyes roam, seeking one sane face that might be able to stop this, and spots Barb as she comes to the edge of the crowd.

She looks around at the other people, bewildered, then catches sight of Kerry. Worry flashes across her kind features. Her mouth opens. She seems on the verge of calling out, but something finally prompts her to glance upward at the sign. Kerry watches her eyes as they move across the words on the billboard.

Barb looks back at him, shock replacing the concern on her face.

Then she scurries away.

"Hey, you look at me when I'm talkin to you, kiddie-fucker!"

This time, Hummer uses both hands to push him. Kerry stumbles backward, managing to stay on his feet. He weasels away from the big man and tries to run, but the crowd is too dense with rubberneckers now, some of them even spread their arms to block him, and a foot flies out and kicks him high up on the thigh. A half second later, something small but heavy comes flying through the air and pounds him in the shoulder, causing agony to boil down his arm.

A can of Caulfield's organic, all-natural green beans rolls to a stop on the concrete beside him.

And then Hummer is on him, grabbing his shoulder, spinning him around, and socking him in the stomach with that meat hook at the end of his arm. Kerry's breath explodes from his mouth; another doesn't come to replace it. He doubles over, gagging on the stale air from the bottom of his lungs, and sinks to his knees as the guy's other fist wallops him in the left eye. A red explosion goes off inside his head.

"Let's see you rape some kids after I stomp your dick into ground beef." Hummer's voice comes from miles away.

There's a roaring noise, followed by the high-pitched blat of a car horn. The crowd scatters before the grill of a beaten up Chevy Tahoe can plow into them. The vehicle squeals to a stop halfway on the sidewalk. The driver's door flies open and then Scott comes hurtling into the crowd with a tire iron clutched in one hand.

"*Get the fuck off him!*" he shouts, swinging the metal bar in wild arcs. Everyone cringes away except Hummer, but even he holds up his hands in surrender when the iron is pointed at his face.

"Move your ass, Denton." Scott yanks him to his feet, then drags him back to the car.

SIXTEEN

One of the cops that shows up to Hopeful Sunshine is a tall, broad-shouldered Asian man with a voice so nasal he'd probably be better off talking out of his nose. The other is Kerry's good friend Officer Prentiss, the cop who thinks humiliation is its own reward. They take his statement about the incident at Caulfield's while Kerry sits at the kitchen table with an ice pack over his eye. Les hovers at his shoulder, interjecting every few seconds.

"And you say this attack was completely unprovoked and one-sided?" the Asian cop, Office Cho, asks. "You didn't swing at him at any point? Maybe push him back?"

"Or mouth off to him?" Prentiss adds, speaking through his teeth.

"What difference does that make?" Les demands. Kerry has never seen him so mad, spots of color high up on his cheeks and a virtual waterfall of sweat pouring down his brow and cheeks. "It doesn't matter if he insulted the man's mother, it's still assault!"

Cho frowns at him. "Sir, we've asked you to please stay out of this. You were not a witness."

"And I told *you*, he's one of my patients! You talk to him, you talk to me!"

Prentiss doesn't take his eyes off Kerry during this exchange. "Answer the question."

"No, I never touched him." Kerry moves the ice pack to a new part of his swollen eye socket and winces. His stomach still throbs from the punch he took there, and a bruise as big around as an apple stretches across his shoulder where the flying can hit him. "Or said anything that could remotely be considered confrontational. I'd have to be a first class moron to goad a guy that big."

Prentiss grunts at this.

"What happens now?" Les asks.

Cho takes a deep breath before answering. "Well, we have the description of the assailant from both Mr. Denton and Mr. Ramirez, but the few witnesses we've found haven't been very forthcoming in identifying him. Neither has the store. They have cameras that we can probably get the license plate from, but the manager is going to make us get a warrant."

"So they're protecting him. Unbelievable." Les looks a little dumbstruck by this idea, and Kerry wants to sit him down and tell him everything that he and Sanders talked about during their first parole meeting, like scarlet P's and universally-hated demographics. The man is too much of an optimist for his own good.

"Call it what you want," Cho says, "but what we need to know is, do you even *want* to pursue charges?"

The question is directed at Kerry, but again, Les explodes with an answer first. It's nice to know the psychologist has his back, but right now he's prolonging this situation while Kerry just wants it to be over. "Of course we want to pursue charges! We want this man arrested and thrown in jail! And we want whoever put up that atrocity on the billboard prosecuted as well!"

The two cops exchange a look. Then Cho steps forward, nodding seriously, and puts a comforting hand on Les' shoulder. "I understand completely, Mister…Norris, correct? If you'll step this way, I need to get a little more information from you …" He gently guides the psychologist away, leaving Kerry in his seat with Prentiss standing over him.

The officer stares at him for a long moment, his eyes two glinting drill bits. When he speaks, it's through his teeth, like his jaw is wired shut. "Sounds to me like you might've gotten what you deserved. What do you think?"

Kerry lowers the ice pack and glares up at him. "Yeah. Maybe."

"Well, in that case, you probably want to forget all about this and not worry with pressing charges. Am I right?"

"Absolutely."

"Good." He strides from the kitchen, calling out, "Cho, we're good here." A moment later, both cops walk through the front door, on their way to the cruiser parked at the curb.

Les rushes back into the room. "What happened, what did they say?"

Kerry gazes at the table. At the same time, Les' cell phone goes off. "It's Brad." Les talks to him for a moment before handing the phone to Kerry.

"You okay?" Sanders asks.

"I'm fine."

"You sure? If we need to get you to a hospital—"

"I said I'm fine," Kerry snaps.

"All right." Sanders switches gears without argument; for that, at least, he has Kerry's respect. "We're going to skip the part where I chew you out for taking an off-the-books job and move on to the sign. I talked to an attorney. That billboard is highly illegal. Not just libelous, either. It could be construed as threatening, especially in light of what happened. He's filing an injunction. Said it should be down by tomorrow morning."

"Whatever." At this point, it doesn't matter. The damage is done.

Sanders is quiet for a moment before saying, "So...you want to tell me what's going on?"

"What do you mean?"

"Nobody does something like that without a serious grudge. I did some checking, and that billboard was rented two days ago by a MacCallum Construction Group. Does that name mean anything to you?"

"Nope."

"You sure? Cause here's the thing, Denton. The victim's name in your case was sealed so I can't check it, but it doesn't take a genius to figure out this must be related to her somehow. Is this her parents, maybe?"

"I don't know what you're talking about."

"Have they contacted with you? Threatened you?"

Kerry says nothing.

"Listen, my friend." Sanders sounds equal parts exasperated and angry over the connection. "This is dangerous water you're treading in. And I can't help you if you don't talk to me."

"When I have something to say, I will."

Kerry ends the call.

SEVENTEEN

A few hours later, after being fussed over by Lorie and made to describe every exhausting detail of the encounter to Ray, Kerry makes his way up to Scott and Mark's room. The former is stretched out in bed with a car magazine open on his chest. Thankfully, his roommate is still at work.

"Yo, that *puta* did a number on you, huh?" Scott remarks, glancing up at Kerry's face. "Eat some pineapple. That's what my mom always used to say for a black eye."

"I'll try that." Kerry stands in the doorway, shuffling his feet. "I wanted to say thank you. For dragging me out of there."

"You're lucky I left work early today, bro. I drove by, saw that sign…shit, I *knew* there was gonna be trouble."

Kerry nods. "I'm kinda surprised. Figured you'd love to see that happen to someone like me."

Scott looks up from the magazine. "We live under the same roof. That makes us family. And where I come from, you stand up for family."

"Even Ray?"

Scott sighs. "Shit, I guess every family needs a dog that humps your leg." He puts the magazine aside and sits up. "Hey…Me and D'leeb give you a hard time, bro, but I know you ain't like that weirdo. And you sure don't deserve havin that sign put up."

A hard lump forms in Kerry's throat. It roughens his voice as he says, "Can you convince the rest of the world of that?"

His housemate sits for a second, rubbing his palms together thoughtfully, then motions Kerry into the room. "If you tell anyone what I'm about to say…yo, I swear, I will cut the rest of your fingers off and shove them up your ass one at a time."

Kerry steps inside and sits on Mark's bed. Scott checks the hallway, closes the door, and perches on the edge of his own bed. He stares Kerry right in the eye and says, "Look, bro…when I was twenty-five…I fucked this fourteen-year-old girl that lived on my block." At the shock on Kerry's face, he holds up a hand and says, "Yo, don't even start judgin."

"Sorry. It's just that you said you hated sex offenders."

Scott jumps up from the bed with hands fisted at his sides. "That's cause I *ain't* no goddamn sex offender," he growls. "You got that?"

"All right, yes, I get it!"

Scott slowly unclenches his hands and sinks back onto the bed. "I didn't do nuthin that any other guy wouldn't do. This chick…she was fourteen, but, Jesus H. Christo, she had the body of a porn star. And *she* came on to *me*. Knocked on my door wearin this skirt so short you could see—"

"Why are you telling me this?" Kerry asks.

"Yo, if you let me finish, maybe you'll find out. Anyway, I just fucked her the one time, cause by that afternoon, the whole neighborhood knew, includin her parents. But I didn't go down for it. Never even saw a cop. Know why?"

Kerry raises an eyebrow and waits for the answer.

"Because I fucked my jailbait…but you fell in *love* with yours."

"Oh please, that's a load of horseshit."

Scott grins. "Bro, the world hates pedophiles, that's true, but unless you're molestin little kids like your roommate, nobody cares. The cops only give a shit about statutory cases if somebody complains. Those laws were made up for rich white folks to keep their precious daughters from runnin off with guys they don't approve of. Think about this, bro: when was the last time you heard a statutory against an older woman?"

"I…I don't know."

"Right? And you're a fool if you think that shit don't happen just as much as the other. 'Cept nobody cares because it's all good for younger dudes to be chasin older tail. Even if a chick gets caught—a teacher bangin it out with her students or some shit—mosta the time they get a slap on the wrist compared to the guys. It's all one big system you gotta know how to work. Like everything else in life."

Kerry squirms, understanding one essential fact: that this man will go through whatever mental gymnastics are necessary to keep from equating what he did to what Kerry did. Scott Ramirez isn't the type who would ever say, 'there but for the grace of God,' because for him, there is only one true sin: not understanding your place in the world. "I think you're oversimplifying things."

Scott waves a hand. "I'm gettin off topic anyways. What I mean to say is, you love this girl, right? I mean, you *still* do. Don't deny it, I saw it in your eyes when you talked about her. You seen her since you got out?"

Kerry hesitates, then shakes his head.

"Yo, it's none of my business, but you should go to her, bro. See if there's somethin still there besides the danger of forbidden fruit." He grins. "I mean, you did *hard time* for this woman. If that ain't a fuckin romantic gesture guaranteed to get a man some pussy, I don't know what is."

EIGHTEEN

Kerry spends the next two days moping around the house, recovering from his injuries. His body heals enough for the pain to fade, but that black eye stubbornly clings to his face, pulsing with sick heat every time he so much as blinks.

As for the shame…he figures that will be with him long after even the swelling goes down.

So much for laying new tracks.

A futile, directionless anger simmers inside him, one that never entirely goes away, that urges him to punch the closest wall every time he thinks about what happened. He wants revenge, not just on the man who did this to him, but on the entire world.

And, on top of that, Scott's advice repeats in his head, over and over.

That's why, on the very next Sunday, Kerry gets up early and logs in to his account on the computer in the media center for the first time. He still feels uncomfortable as he does it, as though a SWAT team is going to descend upon him the moment his fingers touch the keyboard. But with a few minutes of Googling, he finds the address he needs.

Ray is in their room, boxing up the origami creations for his big order. For some reason, he doesn't have on his usual gym shorts and t-shirt, instead wearing a pair of khaki pants and a crisp blue Oxford shirt that's at least a size too small. Kerry hasn't talked to him much since his breakthrough in group last week, but he's seemed more like his old self, just exhausted and harried as he rushed to finish the big job, often working late into the night and even—gasp!—missing his cartoons. Les' attempts to keep him talking about his past in subsequent therapy sessions have also been cheerfully stonewalled. He glances up as Kerry enters the room and perches on the edge of the dresser.

"I've got a deal for you."

"What's the deal, Ron Popeil?" Even his lame greeting rhymes lack their usual enthusiasm.

Kerry points at the huge stack of cardboard boxes in the corner. "I'll help you pack all this up and get it to the post office if you'll give me a ride somewhere."

"Oh buddy, you know I'd give you a ride no matter what!" Ray reaches over from where he squats on the ground, grabs Kerry's ankle, and gives his leg a friendly squeeze. "But this shipment doesn't have to go to the post office."

"Wait, is that why you're dressed up? You're delivering it *yourself?*"

"Yep!" Ray runs a hand down the front of his fancy duds. "It's just downtown. The people that ordered them asked if I could bring the boxes myself, so they don't get hurt in the mail. I found it on a map by myself and everything!"

"Are you sure that's a good idea, Ray? You're not...you know...taking them to a kid's party or anything, right?"

"Nope, I already asked! It's some fancy dinner they needed placeholders for. Les says it'll be good for me to develop my people skills if I want to run a business!"

"Well…okay." Kerry can understand the psychologist's intent; however, he can't help thinking that 'developing Ray's people skills' could be a recipe for disaster. "I can go with you if you want some backup," he offers.

"Thanks, but they said they don't want a lotta people on their property, so only I'm cleared to go through their security." He rolls his eyes. "Rich people, huh?"

"Yeah." Kerry tries on a grin that becomes a grimace as a bolt of pain shoots through his bruised eye. "Maybe you can drop me off as you go. It's not too far from here. I'll find a way to get back."

It takes them another half hour to finish packing the pieces and five trips to get the boxes loaded into the van, mainly because they have to be transported with all the careful finesse of a crate of nitroglycerine. After they're all stacked and secured between the microwave and the empty deep fryer, both men climb into the fried fog hanging over the front seats.

"Jesus, how big is this dinner party?" Kerry asks, looking back at their freight.

"Don't know. I just fill the orders!"

As they pull out of the driveway, Kerry keeps a watchful eye out for red trucks or any other vehicle that appears to be following them, as he does every time he leaves the house. He gives his roommate directions that will get them to the freeway without going by the shopping center. Sanders has assured him that the tarp is down from the billboard, but he feels no need to check for himself, not even to look out his bedroom window. And the very idea of seeing Grindhouse again stokes the flames of that angry furnace in his guts.

When they near his destination, he tells Ray to stop several blocks away, in front of a vacuum store.

"Why'd you wanna come *here*?"

"Part of the house cleanup," Kerry lies. "We need a good shop vac."

"But there's a Wal-Mart like ten minutes from the house!"

"These are better."

"Then…don't you want me to wait, so I can help you get it back?"

Kerry sighs. "No, I'll be fine. Go make your delivery."

Ray stares at him incredulously, which, for him, has all the subtlety of Wile E. Coyote eyeballing the Roadrunner. Kerry gets out of the van, closes the door, goes into the vacuum store, and waits for the other man to drive away before stepping out.

His heart thuds in his chest as he walks the last few blocks. He should've come long before now, he knows this, it's just that the very idea made him queasy. But his talk with Scott finally caused the guilt to outweigh his dread.

A few minutes later, he stands on the sidewalk looking through an ornate wrought iron fence. On the other side sprawls acres of rolling green lawn, broken by huge willow trees whose branches remind him of melting candle wax, and rows upon rows of bronze plaques anchored into the ground on stubby concrete posts. A squat building past the gate displays an unassuming sign that offers the name of the establishment.

Willow Grove Cemetery.

The words bring a distant jolt of pain from the wraith that lives where his finger used to be.

Kerry goes through the gate and stops at the office long enough to check a burial directory. He's been here before, but it was five years ago. After finding the name he seeks, he gets his bearings and sets off across the graveyard.

There are several funerals in progress today, black-clad groups sitting on folding chairs in front of solemn caskets. Kerry avoids them as he hikes. It takes ten minutes of walking and a whole lot of sweat, but he reaches a small hill overlooking a duck pond—surely one of the most expensive plots in the entire cemetery—and stands in the shade of a towering willow as he gazes down at a headstone in front of him.

KAYLA ROBERTA MACCALLUM

The love of Kerry's life is somewhere beneath his feet. The mouth he kissed a hundred times is down there right this second, probably no more than withered flesh and dry teeth. The thought sends a full-body shudder through him. On the plaque, her date of death is listed a few weeks shy of her eighteenth birthday, a year and a half into his incarceration.

The plot to the left belongs to one Katrina Anne MacCallum. Kayla brought him here, to her mother's grave. She'd cried on his shoulder as she told him about the circumstances of Katrina MacCallum's death. Although he's never met the woman, Kerry gives a reverent nod in her direction before turning back to her daughter.

"Why didn't you wait for me?" he asks. The question is surprisingly loud in the still morning air. "I told you I'd come back for you, didn't I? That we would be together. That I would take you away from…from *him.*"

His voice cracks on the last word. He hears Scott in his head, telling him that his love for Kayla brought them all to this place. The implication being that if he'd fucked her and left her and been every bit the piece of shit everyone accuses him of being, then she might still be alive and his life would never have jumped the rails and crashed in this nightmare.

Overwhelming grief rushes him from out of nowhere, a flush of heat and sorrow and weakness, tainted with that anger that won't go away. The taste of it is like ashes on the back of his tongue. He falls to the grass at the foot of the grave and puts his hands against the ground, trying to feel her through all the feet of soil that will keep him from holding her ever again.

"*I tried,*" he sobs. "*I did everything I could. I thought if I could just make him see…*"

Kerry weeps, weeps until his eyes sting and the grass beneath his chin glistens with salty droplets and he's so wrung out that he'll never be able to move. And his finger…god, *it* feels like the lit fuse on a very big firecracker, a burning electric pulse that spreads into his hand, climbs his wrist, and then radiates up his entire arm. Those pain receptors are reaching out, reaching out and finding nothing, and that emptiness is causing them to writhe in agony. He's afraid that pain is never going to stop, that this spectral digit will haunt him all the way to his own grave. He would happily cut off the rest of the finger or his hand or however much flesh is required to stop that pain, to peel away layers of himself like an onion, but something tells him that such sacrifice would make his agony worse.

And then it fades, leaving him weak and shaking. Kerry considers stretching out on the grave to fall asleep, but is stopped by a soft voice behind him that asks, "I-is that her?"

Ray stands a few feet away, beneath the cascading branches of the willow, biting his lower lip and wringing his hands nervously. Sweat stains the armpits of his fancy duds.

Kerry's mouth twists into a snarl. "You son of a bitch, I told you to go!"

"I'm sorry, I'm sorry!" his roommate exclaims, wincing as though already anticipating violence. "I didn't mean to follow you, you were just acting so weird and I thought maybe you were auditioning to be on a game show and by the time I realized that was dumb I was already here!"

Kerry works fast to compose himself, wiping the tears away, rubbing his burning eyes, then climbs to his feet.

Ray waits uncomfortably, still kneading his hands, then stops to gesture at the headstone plaque. "So...*is* that her? The one you told us about? She's...*dead*?" The last word comes out a hoarse squeak.

Kerry moves to stand beneath the willow. The branches form a cave around them, a green curtain that shields them from the world. He leans back against the tree trunk and closes his eyes. "Yeah, she's dead. That's usually the reason people reside under the ground in a cemetery."

"Why didn't you say anything in group? When D'libra said—"

"Because it wasn't any of her business. Of course, it's not yours either, but I guess I can't do anything about that now."

Ray is still staring at the grave as if hypnotized. "What happened to her?"

"Okay, I know you have these problems, Ray. I know that you don't understand people and how society works. But I want you to ask yourself—and take all the time you want—do you *honestly* think I'm the least bit interested in talking about this?"

Ray shrugs without the slightest hesitation. "You might feel better if you do."

"I guess you would know, huh?" Kerry squeezes his temples with his good hand, because the bad one is starting to hurt again. "Fine. She committed suicide while I rotted away in prison. There, you happy now? Or wait, do you need more details? She fucking took an entire bottle of Xanax and curled up in bed. Because I wasn't there for her."

"No!" Ray sounds horrified. "No, you can't blame yourself for what someone else did! Everyone makes their own choices! That's what Les says!"

"Les doesn't know a goddamn thing about it, and neither do you." Kerry looks through the willow branches at the sun-drenched graveyard. "I'm gonna tell you something you may not realize, since you got to spend your sentence in a nice little hospital bed doped to the gills: prison is hell for guys like us. The *only* thing that kept me going was the letter from her that came every week, like clockwork. I couldn't risk calling her, and there was no way she could come to see me—even if she could've gotten away from her father, the prison never would've let her in—but she set up a PO box so we could mail each other. And here's the weird thing. No matter how bad it got in there, the time sort of...flew by. Because I had something to look forward to. Because I knew when I got out she would be there, and this time we would do it right, and no one would be able to keep us apart." He pauses as the phone call from his mother plays in his head, the panic that seized him, the sense of utter helplessness. "But then the letters stopped coming. And after I found out that she...well, each day lasted an eternity. It was like I still moved at the same speed, but the rest of the world was set to slow-motion. I used to daydream about bashing my head into the wall until I was unconscious, just so that a few more hours would've passed by the time I woke up. And now...I don't know what the fuck to do with myself. I can't get a job, I can't go to school, I have no future...and I keep wondering if any of that would've mattered if she was still alive."

A long moment passes before Ray reaches out toward Kerry's neck. He expects the man to pull him into another bear hug, but instead he cups the nape of his neck and says, "It's okay, you've got me now!"

"No offense, but I don't think you're a very apples-to-apples comparison."

The other man gives one of his sweet, goony guffaws. "I was gonna wait to tell you, but, what the heck, you need to be cheered up! With the money I'm making from this order, I'll have enough to rent an apartment! I think I'm finally ready! And I'm gonna get one with two bedrooms, so you can come, too! Then we'll be roommates forever!"

Kerry spins to face him, shoving Ray's hand away at the same time. "Is that what you think I want?" he demands. His jaw clenches hard enough to make his swollen eye socket ache. "To be in some pedophile version of *Bosom Buddies* for the rest of my life?"

"N-no, I—"

"You need to get one thing straight, Leary." Kerry advances on him, jabbing two fingers into the man's flabby chest beneath his ironed shirt. Somewhere far in the back of his mind, he knows he's unleashing all that pent-up anger on the wrong person, but it's like a volcano: the eruption has begun, and there's no stopping the flow of scalding lava. "We are *not* friends. All right? I am *nothing* like you. And there is no way in hell I'm going to fuck up whatever shred of a life I have left by moving in with you. When I get out of that goddamn house—and I will—I'm not ever coming back, not for you or anybody."

Ray continues to stare at him, mouth hanging open. Kerry sees his blubbery chin quiver before the man pushes through the curtain of foliage and begins to run away.

"Ah, for Christ's sake," Kerry groans, then shouts, "Wait, Ray, come back!"

But the other man doesn't stop, just continues to bound away across the endless field of gravestones.

NINETEEN

The driveway at the house is empty. Even Les is gone. Kerry has never had the place completely to himself before, but he feels too shitty to enjoy it. He fixes some lunch and spends the afternoon mowing the lawn, spreading fertilizer, and making a list of materials he'll need for the long, arduous process of painting the siding, which he intends to tackle next week. As the other residents arrive home from work, he goes to shower, change, and seclude himself on the back patio with a book.

He gets three pages read before Les comes to find him. "Where's Ray?"

"No idea."

"Didn't you leave with him this morning?"

"Yeah, but he dropped me off somewhere and then went on to make his delivery."

Les sucks in a long, worried breath. "He's still not back yet. He hasn't been gone from the house this long since he got here."

Kerry keeps his gaze carefully trained on the book in his hands so that his burning cheeks won't show. "Give him a little longer. I'm sure he'll show up soon."

But two hours later, with curfew minutes away, there's still no sign of him. Kerry hangs around the kitchen while Lorie prepares dinner and Les paces back and forth across the room.

"Oh, this is *not* good," the psychologist groans. "We don't have any way to get in touch with him. This is why it's a mistake to not let him own a cell phone. I should've made him take mine."

"Don't panic," Kerry tells him. "He probably got held up."

"I don't know," Mark says, breezing into the room behind them to rummage through the pantry. He sounds more amused than worried as he adds, "That tubbo never misses a meal."

"Maybe they let him stay for their party," Lorie suggests hopefully.

"Oh yes, wouldn't he make a great dinner guest? Nothing completes a black tie affair like stories about cornholing little boys."

Kerry rounds on him. "Would you shut the fuck up?"

Mark steps forward until their chests are inches apart. He's a little taller than Kerry and a little heftier, but most of that weight is pure middle-aged flab. "Did you not get enough of a beating from that billboard, jailbaiter? Cause I can give you another black eye so they match."

"I don't know, how would the good Lord feel about that?"

"I'm sure He'd still let me into heaven. Which is more than I can say for you."

"Break it up, or its demerits all around," Les tells them.

But they continue to stand in each other's faces for a handful of seconds until Lorie squeezes between them. "C'mon boys, you don't have to fight. You can both have me."

Mark makes a disgusted sound and pulls away from her touch, one hand grabbing at the crucifix around his neck. He stomps from the kitchen.

With one last reproachful glower at his backside, Kerry turns to Les. "Maybe he got lost or had a flat tire. I'm just saying, let's not assume the worst."

"I hope for his sake, you're right." Les reaches into his pocket and pulls out his cell phone.

"Woah, woah, what do you mean?" Kerry asks. "Who're you calling?"

"Brad, of course. He'll have to use the ankle monitor to track him and then we'll need to contact the police."

"Holy shit, *why*? He only missed curfew, for Christ's sake! D'libra does it all the time and we don't sound the alarm on her!"

Les rubs his eyes beneath his glasses. "He's not like the rest of you, Kerry. The courts deemed him an extreme public safety risk, even with his...medical procedure. He must abide by the rules of this house and account for his whereabouts every second of every day. And once the police are involved, if he doesn't have a damn good excuse for going AWOL, they'll revoke his release and send him right back to the mental institute first thing in the morning." He begins dialing a number on his phone.

Kerry rushes across the kitchen and grabs the man's hand. "Stop. Please don't do this."

Les watches him for a long moment. Kerry can see the anguish in his eyes. "I'm not going to risk losing my job over this. Let's talk to Brad. If he wants to handle it privately, fine, but it'll be his name on the line." He continues his call. Kerry listens to him explain the situation, then there's a long pause before the psychologist's eyes grow wide behind his glasses.

"*What?*" He rushes to the window and looks out at the front lawn. "No, he is absolutely *not* here."

"What is it?" Kerry whispers.

Les holds the phone away from his mouth. "The tracking signal from the ankle monitor is coming from somewhere in the house. Which means he found a way to get it off without setting off the alarm." He returns to the cell and says, "Okay, yes, I'll call them now."

Kerry snatches the phone out of his hand and presses it to his own ear. "Brad, it's me, it's Kerry. Man, we *cannot* call the cops on Ray."

"What do you want us to do then?" The man sounds exhausted over the phone line. "He's a dangerous child molester loose on the streets."

"No, he's not, he's a person who made a mistake, you said so yourself."

"Yeah, and I also told you that we have to work within the boundaries we're given. And if Ray removed his monitor, he violated a pretty goddamn big boundary."

Kerry steps away from Les and Lorie, to the corner of the kitchen, and lowers his voice. "We…we got into a fight earlier today. I said some harsh shit. I'm sure he's probably just upset."

"That's even more reason for us to find him as quickly as possible."

"All I'm asking," Kerry pleads, "is to give him a little longer to see if he comes back on his own. If he's not here by morning, you can bring on the helicopters and bloodhounds."

The parole officer gives a heavy sigh over the phone. "Nine AM, and not a second later. You'd better be right, Denton. Put Les back on."

With the decision made, they retreat to their rooms to get some sleep, Kerry promising to alert Les the second that his roommate makes an appearance. He closes his door, then rifles through dresser drawers and in the closet, searching for where Ray might have hidden his ankle monitor. He can't remember for sure if the man was wearing it this morning, but if not, that means he took it off *before* their fight, an idea that Kerry can come up with no explanation for. The hunt turns up nothing, so he finally lays down and closes his eyes, but his harsh words to Ray in the cemetery echo in his brain. The room seems empty without that goofy lug snoring from the other bed. It's weird and a little scary how fast Kerry got used to the company after four years on his own.

And, even more strange, he thinks that maybe it wouldn't be so bad to get a place with Ray. He has to live *somewhere*, and that would get him out of Hopeful Sunshine and away from this neighborhood where everybody knows his name, and not in a friendly, *Cheers* kind of way.

Then maybe it's time to stop pissing and moaning about the future you were supposed to have, and start building that new set of tracks with the materials you have at hand.

He can't remember falling asleep, but awakens when sunlight creeps through the window and pierces his eyelids. It's close to seven. Ray's bed is still empty. Kerry jumps up, throws on clothes, and runs downstairs.

Les is up and pacing in the living room. "I've already called every hospital I can think of. Nothing."

"We still have two hours." Kerry heads for the door. "I'm going out to look for him."

Les hurries after him. "Where would you even start?"

"He said his delivery was downtown."

"That doesn't narrow it much."

"I don't know, I'll take the bus along the freeway in that direction and stop at a few gas stations. Somebody might've seen that gaudy ride of his." He stops with his hand on the doorknob and leans his forehead on the jamb. "I can't sit here and do nothing, Les."

The psychologist nods slowly. "Then let me go. It'll be faster with my car. You can walk the neighborhood here. This is literally the only area on the planet that he knows. Surely he'll come back."

"All right, yeah, good idea."

"Get to a phone and call my cell if you find him. Otherwise, I'll meet you back here at nine."

Kerry heads out of Hopeful Sunshine. The sun is hidden today beneath a blanket of fluffy, steel gray clouds. They keep the temperature a bit cooler as he walks, but the humidity is so high on this late June morning, he's sweating almost immediately.

The suburban streets are empty. After traveling a few blocks down the main avenue in the direction of the freeway, past Solomon's house, he begins to see how futile this search is. The neighborhood is huge, and he can't walk every inch of it in every direction.

"Where are you?" Kerry says aloud. He keeps going, wandering out of the neighborhood and into the more commercial district. This is the closest he's come to Grindhouse since the billboard incident, but he doesn't care anymore. A sense of impotent urgency sets his muscles on fire, spurring him to run even though he has nowhere to go. He hasn't felt this helpless since his mother called and told him about Kayla, told him that the woman he loved had taken her own life and he was trapped behind cinderblock walls and steel bars and would never see her again...

The left side of the street opens up, revealing the rectangular expanse of the park with its huge horse sculpture. The rolling green lawn is bounded on both sides by small businesses that are all closed at this time of morning, and the school at the far end. From the corner of his eye, Kerry spots a green pickle zooming through an intergalactic backdrop.

Ray's van is *right there*, maybe two hundred yards away, sitting at the left curb of the park, on the street leading down to the school. And actually, if you divided this street in half, it's on the end closest to the school itself, where long yellow buses are lining up to drop off students. The vehicle's position gives it a perfect, unimpeded view of the building's front lawn, which is covered with roving bands of elementary children sitting in groups and eating breakfast and tossing footballs.

If one were so inclined, it would take a mere thirty seconds to drive forward, turn the corner, stop in front of the school, and drag an innocent youngster into the dark depths of the tinted-window van.

If one were so inclined.

"Shit. *Shit.*" Kerry mutters. He can envision the imaginary boundary line that Sanders drew for him on his first day out of prison, the 500-yard penalty box that begins at the opposite curb from where he stands now. Setting one foot over it is a violation of his parole; do not pass go, do not collect two hundred dollars, but go immediately back to prison for the last two years of his sentence and however much longer the judge tacks on.

Same goes for Ray as well. Except he will probably spend the rest of his natural life in the asylum, with no hope of ever leaving.

And it will be Kerry's fault for driving him to it.

He wants to get Les or Sanders, have one of them come and talk Ray Leary down from whatever psychological ledge he's on. But that would require first finding a phone and then waiting for one of them to get here. During which time his roommate could disappear again.

Or do something far worse.

No, Kerry set this disaster in motion; it's up to him to defuse the bomb before it explodes.

TWENTY

A breeze springs up as Kerry crosses the street, stirring the muggy morning air and carrying a heady whiff of coffee from up the block. It helps dry some of the sweat beaded on his face as he enters the Parole-a Triangle, that mythic land where countless sex offenders have disappeared, never to return. Stepping into the park doesn't make him feel like he has a scarlet P so much as a glowing neon GUILTY sign floating over his head. He denies the urge to glance around, knowing it will make him look like he's got something to hide. Instead, Kerry keeps his head down and walks swiftly—but not *too* swiftly—on a diagonal course across the park toward the back of Ray's van.

He's still twenty yards away when a police cruiser appears at the far side of the school and stops at the end of the park, next to the offloading buses. The driver's door opens and who should step out but Kerry's good buddy, the only cop that apparently works in this city, Officer Prentiss.

Kerry's steps falter. Cold dread creeps through his guts and inches up his spine. Oh god, he's been a fool. Some teacher at the school probably spotted Ray's pedo-van, and now they're both about to be caught red-handed in a two-for-one sex offender special. Or hell, maybe the cop is here for *Kerry*. Most of Hopeful Sunshine's neighbors are surely watching him like a hawk, waiting for him to screw up so they can report him. It seems like the kind of thing Regina Velder would devote herself to full time. He almost sprints in the other direction, but then Prentiss ambles around his car and across the school lawn without giving Kerry a second glance, greeting kids as he goes. He takes up a guard post beside the front door and continues to chat with students as they file inside.

A safety officer, Kerry realizes. Prentiss is just there to watch over the kids before school. The relief is euphoric.

The very conspicuous van still sits at the curb. If anyone's inside, they're apparently unfazed by the officer's presence. Kerry passes behind the vehicle, circling around to the driver's side from a distance so he can review the situation before he moves any closer.

Ray is definitely in there. Kerry can see him through the rolled-down window. He turns to look at Kerry as he edges closer to the van. His eyes are wide and glassy.

"Hey buddy," Kerry says warily.

"H-hi," Ray answers. Just 'hi.' Not 'Hi, pumpkin pie' or 'Hey, Sugar Ray' or one of his other stupid greetings that Kerry would suddenly give anything to hear.

Kerry reaches the door of the van and stands beside it. A putrid, vinegary stench smacks him right in the face, the smell of old piss. It overpowers even the cloying scent of fried food. He breathes through his mouth and gives the interior of the vehicle a cursory examination. Kerry doesn't know what he's looking for exactly…except a small voice in his head—one that has never forgotten the defaced photo of the schoolchildren that still lurks beneath his mattress—insists there could be bloodstains, that the inside of the vehicle might resemble a slaughterhouse, a thought which makes his empty stomach churn. The curtain right behind the bucket seats is drawn closed, hiding the rear compartment from view, but otherwise, the cab looks the same as always.

His roommate, on the other hand, is far from normal. He sits bolt upright behind the wheel like in their therapy session last week, during his breakthrough confession. He's still got on the nice clothes he wore for his delivery, but they're rumpled and stained now, the shirt untucked and missing a button near the bottom that allows his gut to protrude. One particular stain on the crotch of his pants is undoubtedly the source of the urine reek. Dark, purple bags hang beneath his eyelids. Kerry is convinced the man hasn't slept since they last saw each other 24 hours ago.

"We missed you last night, man. Did you make your delivery?"

"Yes."

"That's good. Les and Sanders have kinda been going crazy." He forces a dry laugh. "Me too, actually."

"Sorry." The single word answers sound shell-shocked. Or drugged.

"So, uh…what are you doing?"

"N-nothing." Ray's blank gaze returns to the school a hundred yards away, where kids of all ages continue to mill as they wait for class to start.

Kerry senses movement in the other man's lap. He looks down to find that Ray is pinching his left arm, just as Kerry showed him. The technique may be some bullshit he invented on the spur of the moment, but it gave the man back some measure of mental control. Now though, Kerry is horrified to see that a trail of severe red welts leads from his room-mate's wrist up to where his bicep disappears beneath the sleeve of his shirt. Many of them have busted blood vessels beneath the surface, making his entire arm look bruised and diseased. It's the way he imagines D'libra's arms would've looked, back when the track marks were fresh. As Kerry watches, Ray seizes one of them and twists, hard enough for tiny beads of scarlet to form on his skin, like red sweat.

"Ray...listen to me," Kerry begins. "You can't do this. Okay? You can't listen to...to the voices. Remember what I said? They're not real. They don't control you."

A fat teardrop forms on Ray's eyelid and drips down his cheek. "Go away," he says without looking at Kerry.

"I can't do that. Listen, you need to come back with me. Otherwise, you're going back to the hospital. Forever, this time. Is that what you want?"

"Go away Kerry, you have to go away right now." Panic bubbles up in his words.

"If this is about yesterday, I didn't mean—"

"Please stop! Y-you don't understaaaah!"

The end of Ray's statement becomes a surprised squawk. At the same time, he lurches forward in his seat, as though he's been unexpectedly goosed. His stomach presses the horn in the steering wheel, which, thankfully, comes out as more of a decrepit wheeze. Even so, Kerry pushes away from the van and checks to make sure they haven't gotten Prentiss' attention. By the time he looks back, Ray is twisting the key in the ignition to fire up the rattling engine. He puts the van in gear.

"Stop," Kerry tells him, reaching through the window to grab at the shifter as the vehicle pulls away. "Do not do this, Ray!"

His roommate looks at him and, for the barest of moments, Kerry can see stark fear swimming behind his eyes.

Then he's speeding up the street, past the school, leaving Kerry standing in the middle of the road.

TWENTY ONE

He goes home, feeling as though someone spent the last hour kicking him in the stomach with steel-toed boots. The driveway is still empty, the house deserted. Kerry goes inside, sits at the kitchen table, and tries to decide if he should make an anonymous phone call to the school before classes let out for the day. Then again, if he's that worried about what Ray might do, then maybe it would be best to let the police hunt him down.

Les trudges into the house at 8:45. "It's hopeless. I barely covered any ground and nobody I talked to saw a thing. I'm sorry Kerry, but we have to—"

"I found him."

"What? *Where?*"

"Sitting in his van not far from here." Kerry assures himself this is omission, rather than lying.

"Thank god! Let's go get him!"

"He's not there anymore. He took off after I talked to him."

Les fumes with his hands on his hips. "Then why the hell didn't you call me? I went to every gas station for fifty miles when I could've been helping you back here!"

"I...I tried to convince him to come home. I was hoping he'd be here by the time you got back."

The other man sighs and throws his arms up. "Well, that's it then. I'll let Brad know."

"Let's wait just a little longer."

"*No*, Kerry! This isn't—!"

He's interrupted by the sound of the front door opening and closing. Both men watch in amazement as Raymond Leary shuffles across the foyer. He halts at the foot of the stairs and looks at them blearily.

"I'm not feeling too good," he says, and heads up.

"Hey, hold on a minute, mister!" Les calls. "We need to have a very serious talk about your behavior!"

Ray doesn't stop. Les starts after him, but Kerry puts a hand on his shoulder.

"Just...back off," Kerry says gently. "Give him some time and then you can ream him out all you want."

The psychologist glances at him and then back up at Ray as he disappears onto the second floor landing. "And what if he decides to leave again?"

"He's not walking out of this house with all of us here. If he tries, I'll tackle him. Okay?"

Les reluctantly nods.

Kerry spends the day working on the outside of the house, mowing, reading at the kitchen table, all while keeping the front door in sight at all times. Ray does not emerge from their room, not to eat, not even to use the bathroom. As evening approaches and the other members of the house come home, Kerry sits down on the couch in the living room, where D'libra is watching an episode of *Real Housewives* while talking on her cell. Kerry doesn't know how she pays for a phone without a job, but suspects it has something to do with those other friends she spends so much of her time with.

Les comes out of his bedroom, dressed even stiffer than usual, in gray slacks and a plaid sweater vest with a tie.

D'libra lowers the phone to her bared cleavage and croons, "Oooo, what're you dolled up all sexy for?"

"Does no one read the schedules I post?" Les sighs. "I've got my niece's community theater play tonight. With everything that happened, I'm hesitant to leave, but my sister will kill me if I don't go."

"You mean we get to stay home alone? With no babysitter? Sheeeit, I'm 'bouta turn this place *out*."

"Very funny," Les says. "No parties, no visitors, no rule breaking. If I come home and find anyone gone, it's a straight expulsion." He points at Kerry. "And if Ray tries to leave and you do not alert me immediately, I will tell the police that you aided him."

"He's not going anywhere," Kerry promises.

"All right. Brad and I are going to sit down with him first thing in the morning. Oh, and if you talk to him, try to find out where his ankle monitor is. Brad wants to know how he got it off without setting off the tampering alarm."

So finally, after dinner is consumed, the working residents have all gone to bed, and D'libra is in the backyard gathered around the fire pit with some individuals who look like they might be comfortable wearing Crip blue (one of them, a musclebound black guy with a mane of dreadlocks, has a bulge under his shirt that can only be a pistol tucked into his waistband), Kerry goes up and quietly pushes open the door to his and Ray's room.

Both beds are empty. Not only that, but the many shelves adorning Ray's half of the room are swept clean, the origami models missing.

Kerry's heart leaps into his throat. If Ray is gone, Les is going to roast both him and Kerry over an open flame. He spins around, intending to go for the phone downstairs, then hears a soft rustling from the closet.

He finds Ray in the far back corner, sitting in the dark with his knees up under his chin, a position Kerry wouldn't have thought him capable of. The shredded remains of his paper creations lay all around him in snowdrift piles. He winces away from the shaft of light and covers his face with one thick arm, putting the self-inflicted bruises on display. The line of welts are like purple hickeys in the dim closet.

"Jesus, Ray," Kerry says softly, gazing around at the devastation. "What's going on with you?"

His roommate doesn't answer, just lets his arm drop and stares ahead at nothing. He's still wearing the same clothes; the soiled stench around him makes Kerry's eyes water.

Kerry walks into the closet and eases down into the floor beside him, brushing aside tiny crushed Dr. Who phone booths and torn Egyptian Sphinxes. Ray scoots away, pressing further into the corner.

"Talk to me, man," Kerry presses. "I didn't tell anyone where you were, but you need to be honest with me. Did you...did you hurt anybody?"

Ray shakes his head one time, the movement so small it's barely perceptible. Still, it's enough confirmation to roll a load of tension off Kerry's shoulders. He's about to say as much when Ray's hands steals down his tucked up leg and touches the lump on the side of his ankle. The red light from the monitor is visible even through his khaki pant leg.

"Wait a minute, you're still wearing it?" Kerry asks. "You didn't take it off?"

His roommate doesn't acknowledge the question. He whispers in a thin, strained voice, "I talked to it…begged them to help me…but nobody came."

"It's not a god, Ray. It doesn't answer prayers. I told you, they can't even hear you." Kerry wants to press the issue, to figure out why, if he never removed the device, the signal was coming from here at the house instead of alerting the police while he sat in front of the school, scouting out victims. But he doubts Ray would even know, so pestering him about it won't do much good. "Besides, someone *did* come. *I* came. I tried to help you, and you drove away."

Ray says nothing, but Kerry can feel the tension coiled inside him. He takes a deep breath and continues. "Hey…I'm sorry about what I said yesterday. I'm an asshole, all right? Who am I to judge you? Hell, I guess I'm a little jealous. You got out of an asylum after twenty years and you got your shit together way better than me."

This time, the head shaking is big, dramatic, and frantic. "No. I'm b-bad. Worthless. *Evil*. H-he showed me."

"He…? Who are you talking about? The voices?"

"Nothing," Ray says quickly, then rests his forehead against the wall. A moment later, Kerry hears him sobbing.

"C'mon, man, don't do this, you're falling apart at the seams…"

"Do you think that…that we can be forgiven?" Ray asks tearfully, his words muffled as he speaks into the wall. The question stuns Kerry, mostly because it's coming from Ray. It sounds way too deep for his childlike mindset, more like an idea inserted in his head, rather than growing there on its own.

Ray turns to him, waiting for the answer.

Kerry blows air between his lips as he considers this. "Forgiven by *who*? The people we hurt? The law? God? What do you want, someone to present a certificate that absolves you of all sins? Cause, let me tell you, it doesn't matter. It won't change anything, it won't make you feel any better, and it won't help you get through the days any easier. The only person that can forgive you is *you*. Now, can you deal with that? Cause if not, you need to pack your shit and drive that ugly ass van right back to the nuthouse."

His roommate's jaw tightens. A fire blooms in his eyes, the kind of hard resolution that separates those who keep getting back up from those that roll over and play dead, and the last of Kerry's fears evaporate. Ray swallows hard, then nods.

"Good. Cause I'd miss you around here." He reaches over, grabs Ray in a headlock, and pulls him close, burying the man's head in his armpit. "C'mon, you weirdo, let's get you cleaned up and into bed. This'll all look better in the morning, I promise."

He forces Ray to take a change of clothes into the bathroom, then waits in the hall for him to emerge scrubbed clean and wearing pajamas. Ray allows himself to be tucked in, turns toward the wall, and seems to go to sleep instantly. Kerry stretches out in his own bed across the room. It's barely 9:30, but this day lasted an eternity. Raucous laughter drifts up from outside, the sound of D'libra's backyard party. He closes his eyes, even though he's sure that sleep will never come, and is out before he can finish the thought.

A soft thud awakens him sometime later. The sound of a closing door.

He blinks in the dark bedroom, slowly rising back to full consciousness. Once he's sure of who and where he is, he looks over at Ray's half of the room.

The moonlight streaming through the window reveals that his roommate's bed is empty.

Kerry sits up, cursing himself for not taking more precautions. The clock beside him reads twenty minutes to one. He stumbles out of bed so fast, his foot gets caught in the sheets and spills him into the floor. He checks the closet, finds it empty this time, then runs for the door and steps into the hall.

It's much darker out here, but a paper-thin beam of weak light flickers beneath the bathroom door at the far end of the hall, before it opens onto the media center. Kerry moves toward it, past Scott and Mark's room, feeling his way along the wall. He reaches to knock on the door and then jumps away as he spies movement from the corner of his eye.

A shape hurries across the pitch black media center, six or seven yards away. Kerry can see the barest outline as the figure moves in front of the spokes of the bannister on its way toward the stairs, but he can tell that it's way too thin to be Ray.

"Les? Is that you?" he calls out in a whisper.

The figure pauses at the head of the stairs, a spindly silhouette, then steps quickly down and moves out of sight.

Kerry turns back to the bathroom door. It was probably just D'libra sneaking out, and he needs to find his roommate. He raps lightly and asks, "Are you in there, Ray?"

No answer. Kerry pushes the door open.

A scream swells in his chest and then punches its way out of his mouth, followed by another.

The bathroom is lit by two candles on the sink. Their flickering illumination barely reaches the bathtub, where Ray slumps in water up to his chin, still dressed in the pajamas he wore to bed. His eyes are glassy and fake, like the ones in a taxidermied deer. One arm is propped on the ledge where the tub meets the wall.

The wrist is slashed open to the bone.

In the dim light, the blood spurting from the wound into the bathwater is as black as a moonless winter night.

FAIRY TALES

TWENTY TWO

Hopeful Sunshine is quickly overrun by cops and coroners. A half hour after the body's discovery, news vans from three different networks clog the street in front of the house, along with a loose crowd of neighbors who have drifted from their homes in the middle of the night to gawk. The rest of the residents are rousted from bed—those not already awakened by Kerry's screams—and sent onto the back patio while the investigation is conducted.

Kerry sits hunched on one of the loungers with Lorie beside him, her arms wrapped around her waist as she weeps softly with her head on his shoulder. Across from them, Scott and D'libra huddle together on another seat, sharing a cigarette, their expressions dour. None of them has spoken a word except Mark, who paces through the grass along the fence, muttering to himself. Kerry catches something about 'interrupting my sleep' before tuning the asshole out entirely.

The night is hot and humid, but Kerry's skin stays cold enough to bring on a shiver every few minutes. Every time he warms up, the scene in the bathroom hits him all over again, his roommate, his *friend*, slumped over in a stew of cloudy water with his veins sliced open. The blood was terrible—would undoubtedly occupy a dark corner of his memory for the foreseeable future—but it wasn't even the worst part; that honor belonged to the lifelessness of the body itself. Seeing someone you knew like that made you realize that a human being becomes nothing more than a mannequin after that spark of vitality leaves their eyes.

As much as he's often wished that he could've said goodbye to Kayla, a small, selfish part of him is now very glad that he never saw her lying in a coffin.

Then the back door of the house opens and Les steps out, still wearing the sweater vest outfit for his niece's play. He's followed by Sanders, who's dressed conservatively—for him, anyway—in jeans and a black polo. They approach the group of residents, and the parole officer clasps his hands in front of him as he says somberly, "They're taking him out now. As soon as they're finished, you can come back inside."

"Yeah, and what about that bathroom?" Mark yells angrily from across the yard. "How're we supposed to use that with his fucking blood all over the place?"

"We'll bring in professional biohazard cleaners. Till then, you can use Les' bathroom."

Mark throws up a hand and resumes pacing.

"The police are already leaving?" Kerry asks. "Don't they wanna talk to me?"

Sanders frowns. "What for?"

"I'm the one that found him." At the baffled look on the other man's face, he adds, "Aren't they investigating this?"

"There's not much to investigate. The man committed suicide."

Kerry is on his feet and shaking his head before the sentence is finished. "No, he did not."

Sanders and Les exchange arched eyebrows before the parole officer asks, "Do you know something we don't?"

"Yeah, I just talked to him a few hours ago. He didn't have any reason to do that."

"He didn't?" The sarcasm in the question catches Kerry off guard. "Cause, besides the fact that he was—let's be frank—a convicted child molester that spent most of his life in a mental hospital, from what Les told me, he sounded like a wreck when he came home yesterday."

"No. I mean, yeah, he got upset but he…" Kerry can easily recall that fire-glazed determination in the man's eyes, he just can't think of a way to accurately describe it. "…but he wasn't suicidal."

"Then are you suggesting foul play?"

Kerry hesitates. What, exactly, *is* he suggesting? His declaration had been such a gut response, an urgent need to keep them from writing off the man's death, that he hadn't considered the alternative. But it has to be one or the other. Doesn't it? "I…I don't know. I just know Ray Leary wasn't depressed enough to…to kill himself."

These last words cause a brief buzz of pain to rocket all the way up his arm from his ghost finger, like the wrong answer sound effect from a game show. *Go to hell*, Kerry thinks at the missing digit.

Sanders squeezes the back of his neck. "Honestly, I don't know what to say to that, Denton. The police are ruling it a suicide. They found the knife in the tub with him."

"It's my fault." Les wipes away a tear of his own. "I should've seen it coming, it makes complete sense. He has a breakthrough last week. Years of denied guilt crash down on him. He starts acting erratically and then comes home yesterday acting like a zombie…"

Kerry slices his other hand down through the air. "I don't care about any of that. He wouldn't do it. I mean, c'mon guys, we're talking about *Ray* here. He has—*had*—the brain of a goddamn puppy. Can any of you see that big moron sawing into his own wrists like a Goth chick on prom night?"

He looks around at the others, his fellow residents, but none of them will meet his eyes. Mark keeps pacing. D'libra taps her foot spastically on the ground. Scott sucks on the cigarette like it's the only way he's drawing breath.

After a moment of silence that far overstays its welcome, Lorie says, "You saw how upset he got in the session last week, Kerry. I think that...he had more problems than he let on. Hell, we probably all do. But maybe his got to be too much for him."

Kerry tries to speak, tries to swallow, fails to do either. For a moment, he starts to believe them—not only is it the more logical answer, but it's also much *easier*, to just let this go so that he doesn't have to think about it anymore—but then a burst of that same high-octane anger he felt in the cemetery makes his heart contract into a hard knot in his chest. "You didn't know him like I did. None of you even wanted to."

Mark mumbles something that sounds like, "You got that right."

"Maybe you did know him best," Sanders concedes. "But you said it yourself: you can never tell what's going through a person's head."

Kerry glares at him, his thoughts grinding together like cogs in a rusted machine. He's painted himself into a corner, and he's ready to give up until he remembers one other thing.

"Who was upstairs?" he demands.

"What are you talking about?"

"Someone was sneaking around in the media center right before I found Ray. Who was it?"

Again he looks around at the others. This time they meet his gaze with frank confusion.

He hones in on D'libra. "What about your gang member buddies you invited over last night? Did you sneak someone up to your room?"

She raises a manicured hand. "Fuck you Chester, I was asleep when you started yellin."

"We both were," Lorie adds.

"Kerry, I got home at midnight, but I was still awake in my room," Les tells him. "I didn't hear anybody."

Sanders massages the back of his neck again, this time with his eyes closed and the muscles in his jaw standing out in banded cords. "What's the point of this interrogation? Please do not tell me you're accusing someone here of murder."

Kerry stomps past him toward the house. "I'll talk to the cops then."

"Hey! Goddamn it Denton, get over here!"

He stops with his hand on the door. Sanders is heading to the far corner of the yard, away from everyone else, and gesturing to him furiously. Kerry reluctantly walks over to join him.

"Did you happen to notice the shitload of reporters lined up in the driveway?" Sanders asks. "Because all of them are here to drum up a story about the rash of sex offender suicides that keeps getting juicier every time one of you motherfuckers offs yourself. Hell, this makes two of my charges in the last month alone. I've got a meeting with the parole board in four hours to get my ass chewed. And the last thing I need is you concocting some half-assed story about a phantom murderer, or whatever the hell you're trying to imply."

"I'm not implying anything," Kerry says through gritted teeth. "I just don't want the cops sweeping this under the rug because he's another dead child molester. Ray...he deserves better than that."

Sanders continues to stare daggers at him for another few seconds before taking in a deep breath and huffing it out, as though clearing his anger. His tone softens considerably as he says, "I know. I don't want that either."

"Then listen to what I'm telling you."

"I am, while also keeping in mind that your judgment could be a little clouded here."

"How so?" Kerry demands.

"You had a fight with him before all this, right? I won't even sugarcoat it to spare your feelings: you may very well have rattled his mental state enough that he took his life. So you feel guilty. That's understandable. And now you're trying to make it up to him by clearing his name, to force some kind of meaning into his death." Sanders licks his lips, bows his head. "But let me assure you Denton, these things never make sense to the people that are left behind. You'll never understand it, and you can't take responsibility for his actions. If it wasn't you, something else would've set him off."

Déjà vu descends upon Kerry like dense fog. A moment later, he understands why: Ray said almost the same thing to him at Kayla's grave.

A fist of pure, hard-packed emotion punches him in the stomach, one that carries as much weight as the guy that walloped him in the Caulfield's parking lot. This is all too much, history repeating itself, and none of it makes sense. Suddenly he can imagine the rest of his life as an endless series of being told he's not at fault for driving those around him to their deaths.

Sanders keeps talking, unaware of Kerry's anguish. "We all have to face facts. Ray was coming unhinged. He had a breakdown during therapy and disappeared for 24 hours. And the coroner told me there's a line of severe bruises on his arm that look self-inflicted."

"There's...something else." Kerry chews the inside of his cheek as he mentally kicks himself. Admitting this next part is too much like a betrayal. "When I found him this morning...he was sitting down the street in front of that school, watching the kids."

"Oh Chriiiist," Sanders groans, tilting his head back.

"He was terrified of that place," Kerry rushes to add. "Wouldn't even drive past it. Even when I talked to him he was jumpy as hell, like he didn't want to be there."

"Cause he probably didn't. He felt *compelled* to be."

"But...he was castrated."

"Stopping the urge doesn't always cure the sickness. There's a lot of people that can't understand that concept." Sanders looks a little ill as he says this. "That poor bastard. I hate to say it, but...maybe this is for the best. He's at peace now."

"He was also still wearing his ankle monitor. From what I can tell, he never took it off. So why did it tell you he was here?"

"I don't know. Could've been a glitch of some sort."

"That's a big glitch. He was well within the 500 yard barrier. Isn't the whole point of the damn thing to alert someone if that happens?"

Sanders nods, but it seems uncertain. "Technically, as soon as an alert is triggered—either from proximity or tampering—the police are contacted first, then me. Police will usually dispatch the closest officer to assess and detain. I have no idea why Ray's monitor gave a false signal, but I'll check into it. Between you and me, there's a hundred ways to get around those things. With the right equipment, a tech-savvy person could clone the GPS and direct it wherever he wanted. In ten years, they'll be obsolete." The parole officer clasps his hands in front of him, as though pleading. "But if Ray was down there at that school, wrestling with his demons, then what he did tonight makes even more sense. You see that, don't you?"

"Yes, I know," Kerry relents. His last conversation with Ray comes to mind, about him wanting to be forgiven. "But still…something feels weird about this whole thing. Maybe it would help if we knew where he went last night. He told me he made his delivery. Shouldn't we try to find these people and ask if he said anything to them?"

Sanders' eyes bulge. "No, absolutely not. I don't want to bring anybody else into this. The man committed suicide, Denton. As hard as it is to face, that's all there is to it."

Kerry digs at the lawn with the toe of one sneaker. "So what happens to him now?"

"He goes to the morgue while the state arranges a burial." Before Kerry can balk, he says, "Ray has no next-of-kin. His mother died while he was in the hospital and his father disowned him decades ago. Unless you have the money to pay for a funeral, there's nothing either of us can do about that."

The back door of the house opens. Two men in blazers step out and signal to Sanders. "I need to get this wrapped up. Go back inside and we'll talk more later."

Kerry trudges across the yard. The other residents are standing to file back into the house. As he lines up behind Mark and Scott, Kerry hears the former mutter, "So much uproar over a pedo. World's better off with him burning in hell."

Before even he can understand how it happened, Kerry's arm is wrapped around the man's throat. He yanks Mark backward, keeping him off balance, and crushes his neck in the crook of his elbow.

"You mouthy, judgmental fuck," Kerry snarls in his ear. Mark struggles feebly, slapping at Kerry's face and prying at the limb that's cut off his air supply. "You're not any better than him. You're a drunk and a murderer and a...a shitty father. You think God's gonna roll out the red carpet when you die because you wear a cross?"

"*Kerry, let him go!*" Les roars, his face red. From the corner of his eye, Kerry can see Sanders and the detectives running toward him.

He releases Mark and steps away. The other man clutches his throat, hacking and sputtering as he whirls around. "He attacked me, you all saw it! I'm filing assault charges for that! I'll get a restraining order! You won't even be able to live here!"

"Separate, right now," Les orders them. "Mark, sit down and let's have a talk about decency. Kerry, go inside and I'll deal with you in a minute."

Kerry goes for the door. The others part to let him through. In the house, he stomps past an officer in the living room, keeps going until he reaches the kitchen. A moment later he finds himself at the window overlooking the front lawn with tears streaming down his face.

He peeks through the closed blinds. The street is still filled with police cars, news vans, an ambulance, a coroner wagon, and assorted rubberneckers. Kerry sees several familiar faces, including Velder, wearing a robe so formal it could pass for a business suit. He also catches sight of Solomon's gaunt figure standing eerily still in the crowd, that milky pale skin glowing in the backwash of a reporter's camera light. From this distance, those unnatural eyes of his are gaping holes, like the picture of the children with the bleeding sockets.

"Excuse me?" someone says behind him. Kerry swipes at his eyes and turns around to find a man with a CORONER badge hanging around his neck. "You're a resident, right? I mean, you live here?"

"Yeah."

He holds up a small plastic baggie with something bulky inside. "Is it all right if I leave this with you?"

Kerry comes forward and accepts the bag. Inside is Ray's cheap plastic wristwatch, and the black box of his ankle monitor with the heavy strap folded beneath. Bile rises up the back of Kerry's throat when he notices that the watch's face is filled with pink-tinged water.

"Personal effects," the man from the coroner's office tells him gently. "I called and shut off the monitoring for the ankle GPS. Someone from the company should be in touch to tell you how to return it. Just don't plug in the strap or it'll come back on line."

Kerry nods. The guy mumbles, "Sorry for your loss," and leaves him standing there. A few minutes later, he and another man wheel a gurney with a body bag on top out the front door.

TWENTY THREE

"This house suffered a terrible tragedy this week."

Les sits with his hands on his bony knees, letting his gaze linger on each of them, like he's telling a bedtime story. And that's what this is, a fairy tale designed to fool them into believing that the world gives a shit about the man they're discussing. "It doesn't matter if you hated him or disapproved of what he did, Raymond Leary was a human being. And the death of another human being can make us want to shut down. Retreat. Wall ourselves off from the world. But we can't let that happen. We have to keep the lines of communication open, so we don't fall into despair. To that end, I'd like to devote today's session to Ray, and I'd like us to talk about how his passing makes us feel."

This is the first time Kerry has seen the other housemates in days, since that night on the patio. Their last regular meeting, the morning after Ray's death, was cancelled to give them time to mourn, and the house to get back to normal. A biohazard cleanup company called Aftermath spent six hours scouring the bathroom, removing all traces of blood.

And, after a day camping out on Hopeful Sunshine's front lawn, the reporters finally got bored by the lack of additional developments in what one anchor called 'a grisly rash of self-destruction among the sex offender community.' *Community*; as if they all get together to swap recipes and play golf.

Kerry spent the time in his room, packing up Ray's belongings, suffering from nightmares, emerging late at night to find food. Walling himself off, in other words. That was how he survived in prison, by himself, and he will do the same thing here.

Except, without his roommate, the living space is far lonelier than any of his stints in solitary.

Now they sit in their standard ring of chairs, with one conspicuously empty seat next to Les. Kerry keeps his eyes on the psychologist and pretends not to notice the bitter scowls that Mark shoots his way every few minutes from the other side of the circle.

No one speaks. Les waits patiently. The silence grows so thick that each tick of the clock on the wall makes Kerry wince.

Then Lorie sniffles and wipes a hand across her nose. "It just…it scares me. Cause I've had thoughts like that too. There were a couple times, at my worst, that…killing myself…it seemed like the only way out. But I couldn't bring myself to do it."

"So what, you think what Ray did is *brave* or somethin?" Scott asks.

"No, not at all! I just mean, whenever I think about hurting myself, something always stops me. It's like this voice that tells me, 'wait a little longer, things'll get better.' And I can't help wondering…what's the difference between me and him? Why couldn't he tell himself that, too?"

"We all have an innate self-preservation instinct," Les assures her. "But it can be overridden by adrenaline, by strong emotion, by mental instability."

"And yo, fat boy had all three," Scott mumbles, making the insult sound reverent.

"Well see, *that's* what scares me." Lorie wraps her arms around her waist, hugging herself. "What if next time I'm like that, I keep waiting for that voice to stop me...but it doesn't?"

"Then you pray." Mark sits forward eagerly, makes a fist with one hand, and holds it out toward her as though the solution to all of her problems lies within his clenched fingers. "In your darkest hour, you reach out for Jesus with both hands and you—"

"Shut up with that Jesus shit." D'libra's voice is soft, barely more than a whisper, but her words slice through the room like a samurai sword. Les is so startled by the command that he doesn't even issue a warning for the curse. She closes her eyes and crosses her arms, hiding the old needle marks. Kerry can see her shaking as she says, "I been *reachin out* for him my whole life, tellin other people to do the same like you just did, but the truth is, only person that ever helped me is *me*. If Jesus is listenin, he don't care. So don't make it sound like prayin is gon' solve all her problems."

"D'libra," Les says gently, "do you want to talk about how Ray's passing makes you feel?"

"No, I don't," she barks. This time, her dark eyes glimmer with tears as she opens them. Kerry doesn't know which surprises him more: her tears, or his brief urge to cross the room and fold her into his arms. "I don't wanna talk about how that cracker died any more than the one who did it on a cross. And you can keep my credit for the session if you want."

Les doesn't answer. Scott clears his throat and says, "Well, it makes me feel like it's time to get my life movin. So last night...I asked my girlfriend to marry me." The announcement perks up the room, bringing on a brief round of cheers and congratulations. He grins bashfully and adds, "My parole officer says I can apply for house release in like two weeks. And yo, I'm sorry Les, but I ain't gonna miss these meetings even a li'l bit."

"That's great, Scott," the psychologist tells him. "You're right, life goes on. Mark, what about you?"

"Nope, no way." Mark shakes his head back and forth in big, dramatic sweeps that remind Kerry of a five-year-old refusing their broccoli. "Every time I open my mouth around here lately I get persecuted." He looks pointedly at Kerry. "Or attacked."

"Then maybe you shouldn't let so much bullshit come out of it," D'libra mutters.

Mark jerks a thumb at her. "You see?"

Les sighs and swivels in his chair. "Kerry, you've had some time to internalize what happened. Have you come to terms with Ray's passing?"

"Yeah, I've *come to terms* with it," Kerry told him, pouring sarcasm into the statement. "Doesn't mean I accept it."

"Oh Lord," Mark groans at the ceiling. "How much of this must we endure?"

"So you still believe that Ray did not commit suicide?" Les asks.

"I...I don't know. Maybe he did." Kerry shrugs helplessly, reaching for words, and, as usual, they flee from him. "But either way, I think...there's got to be more to it than that. And this is great, us sitting around and telling each other how his death affects us, but I'd rather do something that matters."

"Like what?" Lorie asks. Even she sounds agitated with him.

Kerry stands up and moves into the middle of the circle, squeezing his hand into a tight, hot ball at his side. For once, he wants to wake up his phantom limb, to feel its pain, to have it wash away his fear and the dam in his brain so that he can say his piece. "They're going to put him in the ground in an unmarked grave somewhere and forget about him. Just like his family and the rest of the world did. We're all he had. I think we owe it to him to make sure the truth is told, that we understand exactly why he did this."

"Yo, he didn't, like, leave a note or nothing." Scott doesn't even try to meet Kerry's gaze as he says this. "You ever thought that maybe he didn't *want* us to understand?"

Kerry sees unspoken agreement on the others' faces. And really, why should they care? Three of them already have one foot out the door, ready to reset their lives and forget about this place. Scott's claim that they're all a family is complete horseshit, as much a fairy tale as the idea that Ray's death is a 'tragedy.'

He pushes through the circle of chairs and storms out of the session. Les can keep his credit for the day, too. Upstairs, the door to the bathroom is closed, but Kerry gives it a wide berth. Even though the crime scene cleaners assured them it's sanitized, he doesn't think he'll ever be able to go in it.

TWENTY FOUR

A half hour later, he's stretched out on his bed, staring at the ceiling. D'libra leans through the doorway.

"Hey Chester," she hisses. She's changed since the meeting, into a skintight sleeveless t-shirt and jeans. "You wanna find out what yo' boy been up to?"

He takes a moment to answer, trying to figure out what she means. "Yeah…"

She rolls her eyes and beckons to him. "C'mon then. I ain't gon' beg you."

Kerry follows her down the hall to the media center, where she peeks over the landing, then comes back and slides into the chair in front of the computer. He watches over her shoulder as she logs in to her profile, then clicks an icon on the desktop and types in another requested password.

"When I first moved in, Les watched me like a fuckin hawk. Or a bald eagle." She snickers as she pops the knuckles on her left hand. "Even used to listen in on my phone calls and shit. And the dummy made me watch him do *this* enough times that I memorized his damn password." She brings up a new screen that asks for a date range, types in the dates for this week, and the screen fills up with what at first seems to be computer gobbledygook; phrases, letters and symbols, sorted in huge blocks of text beneath labels for each day. It's not until his eyes skim over the words 'Willow Grove Cemetery' listed under the header for Sunday that he understands.

"The keystroke log." Kerry whaps himself in the forehead with one hand. "Why the hell didn't we think of that the night he disappeared?"

"Cause you and Les a couple of stupid white boys."

Kerry leans over her to read the screen, his face so close to hers that their cheeks are almost touching. He catches a whiff of some delicate flower-scented fragrance, either perfume or lotion. "So do you have any idea what we're looking for?" The blocks of keystroke text are gibberish to him, with occasional coherent phrases mixed in that must have been typed in a string. For example, *someone* in the house has been googling 'Christian Vixens' on a regular basis.

"Be a lot easier if they added a mechanism to filter by specific profiles." She sounds so different muttering technical jargon that Kerry glances over at her in surprise. D'libra stiffens at the attention, then goes back to scanning the information for a moment before tapping one nail on the screen. "There. That's where he went to his website, so that's gotta be his log in and password."

"You know about this kinda stuff?" Kerry means it as a compliment, but regrets the words a split second after they leave his mouth.

She pulls away and glares at him. "Oh no, the cracked-out black bitch couldn't possibly have any computer skills, right?"

"No, I didn't mean—"

"Uh-uh, no sah, sorry massa! I's get back to moppin the flo' now."

"Okay, stop."

"Fo' *yo* information, you ain't the only one who was tryin to get some education before bein sent up the river. And would you mind gettin yo face away from me? Shit, you breathin on my neck like you 'bout to rump ride."

"All right, all right."

He backs away. Her fingers fly across the keyboard. Ray's garish website comes up, so cheerful and happy it sends a pang through Kerry's chest. A second later, and they're logged in to some sort of administrative back page, with an email correspondence list along the bottom half that displays a subject line for each entry. There are several that have come in since Ray's death, orders for origami knickknacks that will never be filled, but the most recent one from before Sunday is titled 'Product Delivery.'

"Try that one," Kerry tells her.

She clicks on the entry, which is from a generic Yahoo address full of random numbers and letters. On the screen now is a complete back-and-forth account of a correspondence between Ray and someone who signs each email with 'Smith.' They scroll to the bottom where the chain begins and skim through, reading the initial order offering an outrageous sum for 300 world landmark centerpieces for a formal banquet, Ray's excited updates on his progress (complete with multiple exclamation points), and finally, the delivery instructions requesting that Ray bring them himself, along with a Dallas address, to receive payment.

"Jesus, he didn't even get a deposit first," Kerry says.

"Well, there you go, Chester." D'libra scoots the keyboard over for him. "You wanna talk to them, go ahead."

Kerry bites his lip for a moment as he considers this. Sanders forbid him from contacting these people, afraid that it would bring even more attention to a bad situation. And indeed, media interest in Ray's suicide may've waned quickly, but Kerry doesn't doubt the vultures would circle again if they found out a fellow sex offender was playing amateur Sherlock. He *does* think it's important to see what the Smiths can tell him about Ray; however, sending an email seems riskier than going to talk to them in person, where he can gauge their reaction and vary his story as needed. So instead, he brings up Google, enters the address, and memorizes the route it recommends. Then he gives D'libra a curt, "Thanks," and goes back to his room.

The keys to Ray's van are still on his bedside table. Kerry swipes them and also grabs the boxes of his roommate's belongings. Might as well put them in the vehicle until Sanders figures out what to do with all of it. The plastic bag with the ankle monitor is still on the bed. To Kerry's knowledge, no one from the company contacted them about returning it. He takes it out of the bag and puts it on the dresser, then changes his mind and adds it to the top of the load. Having it in here creeps him out, especially when he thinks of how Ray acted like it could hear every word he said.

He goes downstairs, unlocks the van, and puts the boxes in the rear compartment, behind the curtain divider. By the time he goes around to the driver's door, D'libra is already sitting in the passenger seat, with a pair of sunglasses on.

"Lucky for you, I got an openin in my schedule," she says.

"Get out. You can't come with me."

"Oh yes I can. You wouldn't even have that address without me. That means where you go, I go."

Even though the thought of taking a trip with her away from Hopeful Sunshine is oddly exciting, Kerry asks, "D'libra...why would you even *want* to go?"

"Cause all my friends are busy and there ain't nuthin good on TV. Might as well watch you make a fool of yo damn self." She raps her knuckles on the dashboard. "Now get this nasty-ass van movin, or I'll tell Les and Sanders what you doin. Shit, my hair's gonna smell like French fries for a week."

He sighs and climbs in behind the wheel. "Okay, but if we get in trouble for fraternizing, it's on you."

D'libra tilts her head down to look at him over the top of her sunglasses, a coy, purse-lipped smile on her face. "Boy, if I was gonna *fraternize* you, you'd already be in a coma from the anticipation alone."

Twenty minutes later, the vehicle is rattling down the freeway a few exits from their destination. They've kept the windows rolled down to alleviate the ghostly smell of fried food from the back, and so D'libra can smoke. As she finishes a cigarette, she stubs the butt out in the ashtray, then rolls up her window enough to cut down the howl of the wind. "So what're you gonna tell 'em?"

"The truth, I guess."

"Which is?"

"That my friend committed suicide after delivering their order, and I want to know if he said anything to them."

"Yeah, that'll sure put some cheer in they day." She twists in the seat, tucking one foot under her body. The position makes her small and fragile somehow. "And what you think they gon' tell *you*? I mean, c'mon Chester, what could you possibly be hopin to get outta this?"

For the first time, he truly begins to understand how stupid this whole idea is. Perhaps Sanders is right, and this whole crusade is nothing more than guilt. Deep down inside, maybe he wants an excuse to tell himself that he's not directly responsible for Ray's suicide. To make sure that his ghost finger doesn't have yet another reason to haunt him. "I have no idea. I guess I just want to know what he did for his last day on earth."

She props the dark shades on her head and continues to stare at him. Her gaze begins to make his cheeks burn. "What?" he asks.

D'libra scoots closer to him, squatting between the front seats, and points at his left hand on the steering wheel. "So fess up. What happened to it, anyway?"

"Huh? Oh, nothing. Just…an accident."

"Weird accident, to fuck up that finger and not touch the ones on either side."

"Yeah, well, coming from the woman who expressed an interest in chopping off both my dick and my balls, I would think you'd be thrilled that I'm missing body parts somewhere."

In response, she holds out a hand. "Lemme see."

"What? No!"

"Why not?"

"I don't like it touching other people. It…feels weird."

She rolls her eyes. "Give it to me, Chester."

"I said no."

Before he realizes what's happening, she reaches across him, grabs his right wrist, and drags his hand away from the steering wheel. The van swerves a bit on the road before he regains control. "Jesus, you trying kill us both?"

D'libra leans closer to examine his finger, her face close to his crotch. She runs her own fingertip around the edges of the stump. A curiously warm sensation flushes through him, not the psychosomatic pain from his phantom limb, but not exactly pleasant either. The only comparison he can make is having his nipples rubbed, a stimulation that's irksome on its own but feels fantastic during in the throes of passion.

An image takes shape in his head, completely unbidden, of D'libra popping the stub of his ring finger into her mouth and flicking her tongue around it. The idea is as alluring as it is perverse.

"Cut's pretty clean," she murmurs, still squinting at the digit like a jeweler examining a diamond. "Looks amputated to me."

"Uh, yeah. Yeah, it was." Kerry is horrified to realize that an erection is straining at the fabric of his jeans, inches from her chin. He gently pulls his hand out of her grasp. "But…I don't like to talk about it."

He can't be sure, but he thinks that her eyes linger on the growing bulge in his lap as she sits back up and says, "I guess we all got our ghosts."

Kerry takes the designated exit and two more turns into a neighborhood that's not as ritzy as what he imagined. In fact, most of the houses are smaller and dingier than Hopeful Sunshine. He finds the street from the address and cruises along, searching for the house number, then pulls to a stop at the curb in front of it.

The house—a tan one story with stained brick, loose siding, and a badly overgrown lawn—has a FORECLOSURE sign in the front yard.

Something heavy and uncomfortable begins to uncoil in Kerry's stomach.

"You sure this is the right address?" D'libra asks.

"Yeah."

"Cause this don't look like the kinda place that throws dinner parties."

"No, it doesn't."

"Well…we came all the way here, might as well go poke around." She opens the door and hops out before he can protest.

Kerry gets out and rushes around the van to catch up with her. His heartbeats are tripping over one another in his chest; he no longer wants to go anywhere near that house, not even if doing so will somehow magically resurrect Ray from the dead. "Wait, hold on, just hold on a sec! I don't think anybody's going to answer the door here!"

"That's why I ain't knockin." She veers off the driveway into the grass strip along the side of the house. Kerry watches as she opens the rusted fence gate and strolls into the backyard like she owns the place.

"Shit." He stands there, uncertain, glancing up and down the empty street, then follows.

The backyard is even more trashed than the front, with knee-high weeds and sun-faded patio furniture on a cracked block of cement. None of the windows have blinds; D'libra is peering through one beside the patio. Kerry cups his hands on the dusty glass next to her.

The space on the other side was probably a bedroom, but now it holds only a layer of stained carpeting. It's as bare and empty as…

Well, as the kitchen in Solomon's house.

That weight in Kerry's stomach squirms harder, eeling through his guts with tentacles of dread.

He's still staring through the window and trying to understand what it all means when D'libra reaches down, grabs a chunk of the crumbling concrete beneath their feet, and casually tosses it through the glass.

"*Jesus Christ!*" he screeches, scrambling away from the

falling shards. To his ears, the crash sounds as loud as a bomb blast. "What if there's an alarm?"

"Houses like this don't got alarms." She reaches through the broken pane, flips the latch, and wrestles the window up.

"What are you *doing*?" he demands. "We're both on parole, this is fucking breaking and entering!"

"You the one who wanted to do somethin that matters," she tells him, slinging a leg over the sill. Her low-riding jeans slip down enough to reveal the upper strap of a dark blue thong as she ducks under the window. From the other side, she says, "Don't leave no fingerprints and we'll be fine. Considerin you only got nine in the first place, that shouldn't be too hard. Now you comin or not?"

Kerry takes a deep breath to steady his jangled nerves, looks around the yard, and borrows her phrase. "Where you go, I go. I guess."

His foot crunches down on the glass scattered across the carpet. He crosses the room in quick, tip-toed steps with his arms clamped to his sides, as if this will somehow make what they're doing less illegal, and jumps through the door into a hallway beyond, running full-body into D'libra's back side. The bubble of her ass grinds into his crotch, but he's far too nervous to take any pleasure from it.

"Would you relax?" she growls. "Shit, it's like you never broke into nobody's house before…"

Neither of them speak as they walk through the abandoned property, inspecting each silent room. There isn't much to see. The sadness of the place—a stolen home, its owners forced into the street—makes Kerry a little ill. They finally end up in a dust-covered kitchen at the front of the house.

"I think yo boy got played," D'libra tells him, opening up the pantry door with the tail of her t-shirt. "Maybe that's why he did it. Got depressed when he realized it was all a prank."

"Maybe," Kerry agrees. There's certainly nothing to suggest that his roommate ever came inside. He can imagine the man driving up after his fight with Kerry, the sadness on his hound dog face when he finds this place instead of the gated mansion he'd built up in his mind, but, being the eternal optimist, knocking on the door for a good five minutes before trudging away. Maybe the disappointment was the final straw that sent him crashing into the depths of depression.

Something beneath the kitchen sink catches Kerry's eye, a complicated shape that sticks out from the shadows. He walks over, squats down, fishes it out, and stares at the object in his hands.

A squashed paper replica of the Eiffel Tower.

TWENTY FIVE

In an effort to promote 'healing and unity,' Les declares the following Saturday 'House Restoration Day.' Instead of group therapy, they're all made to help Kerry with his project of sprucing up the exterior of Hopeful Sunshine.

The place has improved thanks to Kerry's efforts—cleaned gutters and a budding lawn and trimmed hedges—but with only a few hours of everyone pitching in, they're able to get the shutters replaced and the majority of the siding repainted. And, after some initial grumbling, they seem to be having fun in the summer heat, Scott singing pop songs in Spanish, Lorie spraying them with the hose, D'libra laughing, Les wearing a pair of shorts that make him resemble a stork, the melancholia of the previous week lifting away. Even Mark is caught cracking a smile.

Kerry tries to get into the spirit, but every few minutes his gaze is drawn up the road to Solomon's house, sticking out from the corner lot two blocks up like a rotten tooth. That FORECLOSURE sign is still there, and, now that Hopeful Sunshine's makeover is nearing completion, the other property is far more of an eyesore. It's probably paranoia, but every time Kerry looks in the house's direction, he can feel those unnaturally dark eyes staring back at him.

He said nothing to D'libra about the wild suspicions unfolding in his head as they left the other abandoned house downtown. She considered the matter closed, and he gave no indication that he thought otherwise. It's not that he thinks she wouldn't believe him, he just doesn't want any chance of this getting back to Les or Sanders until he has something more than theories. When they arrived home, he spent the day reading in the back yard, then went upstairs to the media center once the rest of the house was asleep.

His research session lasted the better part of an hour. A quick check of real estate records reveals that no one bought the house up the street since it was foreclosed on eight months ago. As far as the government is concerned, it should be unoccupied. It seems to Kerry that his encounter with Solomon at the residence was an especially vivid fever dream.

If he told the police a possible squatter was living inside it, would they find any evidence of the gawky man with the dark eyes?

Kerry thinks not.

A sudden hunch sends him to the state sex offender registry that Ray showed him on his first morning at Hopeful Sunshine. This time, instead of his own name, he types in DOMINIC ZABAWSKI.

The man's profile is still active on the site, despite the fact that he's been dead for several weeks. Kerry wonders if this is due to the slow process of government red tape, or because society isn't going to let a little thing like death stand in the way of shaming a child molester. P is for Predator; a law as eternal and uncompromising as gravity. There's the summary of the man's crimes, along with his description, weight, distinguishing marks, etc., practically all the way down to his preference for boxers or briefs. But it's the address—displayed so carelessly for the entire world to see—that Kerry is most interested in.

With this information, he goes back to the list of foreclosed homes, and begins the arduous process of entering them into Google one at a time. It takes him a half hour, but he hits upon exactly what he suspected.

There is an empty, foreclosed home three blocks away from the residence where Zabawski lived when he committed suicide.

Kerry doesn't know what it all means, but the similarities are too close to put down to mere coincidence.

The toe of a sneaker nudges him in the side, breaking his quiet contemplation of the house where he met Solomon. "Yo, you gonna hand me the drill or you wanna keep starin into space all day?"

"Sorry." Kerry retrieves the tool and hands it up to Scott, where he balances on a ladder while installing the last shutter. The others are nearby resting in the grass, covered in swatches of baby blue paint from their work. While Kerry steadies the ladder, he lets his eyes stray back to the house, expecting, as always, to find Solomon staring out of one of the windows like a ghost in an Amityville flick. Instead, he finds someone else every bit as unpleasant marching up the sidewalk in front of the house.

"Uh oh everybody, bitch alert," D'libra says from the ground.

Regina Velder's head is held as high and stiff as a military drill instructor. She's dressed as formally as ever—pleated gray pants and a white smock top with ornate gold embroidery—and accompanied by a tall man in a dark suit. She reaches the driveway of Hopeful Sunshine, turns smartly on her heel, and continues striding toward them. A smug grin tugs at the corners of her mouth as her cold eyes sweep across them.

Les jumps to his feet and walks to meet her while wiping sweat from his bald crown. "Good morning, Miss Velder! What can we do for you?"

She comes to a halt several yards away and clutches her hands to her wide bosom as though afraid the psychologist—whom she outweighs by a good fifty pounds—might suddenly lurch forward and grope at her. "I've told you many times what you and your band of miscreants can do for me, Norris. But it never makes any difference."

"Yes, well, uh…" Les swipes a hand through the air in the direction of the house. "As you can see, we're performing some renovations and—"

"Too little, too late, I'm afraid. Your disregard for the decent citizens of this community was apparent since the moment you took possession of this house. That ruckus earlier in the week with all the police and reporters was just further proof." That smirk touches her lips as she steps aside to make way for the man with her. "This is our newly appointed attorney Charles Brimhauer. He has something to give you."

By this time, Kerry and the others have all made their way across the yard and stand clustered behind Les. Brimhauer, a man with ruddy cheeks and bags under his eyes, steps forward holding out a packet of paper at least two inches thick. "Mr. Norris, these documents serve as an injunction to prevent you from taking on any more residents at this facility. A copy has been sent to the state correctional board as well. We're also seeking a court order to revoke this facility's operational license. The hearing is scheduled three weeks from today. You'll find all the details here."

Les accepts the sheaf of paper as though it were a dead baby, holding it out in front of him at arm's length. He can't take his eyes off it as he stammers, "But you can't...how did you...?"

Velder answers the unasked question before Brimhauer can. "The neighborhood committee has partnered with another organization dedicated to stopping suburban decline. One with more than enough money to cover our legal fees." Judging from the unrestrained glee on her face as she says this, Kerry suspects that she came to deliver these documents personally so that she could revel in their humiliation. She leans closer now, craning her head to the side in a comically secretive pose, and says softly, "Did you *really* think we would stand by forever while you stocked our neighborhood with drug addicts and..." Her eyes flick to Kerry. "Sex fiends?"

"*You muthafuckin cunt!*" D'libra howls. She lunges toward the woman, but Kerry moves fast, wrapping an arm around her toned waist to hold her back. Scott comes to help him.

"Don't make the same mistake I did," Kerry says, as she struggles against them. "You attack *her*, and she *will* press charges."

"It'd be worth it to jam my foot up her shriveled cooch! She sure ain't usin it for nuthin else!"

"You'd best keep your dogs on a leash, Norris," Velder says, but Kerry thinks there's a glimmer of fear in her eyes as she does. She marches back down the driveway with Brimhauer following. The Hopeful Sunshine residents wait until the pair is down the street and out of earshot before surrounding Les with a barrage of questions.

"Everyone calm down," Les tells them, but the psychologist seems to be in need of that advice himself as he frantically flips through pages in the document.

"But what does this mean?" Lorie squeals. "Can they really close the house down?"

"I don't know. I'll have to get in touch with the state attorneys and see what they say. Don't panic yet though, this might amount to no more than legal harassment."

"Yeah, and what happens to us if it ain't?" D'libra demands.

"You'll…well, you'll probably have to be reassigned to one of the larger group homes."

They all groan in unison. Kerry remembers only too well what Sanders told him about these places.

"Yo, who's doin this to us?" Scott is breathing hard with anger, his shoulders quivering. "What's this fuckin organization that *puta* was talkin about?"

Les is still flipping pages, scanning through the endless legalese. "It doesn't make any sense. The plaintiff on all of these is listed as some company called 'The MacCallum Construction Group.'"

Kerry needs to hear nothing else. Part of him already knew; after all, how could there be any other maestro to his suffering? He turns away from the others without a word and moves toward the house. None of them notice him leave; they're all still too busy shouting at Les. A horrible numbness spreads through him at the thought of what he means to do, one that makes him feel cold and empty and dead inside. All except for the stump of his ring finger, which begins throbbing in time with his heartbeat.

It takes two phone calls in which he claims to be an investor before some receptionist gives him the information he needs. He grabs the keys to the van and peels out of the driveway before anyone can ask where he's going.

A half hour later finds him sitting in front of a bustling construction yard full of hard-hat wearing men climbing around on the steel frame of what will be a strip mall in downtown Dallas. The sign in front reveals this to be a MACCALLUM CONSTRUCTION GROUP PROJECT. He can see a huge foreman trailer in the back corner, inside the chain link fence that bounds the lot.

Once upon a time, Kerry went to a construction site very much like this one to speak with the same man he's here to confront now. That conversation didn't go as well as he'd envisioned, and the memory of it is still drenched in enough terror that he can only sit in the van and stare for several minutes, his breath coming in slow, heavy inhalations. They make him lightheaded, blurring the afternoon sunlight so this all feels like a dream. He rubs at the smooth end of his severed finger, which has progressed from throbbing to burning, as though someone is holding an acetylene torch on it. But no matter where he touches, he'll never be able to find the source of that discomfort.

How is it possible for something that's not even there to cause so much pain?

Finally he gets out and crosses the street, then steps through the gap in the chain link and heads into the construction yard with his head down. Hydraulic squeals and the rumble of heavy machinery assail him from all directions. He keeps expecting someone to tell him to get out as he hurries across the dirt, but the place is so busy that no one pays him much attention.

At least until he's crossed three-quarters of the lot. Kerry glances up to get his bearings and sees a group of men gathered around a makeshift table created from a wooden industrial spool, reclining on the ground while they drink canned ice tea. One of them does a double take as he walks by. Kerry instantly recognizes the ratlike features and sweaty mullet;

the last time he saw them, they were hanging out of a truck window and taunting him after just having tried to run him down. Mullet elbows the man sitting next to him and points at Kerry. The brim of a green trucker cap sticks out from under this other worker's hard hat.

Kerry keeps walking, but glances back to find that they have both gotten up and are following him at a discreet distance. They remind him of hyenas loping behind a wounded gazelle. He quickens his pace as he approaches the trailer, then hurries up the stairs and throws open the door without bothering to knock.

The interior is huge and luxurious, woodgrain panels and leather couches and enough air conditioning in the middle of summer to keep a penguin comfortable. Robert MacCallum leans over a desk at the far end of the room, dressed in jeans and a plaid work shirt. Two other men in suits sit in chairs in front of him. All three are laughing robustly, the kind of powerful laughter that only men who rule the world are capable of producing.

But when MacCallum sees who burst into his trailer, the grin falls off his sallow face in a hurry, replaced by the dark storm cloud he wore when visiting Kerry in prison.

"What the hell do you want from me?" Kerry demands.

Before the man can answer, Mullet and Trucker Hat rush into the trailer behind Kerry and grab him by the arms. "Sorry Mr. MacCallum," Mullet says. "We'll get rid of him."

Trucker Hat adds, "You want us to call the cops or…" Kerry knows all too well what that unspoken 'or' means for him.

But MacCallum holds up a hand. "Stop. Let him go and wait outside." To the men seated in front of his desk, he says, "Gentlemen, if you'll excuse me. We'll pick this up later."

They stand and file out of the trailer, giving Kerry curious appraisals as they walk by. Mullet and Trucker Hat are the last to leave, the former giving him one last angry glare before closing the door.

Kerry spins back to face the father of the only person he's ever loved and says, "You want me dead, then stop drawing it out. I'm right here. Go ahead and kill me."

MacCallum stares at him—or rather *through* him, his mind somewhere far away. Kerry marvels again at how drastically the man aged. Then he comes back to himself, reaches down, and pulls out a drawer in the desk, each movement measured and deliberate. He draws out a small, snub-nosed revolver, which he brandishes casually in one hand. Kerry's heart lurches at the sight of it, but he allows no emotion to leak onto his face.

"I could, you know." MacCallum's fingers squeeze the handle of the gun. "I could shoot you right now, tell the cops it was self-defense. Every man out there would back me up. Wouldn't spend so much as a minute behind bars. Hell, they'd probably consider it a public service for putting a warped little pissant like you out of your misery." He gives the weapon sober consideration for a long moment, then places it on the desktop in front of him. His lips stretch into a malicious grin that would put Regina Velder's to shame. "But where's the fun in that?"

Kerry throws up his hands. "You want to torture me, fine. If you think you can make my life any shittier than it already is, be my guest. But my friends...the other residents of that house...they don't deserve this. If you want me to move out, I will. I have nowhere else to go. I'll be living on the streets by the end of the week. You can drive by in your BMW and laugh at me in the gutter. Just please...call off the lawyers. Don't take this out on them."

MacCallum shrugs. Even with that gleeful smirk on his face, there's something exhausted in the gesture. Revenge might be a dish best served cold, but it's also one that takes a steep toll on the chef. "You say they're your friends? Then you probably should've warned them what being your friend means. How people who stay around you too long have a way of getting sucked into a tornado of misfortune. Or worse."

Kerry clenches his fist around his ghost finger, welcoming the pain, letting it loosen his tongue. When he's able to speak, the words slide out through clenched teeth. "I'm not the reason Kayla killed herself. *You* did that, with all your screaming and rules and punishments, the ones that left her with a dozen different bruises."

MacCallum's face darkens. "Get out," he growls.

"You drove your wife to alcohol and an early grave, then you went to work on your daughter. And after you took away the man she loved, well…I'm thinking she got away from you the only way she could."

"*GET OUT!*" MacCallum roars. His complexion goes from pale to red to purple in less than a second, like watching an ugly flower bloom. "*Get out right now before I finish what I started with your finger, you fucking pedophile!*"

Kerry turns to leave. Pleas will never work with this man. Nothing will. No amount of retribution could ever quell the rage inside him. It will burn on and on, finding new targets until it consumes him.

As if to prove this, MacCallum screams behind him, "*You think this is over? You think I'm finished with you? Not by a long shot! By the time I'm finished, you'll BEG to go back to that prison!*"

Kerry walks out of the trailer, pushing between Mullet and Trucker Hat, and heads for the van.

TWENTY SIX

Ray's 'funeral' is held on a Wednesday morning, at a state cemetery west of Dallas, almost outside the Metroplex. The place isn't as nice as Willow Grove, just a stretch of flat prairie running alongside a freeway onramp, covered in dead, yellow grass. Graves are squashed together in tightly plotted rows, marked by bronze plaques the size of business cards. Indigents, lunatics, and people with no family; Kerry guesses they all still have to be buried somewhere, a final inconvenience to a world that wants to forget about them. Ray's coffin—a wooden box that has more in common with a shipping crate—is lowered into the earth by a bored groundskeeper while a local Presbyterian minister reads a few Bible verses loudly enough to be heard over the buzz of traffic on the highway.

Kerry, Les, and Sanders are the only attendees. Everyone else claimed they couldn't take off work, and D'libra made herself conspicuously absent to keep from even being asked. The psychologist and the parole officer both wear dark suits, but the one semi-appropriate clothing option in Kerry's closet was a pair of ill-fitting black jeans and a gray, short sleeve, button-up shirt that he paired with a tie borrowed from Scott. They sit on folding chairs in the sun until the minister is finished and the groundskeeper begins shoving dirt into the hole with a miniature backhoe.

"He was a good guy." Les delivers this simple eulogy as they stand and walk toward the cars. He slides a finger under his glasses to wipe at his eyes. "I'll miss his cheerful spirit around the house."

"Definitely one of my more pleasant charges," Sanders agrees.

Kerry remains silent. He stares at the grave markers—the type so small you would have to kneel to read it—and wonders if one of them will bear his name someday.

He and Kayla, forever separated, thrown in holes far away from one another.

There's your fairy tale ending.

"Not to be disrespectful by changing topics," Sanders ventures, "but have you heard anything from the state attorneys?"

Les rings his hands before reaching up to straighten his tie. "They said the actual grounds for the lawsuit are frivolous. But...if they stretch this out with more injunctions and appeals...it would probably end up being far more cost effective to voluntarily close Hopeful Sunshine." He swallows, but it takes some effort. "We'll know more after the hearing."

Sanders nods. They reach the cars, Sanders' Honda and Les' beat-to-shit Subaru. Les opens the driver's door and leans in to unlock the passenger side for Kerry, but Sanders stops him by saying, "Why don't you let me give Denton a ride back? I'd like to talk to him."

"Fine by me. See you at the house, Kerry."

Les putters away on the freeway ramp. Sanders waves goodbye, smiling pleasantly while the Subaru speeds away, then shoves Kerry into the side of his car, holding him there with a hand in the middle of his chest.

"All right, goddamn it, enough with the lies," he barks.

Kerry scowls and shoves his hand away. "What the fuck are you talking about?"

"I'm talking about the fact that this mysterious MacCallum company tries to shut down the home where you live a few weeks after they put up a nasty little sign to get you fired. Go ahead, try to tell me that's a coincidence." He takes a step back, giving Kerry enough room to get off the car. "I don't know why this man is spending thousands of dollars to wage a private war on you, and if you're stupid enough not to ask for help, that's your business. But now the collateral damage is fucking with the lives of the people around you, and I want some answers."

"I asked him to stop," Kerry whispers. "The son of a bitch is insane, he won't listen."

"It's her father, isn't it? The girl you went to prison for." Sanders closes his eyes. The muscles in his jaw bulge rhythmically as he grinds his teeth. "Have you been in touch with her? I *told* you to—"

"She's been dead for three years. Committed suicide while I was inside."

"Oh Jesus." Sanders moves away from Kerry and then slumps beside him. "I'm sorry. I didn't know, Denton."

The only words Kerry can get out are, "Yeah, well."

"So her father...blames you? This is all some sort of revenge for him?"

Kerry nods slowly. If he's ever going to talk about this with anyone, it might as well be now. "You need to understand…Robert MacCallum is a dangerous man. And he surrounds himself with a lot of dangerous people. He beat his wife for years, and after she drank herself to death, he started on his daughter. She…she would've done anything to get away from him." Kerry stops for a breath but can't quite reel it in past a lump in his throat. "Then she met me, and I asked her to marry me. Even bought a couple of cheap wedding rings. She thought it was so romantic, wanted to wear them even though it wasn't official yet. Her father…she tried to tell me he'd never let her go through with it, that we'd have to wait till she turned eighteen and run off. But how could I sit back and…and watch her go through that for another two years? So I went to introduce myself to him. To ask his permission. I just *knew* if I explained it all, showed him how much I loved her, he would understand."

"And his response to you pouring your heart out was to have you arrested."

"Eventually." Kerry chuckles and holds up his mangled hand, like a model on a game show posing in front of the merchandise. His missing digit is surprisingly quiet for a change. "But first three of his guys held my arm while he took the ring right off my hand, breaking my finger so bad in the process that it had to be amputated."

"*What?*" Sanders springs forward from the car with his fists held out in front of him, as though ready to fight the words themselves. "*He* did that to you? I assumed it happened in prison. Why the fuck isn't that asshole behind bars for assault and battery?"

"Because I refused to report it." Kerry takes another deep breath that comes out too much like a shuddering whimper. "I told myself it was my fault, for springing it on him like that. I was so naïve, I thought that, after he calmed down, he might come around. Plus...I got scared. How could I go to the cops when *I* was the one having an illegal relationship with a minor? That's like a drug dealer calling the police to report his stash stolen. It only would've made things worse for me, and probably her, too."

"But Denton, something like that could've turned your whole case around!"

Kerry shrugs. "If it makes you feel any better, it probably wouldn't've mattered. The guy is untouchable. By the time I got out of the hospital, the cops were already after me. MacCallum was friends with the police chief, the DA, the judge...hell, he probably had the bailiff and court stenographer in his pocket. I never stood a chance."

Sanders uses one hand to loosen the knot of his tie. "Wow. That is...quite a story. Much better than the nightmare fodder I usually get from my parolees, anyway."

"Yeah. The same one gets told in a hundred movies, and they call it romance. Patrick Swayze lifts Jennifer Grey over his head and tells her father to fuck off, and a million panties drop. But it happens for real, you get your finger cut off, sent to prison, and blacklisted the rest of your life." Kerry grimaces. "How's that for being a predator?"

"And all that wasn't enough for this MacCallum?"

"Honestly, I think it probably would've ended there, if Kayla hadn't killed herself. Now he holds me accountable for that too, and he's not going to stop until he decides I've paid."

"Okay." Sanders nods resolutely. "First thing we'll have to do is make an official police report. If we can get his pattern of harassment on record, it'll help. Then...what, why are you shaking your head?"

"Did you not hear a thing I said? You can't fight the guy. He's just going to keep coming. You were right before: I have to keep him focused on me so no one else gets hurt. The best thing I can do is leave the house and maybe he'll lose interest in this lawsuit."

Sanders puts his hands on his hips. "Nobody likes a martyr, Denton."

"Nobody likes a sex offender either, Brad. So I might as well be both."

"Promise me you won't do anything rash until I can look into this. There are always options."

Not for me, Kerry thinks, but he nods and gets into the car.

TWENTY SEVEN

Their conversation strays to more pleasant topics on the way back to the house, such as several job leads for Kerry. It's 12:30 by the time they pulls to a stop at the curb. A dark head of thunderclouds hangs to the west, waiting to descend. Kerry sits in the passenger seat as he did on his first day out of prison and gestures at the van in the driveway.

"What about Ray's car, and all his stuff?"

"Why don't you keep it?"

"*Me?*"

"Sure, who else would it go to? Not like he left a will. You were probably closer to him than anybody else in his entirely life." He flashes Kerry a sad grin. "Wherever he is now, I'm sure he'd love to know he's saddling you with that rustbucket."

Another lump swells in Kerry's throat as he steps out of the car. He doesn't know whether to be happy or depressed that he's the closest thing the fat weirdo had to a family.

"Hey," Sanders says gently, before Kerry can close the door. "After what you told me, about this girl...I understand why you got so upset about Ray. But have you accepted what he did yet? No more one-armed man bullshit?"

"Other than the fact that I have no idea what 'one-armed man bullshit' is, yeah, I'm fine."

"Good to hear. Keep your head down and stay away from this MacCallum guy. I'll get back to you."

Kerry shuts the door and walks across the lawn toward Hopeful Sunshine, but he takes his time, waiting to hear the sound of Sanders' car driving away. As soon as it does, he changes directions and hurries toward his newly-bequeathed inheritance, then settles himself behind the wheel.

On the cracked vinyl of the passenger seat is a thick stack of paper printed in the media room upstairs. Kerry picks it up and places it on his lap, then begins to rifle through the individual sheets.

He lied to Sanders; he has not accepted Ray's death. In fact, he is pretty fucking far from swallowing *that* particular pill. The stack of papers sitting on his thighs—the result of exhausting late night research sessions—is testament to that fact.

For the past few days, he used the sex offender registry to catalogue the addresses of every pervert, pedophile, and predator within a hundred mile radius. There is no shortage, either. At first glance, the sheer volume of entries is staggering—enough to make a person want to stay inside, lock their door, and never interact with another human being—but most of them are minor, level one offenders; drunken public urinators, peeping toms, the occasional unsubstantiated rape allegation. In a world obsessed with privacy and data protection, it never stops amazing him how easily this information can be collected. For the purpose of narrowing the results, he restricted his search criteria to level two and above. Then he took each return and painstakingly researched the neighborhood they reside in to see if any foreclosed or otherwise vacant homes lay within a three block radius and have been unoccupied for at least six months, long enough for the banks to have all but given up on selling them. This gave him twenty or so candidates that fit his parameters. He finds this list now, along with a route map he put together that avoids all schools and parks, and backs out of the driveway.

Kerry spends the next several hours crisscrossing the Metroplex—Dallas, Fort Worth, and every suburb in between—to visit each address. What he finds, first and foremost, is that his fellow predators come from all walks of life. They live in urban ghettos, trailer parks, middle class tract housing, and behind the gated walls of mansions. He cruises past each home without slowing, very aware that his vehicle could only be more noticeable if it had a blaring siren on top, then continues to the empty property somewhere in their vicinity.

He has no idea what he's looking for. But this nagging hunch hasn't stopped prickling in the back of his mind since he found the squashed paper sculpture on the floor of that deserted kitchen. No, even before that; when he spotted the FORECLOSURE sign in the front yard, and the uncomfortable déjà vu that came with it. So, after a cursory drive-by inspection of each empty residence, he parks somewhere up the street and then walks back to spend several minutes studying at the sign in the front yard and pretending to write down the information, as though interested in buying. His funeral outfit works to his advantage here; the few people he runs into smile politely, as though he has every reason in the world to be there. A desperate real estate agent even comes running out the front door of one of the more recent vacancies and offers to give him a tour, which he declines. At the others, the seedy and long forgotten ones, he tries to act nonchalant as he gets closer, circling the home and peering in the windows.

Each place is as desolate as the house that he and D'libra visited. Gaping rooms behind locked doors and dust-covered glass. Like museums with no exhibits. And what more did he expect? He leaves them feeling a little more tired and a lot more hopeless and ready to scream at the world.

Those storm clouds bring on a premature twilight as he visits the fourteenth residence on his list, a pleasant two-story on a street called Heather Trail, in a much more middle-class neighborhood than Hopeful Sunshine's. The houses here are quaint but cookie-cutter, the streets full of children being called home before the rain starts, and four blocks away a man named Herman Voss lives with his elderly mother, after serving most of a decade in prison for raping his ten-year-old stepdaughter. A true credit to the human race. Kerry tried to read as little of these peoples' dossiers as possible, but certain stomach-churning facts have seeped through.

He goes through his routine in the front yard, but the light is failing and his pretense for being here seems especially flimsy. Thunder rumbles overhead as Kerry steps onto the dark porch. He glances through the glass set into the door. There are no lights on inside either; why use electricity in a house that's not selling? Of course, this wasn't such a big deal when he still had the sun, but now it renders his entire purpose here moot.

This whole thing's moot. A waste of time, which you have plenty of, and a waste of gas, which you don't.

Still, he's here, so he might as well do what he needs to in order to check the place off his list. Kerry walks down the side of the house, opening the gate and checking each window as he comes to it, more perfunctory than investigative, going through the motions, and, because of this, almost doesn't register what he sees through the last one.

The room beyond the glass is an open dining space with a wide aperture opening onto the stairwell and living room beyond. And the reason he can see this in the dark house is because a bluish light is spilling down the stairs, an electric illumination like the glow of a television. Kerry stands and watches it for a moment while the first raindrops patter down on top of his head. Then he glances over his shoulder, back at the street, and moves around to the rear of the house.

A porch awning is attached to the brick façade here, providing shelter from the strengthening rain. Lightning flashes deep inside the clouds as he steps up to the solid glass pane that serves as a back door. The space beyond is pitch black, nothing within visible. Kerry waits for more lightning, hoping to catch a glimpse of the interior, but none comes. Following instinct just as he has this entire day, Kerry puts his hand on the knob—using his sleeve to avoid leaving fingerprints—and twists.

He expects the tension of a lock, but it turns with the slightest effort, the door swinging open so easily that he jumps away from it.

Kerry steps through quickly and closes it behind him before he can lose his nerve. He's standing on tile now, his eyes adjusted enough to discern the dim outline of a bare kitchen. The house yawns open around him, as though he stands on the brink of a deep chasm. He eases around the island, placing each foot carefully to avoid squeaking the wet soles, and pushes deeper into the empty house, out of the kitchen and into the living room, where he reaches the foot of the stairwell he glimpsed before.

That light is still coming from somewhere up there. He strains his ears, but hears nothing except the steady plink of rain on the roof, punctuated by muttery bursts of thunder. Kerry creeps up the stairs, taking each riser one at a time, muscles so tense and coiled he could probably spring straight through the house and into the stratosphere.

At the top is a half wall that hides whatever lies beyond the staircase landing. His heart thuds painfully behind his ribs as he crouches behind the partition. He takes a deep breath and raises up enough to peek over the top.

An open space sprawls across the width of the house, not much different from the media center at Hopeful Sunshine. The room is bare and empty except for a cheap folding card table against the opposite wall. On top of it sits a bank of three computer monitors connected to a squat hard drive, and it is from these that the glow emanates.

A program runs on the leftmost screen, which displays nothing but black with white type continuously flowing across it, new lines added to the bottom as the rest scroll upward. It reminds Kerry of the random gobbledygook on the keystroke log that D'libra showed him. The middle screen is also cryptic, some sort of GPS mapping system with green throbbing circles spread across a yellow, topographic landscape. But there is no mystery behind what the third monitor shows; Kerry knows its contents quite well by now.

The home screen of the State of Texas Sex Offender Registry sits open on a browser window, waiting to divulge all the dark histories of its wonderful clientele.

Kerry stares at the screens. An ache grows in his chest. He realizes he's still holding his breath and releases it, then hurries back down the stairs. *This* is what he was after; he still doesn't know what it is or what it means, but it's more than suspicious enough to notify the police about, as soon as he can get to a phone. He reaches the bottom of the stairs, makes his way into the kitchen and heads for the back door of the house. The night beyond the glass is now as dark as the inside of the house.

He's still several yards away from the exit when a crooked bolt of lightning arcs down from the sky, revealing the gaunt silhouette that stands on the other side of the door, staring back at him.

Kerry skids to a stop on the tile. The figure outside throws the door open, letting in a blast of wind and rain. Its face is no more than a smear of shadows as it charges into the house.

The sight of the silent figure bearing down on him causes a flood of primal, acidic terror to burn the back of Kerry's throat. He tries to raise his fists, to prepare for a fight the same way he did every time he got attacked in prison, but this overwhelming fear insists that flight is the better option. So he pelts back through the kitchen instead, past the stairwell, even deeper into the house. Pounding footsteps ring out on the tile behind him.

The darkness is suffocating. Kerry flees blindly through it, driven by panic and unable to see further than a foot or two ahead. It takes an hour to cross the living room. He almost runs into a wall on the other side before dodging into the opening of a hallway to the left.

Several other doorways fly by on either side of him, no more than black holes in a black galaxy, but he keeps moving. His breath comes in hiccupy little jerks, more from dread than exertion. The front door; he has to find it, it's the only other way out.

Kerry risks one look back.

A frightened whimper escapes his lips.

His pursuer is yards away, sprinting down the hallway, a gangly boogeyman escaped from a nightmare. The figure holds something in its hand now, a long, thin tube that must be the handle of a knife.

The door swims out of the gloom ahead, the same one that he stood on the other side of ten minutes and an eternity ago. Kerry claws at the deadbolts until they release and yanks the door open to the rainswept night.

An arm encircles his waist before he can step out onto the porch.

Kerry thrashes, then sucks in a lungful of air to scream. Something burns briefly on the side of his neck. Too late he realizes that the object in the figure's hand is a syringe. The world blurs around him, and suddenly Kerry's thoughts are so fuzzy and addled he can't remember *how* to scream.

The arm releases him. Kerry tries to step forward, but it's like moving through the bottom of the ocean. His legs fold, dumping him roughly onto the wooden porch, where he lays in an unmoving heap.

He sees a pair of boots move toward him before his eyes flutter closed.

ATONEMENT

TWENTY EIGHT

Kerry comes to all at once, memories intact, heart racing. He jerks his head up and instantly regrets it. His entire body has been flattened by a steamroller, sliced into quivering segments, and then somehow clumped back into a vaguely humanoid shape. His mouth is made of cotton, his eyeballs pulse in their sockets. He recognizes all the symptoms of a hangover, even though he hasn't had one in years. To make matters worse, the pain and discomfort serve to increase his confusion about his present predicament.

Because he's awoken in an upright position, head lolling on his chest, his body supported by some sort of harness that might have started life as a straitjacket. The dingy gray coat engulfs his entire torso, from neck to nuts, with a strap that passes between his legs and wedges deep in the crack of his ass. His arms are strapped uncomfortably tight against his waist inside long sleeves that cross over his stomach and attach somewhere in the back. From what he can tell, leather straps run through thick metal eyelets at his hips and up to sturdy rebar imbedded in the concrete ceiling a few feet overhead, which must have supported his weight while he was unconscious. The whole contraption resembles one of those swings for babies to bounce around in. Kerry might be able to do the same, to twirl and leap like a circus acrobat, if his ankles weren't strapped with metal blocks that weigh a ton and prevent him from lifting his legs. The harness keeps him suspended at a height where the toes of his sneakers can graze the floor, but not enough to get any leverage. He takes all of this in quickly before raising his aching head further to examine the room that he hangs in like a side of beef.

The space around him is dim, lit by a single bulb dangling from a chain off to his left that leaves the farthest corners of the room in deep shadow. It appears to be a bare, concrete rectangle, perhaps the size of a double car garage, the walls and ceiling and floor all a smooth gray that instantly reminds him of the solitary confinement cells. It smells like them too, dank and mildewed, but with a pungent, musky under-aroma, and it's cold enough to make his breath plume. He can see no entrance or exit either; if there is a door, it must be behind him, but Kerry is unable to twist his head far enough around to check.

Directly in front him, barely visible, is another bank of dark computer monitors on a rolling cart, although it's not the same one he found before in...this house? Is he still inside the property on Heather Trail? Somehow, he doesn't think so, and that idea makes his blood run cold.

How long has he been unconscious anyway? An hour? *Two?* Long enough to be brought here, wherever here is, but not long enough for him to be hungry. Hopefully long enough, however, for him to be missed at the house.

Yeah, and what if you are? You didn't tell anyone what you were doing or where you were going, genius.

D'libra. She'll tell them to check the keystroke log, the same way we did for Ray.

Why in hell would she do that? And even if she did, and they somehow figure out your search methods, that only gets them a long list of houses to check. And you're probably not at any of them anyway.

The logic is cold and brutal, but Kerry still clings to the fantasy of rescue as he tries to move, gingerly at first and then with increasing fervor. The harness keeps him entirely immobile; even his fingers have little room to wiggle inside the sleeves. He keeps struggling though, hoping to loosen some part of the bindings. When that fails, he tries to kick his legs enough to start swinging, to initiate any motion that might give him some freedom, but the heavy weights on his ankles drag at his momentum and exhaust him immediately. His breath spews from his nose in bullish, crystalline spurts. Claustrophobia turns the jacket into a vice, crushing the life out of him.

He opens his chapped lips and is preparing to shout for help when one of the shadows in the corner of the room peels away from the others and glides toward him.

A figure enters the wan ball of radiance thrown by the room's only light source, a tall, skinny form dressed in dark boots, pants, hoodie, and thin leather driving gloves. All of that by itself might be enough to unsettle him, but it's the face that makes Kerry gasp as it emerges from the darkness.

The figure's entire head is covered by a skintight, flesh-colored latex mask with large, moist eyes, rosy cheeks, and a pouty, frowning mouth. It gives the effect of a toddler on the verge of tears, a look that might be amusing in a cartoonish context, but the hyperreal features atop an adult body results in a creepy, fetishistic vibe. The other person stands watching him from several yards away for a long moment before saying, with flat, measured cadence, "Kerry Samuel Denton."

"Let me go," Kerry says. He means the words as a demand, but they come out sounding more like a plea.

"In time." The rubbery lips mold perfectly to his own as he speaks. If you could see only that face, you would think that raspy, uninflected voice is coming out of a three-year-old. He says nothing further though, just remains as still and rooted as an oak tree. The calm demeanor is as unnerving as the child-faced mask...but familiar all at the same time.

"Let me *go*," Kerry repeats, and this time it comes out harsh and angry. He thrashes in the harness, straining with all his might to no avail, and then fixes the other man in a furious glare. "What, am I supposed to be scared because you know my name and wear a cheap Halloween costume?" He receives no answer, and raises his tone to add, "*You can't keep me here! What the* fuck *do you even want from me?*" The shouts rings off the concrete around them and buzz in Kerry's sore brain.

After another span of long heartbeats, the man answers, in his maddeningly slow voice, "I don't want anything from you. In fact, I'm going to give you far more than I take. Far more than you deserve. But, before we begin our session, I do need some information. How you found me, for instance, and if anyone else knows where you went."

"*EVERYONE knows!*" Kerry howls, his anger serving to hide the desperation growing in him. "*I told everyone I know, and they probably called the cops the SECOND you fucking drugged and kidnapped me! They're gonna track me down and—!*"

Now the man moves, surging forward with ghostly speed, as he did while chasing Kerry through the empty house. He comes close enough to reach out with one gloved hand, twines his fingers through the back of Kerry's hair, and pulls so hard that his head snaps backward. He hisses in pain. The child mask is thrust forward, floating in front of Kerry's face.

"The next time you tell me something I think is a lie," the man says, his serene voice belying the violence as he pulls even harder, "I am going to leave this room, get in a car, and drive without stopping to the city of Milwaukee, Wisconsin. Once there, I will go to 1284 Treetop Lane, where Timothy and Margaret Denton reside, and I will open up their throats while they sleep. They will probably thank for me doing this, as I'm sure they have lived in nothing but shame for the past five years over giving birth to an embarrassment like yourself. While I am gone, you will remain in this room, where you will most likely die of dehydration. That is not what I want, but it is what I will do if you leave me no other option. Do you understand me?"

Kerry forces himself to breathe through the agony of having his hair slowly ripped from his scalp as he stares at the mask over his captor's face. This close, he can see that the irises of the oversized eyes are cutouts, and, from within, two smaller eyes with impossibly black centers meet his gaze.

"Yes," he hisses, unable to keep the pain from his voice. "I understand."

"Good." The man releases Kerry and steps back. "Because we both know that you found me by cross-referencing the registered sex offenders in the city with listings of vacant homes." Kerry's obvious surprise causes him to clarify, "The research was in your van. That list is quite handy, isn't it? A roster of the lowest forms of life on the planet, and exactly where to find them." He leans forward, and Kerry pulls his head away, anticipating more torture. But the man only says,

"What I cannot figure out is how you knew to do that in the first place. What set you upon my trail?"

"N-nothing. I...I wanted to know what happened to my roommate. There's a keystroke log on our computer, so I read his emails and went to the address for his delivery. When I saw the place...I just suspected."

"Suspected *what*?" Kerry can't tell if the mocking edge the question carries is in his imagination. "Tell me, what do you believe happened to Raymond Leary?"

Kerry hesitates for a long moment. This situation can only get worse if he gives voice to his suspicions...but he doesn't want to risk another lie, either. "I think...you murdered him. Him, and a lot of other sex offenders that you stalk with the registry, and then make their deaths look like suicides."

The edges of the rubber mouth twitch upward as the lips beneath them smile. "You know so much, yet you understand so little."

The statement—smug and superior and fortune-cookie-philosophical—annoys Kerry. Reignites his anger. Perhaps part of him has already swallowed and digested the idea that he's never going to leave this room alive, and, if so, it's surely this part that spurs him to open his mouth and say the one thing he probably shouldn't.

"Whatever. You're no genius. Because I also know who you are under that stupid mask. *Solomon*."

He expects more violence, or, at the very least, denial, but the other man takes a long, considering breath. Then he speaks, in a whisper so low Kerry can barely hear him. "It was a risk, talking to you. I don't often take risks. But when I saw you going door to door, I couldn't pass up the opportunity. And I'm not sorry either. I very much enjoyed speaking with you as equals. Usually my conversations with your brethren are tainted by so much fear."

"So you've been stalking me, too. Did you send me that photograph?"

"A reminder that you can't hide what you are. That even our demons have eyes." 'Solomon'—it may not be the man's real name, but Kerry can imagine the hawkish face and pale skin lurking beneath the mask now—bares his teeth after uttering this gibberish, an expression made even more ghoulish through the crying child mask. "But I was never after you, Mr. Denton. If I was, you *never* would've seen me coming. I was already working with your roommate when you arrived fresh from prison, and taking on two clients from the same house is more risk than I'm comfortable with. No, it's your meddling that brought you here. Your amateur detective work places me in…an awkward position."

"I'm dangling from the ceiling in a sex swing. Maybe don't talk to me about awkward positions." Despite his growing panic, it occurs to Kerry suddenly that all the answers he sought are here, and that maybe he can get them before this psychopath rapes him to death and cuts off his head, or whatever the hell he has planned. "Just tell me… what the fuck did you do to Ray? I know you lured him out with those emails, then, what, held him overnight and sent him home? Then came back to kill him? I've been over it and over it in my head and it doesn't make any goddamn sense."

Instead of answering, the other man stands up straight and begins to walk. He stares up at the ceiling as he paces around Kerry's left side, the same sort of overly casual strut that Pedernales and some of the other guards used to perform before shoving an inmate into the wall or clubbing him across the back of the knees. He disappears out of view behind Kerry before speaking. "Do you know why I chose the name Solomon? Because he was a wise king. A protector of children. The world needs more of those, don't you think? People willing to safeguard innocence."

Kerry says, "I have no idea what the hell you're talking about." But in his head, he hears, *corruption of the innocent...that's a* taboo.

The baby face floats into Kerry's field of vision on his right as Solomon leans around him from behind. Kerry cries out in surprise and flinches away, but the harness keeps him from moving very far.

"That's what I am, a protector," the man whispers, inches from Kerry's ear. "You accuse me of murder, but that is far from accurate. I kill only if I have to. It's a choice that I always, *always* put in the hands of others. What I offered them—what I offer you now—is an opportunity."

"F-for what?" Kerry asks.

Solomon moves even closer, his breath a warm fog in the chilly room. The latex cheek brushes Kerry's neck. He speaks in a tone reserved for the most intimate of lovers. "Atonement. The chance to make up for what you've done."

"Funny, I thought that's what prison was for."

"Prison repays your debt to society. I'm talking about forgiveness. *Real* forgiveness. Perhaps even the chance to forgive yourself."

Now it's Ray's voice that drifts through Kerry's head, asking him if he thinks they can be forgiven as they huddle together in the floor of the closet. It is this man—this lunatic—that put such ideas in poor Ray Leary's head. Kerry's panic blossoms into full-blown fear. "I don't need to forgive myself."

"Last time we met, I believe you said it depends on the day. Seems you're making progress. In the wrong direction."

Solomon walks back around Kerry and continues on, heading toward the computer set up on the cart in front of him. He asks over his shoulder, "Do you know what the deep web is?"

Kerry shudders, relieved to be free of the contact, but that fear is still churning in the pit of his stomach. The question is so abrupt and off-topic, it takes him a moment to recover enough to answer. "Yeah, it's…it's some hidden part of the internet. For hackers or something. You need a special browser to get there."

"It's a den for criminals and filth. The sick underbelly of society. Human monsters that thrive on anonymity. People much like yourself." He brings the center monitor to life on a command prompt and begins typing quickly on the keyboard as he adds, with his back still to Kerry, "If there is a place where true evil exists, it is within that dark crevice beneath mankind's greatest technological achievement."

Kerry remains silent, unsure where this is leading. He needs to pee now, and the harness is becoming more uncomfortable each passing second. His muscles cramp and burn with the need to stretch, but, at the same time, the cold is working its way into him, causing him to shiver every few seconds.

Solomon finishes whatever he's doing at the computer. He comes back to Kerry and stands on his right, ramrod straight with his hands clasped at the small of his back, and watches the monitor. Kerry does the same.

The black screen suddenly brightens to display a picture. A young girl no older than five sits on the corner of a bed, dark hair in curled ringlets down to her shoulders, dressed in a nightgown with Tinkerbell on the front. For some reason, lipstick as red as blood lines her small mouth, as though she's gotten into Mommy's makeup. At first Kerry thinks the photo is vibrating, but then tears slip down the little girl's cheeks and he realizes that this is a video, and that she's quaking with fear. A stifled sob escapes her, but the sound comes not from the monitors but all around Kerry, echoing off the concrete with perfect clarity. There must be hidden speakers mounted in the corners of the room, where the light cannot reach.

A man wearing nothing but a pair of jeans steps into frame, walking backward and staring into the camera as if to make sure it's recording. He's an imposing figure, big and musclebound, abs standing out in definition on his stomach, and a grizzly black beard clinging to his chin. He crosses the room, kneels next to the girl, puts a hand on her bare knee, and says, "Go ahead and take off your clothes, sweetheart."

"Oh my god," Kerry moans. A greasy worm of disgust writhes in the pit of his stomach as the video's subjects both begin to disrobe. He closes his eyes and turns his face away, but Solomon grabs him by the hair and forces it back.

"You will watch or I will cut off your eyelids and make you watch," he says, as conversational as a stranger at a bus stop remarking on the weather.

Kerry watches.

The video can't last more than a few minutes, but it feels ten times as long. When it's over, Kerry's guts are tangled in a hard knot at the center of him. The last frozen frame—a close-up of the nude girl lying on the bed with her lipstick smeared and her whole face wet with tears—causes bile to creep up his esophagus.

"The deep web crawls with such atrocities," Solomon remarks. "There is no end to them."

"What the fuck is wrong with you?" Kerry whispers, each word visible as a white plume. A sudden wave of black nausea makes his stomach clench until he's sure he's going to puke.

"Nothing is wrong with *me*," Solomon answers. "Tell me, did the girl you violated cry like that?"

Kerry fights to hold down the remains of his lunch as he mumbles, "I didn't violate anyone."

"You raped her."

"No. It was...statutory..."

"Pretty legalities. You raped her."

"No, *I fucking did not!*" he screams, his voice cracking halfway through. He thrashes in the straitjacket. "*She was my goddamn girlfriend! Why the fuck can't you get that through your head?*"

Solomon raises one finger and points at the monitor in front of them. "That's what he said, when he was hanging where you are now. *She wanted me*; that's what he told me. Of course, that's what they all say, after the light of day is thrown across them. *She liked it. He asked me to. You don't understand.*" He lowers his arm and steps close again, close enough for Kerry to see his horrible eyes through the mask. "Mr. Leary's exact words were, 'I never, ever meant to hurt them.'"

"You son of a bitch." Kerry's throat is full of broken glass from screaming; the words come out as a torn croak. This theory could go hand-in-hand with the one Scott put forth about love being his crime, but twists it into something dark and sick and impossibly ugly. He thinks of D'libra saying in that long ago therapy session, *That's why they made the law, to keep freaks like you from havin sex with babies and callin it a* relationship. "Oh, you miserable lunatic asshole."

"You are not a unique case, Mr. Denton," Solomon tells him. "I know all about the girl and her death. I know about her father, and his vendetta. None of that matters. If you reduce your actions down to their core, there is no fundamental difference between what you did, and what the man in that recording did. And it's time you learn that."

He squats down abruptly, and Kerry gets the horrible idea that the guy is going to unzip his jeans while he squirms helplessly, pull out his dick, and stick it into the pouting mouth of that rubbery child mask as some kind of symbolic reverse molestation. But Solomon grabs the Velcro straps that secure the weights to Kerry's ankles and rips them off one at a time, then lifts the heavy blocks away.

The relief is immense. As soon as they are removed, Kerry is instantly free to stretch and kick…but at the same time, the room begins to shift and spin as he tilts forward in the harness, his center of gravity altered. He cries out as his knees and shoulders change places, and then he is completely upside-down in the harness, staring at the back of the room for the first time, where a heavy steel door is set into the wall. He flails his legs and then draws his knees up, trying to right himself, but only succeeds in rocking back and forth and adding to his nausea.

Solomon comes around and looks down at him. "This harness is designed to keep you top heavy. If you turn over, it's impossible to get back upright. In this position, the blood rushing to your head would cause you to pass out after an hour or so. Then you would either suffocate or suffer a brain hemorrhage."

He puts a hand on the back of Kerry's thigh and shoves, spinning Kerry back up. The dizzy swirl of motion is the last straw, and Kerry lets loose a string of brownish vomit that spatters across the concrete in front of him.

"Stretch out with your toes. You should be able to touch the floor."

Head still reeling, Kerry does as told. As he discovered upon first awaking, if he strains and flexes his calf muscles, the tips of his sneakers can skim the smooth cement beneath him. The slight contact is enough to keep him from capsizing.

Solomon heads back to the computer to continue typing. "I'm sure you've had a lot of therapy at that house of yours. Sitting around, talking about your feelings. *Your* feelings; never the feelings of your victims. But now, you'll experience a more effective method. You're going to spend a night immersed in the horrors your fellow deviants inflict on the innocent. Even though these things might normally arouse your diseased mind, I don't imagine you'll enjoy this much. They call it 'overload therapy'. It's the same idea behind forcing someone to chain-smoke an entire pack of cigarettes so they develop a negative association. While you watch, try to think about the poor girl that *you* abused."

He finishes at the computer, then starts to walk past Kerry again, but stops beside him, beneath the room's single lightbulb.

"I'll be back in the morning, and we'll see if your views have changed," he says. "Of course, if the guilt becomes too much for you, you can always...lift your feet. I'll have to bury you in an unmarked grave, but you can be comforted in the knowledge that your disappearance would be a great relief to many people, including your parents."

"Fuck you," Kerry growls.

"Make no mistake, Mr. Denton: everything that happens from here on is *your* choice. So take some responsibility for your actions."

Solomon gives him another tight smile through the child mask and walks out of sight behind him. A moment later, there is the sound of that steel door squalling open and closed, and then Kerry is alone as the monitors in front of him come to life.

TWENTY NINE

Books were a luxury that could be earned in solitary confinement, but the first time Kerry was sent there, barely a month past Kayla's death, insanity always felt a few short breaths away. As he'd told Ray, being locked in that empty gray cell with nothing to do and, more importantly, no way to tell time, made the seconds soggy, runny, a sticky molasses that clung to him and smothered him and dragged him into a black pit of despair. Kerry had been a loner for his entire incarceration up to that point, avoiding other people like the plague, but a single day in isolation made him hunger for human interaction, if only to relieve his mind of that constant temporal disorientation.

His night spent in Solomon's care proves to be far, far more horrible.

First of all, keeping himself from turning upside down in the sling requires constant attention. If his toes lose contact with the ground for even a second, he starts to shift, his upper half leaning forward into a tumble that will mean his death. And yet, maintaining that contact itself is a chore, as he is forced to stretch his feet out to reach the concrete. After a few seconds of this, his calves burn and tighten, threatening to cramp. It takes him another—fifteen minutes? half hour? fifty years?—to realize the only possible way to sustain himself long term will be to alternate, holding himself stable with one foot for a bit while the other rests.

As the hours pass—and they *do* pass, he reminds himself that this is true no matter how much it might seem like he's stuck in a frozen pocket of time—his stomach empties, begins to growl. His throat dries and shrivels and begs for liquid. The cold numbs his extremities, carves its way into his bones. His already-full bladder fills until he has no choice but to let it spill down his leg and spatter on the concrete, creating a slick puddle that further hampers his attempts to stay alive.

And, through it all, the monitors show him an endless litany of nightmares.

They play simultaneously, a three-ring circus of abuse, molestation and rape perpetrated against minors of all ages, sexes and races, one video rolling as soon as the last one ends. Some of them are home movies captured on wobbly, grainy footage, which is terrible; others are slick, multi-camera affairs with professional pornography level production value, which is worse. Like any modern, red-blooded American male, Kerry has seen his fair share of filmed fucking, but he doesn't know how any human being with a soul could enjoy filth like this, let alone create it. With Solomon gone, he can, at the very least, escape the images themselves by looking away. But the audio pumps through those blazing speakers overhead, bathing him in every whimper, every cry, every plea and, worst of all, every grunt and groan of pleasure from the adults taking part in the pedophilia.

He tries to ignore it. Tries to let his mind wander. But the harness and the constant pain in his calves and ankles keep him in the here and now, as he's sure his captor intended. At least in solitary confinement he could escape the mental torture for a bit by drifting into wary sleep, but now, even though he's utterly exhausted and his eyelids weigh a ton, giving in to that urge would mean death.

Four years and a hundred lifetimes ago, Kerry took a course in psychology his sophomore year of college. One of the units that fascinated him the most dealt with brainwashing. The quickest and easiest way to get a person to accept an unwanted dogma is to expose them to it constantly while making them uncomfortable, through hunger, pain, sleep deprivation or humiliation.

Solomon's ingenious 'therapy' utilizes all four.

Well, it sure as shit won't work on Kerry. The fact that he understands the intent serves to harden his resolve. Kill himself? Oh no; he won't give that crazy son of a bitch the satisfaction. He refuses to buy into the delusion that he deserves this, that he must grovel for forgiveness from some psycho in a mask.

That he's anything like the vile people in the videos playing in front of him.

Staying alive; that's his choice, and he will goddamn take some responsibility for it.

And then, some unknowable number of hours into his torture, while Kerry lets his head hang to avoid watching the terrible images onscreen, his weariness finally outweighs his caution, and his eyes slip closed.

The sensation of falling causes him to snap awake. He's tilting forward in the harness. Blind panic steals his breath as he scissors his legs, reaching for the ground. For one strung-out moment, he thinks he's already spun too far, but then the very tip of one sneaker skates along the urine-stained concrete, enough to stabilize him.

He takes sloppy, panting breaths as his heart thunders in his chest. It was close. Too close. He can't risk it again. If he doesn't keep his mind active, he won't be able to stay awake.

Except in here, there's only one way to do that.

Kerry reluctantly raises his eyes and focuses on the monitors.

And receives yet another gut-punching shock.

The screen on the left plays a video of a dark-haired girl, perhaps thirteen or fourteen, face down on a filthy mattress. She rests her chin on her hands and stares blandly into the camera except for every few seconds when she winces with pain, while some blurry form can be seen moving over her shoulder. Kerry knows she isn't Kayla, knows she can't be, but the resemblance is close enough that his weary brain overlays her face on this one, and then tears are spilling down his face as he weeps. The sobs are so great and heaving, they cause the harness to jangle on the rebar above him.

That's what people think of you. His interior voice drips with contempt as it sweeps in from the dark corners of his mind, bringing with it a raging electric storm of agony that begins in his severed finger and then consumes his entire arm. *The other convicts, your housemates, the neighbors, all those employers you begged for a job. Barb from Grindhouse. Robert MacCallum. Your parents. In their heads... you held down a little girl and raped her.*

"No," he says aloud through the tears. That pain from his stump is white-hot and still spreading through his body, it's going to burn him to a cinder, and he doesn't care what the doctors say about misfiring pain receptors and psychosomatic attacks, he's convinced in that moment that he's being haunted by the spirit of his own ring finger. "He's full of shit and so are you. Mom and Dad do *not* think that."

They do, though. They all do. And you'll never convince them otherwise. P is for Predator, and that's all you are, a predator who preyed on the wrong sheep. Jesus, can you blame that guy in the parking lot for beating the shit out of you? And if this is what the rest of your life is going to be like, then maybe you really should…pick up your feet.

He can suddenly envision how easy it would be to let go, to grant himself a release from not just these hours of physical torment, but all the fear and uncertainty and regret that have ruled his life since he walked through the cold, hostile gates of Wayne Clifford and back into the cold, hostile embrace of the real world.

If nothing else…maybe he'll even get to see Kayla again.

A new image cuts through the maudlin haze of sorrow and self-pity: Solomon returning to find his corpse upside down in the harness. He stands and admires his handiwork and nods knowingly, as if all his accusations have been validated.

Kerry grits his teeth and shakes his head violently, keeps shaking while spittle flies from his lips.

"*OLD MACDONALD HAD A FARM!*" he bellows through the pain, loud enough to drown out the repugnant audio streams. His feet begin to move, alternating taps on the ground so rapidly it's like he's jogging in place. The movement helps chase away the cold. "*E I E I O! AND ON THIS FARM HE HAD A DUCK, E I E I O!*"

He runs through every animal he can think of, then sings a new song, and another after that. Eventually the painful fire inside him gutters out, but he doesn't let up. Each song is another few minutes gone by, and those slowly stack up into hours, and he's still flitting his feet like a hummingbird and singing—albeit, in a hoarse, cracked, whisper-of-a-voice—when the heavy door behind him groans open. Solomon comes around to stand in front of him, still wearing the crying-child mask. Kerry ignores him, doesn't stop moving, doesn't stop singing. The other man's unnaturally dark eyes regard him for a long moment before speaking.

"What about now, Mr. Denton?" he asks. "Do you feel any spark of guilt for your actions?"

Kerry breaks off his strained rendition of "Jimmy Crack Corn" long enough to meet the man's gaze. "You're gonna have to...do a lot worse...than this."

Solomon remains as still as the Sphinx. It's hard to tell beneath the mask, but Kerry thinks he sees annoyance, perhaps even anger, flash behind those perpetually impassive eyes.

Then he reaches out with both gloved hands, releases some kind of catch on the harness ringlets, and Kerry drops to the floor.

The fall is barely a half foot, but Kerry's overtaxed legs fold beneath him like wet tissue paper. He crashes to his knees and then topples forward. With his arms still bound in the straitjacket, he can't prevent himself from smashing face first into the concrete. New pain explodes across his nose and tender eye socket, but his relief at being free of the dangling harness is so immense, he barely notices.

The comfort is short lived. Solomon is on him immediately, pulling a thick canvas hood over his head and cinching it tight around his throat, like a military prisoner at Guantanamo. The world goes dark. He grabs Kerry under his bound arms and hauls at him.

"Get up."

Kerry tries and fails. His legs might as well be made of rubber. The rest of him isn't in much better shape; he could happily close his eyes and sleep for a year. It takes a minute of manhandling, but Solomon gets him into a standing position.

He's shoved forward. His calves cramp up hard after a few steps, the muscles as tight as steel cables, but there's no time to baby them. Solomon drives him on at a brisk pace, guiding him with one hand clamped around the back of his neck. Kerry wants to ask where they're going, but besides the fact that he's terrified of what the answer will be, he's having trouble getting fresh air inside the thick cloth hood.

Without sight, he's forced to rely on what his other senses can tell him about the surroundings. The grunts and whimpers of the obscene pornography fade away, replaced by the ringing of their footsteps in a narrow, echoing passage. As Kerry stumbles on, the floor beneath his feet goes from concrete to creaking wooden boards. Eventually they mount a long staircase, Kerry able to keep his balance only because Solomon holds the back of the straitjacket. There's the creak of another door, and then the darkness inside the hood grows sharply brighter.

A breeze rustles his hair. The freezing cold air is gone, replaced by delicious warmth.

Kerry realizes with shocked awe that they're outside.

He opens his mouth and screams for help, over and over. Solomon makes no move to stop him, just stands still, holding him at the collar and bottom of the jacket, like a bouncer getting ready to toss a drunk. Kerry's cries wind down into ragged whispers. "Are you finished?"

Kerry nods slowly. He can hear no noise, no people, not even a single car engine. Wherever Solomon took him, it's far from civilization. His heart sinks.

They walk. The ground becomes dirt. A few steps later, Kerry runs into a thigh-high barrier, and Solomon pushes until he topples over onto it. Kerry lands hard on a surface covered in thin padding. He can tell from the change in ambient noise that he's inside a much smaller enclosed space than the harness room. His legs are bent and shoved in with the rest of him, then there comes the sound of double doors slamming shut behind him.

Even inside the hood, Kerry's nostrils have no problem detecting the undying stench of old fried food.

THIRTY

Kerry lies still on the floor of the van and strains his ears. His trapped breath has converted the interior of the cowl into a sweltering, humid jungle, causing sweat to break out on his face. He hears the driver's door open and then a creak as Solomon settles himself behind the wheel and starts the wheezing engine. There's a lurch when the vehicle begins to move.

Escape flashes in his mind like a neon sign. This might be his one chance to get out of this nightmare. But his options are severely limited at the present, what with being bound and blind.

Although the latter might not be such a hindrance. Now that he knows where he is, Kerry can envision the countertops and cooking stations to either side of him, but doesn't know what good it would do to roll toward them with his arms still strapped across his abdomen. Instead he braces his feet on the rear doors of the van and pushes. He's still as weak and uncoordinated as a newborn foal, but Kerry manages to inchworm across the dirty carpet on his stomach.

Maybe if he can stand up, someone will see him through the front windshield, the only glass on the vehicle not blacked out. But he's barely moved more than a foot before the top of his head bumps into a flat, slightly yielding surface. It takes several minutes of weary rumination before he realizes it's one of the cardboard boxes filled with Ray's belongings.

"Stop." Solomon's mild admonishment floats down from somewhere above.

"Where are we going?" Kerry asks, but his voice is so thin and strained he can't even hear it himself over the rumble of the engine. He licks his lips and tries again.

At first, he thinks the other man still didn't hear him. Then Solomon says, "To the next step in your therapy. No more talking now. Get some sleep."

Fat chance, you asshole, Kerry thinks, but then, what feels like a half second later, he's jerking awake as the van brakes to a halt, with no clue as to how long he's been out. A wave of drowsiness tries to pull him right back under, but he fights it, struggles to full consciousness and all the pain that comes with it.

The engine shuts off. Fingers scrabble under his chin and rip the hood away.

Kerry blinks at the dazzling morning sunlight pouring in through the van's front windows. Even now, he can't help but feel another swell of appreciation that he's still around to see such a beautiful sight. Then the view is interrupted by Solomon, who twists around to lean over him between the bucket seats.

"This is where we show each other some trust," he says from inside the mask.

Kerry thrashes on the floor, rolling away from him. Solomon reaches for him and misses. Kerry shouts and screams as he spins around and pushes toward the rear doors on his back. There's nowhere to go, he's aware of this, but desperation and fear of whatever this man has in store for him next overwhelms his good sense. His foot catches one of the cardboard boxes in his flailing and sends it crashing over, the contents scattering across the floor and under the seats.

Solomon doesn't allow him to exhaust himself this time. He squeezes his lanky frame into the cargo space and leaps atop Kerry. One gloved hand closes around his throat, pinching his windpipe shut. The other produces a narrow stiletto and holds the incredibly sharp tip below Kerry's left eyeball.

"*That* is not the way to begin," he says, the rubbery nose of the mask squashing against Kerry's. "Make another sound, attempt to escape, do anything at all other than follow my instructions to the letter, and I will stab you through the heart and then go and do the same to your parents. Their death will be a direct result of your decision to test me. There will not be a second warning. Do you understand?"

He releases Kerry's throat long enough for him to drag in a breath and gasp, "Yes, god yes."

"I am going to remove this jacket. You are to crawl past me and climb into the driver's seat. The inside door handle is removed, so don't bother trying to open it. Sit there and touch nothing."

Solomon doesn't wait for confirmation this time. He rolls Kerry roughly onto his stomach, and undoes the bindings on the back of the straightjacket. His arms fall out of the sleeves like dead pythons; allowing them back to their natural position at his sides causes a fresh round of sharp muscles spasms. Once he's completely unbound, Kerry gets to his knees with some effort, shuffles past Solomon in the tight quarters, stumbles through the minefield of Ray's clothes and other belongings that are strewn across the cargo area, and then flops bonelessly into the front seat. It takes him another minute to get turned around and sitting upright behind the wheel so that he can take in the scene outside the van.

A hundred yards ahead and a bit to the right sits a familiar red brick building. Gaggles of children mill around it, talking, laughing, huddling on the steps in small groups, as SUVs and yellow buses drive up to drop off more. They are currently parked two blocks away from this structure, beside the curb of an open grass strip that rolls past the passenger side of the van with a huge bronze sculpture of running horses in the middle of it.

It's the school. The one down the road from Hopeful Sunshine. He's back inside the dreaded Parole-a Triangle. Some connection tries to click in Kerry's brain, but he's too frazzled to nail it down.

An open plastic water bottle is thrust in front of his face. Kerry's entire body cries out at the sight of the sparkling liquid. He snatches it away and drinks, downing the entire bottle in a series of greedy gulps. It soothes his scratchy throat and aching head, sends the smallest trickle of strength back into his overtaxed body.

"I am going to close this curtain," Solomon says behind him. "This is for my protection, not yours. Try to roll down the window or signal anyone, and I will have more than enough time to make good on my threat. Comply, and you will be sleeping in your own bed before the day is over."

The curtain sliding closed behind his seat is what suddenly snaps everything into place for Kerry.

"You were there," he murmurs. "I mean, *here*. In the van with Ray, the day I found him. You were...shit, you were right behind him while I was talking to him."

He can hear that small, preoccupied grin in Solomon's voice when he speaks from the other side of the barrier. "You cut our session short that day, but it still had the desired effect on Mr. Leary. At the time, I didn't expect to ever be back inside this foul-smelling vehicle. Life...has a strange synchronicity sometimes."

"He didn't want to be here." Kerry grimaces as he remembers the stark terror on his roommate's chubby face. It makes sense now, all of it. Ray didn't come here with the intention of hurting anyone; he'd been *forced* to come here, no doubt after enduring everything that Kerry himself just went through. The thought of him hanging in that dank basement, blubbering his heart out while he fought to stay alive, makes Kerry sick. *Jesus man, why didn't you say something? If you were too scared to do it in the van, then why not at the house, after he let you go?* He bows his head, overcome with sorrow and guilt at not having seen the truth, and that's when his eyes land on a strange shape in the floorboard between his feet.

"No doubt you know where you are," Solomon says. "Since you're so determined to follow in Raymond Leary's footsteps, I figured I might as well oblige. Though I can't help wondering if your foreknowledge of my methods will impact the value of the therapy."

Kerry ignores his babble, focusing on the object in the floorboard. It's familiar, but he can't figure out why until he nudges it with his foot. Even then, after he's identified it, he can't understand how it came to be here, next to the gas pedal, then remembers the box he kicked over during his futile escape attempt.

His head is yanked back up by the hair.

"Don't you dare look away," Solomon says. "You keep your eyes on all those happy faces."

"Okay," Kerry agrees, and his hair is released. He does as commanded, letting his gaze wander across each elementary school kid, wishing like hell he was one of them instead of caught in this nightmare that won't end. He doesn't know what he's meant to see, but at least this forced viewing is easier—and more pleasant—than the last.

As he watches, the front door of the school opens and good ol' reliable Officer Prentiss emerges to resume his morning guard post. Kerry's heart leaps into his throat at the sight. Not because he's scared of being discovered this time, but because he would give anything for it to happen. It takes every inch of willpower to not press his hand down on the horn in the middle of the steering wheel. He has serious difficulty believing Solomon's promise that he'll be let go after this is over, but he can't afford not to take the threats seriously. For his parents' sake, if not his own.

Directly on the heels of this thought, a plan springs into Kerry's head, so fully-formed it should have a bow on it. It's a longshot dependent entirely upon the object at his feet, but it gives him his first spark of real hope.

Solomon speaks behind him. "What do you see, when you look at them?"

"I...I don't know. Kids."

"Yes, kids. *Real* kids. Not just faces on a screen. They have lives and hopes and dreams that can be shattered so easily. I want you to see every one of them. And I want you to imagine them being hurt, like the children in those videos."

Kerry finds that, after an entire night exposed to Solomon's deep web pornography, this is entirely too easy. He understands the ingeniousness of this 'therapy,' how someone like Ray—already conflicted and regretful over his past—would be overcome with guilt when put through these exercises. It's the extreme opposite of Les' sessions, designed to tear someone down instead of lift them up.

But Kerry doesn't feel guilty. He just feels angry and insulted all over again.

Solomon is still speaking, his droning voice somehow like a newscaster. "Statistics say that one in eight of them has already been abused. And that ratio goes up significantly if you restrict it to the females."

"Then go string up the people that did it to them."

"I would love to. And in a way, I am. Because this is a societal problem. Whether we want to admit or not, we give implicit approval for this kind of behavior through books and movies that blur the line. By pairing television husbands with women far too young for them. By sexualizing underage pop stars."

"Yeah, you know what, I agree with you there. But what does that have to do with *me*? Why do I have to pay for the rest of the world being fucked up? Or what some other shitheads did to those kids?"

"You're not. You're here because of your own sins. But I like to think that your guilt is their guilt. By helping you, I help them."

"That is fucking retarded. I want to be very clear, the things you're talking about...what you made me watch last night...it completely disgusts me."

"If that's true, it's because you've been caught. Your kind thrives in darkness, behind closed doors. Only after you're pulled into the light does shame begin to blossom. I can prove it to you. Unzip your pants."

Kerry's attention has only halfway been focused on this conversation. The rest has been diverted to using his feet to manipulate the object in the floor without making his actions obvious. Now he looks in the rearview mirror, at the narrow part in the curtain where one of Solomon's unnaturally black eyes peers out. "Wh…what?"

Something jabs him in the back, as surprising as it is painful. Kerry jumps and lets out a yelp before realizing that Solomon poked him with the switchblade right through the vinyl seat, the same thing he must've done to Ray to make him drive off that day as Kerry stood outside the van. He clings to the steering wheel, afraid to lean back.

"Unzip your pants and take your genitals out," Solomon says, the utter lack of emotion in the words making the request sound clinical.

Fear utterly envelops Kerry, sinks through his skin and freezes his muscles. He served his entire four-year sentence without being sexually assaulted, mostly because of his stints in solitary, and damned if he's going to let it happen now. His voice is a squeak as he asks, "Why? What are…what are you going to do?"

"I'm going to show you what it's like to indulge in your deviancy while someone else is watching. You're going to masturbate to completion while staring at those children."

A fat bead of sweat trickles down Kerry's temple. For some reason, he sees the girl that resembled Kayla in his mind's eye, looking bored as her innocence (*taboo, it's a taboo*) is taken. "No. No I…I can't do that."

"Then you will go back for another night in the sling. Your decision, your responsibility. You have three seconds to decide."

"Wait, wait, just wait!" The panic is enough to make Kerry want to bash against the inside of the van, like a bird that flies inside a building and can't find its way out. Somehow this option is even worse than the molestation he feared, and the son of a bitch knows it, too. Words flow out of him even as he renews his efforts in the floorboard. "Man, I can tell you…whatever the hell you want to hear. Tell me what it is, and I'll say it. I'm sorry, I'm regretful, I'm reformed, I'll never do it again. Please, *please*, believe me."

"This isn't about *me* believing, Mr. Denton. I want to help you, I want to set you on the path to your forgiveness, but I can't until you show some glimmer of true remorse."

Kerry raises his voice to cover the click as he connects the two ends of the item between his feet. The floorboard lights up with a dull, red glow that he tries to cover with one sneaker. "My *forgiveness*? What are you, a goddamn preacher? What does that even mean?"

"What does it mean to you?"

"Oh, for Christ's sake," Kerry groans. "Stop pretending like you're fucking Buddha because you go around murdering sex offenders. You're a serial killer. If you want to watch me jerk off, then how the fuck are you any different from any of those sickos in your private collection?"

This time Solomon's hand emerges from the curtain to cup his cheek and shove his entire head sideways. Kerry's left temple smashes into the driver's window hard enough to make stars burst across his vision. Solomon holds him there as he snarls, "I am *nothing* like you people. You think I want to do this? I do it because no one else will, because no one else cares enough to. This is my duty, not a pleasure. I am offering you a chance to be free."

It's the first break in his eerily calm demeanor, and it somehow makes him *less* scary, humanizes him. "Let me guess, that ends with me dead in a bathtub, right?"

"I told you, where it ends is entirely up to you. But if you're implying that I killed your friend, I tell you again, I did not."

"Bullshit, I saw you in the house that night."

"Yes. Because I came to show him the way. To hold his hand through the last step. But I assure you, he took his own life; otherwise, this exercise is all for naught." He takes a sharp breath that sounds a bit like a sob before continuing. "You should be proud of Raymond Leary. He found the courage to make the ultimate sacrifice in order to find peace. To make this world a better place. Like so many of my other clients."

"Jesus, *that's* what this is about? Getting us to *actually* commit suicide? Boy, I've got a neighbor you need to meet." Kerry chokes on laughter. "You're even more pathetic than I thought. Ray might've been chemically castrated, but you're just plain neutered."

Solomon doesn't answer, but he doesn't let go either. With his head held against the glass, Kerry can cut his eyes over to the side enough to see Prentiss still standing on the steps of the school. The officer issues high fives to several older boys as they walk by him on their way inside. The class bell must have rung at some point, because the schoolyard is all but empty now.

Come on, Kerry thinks. *Please work*, please *goddamn work*.

And then, as if he mentally willed it, the cop cocks his head, then thumbs the radio on his belt and says something into the mic attached to his collar. A second later, his head swivels around, scanning the park. His eyes land directly on the weird van with the blacked-out windows parked a couple of blocks away, the one vehicle on the street amid the closed businesses. He says something else into the mic and then heads across the schoolyard on a beeline toward them.

Solomon takes his hand away and withdraws behind the curtain. Kerry prays the man's attention is still on him, that he hasn't noticed the cop yet. And indeed, when Solomon speaks, his composure is restored. "Think what you want about me. But soon you're going to be offered a choice. The last choice you will ever make."

Kerry sits up and leans across the gap between the bucket seats, further blocking Solomon's view of Officer Prentiss as he cuts through the corner of the park and marches down the street directly at the van. The bald cop snorts like a bull through his thick mustache, and his hand rests on the butt of his gun, like he's about to enter an old west gunfight. Kerry is giddy with excitement, so much that he can't resist asking, "When you kidnapped Ray…you messed with his ankle monitor, didn't you? Cloned the signal or something, so it would show a false location for him."

"Those devices present little challenge for me." Solomon seems annoyed at having the conversation hijacked yet again. Kerry suspects he probably has a mental script for these therapy sessions, and they have far deviated from it.

"Yeah, you're real handy with computers," Kerry continues. "But I guess you have to know a monitor is around before you can do anything about it, huh?"

For the very first time, Solomon sounds genuinely confused as he says, "You don't wear one. I checked."

"Nope." Kerry leans forward to grab the heavy band of the object on the floor and holds it up for Solomon to see. "But Ray's was packed up with the rest of his stuff, and I turned it back on."

A heartbeat later, Prentiss bangs a hand down on the hood of the van and shouts, "*Step out of the vehicle!*"

"You have made a mistake," Solomon hisses, crouching even lower in the cargo space.

Prentiss circles the van, coming around to the driver's side but keeping his distance. His eyes suddenly light up with recognition as he recognizes the driver. He pulls the pistol from the holster at his hip, points it at Kerry through the glass, and repeats, "*Step out! Right now! Let me see your hands!*"

"Get rid of him," Solomon whispers from behind the curtain. "You will not like what happens if he tries to take you from here."

Kerry begins frantically rolling down the window, trying to figure out what he's going to say. In his head, he envisioned the sequence of events so clearly: the signal from the ankle monitor alerting the police that it was within 500 yards of the school, the nearest officer being dispatched to investigate as Sanders said, and then himself being magically rescued on the back of a white stallion. The fantasy somehow skipped over the part where he had to find a way out of this situation without Solomon stabbing him right through the seat.

In the end, the decision is taken from him. Officer Prentiss rushes forward and yanks the door of the van open. He grabs Kerry's upper arm with one hand while keeping the gun pointed at his chest and drags him from the vehicle.

Kerry is too weak to fight. He stumbles out onto the street, his exhausted legs wobbling. In one smooth, practiced chain of motions, Prentiss holsters his gun, spins Kerry around, slams the driver's door, and throws him into it face first. A moment later he runs both hands around Kerry's waist and down his legs, a rough frisk.

"Officer, listen to m—!"

"Shut up," the cop cuts him off, in a voice that's half-growl, half-glee. "You screwed up this time, my friend. You ain't going back to your little convict clubhouse now. Oh no, you're on your way directly back to the slammer, where you will stay a very long time, you kiddy-diddling fu—"

He's interrupted by a ratcheting squeal from their right. Kerry turns his head in time to watch the side door of the van finish sliding open beside them. Solomon lunges from the dark interior. The warm light of day should render his mask fake and cheap and plastic, but it doesn't, not at all. The tapering blade of the stiletto flashes as the killer stabs out.

Over his shoulder, Kerry sees Prentiss spin to meet the threat.

The knife slides through one side of the cop's thick neck and out the other, so nice and neat the whole thing is like some optical illusion. He grimaces and raises one hand to grab at the blade, but Solomon jerks it back out of his throat. A single jet of brilliant crimson squirts from the half-inch slit and splatters on the driver's window beside Kerry's face.

Solomon turns to him next, snarling, and swings the knife in a short arc. Kerry pushes away from the van, narrowly avoiding a slash across the chest, but his abused legs give way. He falls past Prentiss—who's still clutching at his neck, where a raging torrent of blood flows between his fingers to darken his uniform shirt—and lands on his back in the street.

The killer glances around hesitantly before stepping completely out of the vehicle. Unfortunately, now that school is in session, the entire street is deserted. He moves toward Kerry, but is stopped by Prentiss, who suddenly lurches forward to grab at him. His hands latch around the killer's throat. The squat, musclebound officer still has enough life in him to drive Solomon's scarecrow-ish form backward. Both men fall through the side door of the van, grappling with one another in the cargo space.

Kerry gets to his feet and runs.

THIRTY ONE

The holding room at the police station is a ten foot wide square, with a tile floor and nothing to occupy the space but a table and chairs. Strangely, being locked in it all alone as time ticks by doesn't bring uncomfortable flashbacks of the months Kerry spent in solitary confinement so much as it does his one night in Solomon's dungeon, a dismaying fact that shows how much the motherfucker got to him. Kerry wolfs down a jailhouse breakfast of runny eggs and over-cooked hash browns to appease his raging hunger and then begins pacing around the interior of this room. He's completed roughly two-thousand circuits and is covered in a film of greasy, nervous sweat before the door finally unlocks and opens again. He expects the dour, overweight detective who questioned him for an hour before leaving to 'check into his story,' but is relieved to see Sanders walk through instead.

"Brad, thank god," Kerry gushes. It isn't until this moment that he understands how much he truly expected to die today. He scrambles around the table but stops short of throwing his arms around the man because it reminds him too much of Ray. "What's happening? Do you know if they found him? Did they get the guy?"

Sanders takes a half second to look him over. Kerry sees the twitch of disgust that he tries to hide. Not surprising. The nice outfit he wore to the funeral yesterday is now attire fit for the homeless: filthy, stained and smelling badly like old piss. Then the parole officer gives a conciliatory smile and gestures to the chairs. "It's a relief to see you, Denton. We all got scared when you didn't come home last night. Why don't you calm down and let's have a seat."

"'Calm down?'" Kerry blinks at him as if he's just spoken another language. "What're you talking about, did they fucking catch him or not?"

Sanders swallows, the action taking some effort. "They haven't found anyone like the man you described."

A cold hand grabs a fistful of Kerry's guts and squeezes. "They went to the school, right? What about Prentiss, is he...?"

"Officer Prentiss is officially listed as missing." Sanders takes great pains to choose his words. "No sign of him or Ray's van at the school. They're canvassing the neighborhood for anyone that might have seen...well, anything. From what I understand, they also went to these other addresses you gave—the house up the street from Hopeful Sunshine, the one on Heather Trail, this place downtown—and all of them are completely empty."

"Jesus..." Even though it's no less than what Kerry expected, the confirmation makes the room give a sickening lurch around him. He reaches for the table to steady himself with a trembling hand. He regretted leaving the cop behind, but only after the shock wore off. Most of his panicked flight is a half-remembered blur. Kerry apparently sprinted four blocks away from the school to a gas station, gibbered at the clerk to get the poor man to call 911, and then shivered behind a dumpster until a squad car arrived. "M-my folks. Do you know if they're okay?"

"Yeah, Milwaukee PD has them. The chief up there agreed to a temporary protective detail until we can get this sorted out. They're gonna be okay."

Tears of relief sting Kerry's eyes. He sits down heavily in one of the chairs and rests his forehead on the interrogation room table. After they'd gotten him back to the police station, he'd told the detective that his parents were in danger, but insisted he be allowed to call them himself. There was no way Solomon could've gotten to the other side of the country already, but Kerry couldn't rule out the possibility that the maniac has accomplices or some other way to make good on his threat. He didn't even try to explain the situation to them, just insisted they get out of the house immediately and go to the police. His mother sobbed and begged to know if he was all right, if he'd 'gotten himself into trouble again.' Kerry didn't need to talk to his father to know what the man must be thinking: that their pedophile son is out of prison less than three months, and their lives are being upended yet again.

Sanders grabs the chair from the far side of the table and slides it around to the corner right next to Kerry. He sits down and says, "Denton, man, I'm sorry, but we don't have time for you to fall to pieces. It took some serious convincing for them to let me come in here and talk to you."

Kerry sits up and swipes a hand across his face as he tries to interpret this. "Wha...? *Why?*"

The parole officer takes a breath. "I got the bare bones of this thing, but, from what I understand...there are quite a few holes in your story. And a lot of people out there would love to fill those holes with pieces of your scrawny ass."

An angry warmth rockets up Kerry's neck to boil inside his cheeks and forehead. "*What the fuck are you talking about?*" he screams. "*Me?* They're trying to blame this on *me?*"

"Calm. Down," Sanders says through clenched teeth. "I'm doing my best to help you, but if you go nuts, they'll drag me right back out of here."

"But you're my parole officer!"

"Yes, your *parole officer*, not a detective. Which means they want me far away from this investigation in case I decide to cover for you. Which, I might add, I most certainly would *not*. But there's protocol to follow. They only let me in because time is of the essence and they think I can get some answers out of you."

"Okay. Fine. Sorry, I haven't slept in a goddamn day and a half." Kerry takes a shuddering breath intended to calm himself, barely reigning in his fury. He motions at the holding room around them. "Is this an official interrogation then? Should I be calling my attorney?"

"If you did something wrong, then hell yes, don't say another word to me or anybody else until you do."

Kerry closes his eyes and clenches his jaw. His teeth are on the verge of shattering. "This doesn't make any fucking sense! I already told them everything! What else do they goddamn want?"

"You need to understand something." Sanders' voice is steel as he scoots forward to the edge of his seat, their knees almost touching. "There's a cop missing and, from what you're claiming, probably dead. That kind of thing tends to make *other* cops very eager to string someone up by the scrotum. And an ex-con sex offender who's been missing for 24 hours, who, by his own admission, was the last one to see the missing cop after being caught in a place that violates his parole, and who is now telling an absolutely insane story to explain all of it, makes for an appealing target."

"Always a predator," Kerry whispers.

"That's right, and don't you forget it. So you better appreciate the few people in this world who will look past it." He grabs Kerry's shoulder. "Hey, *I'm* on your side, until you give me a reason not to be. I've already assured them you're not the delusional or homicidal type. So pretend I'm coming in fresh and help me understand what's going on. Who the hell is this guy you told them about?"

"He's the reason all your sex offenders are committing suicide. He's...he's the reason Ray's dead."

"And his name is Solomon?"

"That's what he called himself. I met him a few weeks ago, during my parade around the neighborhood. He was living—squatting, I guess—in that foreclosed house down the street from Hopeful Sunshine. That's his MO. He finds sex offenders on the registry and uses empty properties close by as a base of operations, to keep tabs on them or something. Then he...he kidnaps and tortures them."

Kerry gives a quick outline of the sequence of discoveries that led him into Solomon's clutches, while once more leaving out D'libra's involvement—if there's a price to be paid for breaking into the empty house, he doesn't want a bit of it to fall on her—then starts into an overview of the past day. He gets as far as explaining the first iteration of the killer's 'therapy' before Sanders interrupts with a low gasp.

"Jeeeesus Christ, Denton. He left you like that *all night*?"

"Yeah. And I'm not making it sound nearly as bad as it was."

"But why? What's the point of all this?"

"He thinks he's some kind of crusader. Stopping evil in the world, savings us from ourselves, basic delusions-of-grandeur type stuff."

"And stringing you guys up and forcing you to watch child pornography is, what? Some form of punishment?"

Kerry tries to shrug, but finds the effort needed to roll his shoulders is more than he can manage. The only thing that's kept him awake this long is tension and worry about his parents, but now that both are dissipating, his exhaustion is like a bowling ball tied around his neck. "It's more like brainwashing. Supposed to bring out our guilt. That's how he got these people to kill themselves. He told them they could find *forgiveness*."

Sanders arches an eyebrow. "Go ahead and tell me the rest. How did you end up at the school with Ray's ankle monitor?"

Kerry finishes the story, but leaves out one important detail about the events in the van, as he did with the detective. Every time his mind dredges up what Solomon wanted him to do, a flush of shame and embarrassment makes his stomach churn.

And then rage flushes it away as he remembers that this is exactly what the psychopath would want.

When he's done, Sanders sits back in his chair and interlaces his fingers in his lap. He sits that way for a very long time, brow knitted as he stares at his knees.

"I'm trying to approach this like they will," he says with a pensive frown. "So let me ask, are you assuming, or did this guy *say* that he did all these same things to Ray?"

"Yes, definitely. He even admitted to being in the house that night. Said he was 'helping Ray through the final step' or some bullshit."

"If that's the case then…you no longer believe he was murdered?"

Kerry uses an open hand to smack the top of the table, the jolt spilling a half-empty plastic cup of water that came with his meal. "I never said he was murdered, I said something was off! And I was right. *God*, was I right." He squeezes the knob at the end of his finger, trying to massage away the ache growing there. "Ray…he was more of a fighter than most people would give him credit for, including you. But now that I know this lunatic was constantly dogging and coercing and threatening him, his suicide makes a lot more sense."

"But he wasn't, right?"

Kerry stares at him, confused.

"Let me clarify that. I'm not saying that putting someone through all that—especially someone with a mental instability—wouldn't be enough to shame them into suicide. What I mean is, the treatment isn't 'constant.' Ray disappeared overnight, but then he came back to the house the next morning on his own, free and clear. You saw him, and so did Les. So the problem is, if he was kidnapped and subjected to everything you described, why didn't he—or any of these other offenders—say anything? For that matter, why would this Solomon person let them go and just…trust that they'd keep their mouths shut?"

Kerry grows still, his shortened digit throbbing. He can't meet the other man's eyes as he says, "Solomon wanted me to…do things to myself. While he watched. Maybe he did a lot worse to the others, and I escaped before he could do it to me. Not too many people would admit something like that, if they thought it was over. Especially not a group that's viewed as somewhere between Hitler and dog shit on the socially acceptable spectrum. Jesus, most people would say we deserved it. A lot of *them* probably thought they deserved it. And you know it."

The parole officer's stern expression melts into something indecipherable. He clears his throat and says, "All right. Maybe. But there's a world of difference between keeping your mouth shut and feeling guilty enough to kill yourself. You talk about forgiveness, but a lot of the ex-cons I know wouldn't give a shit about some namby-pamby, therapeutic crap like that. They're notoriously selfish people; that's usually why they go to prison in the first place."

"I don't know, maybe Solomon only goes after the people he thinks will be susceptible. I can only tell you what happened to me, and what he said."

"Still...you understand how crazy it sounds, right? And how utterly unprovable? Unless they find this guy, all you've got is a story."

"The keystroke log," Kerry says quickly. "I told the detective about that, too. It'll show the emails Ray exchanged with him. That should at least prove he exists."

Sanders squirms uncomfortably in his chair for another moment. "I spoke to Les while I was on my way here. He said the cops already asked him for a full transcript of the log. Neither of us knew why at the time—since you were in custody, we were afraid you'd...well, never mind—but then he went to check the computer and...it had crashed."

Kerry sighs and nods. "That's our guy. He's very technologically gifted."

"I'm sure we can turn it over to digital forensics though, if they push the investigation that far."

"Won't matter. If Solomon wanted it wiped, it's wiped."

Sanders regards the puddle of spilled water in the middle

of the table as he says, "Are you sure there's nothing you're missing?"

Something about the way he asks the question causes Kerry to blurt, "What's that supposed to mean?"

"Changing your story now…it wouldn't look bad, it would just be you, you know, remembering something more clearly."

"So you still don't believe me."

"I'm not saying that. At all. But I want you to ask yourself, instead of some big conspiracy involving all the sex offenders in the city under attack by an incredibly brazen, computer-hacking ghost, maybe this is just your girl's father messing with you."

"I wish it was," Kerry tells him. "Cause I'm a lot less scared of Robert MacCallum now."

THIRTY TWO

Kerry is kept in the holding room another two hours before the detective returns. They have nothing to corroborate his story—no information on the whereabouts of Prentiss or the van, not so much as a single fingerprint to show that Solomon even exists—but they also have nothing to implicate him in the officer's disappearance. He's warned that this matter is far from over, but that they have no further reason to keep him.

"No further reason?" Kerry demands. "Uh, what about protecting me? This guy is still out there, he could be coming for me!"

"At least then we would have something to go on," the detective says, with an unmistakable note of hostile sarcasm. The man has no more interest in helping him than Prentiss and Cho did after he got the shit kicked out of him in the parking lot of Caulfield's. Even if Solomon walked in here right this second and confessed, they would still find some reason to hassle him. "An officer will be parked out in front of your place for a while. You better hope this one doesn't disappear too, or you're gonna be in a world of misery."

Kerry refrains from telling him that wouldn't be much of a change. "What about my parents?"

"Whatever Milwaukee PD does is up to them. My goal here is to catch the bad guy. *Whoever* he may be."

Kerry is led out to a lobby where Les waits. He has a brief flashback to the night his parents bailed him out of jail, his shame when facing them. At least back then, he knew the pain in his severed finger was real.

"You have another exit we can use?" Les asks. "There's an entire press conference waiting outside."

The detective motions at another door. "Go through prisoner processing. Once you're away from here, you should be safe from the media, at least for a while. The chief is keeping a lid on Denton's name so it doesn't derail the search for Officer Prentiss, but there's no guarantee how long that will last. If they're on your doorstep tomorrow morning, I think your lawyer would probably advise you not to speak to them."

They smuggle him out with his shirt pulled over his head, until Kerry can get ducked down in the back of the psychologist's car. Les is drenched in sweat by the time they pull out of the police department parking lot past a slew of news vans.

On the way back to the house, Kerry borrows Les' cell to call his parents. Now that the urgency is gone, he tells them the entire story, with some careful edits for decency. By the end, his mother is outright weeping and declaring that she'll be on the next flight back to Texas.

"No, do *not* do that," he tells her. "You're safer there than here. This guy was probably bluffing about going after you, but just in case, get away from home for a while. Stay somewhere else and don't use your credit cards."

"But Kerr-Bear," she cries, using a nickname he hasn't heard since grade school, "what about you?"

"I can take care of myself. This is my problem, not yours, so don't make it worse than it already is."

He hangs up before he can plead for her to come, to take him in her arms and rock away all the awfulness like she did back in the Kerr-Bear days.

Hopeful Sunshine is empty when they arrive. A police squad car pulls to the curb in front of the house as they get out of the Subaru. The officer behind the wheel gives them a nod.

"Do you want to talk about anything?" Les asks him in the foyer.

"Not now. I just want to sleep."

"Okay. Not to add more stress to what you're already going through, but, when you get a chance, you might start packing up." Kerry throws him a sharp glance. "I got the word this morning. The state is shutting down the house to settle the lawsuit from the neighborhood. We're out of here in two weeks. Everyone will be assigned a new group home. Including you, if you want it."

"Of course I want it. I don't have any place else to go."

Kerry trudges up the stairs, but stops when Les calls out to him.

"For what it's worth," the psychologist says slowly, "I'm sorry I didn't believe you. About Ray. It...it makes me happy to know that maybe...I didn't fail him."

"You didn't, Les. That poor bastard probably wouldn't have made it as far as he did without you."

Kerry feels like a light breeze could blow him over by the time he makes it upstairs, but forces himself to stay on his feet long enough to take a scalding hot shower. The water is heavenly, sluicing away the horrible stink of fear sweat and stale piss, but it can do nothing for his memories. At one point during the shower, he realizes that he's standing in the same place where Raymond Leary took his own life and then he's wheezing and his shoulders are shaking and he collapses into a sobbing heap on the bottom of the tub with the banshee that haunts his hand wailing.

In the past four years, he never considered killing himself, not once, not even when Kayla died. If anything, her death hardened his resolve to survive prison. Even his moment of weakness while strung up in Solomon's basement was a passing whim, a response to physical pain and discomfort.

But he understands the *true* appeal of suicide now. How there are some things in life that only death can erase. And if too many of those things attach themselves to you, like barnacles on an old ship, you might be willing to do anything to hasten that release along.

It takes the last of his willpower to climb back up, change into fresh jeans and a t-shirt, and tumble into bed. His head is on the pillow all of three seconds before sleep takes him.

A nightmare jerks him awake. Late afternoon sunlight scrabbles at the windowsill, bright enough for him to see D'libra perched on the dresser, watching him. She's wearing a thin spaghetti strap top and a pair of jean shorts that showcase her smooth, dark legs as they hang off the front of the dresser. He's surprised to find that his heart gives a happy lurch at the sight of her.

"You don't seem to be bleedin," she says.

"Huh?"

She taps a finger on the air in the direction of his crotch. "Les told us what happened, that you got kidnapped by the psycho that murdered Ray, or somethin like that. They's a rumor goin around that he cut yo' dick off."

"A rumor?"

Her mouth curls into a wicked grin. "Well, I started it. But still."

"What is your obsession with people having their genitals cut off?" Kerry makes a show of grabbing at his groin as he sits up. "All present and accounted for. Feel free to check for yourself when you suck it, bitch."

She smiles and raises a sculpted eyebrow. "Whip it out, Chester. You couldn't handle these lips wrapped around yo' white meat." The grin falls off her face. Her eyes narrow accusingly. "Why didn't you say nothin?"

"Cause I didn't want you to get in trouble for helping me. I told the cops I broke into that house by myself and—"

"Not to *them*," she snaps. "To *me*. We started this Hardy Boys bullshit together. Then you pretended like it was over, mystery solved, all the while sneakin 'round behind my back to keep playin detective by yo'self."

"I wasn't sneaking! I just...didn't think you cared."

D'libra scowls at him. "That's a real shitty thing to say."

Kerry gives a bark of disbelief. "Since when have you given a damn about Ray?"

"Never. But I wasn't doin it for him."

"Oh." Kerry's gaze drifts to the foot of the bed. "I'm sorry. Tell you what, next time I get tortured overnight, I'll make sure you come along."

She hops down from the dresser, crosses the room, and eases down on the bed beside him. He catches a whiff of that wonderful lotion. "So...you okay or what?"

He considers that. "I'm dealing."

"What'd he do to you anyway?"

"Tied me up. Made me watch a bunch of kiddie porn."

"*Ugh!*" Her nostrils flare as she gags. "What for?"

"He wanted me to feel guilty. So I would kill myself."

"Well...that's fuckin stupid."

"Worked on Ray, apparently."

D'libra leans closer, close enough to give him a shove with her bare shoulder. "Then it best not work on you, Chester. We got two weeks left in this shithole, and I ain't gon' spend it alone with the rest of these assholes."

He studies her deep brown eyes from a foot away—such a prettier shade than Solomon's—her full lips and the streak of purple hair that falls down her forehead like a ribbon. He wants to say something, to explain that she's come to mean something to him, or, if he can't get that out, just to thank her, but then her cell phone buzzes and she's gone, standing up as she reads a text.

"I'm 'bout to bounce," she says. "But I'll be back later on. We can...shit, I don't know, we can talk or somethin, if you want."

"Yeah. Okay." The words 'or something' encompass an ocean of possibility to Kerry. "You gonna be back before curfew?"

She rolls her eyes at him. "C'mon now, let's not get all crazy." One hand touches his shoulder as she walks out of the room.

He hangs around upstairs a little longer, until the sun is down and he can't stand to be alone with his thoughts any longer. Kerry emerges from his room, still weary and sore but at least the few hours of sleep he got have relieved his exhaustion. The door to Mark and Scott's room is closed, but soft hymnal music can be heard within, and the sound of the former humming along. Other voices float up from downstairs, punctuated by laughter. Kerry moves toward them, noting that the computer in the media center is missing its hard drive, undoubtedly now in police custody.

Les and Lorie sit at the big dining table outside the kitchen, playing a game of Monopoly. They smile as he walks past.

In the kitchen, he grabs a soda from the fridge and then goes to the window. The cop car is still parked at the curb, the officer within bathed in the glow from his dashboard as he leafs through a magazine. Seeing him eases a nervous flutter in Kerry's stomach. He suspects he's going to be looking over his shoulder for a long time whether they catch Solomon or not.

"Five-oh still out there?"

Kerry turns from the window as Scott strolls into the room, dressed in his suit from work. "Yep."

"Yo, I bet the neighbors love that shit." He opens the fridge, takes out a bag of marinated chicken breasts and the ingredients for a salad, and starts preparing their dinner on the island in the middle of the kitchen. "Fuck 'em, we're all gonna be outta their hair in a couple weeks anyway, right?"

Kerry moves to help him, taking out a pan from the drawer beneath the stove. "Yeah. And, to tell the truth, that's sort of my fault."

"What do you mean?"

"That construction company that's footing the legal bill? That's the father of the girl I went to prison for. He's doing this because of me. So I apologize in advance for you having to go to one of those shitty group homes."

"Not me, bro!" Scott turns on one of the oven burners, slides the pan onto the coil, and dumps chicken into it. "Les talked to my parole officer, and he signed off on my release early. Didn't make no sense to force me to move when I'm a free man next month anyways. I'm gettin the fuck outta here and movin in with my girlfriend. I mean fiancé, shit, I keep forgettin. Yo, if anything, you did me a favor!"

"Oh. Well then…I guess we're even?"

"Fer sure." Scott works his way around the island, to the big walk-in pantry on the far side of the room. "Hey, I heard about what happened with that whacko. Your dick okay, bro?"

Kerry sighs and rolls his eyes as he dumps the salad ingredients into a bowl. "Yes. My dick is fine."

"Cool." Scott pulls open the pantry and stands in the dark doorway as he says, "Yo, too bad that cop's hangin around, cause I'd love for this fucker to come back and let me get my hands on 'im, you know?"

This cheerfully naïve statement is followed by an odd gurgling sound, and Kerry looks up from his work to discover that the thin handle of a knife has magically sprouted from Scott Ramirez's Adam's apple.

THIRTY THREE

It all takes on the horrible, sticky slowness of a night-mare: Scott flailing away from the pantry door...lurching to-ward Kerry...reaching up to clutch at the object sticking out of his throat, eyes full of confusion and pleading. His mouth opens and closes as though trying to speak, but not so much as a whisper comes out. Even though Kerry's mind seems to be moving at one-third its normal speed, instinct causes him to step forward and catch the other man before he collapses. He's rewarded with a rush of hot blood that sprays across his neck and chest.

And then, over Scott's shoulder, Kerry sees Solomon emerge from the depths of the pantry, a boogeyman in a weeping toddler mask. His heart shrivels at the sight even as his brain insists that he must be hallucinating.

"Remember, you chose this," Solomon says in that cool, utterly detached monotone.

He moves forward, raising the syringe in his hand.

Kerry tries to retreat, but all of Scott's weight is still on him. His Hispanic housemate is shuddering violently now as he bleeds out on Kerry, his eyes rolled back in his head. Solomon puts a hand on his shoulder and shoves him aside. Scott stumbles across the tile, trips over a chair. He topples face down on the small breakfast table with the stiletto still buried in his throat, splashing maroon droplets in all directions.

Distantly, like the real world bleeding into a nightmare, Les' voice drifts in from the dining room, asking if everything is okay in there. Kerry wants to tell him no, that everything is most assuredly not the fuck okay, but can't figure out how to form the words. Terror eclipses every instinct except the need to flee.

Solomon's gloved fingers snag his wrist before he can take a step. Kerry tries to plant his feet and yank free, but the tile beneath him is slick with blood. The other man's hand is a manacle clamped around his arm. The two of them play tug-of-war with his appendage in the middle of the kitchen. Kerry watches helplessly as Solomon uses his free hand to move the syringe toward Kerry's forearm.

The needle slides beneath his skin with a sharp pinch.

Instead of pulling away, Kerry lunges forward. The movement catches his attacker off guard. Kerry feels the tiny snap as the needle breaks off in his flesh before it can deliver the contents of the syringe. Then he's smashing into Solomon's chest with the heels of both hands, driving him backward into the large oven, where he sprawls across the stovetop before catching himself.

There's a low *whoosh*. Wings made of flame burst out of Solomon's back. Kerry expects the man to rise into the air for a half second until he realizes the lit burner caught the back of his hoodie on fire. Whatever material the garment is made of, the flames must be hungry for it; between the blinks of an eye, the killer's left half is engulfed in red and yellow tongues high enough to lick at the cabinets over the stove. Solomon doesn't give so much as a whimper as he struggles with the zipper.

Kerry runs from him yet again, as he did in the foreclosed house yesterday and at the school this morning, a synchronicity of events that overlay one another in his mind despite the fact that they're separated by a million years and a billion miles. One foot skids in the puddle of blood on the tile before it finds purchase, and then he's off. His only thought now is reaching the cop in front of Hopeful Sunshine, getting to someone who can protect him, who can stop this maniac once and for all. Kerry rounds the island, sees the foyer and the front door of the house ahead. He sprints even faster, carried by hope...

And collides full-body with Les as the other man comes around the corner.

The impact sends them bouncing in different directions, Les into the wall beside the front door, Kerry across the foyer, where his blood-slick shoes slide out from under him on the tile. He lands on his right hip and elbow with a bone-jarring crunch, then scrambles back up as Lorie enters the foyer from the dining room.

"Hey, what's—!" Les's admonishment dies as he adjusts his glasses to get a look at Kerry. "Good god! What happened, are you all right?"

Solomon appears in the kitchen doorway behind him, amid a thin pall of smoke.

The left side of the toddler mask is a charred horror.

"*Les, watch out!*" Kerry shouts.

Understanding dawns on the psychologist's face as a gloved hand slips over his mouth. Solomon wrenches Les's head to the side and draws the stiletto across his throat in one swift motion, like a pig at slaughter. A vicious red slit appears beneath the psychologist's chin and spews forth a steaming waterfall of blood.

Lorie screams, but the sound is lost under the shrill blat of the smoke alarms.

Kerry grabs her hand and pulls her away, further into the house. With Solomon next to the front door, there will be no escape that direction. The stairs are to their right, and Kerry heads toward them on impulse, still dragging Lorie, who won't stop shrieking. Once he's sure that she's moving up the steps on her own, he chances a look back.

Solomon is coming up, not even bothering to run, dragging the tip of the knife along the bannister. The killer's hoodie is gone, replaced by a singed black sweatshirt. His mask is still dripping with molten rubber that makes him resemble a lit candle. Beyond him, Lester Norris's body lies in a spreading crimson pool. Greasy black smoke belches out of the kitchen doorway, where the crackle of flames is audible. Kerry tears his gaze away from the horrible scene and plows up the steps, with Lorie sobbing as she scrambles up at his heels.

"What's all that noise?" a voice shouts from somewhere ahead. "What's going on down there?"

The media center is dark, but Kerry sees a shaft of light from an open door on the far side, where Mark is sticking his head out of his bedroom. He sees Kerry coming up the stairs covered in blood and his eyes nearly fall out of their sockets. "*I knew it!*" he bellows. "*I told them you were nuts! Stay away from me, you psychopath!*" He pulls his head back into his room and slams the door.

"Mark, get out of the house!" Kerry yells. "Go out the window, get the cop!" The drop from the second floor isn't too high; Kerry hopes the man will be smart enough to jump.

The first door he comes to is also the only one in Hopeful Sunshine with a lock: the bathroom, the place where Ray died, either by his own hand or that of the man who just murdered two of the other residents. Kerry lurches inside, waits for Lorie to make it through, then slams the door and locks it. Lorie rushes to the entrance on the opposite side and does the same after flipping on the light.

"Who w-was that?" she sobs. "Oh my god, h-he killed Les!"

Kerry doesn't bother answering. Now that he has time to breathe, his mind catches up to the rest of him, and it's pointing out the major flaw in locking themselves away.

"Do you have your cell phone?"

She pats her pockets. "I-I think it's downstairs."

"Fuck!" He goes to the cabinets beneath the sink and digs through them.

"What are you doing?"

"Looking for something we can use as a weapon."

"Y-you think he'll break in here?"

"Maybe. Even if he doesn't, we're gonna have to go back out."

"No no no! Let's wait in here until Mark gets the police!"

Kerry waves at the door, where tendrils of gray smoke are already creeping through the gap at the bottom. Even muffled by walls, he can still hear the alarms blaring downstairs. "The place could be burning down. We can't get trapped in here."

Kerry comes up with an ancient hair dryer as heavy as a brick, and Lorie arms herself with one of D'libra's long nail files. Then they huddle next to the door on the girl's side of the hall, opposite from where they entered.

"I don't wanna go," she tells him.

"I'm sure he's gone by now. He has to be. Just…run for the stairs and don't stop until you're outside."

He throws open the door, then follows close behind Lorie as she rushes through.

Hazy smoke fills the air. Kerry chokes on his first lungful, tries to wave it away, then pulls his shirt over his mouth to help him breathe. Lorie stops at the end of the hall, and, as he catches up to her, Kerry understands why.

There will be no going down the stairs. The entire front wall of the house is ablaze, a shimmering, two-story high curtain of flame. The smoke alarms short out and die as they stare at it, leaving them in the crackle of the fire. He wheels around, realizing that they will have to leap out a window also, but sees Solomon materialize from the smoke, rushing down the hallway toward them.

His lanky form barrels into Kerry with the force of a dump truck, driving him across the second floor landing. He's stopped by the wooden bannister at the edge of the drop off, which slams into Kerry's back hard enough to wallop the air out of him.

The shifting firelight plays across the remaining half of the mask and liquid black eyes beneath as the killer leans over him.

"*You* will *take responsibility!*" he growls, spitting each word into Kerry's face.

And then Lorie's arm snakes over his shoulder and stabs the nail file into his left eye. Kerry watches as one of those black orbs winks out in a gush of gooey fluid.

Solomon stumbles away from Kerry, the nail file sticking out of the eyehole in his mask. He pulls it out and tosses it away as Lorie waits behind him, arms held up like she's ready to fight. Kerry tries to tell her to run, but can't suck in enough air to speak.

The killer turns to her. The wickedly thin knife appears in his hand like magic. Lorie sees it and shrinks away, confidence forgotten. He surges forward and rams it into her lower abdomen in one brutal movement, twisting and wrenching the blade upward before yanking it free. She falls to the floor with a dark mass spilling through a gaping hole in her stomach.

Kerry stands as Solomon faces him. Blood streams down the burned side of the mask. The entire upper story of Hopeful Sunshine is filled with smoke as dense as fog. Heat from the flames warms Kerry's back. But the knife in the other man's hand is his sole focus.

"I can still help you," Solomon says, his voice quavering. To Kerry's amazement, he folds the blade and slips it back into his pocket. "Make the right decision. Come with me, or there will be more death on your head."

"You're right about that," Kerry agrees, and swings the hair dryer he's holding behind his back.

The appliance comes in from the other's man newly blind side. It smashes against his temple hard enough to crack the casing. Solomon grunts and stumbles away. Kerry stays on the offensive, hitting him again, using the hair dryer like a hammer. The killer makes a weak move to block the blow, but seems too woozy to keep up the defense. Kerry continues the barrage as he circles around, moving between Solomon and the stairs.

"If you want me, you're gonna have to drag me out of here," Kerry tells him.

Solomon makes a move to do just that, lunging forward with his gaunt arms outstretched. Kerry easily dodges aside and brings the remains of the hair dryer down on the back of the killer's head. The force of the blow sends him tumbling down the stairs in a whirlwind of gangly limbs. Kerry watches the inferno at the bottom swallow him up, then hurries back to check on Lorie.

She's dead, her eyes open in the smoky darkness, guts in a puddle beneath her. Kerry touches her cheek and then moves back into the hallway, coughing into his shirt.

He enters an empty bedroom and goes to the window. On the girl's side of the house, all of them look out on the back yard. He slides up the glass, sits on the sill, and jumps without hesitation, landing hard on the lawn beside the fire pit.

Kerry takes a few shaky steps away from the burning house and hears, *"Freeze, police!"*

Behind him, Hopeful Sunshine is shrouded in an amorphous cloud of smoke, with ten foot high flames waving on the rooftop. The gate where the fence meets the side of the house is open. He can make out a silhouette in the smoke, pointing a pistol at him, and another behind it that sounds like Mark as it shouts, *"That's him, he killed them, he's crazy!"*

Before Kerry can speak, he simultaneously hears a boom and sees a burst of light from the gun barrel. Something hot passes by his shoulder. The realization that he's been shot at snaps something inside him, an inner vial like one of those glow sticks at a rave, but instead of releasing phosphorescent chemicals, he experiences a rush of desperation and raw animal panic that wipes away all rational thought. Kerry breaks into motion as a second shot goes off, ducking his head and limping down the rolling decline of the yard, toward the other gate at the rear edge of the property. He holds both hands up while he runs, begging for the officer to stop, stop shooting, but he doesn't know if he's saying this aloud or only thinking it. In any case, the bullets keep coming even while he throws open the gate and falls through into the alley on hands and knees.

A few feet away from him is a tire with a shiny gold hubcap that winks in the glow from a nearby streetlight. A midnight blue Honda is idling in the narrow alley behind Hopeful Sunshine. The rear door opens.

"What the fuck is goin on?" D'libra asks. There's uncharacteristic bewilderment in her voice as she stares at the flames visible over the top of the fence.

"Help me," he pleads, crawling forward to clutch at her. The car is packed with other bodies, at least two others in the back seat next to D'libra and two more up front, but he doesn't pay them any attention as he clings to her waist and begs for mercy.

"Where's everybody else, what happened?" she demands.

Another gunshot cracks on the far side of the fence.

"Somebody shootin!" a deep, rumbling voice inside the car declares. "Get dat muhfuckah in here and let's go!"

Kerry is pulled into the vehicle, sprawling across D'libra's lap, and then the car squeals away into the night, taking him with it.

FORGIVENESS

THIRTY FOUR

Solomon emerges from the hellish inferno at the bottom of the staircase and mounts the steps, as relentless and unstoppable as Schwarzenegger in those killer robot flicks. Kerry tries to move his legs to run, but he's rooted in place, transfixed by the horrific sight. The killer's mask is entirely burned away now, along with his face, leaving a leering, scorched skull. But those black eyes are still in there, skewering Kerry as Solomon grabs him by the throat. Kerry struggles and flails and tries to scream and then he sits up and the nightmare shreds away, the blazing interior of Hopeful Sunshine replaced by an unfamiliar room.

The couch where he slept is filthy and threadbare, with uncomfortable lumps, exposed springs, and—judging by the tiny red welts on his legs and chest that remind him of Ray's self-pinching—probably infested with bed bugs. He was so exhausted by the time it was offered to him, he fell onto it without a single complaint and passed out for…Jesus, close to twelve hours, according to his watch. As he rubs sleep out of his eyes, he wonders if he was in shock, his body sending him into a mini-coma so his brain could reboot. In any case, he still feels like shit, but well-rested shit, at least.

Enough sunlight slips between the boards nailed across the room's window for him to take in this place for the first time. Not that there's much to differentiate it from the mental picture conjured in his head by the words 'crack den.' Stained carpet, bare plaster walls layered with graffiti, and a sickly sweet smell that must be a combination of mildew and weed. A far cry from the luxury of Hopeful Sunshine. Last night, as he was ushered inside, the interior of the house was lit only by small LED lanterns. At the time, he thought the occupants might be squatters. That may still be true, but, seeing it now, he suspects the place probably doesn't have working electricity either.

Kerry swings his legs off the couch, stands up, and is nearly swept back off his feet by a dizzying barrage of pain. His entire body is wracked by various aches and bruises, most of which he can't even recall getting. The worst, by far, is a low throb in his right hip from where he slipped and smashed into the tile, the sort of injury that frequently puts elderly people down for the count. But there's also a curious burning sensation across the top of his forearm that he can't even find a source for.

A pair of jeans and a plain black t-shirt have been left on the back of the couch. D'libra made him surrender his bloodstained clothes to her, leaving him with nothing but underwear and sneakers. Kerry picks up the clothes and carries them with him as he limps to the door.

He's afraid it might be locked or barred from the outside, but the knob turns. Kerry pulls it open a crack and peeks through. The hallway is just as trashed. An open door on the opposite side reveals a filthy bathroom. He can hear distant voices talking and laughing but can't tell from where. Even though he obviously isn't a prisoner, he's still hesitant to step out of the room.

His hosts made it clear last night that he is not welcome here. After racing away from Hopeful Sunshine through endless alleys and back streets—during which he babbled the entire story to D'libra and her friends, all of them sandwiched together in the small Honda—the young black man driving the vehicle pulled over. Kerry was left inside the car while everyone engaged in a very loud, very heated argument with D'libra in the cones of the headlights. He caught a few insistences from the driver about them 'not needin this kinda heat,' before D'libra jabbed a finger into his chest and told him something that caused him to back down. A half hour later and Kerry was being chauffeured through a downtown Dallas neighborhood with dead trees, barred windows, and burnt out cars at the curb. The house they brought him into had tiny holes all across its brick exterior, and he didn't need any Spike Lee movies to tell him what they were.

His full bladder is what finally spurs him to leave the room. Kerry steps into the hallway in his underwear and scurries across the hall. The bathroom is terrible, spray-painted and stained, the floor rough and uneven from missing tiles, the tub filled with stagnant, algae-ridden water. As he suspected, the light switch doesn't work, but an unblocked window over the cracked toilet lets in plenty of light. Kerry sets the clothes on the toilet tank and faces the mirror over the sink, which is shattered except for one jagged corner.

A gaunt, bloodstained ghoul stares back. Purple bags hang under his eyes like fat leeches. Bruises decorate his torso and left temple. Scott's dried blood is on his neck and chest, and caked in the creases of his fingers. The sight of it makes Kerry's gorge rise. Their dead faces flash behind his eyes, Scott and Lorie and Les like wax mannequins, accompanied by arrows of regret and sorrow. This is his fault, all his fault, just as Solomon told him, and maybe things would be better for all of them if Kerry had listened to the man in the first place and followed Ray's example.

As he wallows, Kerry reaches for the faucet, desperate to scrub that disgusting blood from his skin, and experiences a moment of blinding agony from the motion of twisting the spigot.

He brings his forearm up and rubs at the burning spot he noticed earlier. If he presses down, he can feel something thin and hard beneath the flesh, rolling against the bone. He squeezes, biting down on a scream as pain boils up the appendage, and is rewarded by a shiny bit of metal that pokes through his skin amid a burst of pus. Kerry pinches it between thumb and forefinger and slides out the two inches of needle that broke off inside his arm from Solomon's syringe.

"Rot in hell, you sick asshole," he whispers. Knocking the man down the stairs into the flames is one of the sweetest memories of his life. "I hope you were still conscious when that fire burned you up."

The water in the sink is clear, but it never warms. He uses it to get himself as clean as possible before putting on the fresh clothes, which are a size too big, then heads down the hall toward the voices.

At the end he finds the house's living room, as used and abused as the rest of the place. A couch in about the same shape as the one he slept on is against one wall, except this one is currently supporting a huge pile of plastic baggies filled with white powder; cocaine or, more likely, heroin, prepackaged for sale on the street. A card table sits in the middle of the room, with two black guys gathered around it in lawn chairs, hunched over a laptop and laughing at something on the screen. Kerry doesn't know if either one of them were in the car last night, but he recognizes the big, dreadlocked dude lounging in the doorway on the far side of the room as the driver. All three of them grow quiet and stare when he comes around the corner.

"I...I'm sorry," he stammers, trying not to stare at the drugs. "I was...looking for D'libra."

"She left last night, after makin you *my* problem," Dreadlocks says. "Went to go check in with her parole officer so she can get a new place to live. You know, since somebody murdered all her roommates and burned her fuckin house down."

"So you the big deal psycho killah, huh?" one of the guys at the table asks with a smirk. "Shit, my grandma scarier'n you."

"That's how it works, muhfuckah," the other one tells him. "The craziest dudes is the ones that don't look crazy at all. That's how they get close enough to slit yo throat'n shit."

"Right right right."

"I didn't kill anybody," Kerry says.

"Yo, that ain't what the news is sayin." The second guy goes to work on his laptop, typing quickly, then spins the device around to face Kerry. A pre-recorded news segment from a local affiliate begins playing, and Kerry hunches over the table to watch.

The female reporter begins speaking over nighttime footage of Hopeful Sunshine, but the entire front of the house he spent so much time restoring is burnt to cinders, all but unrecognizable. Dozens of cops and fire fighters comb the smoking wreckage. There's some details on the fire, then

Kerry's own face fills the screen, that mug shot which has become so handy for so many people.

"Police are not releasing details about the number or condition of the bodies found inside the group home, but house resident Kerry Denton is considered the sole suspect at this time. Denton, a convicted sex offender, fled police at the scene, possibly with the help of others, and is being sought for questioning."

"I saw it! I saw it all!" Suddenly Mark is there, shouting frantically into a microphone while he sits on the back of an ambulance with a blanket around his shoulders. "Kerry went nuts and killed them all, then torched the house! There was blood all over him! He even attacked me one time! Probably killed his roommate, too! He's completely crazy!"

"*You lying asshole!*" Kerry smashes a fist into the laptop screen before he can stop himself, sending the device sliding across the table.

"C'mon, man," the guy who played the video for him says reproachfully, pulling the computer away. "Do I come over to yo crib and punch shit?" He stops the playback as the reporter begins rehashing the circumstances of Ray's death.

"It's not true," Kerry says, but the reassurance is mostly for himself. "They'll figure it out. They probably haven't ID'd Solomon's body yet. Soon as they do, they'll understand."

"You. In here," Dreadlocks tells him, pointing into the room behind him. Kerry follows him into the kitchen, which seems to be the cleanest room in the house, although that doesn't mean much. He crosses his thick arms and says, "I don't know you, man, and I don't give a shit 'bout you or what you did or didn't do. If I knew it was the cops shootin at you last night, I never woulda let you in the fuckin car. D'libra vouched for you, so I took you in as a favor, but this ain't no bed and breakfast. The last thing I need is the pigs trackin a fugitive to my doorstep. One night is all you get. Soon as Leeb gets back, yo ass is out on the street. Feel me?"

"Yes. Absolutely. Thank you." *Fugitive*; the word carries a strange, foreign weight in Kerry's mind. Jesus, is that what he is? After the shock of his encounter with Solomon, his only desire was to put distance between himself and anyone who wanted to kill him. Unfortunately, that group included the police, although he's sure that a shoot-first-ask-questions-later disposition is typically frowned upon for officers.

"Good. And keep in mind, you tell anyone 'bout what you saw up in here, I will find you no matter where you are and shoot you in the fuckin face."

"My lips are sealed."

"Then we square." Dreadlocks nods and walks away, toward a cooler on the counter. "You want somethin to drink? I got water and Coke. Oh, and some beers."

"Water, please."

Dreadlocks tosses him an ice cold bottle. Kerry chugs most of it while the other man studies him. "So what the hell'd you do to get on Leeb's good side anyway? Cause she wadn't takin no for an answer 'bout you stayin here last night."

Kerry shrugs, but something in the man's tone causes a thought to pop into his head. "How...how do you know her? Are you two, uh...?"

"*Sheeeit* no." Dreadlocks chuckles. "Prob'ly be like stickin my dick in a bear trap. We just went to school together, man. She helped me get started sellin, but couldn't keep away from the product. When she got nailed, the pigs offered her a deal to sell me out, but she never said a word. Did her time like a champ. And I guess she ain't ever gon' let me forget it, cause…here you are." He raises an eyebrow. "'Zat what you wanted to hear, that I wadn't fuckin her?"

"What? *Me?* No, I don't—"

"Yeah, I think you do," the other man interrupts. "And lemme tell you somethin, I don't know what that group home did to Leeb, but she ain't the kind to stick up for a white boy. 'Specially an offender. Then again, she always did have a thing for poor lost puppy dogs, and you 'bout the lostest muhfuckah I evah saw."

Kerry considers this as he returns to the stinking bedroom and stretches out on the couch to wait. He wants to ask for a phone to call his parents so he can tell them the truth, but he's so tired of explaining himself, of hearing his mother cry and plead. An hour later the door opens and D'libra slips into the room.

Her purple-streaked hairs is tied back in a ponytail, and she's wearing a pair of baggy jeans and an ill-fitting white polo, the clothes far more subdued than her usual fashion choices. The change is so drastic it makes her look ten years older. Kerry smirks.

"Yeah, I know," she says, plucking at the hem of the shirt, "but guess what? The girls' side of the house got burnt to shit, so everything I own is ash. Red Cross donated this lovely outfit until I get settled in my new home. Like somethin my damn mama would wear."

"Where they sending you?"

"Some big women's group home downtown. My parole officer said they got a gang problem, but that's okay. Any of those stone cold bitches come at me, I'm gon' take they eyes out."

"God. I'm so sorry."

D'libra sniffs, a tough display, but there's a heavy, far-away look in her eyes as she says, "Can't complain, can I? Considerin everybody else from the crib is fuckin dead."

The words hit him like punches to the chest. He doubles over for a moment on the couch, clutching his stomach, before forcing himself to sit up. There will be time to mourn when he's free of this situation. "What'd you find out?"

"Not much." She shifts her weight from foot to foot as she speaks, an uncharacteristically nervous gesture. "They brought me in, questioned me for like an hour 'bout you. They think...they think you killed Scott and Les and Lorie and then set the fire to cover it up."

"For Christ's sake, didn't you tell them the truth?" Kerry demands.

She scowls at him. "How the fuck was I supposed to do that? I wadn't there, I didn't see it, and if I'd told them I got it directly from you, they woulda arrested me too!"

"But what about Solomon? Surely they have his body too, that's got to prove *something*!"

D'libra's dark brow furrows, and then she says the one thing he's feared this whole time.

"I...I don't think they found the guy."

"No." The word comes out as a moan. "No way is he still alive. No way did he make it out of that house." But already he's wondering, replaying that moment full of confusion and smoke. The knowledge that the psychopath might still be out there makes him feel split in half between terror and a fury so bitter it makes his eyes water.

"There's somethin else." D'libra stands stiffly at the opposite end of the couch, closest to the door. She keeps her eyes on the filthy carpet and says uncomfortably, "They found somethin in yo bed, under the mattress. The cops showed it to me. This sick picture of some kids with they eyes cut out…"

"Solomon sent it to me. Shit, I should've given it to them yesterday, but I forgot all about it."

"Yeah, well, now they think it proves that you a fuckin lunatic." She murmurs this, still staring at the ground.

Understanding begins to dawn on him. "Wait…you don't believe them, do you?"

"Well…you *was* covered in blood last night, and Mark's sayin he saw you do it…"

"Mark is a goddamn liar."

"But that story you told me. It sounded like this dude had every chance in the world to kill you, too. So why rip through all the others and leave you alive?"

It's the same question he's been asking himself. "I don't know. He tried to drug me. Told me that I had to atone, that if I didn't go with him worse things would happen." He sighs and pulls at his hair. "You know, at first I thought he wanted sex offenders to commit suicide because he was too scared to kill them himself. Or maybe because murder is too much of a risk for a guy that's invisible. But obviously he doesn't give a shit about either. So what if getting me to off myself is…I don't know, a key part of whatever delusion is playing out in his head?"

"Like…he doesn't want you to die unless you do it yo'self?"

"Yeah. The only path to 'forgiveness' that he'll accept. And let me tell you, that idea scares me more than any-thing." Kerry sinks down on the couch. He can feel tears welling, and closes his eyes to stop them.

D'libra comes forward—cautiously, almost timidly—and eases down onto the cushion next to him, so close their hips touch. Her hand slides up his wrist to the elbow. The contact sends an electric tingle up his arm that is the polar opposite of the sensation his ghost finger broadcasts. "If you didn't do it, then every second you stay on the run makes it worse, Chester. You gotta turn yo'self in."

He opens his eyes, then hesitantly moves his other hand on top of hers. "Will you come with me?"

Instead of answering, she lunges forward and presses her lips against his. Her hand moves to his lap and squeezes him through his jeans. Kerry kisses her back, urgently, their tongues engaging in a slow, languid massage that pushes every bit of pain and fear and doubt from his head. He catches a faint whiff of that flowery lotion, but he's close enough now to smell her beneath it, a clean, earthy, natural musk that awakens a hungry arousal inside him.

Kerry revels in the scent as she pushes him down on the couch with their mouths still locked together. She somehow unbuttons the oversized jeans and squirms out of them without breaking the kiss, then straddles him. Her long, dark legs crush his waist with a needful pressure. He runs his hands up her bare thighs, across her hips, and around to her ass, which is smooth and soft in his palms. He's rock hard, more aroused than he can ever remember being in his life, although four years in prison undoubtedly contributed to this. She unzips his borrowed pants and reaches inside now, using one hand to stroke that length of steel at his groin. It takes every ounce of willpower not to explode right there in her delicate fingers.

A moment later he's buried in the moist warmth of her, the two of them rocking back and forth, and god, her dreadlocked friend was wrong, because fucking this woman is nothing at all like sticking his dick in a bear trap.

THIRTY FIVE

A half hour later, as they lay naked in a sweaty embrace, Kerry reaches down and runs a finger along the puckered circles crowded around the inside of her elbow.

She jerks away from the contact. "Don't."

"Why not?"

"Cause I don't like nobody touchin 'em."

"So you get to poke and prod at my finger, but I can't touch your precious needle scars?"

D'libra turns her head on his chest to squint up at him. "Why would you even want to?"

"Because it's you," he says simply.

"That's some cheesy ass shit." After seeing a flash of hurt pass over his features, she sighs. "Fine. Go ahead."

He resumes, grazing each track mark with his fingertips. She watches his face as he does it, shivering against him. "So are we on the right side of the line?" he asks.

"Huh?"

"The love line. Where it's wrong on one side and right on the other. You're the expert, you tell me."

"First of all, ain't nobody said nuthin 'bout 'love,' Chester, so cool yo' fuckin jets." She lays her head back down on him. Her voice softens as she says, "Maybe there ain't no sides. Shit, maybe there ain't even a line. Or a purpose or a God. Maybe we all bacteria in a petri dish, floatin around and bumpin into each other, and when shit happens to you, it just happens. Nobody cares, and anybody that pretends to is just doin it to make themselves feel better. And if that's the way it is, then askin for forgiveness is a waste of breath."

The sentiment is close to what he told Ray, but now he understands how wrong it is. Kerry is about to tell her that he cares, when a knock at the door shatters the moment into a million jagged shards. Dreadlocks' rumbling voice drifts through. "You two are way past check-out time, Leeb. Get him the fuck outta here. *Now*."

"Jesus, all right, we're goin! Sheee-it." She stirs and sits up on the couch. Kerry watches her get dressed and wishes desperately they could stay here, in this room, for at least another week. "Don't go gettin another hard-on lookin at my ass. Ain't no time to take care of that thing again."

"I was thinking it's good that we're not living at Hopeful Sunshine anymore. Cause we just violated that 'no fraternizing' policy all to hell."

D'libra grins grudgingly—the expression is rare, and so lovely on her dark face—then leans over to give him another kiss, one much softer and shorter than the last, but that lingers on his lips. "All right, let's get you surrendered, Mr. Outlaw."

He stares at her. "So you'll go with me?"

"Of course. Where you go, I go, shithead. So how you wanna do this?"

"That depends. Can I borrow your phone?"

"Hell no. Sex offenders ain't allowed to use no cell phones. You think I wanna go to jail fo' *yo* scrawny white ass?"

After squeezing a handful of her not-so-scrawny black ass, she hands over the phone.

He dials the number from memory. D'libra listens over his shoulder as the other end is answered and Kerry says, "It's me."

"Fucking shit, Denton," Sanders growls. "Where the hell are you?"

"Someplace safe."

"You think I give a rat's ass if you're 'safe' or not? *Where are you?*"

"I didn't do it."

"Then why the fuck did you run?"

"Cause the cops were shooting at me!"

"Gee, could it be because you murdered three people and burned down a house?"

"He was there, Brad." Kerry strives to keep his voice even. The accusation coming from this man—the one person who's been in his corner from the moment he walked through the prison gates—stings worse than being snubbed by Barb.

"Who?"

"Solomon. The son of a bitch hid in the fucking pantry, waiting to get to me. I wouldn't be surprised if he went straight there after I escaped yesterday. He murdered the others and started the fire. Please tell me you believe me."

Sanders takes so long to answer, Kerry is afraid he hung up. "I want to, Denton. I really do. You seemed like one of those rare ex-cons who was truly trying to get their life straightened out. But for all I know, it was an act, and underneath it you're a raging sociopath. If you're telling the truth, and you're innocent, then running was the shit-all stupidest thing you could've done."

"I told you, the cops tried to shoot me, what was I supposed to do? Besides, I thought Solomon was dead, too. I beat the hell out of him and pushed him down the stairs into the fire. All of this should be over by now. But if they didn't find his body, then…" Kerry lets the thought hang and takes a deep, shuddering breath. D'libra strokes the back of his neck.

"You need to surrender. Immediately. That's the only way to sort through this."

"That's why I'm calling. I'm kinda nervous about getting my jaw broken or a bullet in my stomach before I ever see the inside of a cell, you know?"

"Fine, I'll take you in myself. Where are you?"

Next to him, D'libra begins frantically shaking her head.

"I can't tell you that. Can you meet me somewhere?"

His parole officer makes a grunting noise of disgust. "I'm beginning to wonder why I keep sticking my neck out for you, Denton. Can you make it back to the grocery store down the street from the house?"

"I'll find a way."

"Okay, it's…three o'clock now. Let's try to keep you out of public so you don't get arrested before you can surrender. Meet me in the back parking lot at 7:30, after the place closes. After I see that you show up, I'll call ahead to the detective working the case and let him know I'm bringing you in. If you get caught before then, you're on your own, we never had this conversation."

"All right. I'll be there."

"And Denton?" Sanders' voice hardens to steel. "I *will* have my gun. If you try anything, I will not hesitate to take you down." He hangs up before Kerry can reply.

With a little bullying, D'libra convinces Dreadlocks to loan her a car, a beat-up Toyota with deeply tinted windows and the serial numbers stripped off. They leave the drug den and spend the next few hours motoring around Dallas, getting food from a drive-thru, then eating in the car at a public park, too afraid to get out in case someone should recognize him. They talk the entire time, easy, pleasant conversation that it somehow feels wrong to be having in their current situation. He should be freaking out about the police, about Solomon, wracked with guilt over the horrific deaths of the people he's lived with for the past two months, but being with her keeps him from sliding into self-pity. She's so unlike Kayla, unlike any female he would normally go for. Kerry has no idea what this is between them, where it can possibly be going, and finds that he doesn't much care. If the last four years have taught him anything, it's that only this moment matters, only this snapshot of happiness is guaranteed.

And, when the moment finds their lips together again, he pulls her into the vehicle's cramped back seat, where they screw each other once more, until his sore hip is screaming from the repeated thrusting.

It's 7:15 by the time she drives them into the parking lot behind Caulfield's. Kerry hasn't been here since the day he almost got lynch-mobbed in front of the store. They sit holding hands and watch the employees come filing out of the grocery store for the night. Back here, they're hidden from the traffic on the main road and the freeway access. The sun is down, and the darkness beyond the parking lot lights grows steadily deeper, adding to a buzz of anxiety in Kerry's chest. Anything can be out there in that darkness, waiting for him.

At 7:35, Sanders' white Honda pulls into the lot and parks facing them with the lights on.

D'libra squeezes Kerry's hand, her palm brushing the stump of his ring finger. "I'll go with you as far as I can, Chester. And I'll be waitin when they let you go."

"Don't make promises," he tells her.

They get out of the car and walk across the pavement, still holding hands. Sanders opens his door and stands there in another one of his quirky t-shirts with his jaw unhinged. "D'libra…is that you? Christ, *you're* the one that got him out of there? You realize, if they find out you lied when they questioned you, you could get your parole revoked."

"Then make sure they don't find out. Far as they know, I'm just escortin my man to prove his innocence."

The parole officer's eyes stray down to their clasped hands. "You two…are an item?"

"You got a problem with ebony and ivory?"

"Generally speaking, no. But if a meteor came out of the sky right now and hit me dead between the eyes, I think I'd be less surprised by that than I am by the idea of you two cozied up in front of a fire with a glass of chardonnay."

"Damn, is that what you white people do in your spare time?"

"Honestly, I'm fascinated. How in the world did this hap—?"

"Shut up and drive, Sanders."

She opens the back door and climbs in, shoving the mountain of file folders out of her way. Kerry goes to follow her, but Sanders puts a hand on his shoulder. The parole officer holds up a pair of handcuffs. "Sorry, but I can't look complicit in this. You're technically under arrest."

"Oh, this is bullshit!" D'libra screeches from inside the car.

Kerry puts his hands behind his back. The snap of the cuffs closing and the cold steel on his wrists sends a sharp spike of claustrophobia through his chest.

Suddenly, the idea of going back to prison is very real, and he wants to kick and scream and run away until it fades back into an abstract.

Sanders escorts him around to the passenger door, saying that he'll have more room up front than in the back. He leans the seat back a little before helping Kerry duck his head to get inside. As he fastens the seatbelt over him, the parole officer says, "For what it's worth, I *do* believe you."

"Yeah, I can tell."

"I want to do this by the book so we don't give them anything else to use against you. The sooner we clear your name, the sooner the cops can find the maniac responsible for all this."

The parole officer goes around, gets behind the wheel, and starts the engine. The reclined seat definitely helps, but Kerry still works to get his cuffed arms into a comfortable position under him as they drive across the dark parking lot toward the street. D'libra leans forward and trails a fingernail down his cheek.

"You know, the bright side to this," Sanders begins, "is that you're gonna make a shitload of money selling the rights to your story."

Kerry twists his head to tell him that he wants to be played by Chris Pratt, but is dazzled by a pair of high beams that burst into existence through the driver's side window. He has enough time to register that they're quickly growing bigger before a thunderous, grinding crash envelops him. The world lurches in dizzying circles that first strain him one way and then fling him the other direction at the passenger door. He rolls face first into the hard plastic. A bright flash of pain blots out all sensation.

The car's spinning motion comes to an abrupt halt. Kerry can hear the engine making a sickly sputtering noise. He's aware of something wet dribbling down his lips and chin, but it takes another few seconds before the disorientation clears and he can make sense of the situation.

He's laying sideways in his seat now, cuffed arms wrenched uncomfortably behind him and head jammed between the headrest and the window. The blood running down his face left black streaks on the glass, but he can see Caulfield's on the other side, across a dark stretch of tarmac. His nose throbs and, when he tries to move, a heavy boulder rolls around behind his forehead. He keeps squirming though, trying to roll over far enough to check on the others.

The front quarter of the car on the driver's side is crumpled, with ribbons of smoke leaking out around the mangled hood. In the seat next to him, Sanders groans as he uses the steering wheel to pull himself upright and then falls back clutching his chest. "Aw shiiit...I think I busted some ribs," he mutters through clenched teeth.

Kerry swallows a mouthful of coppery blood and cranes his head around. "Leeb, are you all r..."

She's sprawled across the back seat amid the scattered files, breathing but not moving. A crimson sheet runs down her face from a swollen gash on her forehead.

"*D'libra!*" Bright, hot fear fills his veins. Kerry thrashes in his seat, struggling against both the seatbelt and handcuffs, unable to think of anything but reaching her.

"*Get outta the car!*" a deep voice from outside shouts.

Kerry peers through the rear window and sees the vehicle that slammed into them sitting ten yards away: a big red pickup truck with a sturdy front grill that's barely even damaged from the collision. The headlights are still on, but through the glare Kerry can see two shadows in the cab, their heads peeking over the dash. Even though he can see no details, it's not hard to imagine one of them wearing a trucker hat and the other sporting a mullet.

"Is that your guy?" Sanders asks.

It takes a moment for Kerry to understand that he means Solomon. "I don't think so," he whispers. "Get me out of these cuffs."

"Hold on." Sanders rolls down his window as the engine of his car gives a last wheeze. "What the hell do you think you're doing?" he yells, his voice strained. "I'm a cop!"

"*Yer a parole officer!*" the other replies.

"*We just want the pervert!*" a second voice adds. "*Send him out here and you can go!*"

"Fuck you, I'm calling for backup!"

A flat crack rolls across the empty parking lot, and Sanders' side mirror explodes.

"*Jesus, get down!*" the parole officer shouts, hunching lower.

Thanks to the reclined seat, Kerry is already low, but now he scoots down, kneeling in the floorboard, and bends over to lay his head on the center console. "Take the cuffs off!" he pleads.

Sanders reaches over, but instead of freeing him, he opens the glovebox and takes out the pistol inside. He leans forward and opens fire through the window, three quick, barking reports, then ducks back into cover. "*Put your weapons down and get on the ground!*"

"Brad, listen to me! Those guys work for MacCallum!"

Sanders blinks at Kerry in the dim car as this information registers. Finally he reaches forward and pulls his keyring out of the ignition. "I'll cut you loose, then I need you to use my phone to call for help while I hold them off."

As he reaches for the handcuffs, a figure appears in the open window beside him.

Kerry's breath catches in his throat as the barrel of a rifle slides into the car through the open window, pointed at the parole officer's chest. Fire blossoms from the end, accompanied by a ringing boom. Sanders jumps before slumping over against the door with a red circle spreading across the front of his t-shirt.

His killer leans down to the window and leers at Kerry from beneath the brim of a green trucker hat.

"Mighty nice of him ta gift wrap ya for us," he says with a sneering grin.

"*You son of a bitch!*" Kerry screeches, his voice so shrill it comes out a scratchy whisper. He thrashes in his bindings as the passenger door is opened behind him. A hairy arm slips around his neck in an air-stealing headlock. He's yanked backward. Kerry looks up into the leathery face of the man with the mullet.

"Keep your mouth shut, pedo," he growls, "or this is gonna get a lot more painful."

Kerry is dragged out of the car by his throat. Once he's on the ground, the pressure on his windpipe disappears, allowing him to pull in a gasping breath. Mullet hooks an arm through his elbows and drags him across the pavement toward the truck. "Grab the keys to these cuffs," he tells Trucker Hat. "And don't leave any fingerprints, for fuck's sake!"

The other man hesitates at the rear window of the car. "What about the black girl?"

"Dunno. Boss didn't say anything about her bein here."

"Well, we can't leave 'er. Not alive, anyway."

"*Don't you fucking touch her!*" Kerry screams, and receives a swift kick in the side with a steel-toed boot.

Mullet sighs as if this is all one of life's minor inconveniences. "Bring 'er along, I guess. I'd rather Rob Mac make the call, if he wants 'er dead."

Kerry is dragged to the bed of the truck, where both men lift him up by arms and ankles. He glimpses the shiny metal cargo box behind the cabin before he's dumped inside and the lid is slammed shut, sealing him into absolute darkness.

THIRTY SIX

He doesn't know how long he rides in the stifling steel coffin. Millennia, it seems. He only manages to not succumb to outright panic by reminding himself that, compared to Solomon's machinations, this isn't a terrible confinement. At least he can relax his muscles without fear of death.

And he keeps his mind busy by trying to figure out how, exactly, these two murderous rednecks knew where to find him.

At last the swaying of the truck stops. Kerry strains to catch outside sounds but hears nothing until the lid of his tomb is thrown open a few seconds later. After so long in the dark, the flood of moonlight is bright enough to momentarily blind him. Both men yank him out and carry him roughly between them as before, like villagers with a human sacrifice to toss over a cliff.

His eyes clear, and Kerry sees that they are at another of Robert MacCallum's construction yards, this one closed and empty for the night. The footsteps of his captors crunch loudly in loose gravel as they cross the dark lot, cutting through the chirp of crickets. Kerry can't see beyond the boundaries of the yard because of the high fence surrounding it, but, based on the silence and the fact that they haven't bothered to gag him, he doesn't see any point in yelling for help.

The structure in the middle looks like it might end up a huge, cube-shaped, multiple story edifice—perhaps a condo block or office complex—but at the moment only its lower two floors are closed in. The upper two-thirds are comprised of partially completed walls that climb up one side of the building in a jagged arc, like a giant took a bite out of the structure. The missing exterior exposes the skeletal innards of the building, ladders and scaffolding that lead upward through a tangle of steel beams that remind Kerry of a gigantic, three-dimensional game of Donkey Kong. A crane parked next to the building towers over him in the night sky as he's carried inside.

This bottom floor is a maze of sheetrock hallways that all look the same, lit by a few electric lanterns left atop stacks of building materials like a trail of glowing breadcrumbs. They go through a door into a dark stairwell, then up a single flight of steps. Both of his captors are panting and grunting with effort as they carry him onto the second floor of the building and into a wide atrium covered with painting tarps. Kerry catches site of several rooms walled-off by frosted glass that will probably become lavish offices for some corporate tycoon before they pass into more dim, cluttered hallways. Cameras of the closed circuit variety are already mounted in strategic corners, along with speaker boxes for a PA system. Finally, he's brought into an unfinished space lit by a single row of bare fluorescent lights overhead that create crisp shadows. Trucker Hat and Mullet carry him past a tiny desk and filing cabinet and slam him down in a low office chair. The handcuffs are unlocked and then quickly replaced after his arms are pulled behind him, through the armrests and around an exposed pipe, simultaneously attaching him to the wall and the seat. The keys go in Mullet's shirt pocket, then both men walk out of the room and close the door. There's the unmistakable click of a lock engaging.

Kerry immediately strains until his back hurts and the handcuffs threaten to dislocate his wrists, but neither gives in the slightest. He could probably tip the chair over, but the way his limbs are positioned, the maneuver would end up breaking his arms. And even if he got free, there's nowhere to go, nothing that can help him, not even a telephone. Up in the corner, one of those cameras watches him with a blank, glassy eye.

Don't panic, he tells himself as his breaths begin to shorten. *Please don't panic.*

Oh no, why should you panic? This is the second time in two days you've been kidnapped and tied up; it's getting to be a lifestyle for you by now.

He's still desperately searching for options when the door unlocks and in walks Rob Mac himself, flanked by his henchmen.

The man looks better tonight. Or less like a walking corpse, at least. Although part of that might be the gleeful fury that infects his eyes as he catches sight of Kerry. The emotion isn't pretty, but it does bring some life to his face. He's wearing khaki pants and a polo emblazoned with the name of his self-made company, which, of course, is just his own name, a testament to his ego. One hand clenches a folded slip of paper hard enough to crumple it.

The sight of him starts Kerry's shortened finger throbbing, a pain that quickly gains enough strength to compete with his swollen nose and various other aches and pains.

Mullet and Trucker Hat—the former with a pistol, the latter with the rifle he used to kill Sanders—wait beside the door like sentinels while their boss comes forward, drops the paper onto the desk nearby, and stands in front of Kerry with arms crossed. The burning lights in the middle of the room stream across his face, carving deep lines into his craggy skin and throwing a shadow version of him onto the wall to Kerry's left, like an escaping prisoner caught in the spotlight from a guard tower.

"I have to say," MacCallum begins, the barest hint of a smile playing around his chapped lips, "it's a real pleasure seeing you like this. Does my heart good."

"The only thing that would do your heart good is having someone put a stake through it," Kerry snarls. "Where's D'libra?"

"That the jungle bunny? She's alive, for now. Not that it concerns you much."

"You can let her go. She didn't see anything, she doesn't know anything. You...you can just let her go and then we can do...whatever this is."

"Whatever this is," the other man repeats, and makes a hoarse barking noise that Kerry almost doesn't recognize as laughter. "You know Denton, you're a real piece of work. *Whatever this is.* As if you have no idea why you're here right now." The laughter dies and he swallows hard enough for his Adam's apple to yo-yo. "I promised you this would happen. Didn't I? And I always keep my promises."

"Listen to me," Kerry says slowly. He'd told Sanders that he was a lot less scared of Robert MacCallum after facing Solomon, but he finds such a fact still leaves a lot of wiggle room. He's careful to keep his voice confident and calm though. Something tells him that giving this man a whiff of his burgeoning panic will be like blood in a shark tank. "You need to stop and think about what you're doing before this goes any further."

"Oh, I have. I've thought about nothing *but* this for four years. In fact..." He points at the camera mounted in the corner, taking in the entire room. "That's why I brought you here. To record all of this. So I could relive this moment over and over and over again."

Kerry shakes his head. "God, you're so fucking sad."

"*Me?*" The word comes out as an incredulous squawk. "I'm not the ex-con living in a goddamn halfway house! Let me tell you something fuckhead, life may've taken my family, but I still got more money and power than you could ever dream of!"

This proclamation so perfectly encapsulates the man's entire world view that Kerry can imagine him giving such a succinct elevator pitch to his investors. No one could ever be pathetic or alone as long as they have wealth and control. And, of course, he alone is personally responsible for all of his good fortune, while the nebulous specter of 'life' is at fault for the bad. But explaining this to him would be like trying to convince a salmon it would be easier to spawn downstream, so Kerry continues with the point he's trying to make.

"Not for long, you don't." He shifts his gaze past Mac-Callum to nod at the two men across the room. "What you said last time...you might be right. You could probably put a bullet in my brain on the steps of the White House and no one would give a shit. I'm a sex offender, right? P is for Predator. But your boys over there...they killed a cop tonight. You know that, right?"

"He wasn't a cop, he was a babysitter for human garbage. That's what he gets for trying to help scum like you."

"Tell that to the police when they hunt all three of you down, see how much good your money and power do you. If they find out you put these two geniuses up to it, you'll go to prison right along with them. Maybe you can have my old room at Wayne Clifford."

MacCallum cocks his head a few degrees to the side, scattering those shadows on his craggy face. "Son, there's nothing connecting me to any of this. No one even knows what your parole officer was doing there. And if they figure that much out, well…what's to stop them from thinking *you* did it?"

Kerry doesn't realize there's dismay on his face until MacCallum's lips wrinkle back in a bizarre, rictus-like grin of triumph. The expression is so feral, it's like this man forgot how to exhibit a genuine human smile.

"Yeah, that's right," he continues, speaking through his bared teeth. "Everyone in the state is hunting for your ass as we speak. Way I hear it, you mighta killed a cop yourself. Along with half those dirt bags you were shacking up with."

He comes closer, bends down to move that terrible grin level with Kerry's eyes.

"Funny, I always knew you were a pedophile, Denton. But I never pegged you for a psychopath, too. That a hobby you picked up in prison?"

"I didn't do it." The familiar phrase rasps over Kerry's dry, blood-crusted lips, a sentiment that will be etched on his tombstone. He shrivels like a snail with salt poured on it while MacCallum is more alive with every passing second. "I didn't do any of those things they're saying."

"Sure you didn't. Like you didn't rape my daughter."

Kerry has heard that word a thousand times—in court, in prison, from Solomon. Total strangers have condemned him for this and so much worse. And it stung every time, even with that clunky, legalese 'statutory' in front of it. But somehow, coming out of this man's mouth, the accusation jolts him worse than ever before. His phantom finger sends a blast of imaginary lightning up his arm.

"That's not what happened. We were in love. You can deny it all you want, but somewhere inside your twisted brain, you know it's true."

"Oh really? You believe she loved you? Cause you seem to think I was an awful father. But if I was so terrible, then maybe she just used you to get away from me. You ever think of that?"

Kerry nods. "I have. And maybe she did. But this isn't about her. It's about me. And I know what I felt."

MacCallum takes a long moment to answer, studying Kerry's face as he does. "I've spent such a long time hating you, Denton," he says quietly. "I paid that guard Pedernales to make sure your life was torture. Paid the warden to keep putting you in solitary, to see if you'd crack. All the things I've done since you got out…they were all for my daughter. I've never forgotten her, never let her face slip from my mind for a minute. Now, *that's* love. *That's* devotion. Whatever you felt for her wasn't anything close. You've proven that."

"How do you figure?"

"Let me ask you something." MacCallum relents at last, backing away toward the desk. "You and that black girl fucking? What am I saying, of course you are. Only trash like her would let that child-raping dick of yours inside them."

He grabs the small square of paper he brought into the room with him, unfolds it, and holds it up. Kayla stares out from one of her school pictures, freshman or maybe even sophomore year, just before she met Kerry. He realizes he hasn't set eyes on her since the night before his arrest. She's different than the memories he's clung to, less vibrant somehow. Almost plain. As if the reality of her could never live up to the ideal he's built. Nevertheless, the image dumps an oozing bucket of warm guilt over the top of his head. The throb in his finger kicks up a notch, bad enough to make his teeth grind…but the pain also serves to dampen his fear.

"Oh, so you remember her?" MacCallum holds the picture out. His hand trembles in front of Kerry's face, making the image blur. "I'm surprised. All that talking you did… bringing me that stupid fucking ring…jabbering on about how you wanted to spend the rest of your life with her… But that didn't last too long, did it? You moved on to the next piece of ass that jiggled by, like I knew you would."

"Are you goddamn kidding me?" Sweat beads on Kerry's forehead, drips down his cheeks. "First you hate me because I dared to fall in love with her, now you hate me because I'm not still pining away for her? What, was getting me thrown in prison some kind of elaborate test to see if I was quality son-in-law material?"

"If it was, you failed."

"What. The fuck. Do you want. From me."

"*I want you to cherish her, goddamn it!*" MacCallum shouts. "After my wife died, I never so much as *looked* at another woman! You say you loved Kayla, then show some faithfulness! It's the least you could do since you got her killed!"

"That is not fair," Kerry whispers. But part of him thinks it is though, *knows* it is, has *always* known, and that part is his ghost finger, the piece of him which wore his commitment to Kayla MacCallum, a circular shield that proved he was more than a predator. Now it will never wear a ring again, will never stop haunting him, and the burning pain that radiates up his arm is excruciating.

"No." The other man comes forward, holding the picture out like a cross against a vampire. "'Not fair' is trying to raise your daughter—your one child—by yourself, only to have her seduced by a perverted piece of shit. 'Not fair' is even when you manage to get the fucker away from her, she k…kills herself…" His fury breaks like a wave on a rocky shore, the last two words coming out a gasp.

Kerry tears his eyes away from the picture and meets the man's gaze as directly as possible. "I meant what I said. I never wanted to hurt her."

"But you did. You did hurt her. And I want to hear you say it." He comes closer, shoves the picture in Kerry's face. His voice slips into a reedy, breathless register. "You look at her, and tell me it's your fault. All of it. You're responsible. I want to hear it from your own mouth."

"What difference will it make?" Kerry pleads. Responsibility; it's all anyone wants from him. "It won't change anything. Don't you see that?"

"Let's find out. Admit you abused her, you son of a bitch. Admit you got her killed. I deserve the truth."

"I did," Kerry says, tears mingling with the sweat on his cheeks, "I got her killed because I wasn't there to save her, but the only one who abused her is you. You gave her more bruises than—"

The blow comes so fast, Kerry doesn't even register it until a half second after it happens. Pain boils across the right side of his face. His mouth fills with fresh blood; two of his teeth wiggle when his tongue brushes them. He probably would've fallen out of the chair if not for his cuffed hands.

"*Shut the fuck up!*" MacCallum roars. He's shaking all over, and crushes the picture in his palm as he leans over Kerry, eyes bugged out of his skull.

"You're delusional." Blood dribbles into Kerry's lap as he speaks, from what he suspects is a split lip. An overwhelming weariness steals over him. All he wants is for this to be over, to be finished with fear and doubt and pain and phantom limbs. To find peace, one way or another. In that moment, he truly wishes he'd let himself flip over in Solomon's harness. "You think you're the hero of this story, but you're not. Punishing me is just a distraction so you don't have to face your own guilt. You beat your wife and you beat your daughter, and they both killed themselves because of it. Jesus Christ, if you need help understanding why Kayla committed suicide, look at yourself. Imagine how she would look at you if she were here. So if you think you're gonna bully me into saying whatever you need to hear, you can think again, motherfucker. Cause I've been tortured by a lot worse than you."

Each word out of his mouth adds a darker shade to the red color creeping up Robert MacCallum's neck and into his cheeks. He's still shaking, his teeth grinding together audibly. The picture falls out of his hand and flutters to the floor.

"*Then I'll fucking KILL YOU!*"

MacCallum wades into him with mindless fury, raining blows down from all directions. His big fists pummel Kerry's defenseless head back and forth, back and forth, each punch scrambling his brains a little more. The pain is sharp at first and then begins to fade, like a stereo with the volume slowly being turned down. Then those hands go to his throat and squeeze, crushing his windpipe, and, as a veil of darkness drops over Kerry's vision, he understands that the last thing he will ever see in his life is Robert MacCallum's snarling, red-hued face.

But he's still conscious enough to hear the disembodied voice that booms across the room.

"Mr. MacCallum," it says, "please remember that killing him would be a violation of our agreement."

THIRTY SEVEN

Robert MacCallum's mouth drops open in shock as he lets go of Kerry's throat. The desperate breath he sucks in and coughs out is like hot coals. Across the room, the two meatheads gape at the ceiling in amazement, as if the voice of God Himself just spoke.

"I apologize for interrupting," the amplified voice continues, as polite as a waiter letting them know their table is ready. Even as he tries to pull air through his bruised throat, Kerry recognizes that monotone, gravelly cadence. "But your anger seems to have gotten the better of you. I understand how frustrating that young man can be, however, I knew you wouldn't want to end things prematurely. Especially since the terms of our arrangement were so clearly defined."

MacCallum recovers from his surprise, and turns to the PA speaker mounted in the corner of the room, beneath the camera. He stands up with his hands fisted at his sides.

"You listen to me, you bastard," he announces. Trucker Hat and Mullet stare at him as if he just started writing on the walls with his own feces. "I don't make deals with people who call outta the blue and refuse to give me so much as a name. You may think you got some balls coming here, but this boy is *mine*, and I'll do whatever I want with him. You got that?"

A heavy sigh comes from the speaker. "I thought we were on the same page. I guess I was wrong. Of course...if what Mr. Denton said about you is true...then perhaps you and I need to have a very different conversation."

Without another word, MacCallum marches across the room and wrenches the pistol from Mullet's hand. He aims it into the corner of the room and opens fire wildly, each gunshot loud enough to claw at the eardrum in the enclosed space. It takes four bullets, but the camera and PA speaker finally explode in a shower of plastic and circuitry.

"He's in the goddamn control room!" MacCallum bellows at his henchmen.

"Uh...*who* is, Boss?" Trucker Hat asks, shooting a nervous glance at his cohort. "Who was that?"

MacCallum clenches his free hand in front of his face while jabbing the barrel of the pistol at the ceiling. The other two men draw away from him. "I...I don't know! Just get down there and *bring that shitheel back to me!*"

They open the door and rush out of the room looking both reluctant and relieved, Trucker Hat with his rifle, Mullet unarmed now that his pistol has been taken. As soon as they're gone, MacCallum begins to pace beside the door, with the nervous agitation of a caged lion.

Or a convict.

"What deal did you make?" Kerry croaks. The question is coated in shards of broken glass. His face is hot and tight, and he thinks one of his eyes is swelling closed. The other man doesn't answer, so he forces himself to continue. "That's him, you know. The lunatic who killed all those people."

MacCallum stops his pacing and looks at Kerry without speaking, eyes glassy and face unreadable.

"*He* told you where I'd be," Kerry whispers, as understanding dawns on him. "That's how you knew. Of course, he…hacked Brad's phone or something, in case I called. He tells you, you get to beat up on me for a while and, in exchange, you have to give me to him after you're through."

"Or the police." MacCallum's voice is even quieter than Kerry's. "He just wanted you hurt. Beyond that, he didn't care what I did with you, so long as I didn't kill you. Said… only you could decide when the punishment was over."

"He used you. Got you to do his dirty work. And you did it, without knowing a thing about him."

"Honestly…I didn't care. I just wanted it to be over." His eyes lose focus, staring through Kerry, beyond the wall, into a world less cruel and unfair than this, perhaps. "Whoever he is, I think he hates you as much as I do."

"Yeah, well, he doesn't sound too happy with you right now either. In fact, I think you and I are probably in the same boat, as far as he's concerned."

The other man continues to gaze through him for a long moment, his brow drawing together in thought so that it forms a deep valley down the center of his forehead. Kerry's never seen him so contemplative. He opens his mouth, as slowly as he did that day in the prison visitation booth, and what comes out is as much of a shock. "She…she left a note—"

Whatever he means to say is interrupted by the distant crack of a gunshot that echoes up the hallway, followed by a scream.

MacCallum charges across the room at him. Kerry closes his eyes, bracing himself for the beating to resume or for the man to put a bullet in his head, but instead he hears a jingle and peeks through his one good eye to find MacCallum removing Sanders's keyring from his breast pocket. He kneels beside the chair, and, a second later, Kerry's arms are free from the handcuffs.

"Stand up!" MacCallum orders, hitting the back of the chair with the pistol. At first, Kerry can't remember how to make his body work, but then, somehow, he's on his feet. The floor lurches from side to side beneath him, like the deck of a ship in rough seas. He catches sight of Kayla's picture a few feet away, staring up at him. MacCallum steps on it as he slips behind Kerry, wraps an arm around his throat, and puts the gun to his head. The man maneuvers him across the room and through the door at a pace that Kerry can barely keep up with.

The hallway outside is dim except for a single electric lantern sitting atop a stack of tile, creating a globe of radiance. MacCallum turns him to the right and halts, so that both of them are staring into the deeper darkness that waits further down the hall.

Someone is coming. Kerry hears rapid, shuffling footsteps approaching across the bare concrete corridor, can see flickers of movement weaving through the maze of construction debris. Fear burrows deep into his guts.

"*Stay back!*" MacCallum screeches, his mouth next to Kerry's ear. "*You want him alive? I'll kill him right now if you come any closer!*"

But the figure keeps coming, emerging a moment later into the circle of illumination cast by the lantern.

Mullet stares at them with wide, pleading eyes. Both hands are wrapped around his throat, where blood as black as oil pours between his fingers. He stumbles forward another step, gurgling deep in his throat, before falling against the wall and sliding into the floor.

"Ahhhhh. Ahhhhh." MacCallum begins making a distracted moaning noise that slowly spirals higher, like a man on the verge of sneezing. The gun falls away from Kerry's temple, first aiming over his shoulder at Mullet's corpse, than rising to waver wildly down the hall.

Kerry swings an elbow into his side.

MacCallum grunts in surprise and steps away from him. Kerry follows through with the motion, shoving him into the wall and then lurching past. Every part of his body screams with pain, vertigo turns the world on its side, but he pushes through it all and flees down the hallway toward the atrium and conference rooms he was carried through a half hour before.

"*You chickenshit babyfucker, get back here!*" MacCallum howls.

The gun goes off behind Kerry. Ahead of him, one of the fancy glass wall partitions shatters into a million tinkling shards. Kerry ducks his head as another gunshot sounds and a can of paint explodes to his left. He falls to his hands and knees and then he's crawling around the corner, out of the line of fire, but MacCallum continues to blast away until the hammer clicks empty.

Kerry keeps moving around the periphery of the atrium, using a construction sawhorse to regain his feet. He pulls aside a plastic curtain to reveal an opening in the sheetrock wall and plunges through. Ahead of him is another long hallway, lit by moonlight coming through a window at the far end. This isn't the way he came in, but there's no going back now, he needs a place to hide before his body gives out. He keeps one hand on the wall to steady himself as he stumbles along, trying every door he comes to and finding them all locked.

"*DENTON!*" MacCallum roars behind him. Kerry sees the man's silhouette approaching the plastic sheet across the hallway. There's something long in his hands, and, as he tears the tarp down, Kerry sees it's a fire axe.

"*I'm going to chop you into fucking pieces!*" he screams, voice so shrill it breaks on the last word. "*Then I'm going upstairs to do the same thing to your little black girlfriend! I will bury both of you in the foundation of this building and for the first time since my daughter died I WILL BE ABLE TO SLEEP AGAIN!*"

Kerry runs, drowning in terror, rattling doorknobs as he makes his way down the hall. The far end of the corridor appears to be a dead end. He spots another dark opening in the wall to his right and rushes toward it, steps across the threshold even as he registers the fact that the room beyond is nothing but a small square like a closet and—

His hand catches the edge of the opening as his foot plummets through empty space. The room has no floor. It takes Kerry a heartbeat to realize this is an elevator shaft with no elevator. Two stories below, in what must be a basement level for this building, is a jagged bed of construction debris.

He spins around, spots the staircase that opens on the opposite side of the hallway from the elevator. Kerry moves across to it, starts up, but can't raise his exhausted legs high enough to mount the steps. His foot catches on the second riser and sends him sprawling face down. He doesn't even try to get back up this time, just slithers on his belly, clawing his way up one stair at a time.

A hand latches on to his ankle and yanks him back down.

Kerry turns over in time to see the axe swinging down in a long arc toward his skull. He rolls to the side, and the heavy blade smashes into the concrete steps beside his ear.

"*It wasn't my fault!*" MacCallum is sobbing now. He raises the axe, holds it wobbling in the air above his head. A lightning-fast realization occurs to Kerry: this man has come to believe that killing him will also kill his own guilt. "*She was all I had…and you took her from me!*"

A shadow glides through the hallway behind him. Kerry sees the gaunt form as it approaches, catches the glint of a knife before it rams upward into MacCallum's side.

Robert MacCallum gives a high-pitched whimper. The axe falls from his hands, tumbling over backwards to clatter on the hallway floor. His mouth stretches into a round, shocked O as he clutches at the knife sticking out of his side.

"What did you do to your child?" Solomon asks him. He's still dressed in black but not wearing the toddler mask anymore. Even in the dim light, Kerry can see the hideous burns that stretch across the right half of his face, but the eye that Lorie gouged out is covered by a thick pad of gauze.

"*N-nothing!*" MacCallum insists. He flails away from the killer, backing across the hall as he pulls the knife out of his side and lets it fall from his hand. "*I didn't do anything! I loved her, damn it! I'm not like him!*"

Solomon lunges, grabs him by the front of his shirt, and whispers, "There are other ways to abuse."

He rears back and hits the man in the face with an open palm. The crunch of MacCallum's nose breaking is sharp. He stumbles away in shock, then backpedals in an effort to put space between him and his attacker, one frantic step after another…

And walks right into the yawning elevator shaft.

Robert MacCallum drops out of sight with a confused cry, his money and power doing nothing to save him. It takes an eternity before the crash of his body hitting the bottom echoes back up.

Kerry doesn't wait for it. He flips over and scrambles up the steps on all fours. The staircase folds back on itself half-way between floors and, as he turns the corner, Kerry can see Solomon hurrying up.

The top of the staircase has a collapsible security gate attached to one wall that's been left open. Kerry rushes through it, grabs the metal lattice, and hauls it across the landing with a rusted screech. An open padlock dangles from the latch, and he snaps it closed as Solomon reaches the other side of the gate.

They stare at each other through the steel bars. Solomon's delicate-featured face is a misery, the flesh blackened and covered in oozing blisters. The more severe burns even appear to be infused with melted plastic from his mask, like veins of gold in a rock face. His left eye is covered by that blood-soaked gauze, but the right one fixes on Kerry, its dark iris as impossibly black as a maelstrom. He holds his right arm awkwardly against his body as well; Kerry suspects he was injured in his tumble down the stairs at Hopeful Sun-shine. Now it makes sense, him reaching out to MacCallum for help.

"You're not gonna kill me," Kerry pants. "And we both know it. That's not how your little game is supposed to end."

"No, never you," Solomon agrees. "But let's see what else I can take from you before you finally see things my way."

He spins around and goes down the stairs two at a time.

THIRTY EIGHT

Kerry doesn't even pause long enough to catch his breath, just continues down the new corridor as quickly as his weary legs can carry him. He would love to believe the danger is over, that he bested Solomon yet again, but he's sure the killer isn't leaving. In fact, his parting threat turned Kerry's bone marrow to ice, because he has a strong suspicion what it means.

D'libra. Kerry has been too busy running for his life to worry about her, but now she looms in his mind. Solomon must know she's here, probably even knows where, if he accessed the cameras in the building. Kerry's got to reach her first. Nothing else matters except making sure she's safe.

No one else will die because of him.

MacCallum's unhinged shrieks echo in his head. The man said he would go upstairs to kill her. Maybe she's close.

"Leeb!" Kerry calls her name in a whispered shout. Those waves of fiery pain radiate up his arm from his missing finger; he squeezes his hand into a fist and ignores them. This corridor is shorter than the last, with only a few turnoffs into empty rooms. At the end is a steel door with a push handle. A yellow caution sign proclaims, in big black letters, HARD HATS BEYOND THIS POINT! Kerry shoves the door open and bursts through, then comes to an abrupt halt as a stiff breeze hits him.

He's outside, in the open, unfinished portion of the building. The area in front of him is nothing but a bare metal plane that stretches away in all directions like a football field. Construction equipment and haphazard stacks of material sit everywhere, blocking his view of whatever lies ahead, but to his left, the edge of this temporary roof ends in a sheer concrete lip, beyond which he can see the dark spire of the crane that must have lifted all this up here. Over his head is that network of steel girders hanging in space. Moonlight trickles through them to form a complex pattern of grids on the metal floor at his feet.

Kerry is on the verge of hurrying into one of the other rough hallways that opens onto this construction zone when he hears a muffled cry.

"D'libra!" He shouts it louder now, but the words are snatched away by the wind. It's a warm spring night, but up this high, the breeze whistles through the exposed ribs of the building, cool enough to goosepimple his bare arms. Kerry rushes into the maze of construction debris, following the garbled shouts. He doesn't have to go far before he finds her at the base of a concrete support pillar, her hands duct-taped over her head to a piece of rebar and an oily rag in her mouth, tied around the back of her head. She's struggling like a maniac, throwing her entire body side-to-side as she growls through the gag, but, when she catches sight of him, her eyes grow huge and she drums her feet angrily on the ground.

He crashes to the metal floor beside her in a painful heap, then yanks the gag off her head and presses his lips to hers.

"Jesus Christ Kerry, you look like the end of a *Rocky* movie," she says after they separate.

He waves her concern away, aware of two things at once: that she used his name for the first time, and that he actually prefers 'Chester.' "Are you okay, did they hurt you?" She appears to be in good condition besides the swollen cut on her forehead.

"I don't even know who the fuck 'they' is, I just woke up tied to this fuckin thing! What happened, where are we, where's Brad?"

"Brad is dead." For the first time since he's known her, fear steals into her brown eyes, and he hates that he's the reason for it. Regardless of who's at fault—who's *responsible*—Solomon is right about one thing: all of these people would be much better off if Kerry Denton had never come into their lives. "We need to get out of here."

Kerry goes to work on the duct tape, tearing it away and unraveling enough that she can slip her hands free. She throws her arms around his neck and kisses him, so deeply her tongue grazes his tonsils. As much as he wants to let her keep spelunking, he grabs her shoulders and forces her gently back. "Later, I promise."

"You better."

They stand. Kerry takes her by the wrist and leads her back toward the finished parts of the building, but his legs quickly give. D'libra catches him before he hits the ground, then brings one of his arms around the back of her neck to prop him up. They continue on, Kerry leaning on her and doing his best to keep from blacking out.

The slam of a door brings him back to full consciousness.

Solomon found his way onto the roof from one of the other hallways. He spots them across the construction field and surges forward, scrambling over a stack of sheetrock panels and anything else in his path while still favoring his injured arm.

"Go back!" Kerry shouts. They about-face and plunge into the maze, D'libra dragging him. Kerry regains his balance and pushes her ahead of him, through the narrowing passageways lined with cinderblock pallets and towering piles of sheet metal. He focuses all his energy on keeping up with her as they hurry past a row of silent mini-forklifts and squeeze between two industrial a/c units.

"Was that him?" D'libra hisses as they stop to huddle in the deep shadows beneath a stretch of ductwork. "That Solomon guy?"

Kerry nods and then closes his eyes long enough to sharpen his blurring vision. He could easily fall asleep sitting up. For the first time, he wonders if he has a concussion. "I'm slowing you down. Leave me here and…find some way out of the building. I'll try to lead him away from you."

"Nah uh. That ain't happenin."

"No, it's okay, he won't hurt me, remember?"

D'libra reaches out and flicks him right on his swollen eyelid. The pain is a shockingly crisp bolt of lightning in his brain…but it also chases away the fog. "How many times I gotta tell you, dumbass? Where you go, I go."

She pulls him up. They continue picking their way through the construction at a more deliberate pace. The night is silent up here except for the moan of the wind, offering no clue to Solomon's location. Ahead of Kerry, D'libra rounds a huge power transformer and gives a little squeak of surprise.

They've reached an abrupt edge to the roof. The metal plating ends, revealing more naked girders that make up the remainder of the third floor. Directly below them, the guts of the building are visible all the way to the ground. Kerry can see the construction yard in the moonlight, but the land beyond the fence is a dark smear in all directions, aside from a bright swell of lights on the horizon. Kerry wonders if it's Dallas.

"I know it ain't never come up in conversation," D'libra whispers, "but I got a thing about heights."

"Then don't look down."

"Oh yeah, thanks for that completely original advice. Where to then?"

Their options are limited. They can try to sneak back through the construction. To their left is a scaffolding staircase that leads up into the forest of rafters. To their right...

Solomon steps out from behind a bundle of PVC piping, twenty yards farther along the edge of the roof. He has the thin knife in his hand.

"Goddamn it, leave her alone!" Kerry moves in front of D'libra and stands with his fists balled.

D'libra tugs at him, pleads with him to come. He lets himself be pulled away from the standoff, turns to see her going up the rickety steps of the scaffolding. He follows. The landing at the top opens onto a thin metal strip no more than a yard wide and several long, a loose corrugated panel thrown down so that the workers have something to stand on up here. Girders snake outward in all directions, forming a grid of support beams for the fourth story.

D'libra clutches at his arm. "Shit, there ain't nowhere to go!"

Below them, Solomon reaches the base of the stairs and starts up.

Kerry looks around in desperation and says the only thing he can think of. "We have to go out."

"What?"

He points at one of the steel girders, a foot-wide strut that extends off the incomplete edge of the building. It hangs over nothing but empty space for a stretch before joining to another thick concrete support pillar.

"No, no, no!" D'libra's eyes stretch wide. "Are you fuckin crazy?"

"It's the only way I can protect you."

She shakes her head violently, flinging her purple-streaked hair.

"You just have to make it to the other side."

"I can't! I can't go out there!"

"Hey." Kerry grabs her face. "Where I go, you go. Right?"

D'libra glances from him, to Solomon mounting the steps, and back again. She nods hesitantly.

"Then hang on to me," he tells her. "I will *not* let you fall."

They move to the head of the girder. Kerry takes her clammy right hand with his mangled left and holds on tight as she steps out sideways, sliding each foot along the smooth steel surface. She stares straight ahead, never down. He does the same. As soon as his feet leave contact with the panel, the breeze seems to increase into a gale-force wind, buffeting him back and forth as he strives to keep his balance.

The first few steps are the hardest. Kerry holds his breath as they move further out. From the periphery of his vision, he sees the solid construction floor slide away an inch at a time, until there is nothing below them but the long fall to the ground. D'libra bears down on his hand hard enough to grind the bones. The stump of his ring finger burns between their palms like a hot coal.

He knows when she reaches the far end because she lets go of his hand and wraps both arms around the pillar in a panicked bear hug, pressing her face into the concrete. Kerry puts one hand on her shoulder to steady himself and looks back.

It felt like they must've slid along the girder for miles, but, from out here, Kerry sees it was little more than three yards. Solomon stands at the opposite end, safe on the metal panel, regarding them with his remaining eye. The moonlight makes the pustules on his face look like reptilian scales.

"You can't get to her without going through me," Kerry tells him, speaking loud enough to be heard over the whistle of the wind. "And if you push me off this, it sure ain't gonna be suicide."

"But I *will* get to her," Solomon says, the phrase as simple and matter-of-fact as the sun rising in the morning. "If not today, then tomorrow. Or the next day. And your parents as well. I will make it my business to ensure that you never possess anything good again." He gestures at the girder with the knife. "Or this could all end now. All you have to do is find the courage to…step off."

Kerry chances a look down. The toes of his sneakers stick off the edge of the girder, a fact that sends his balls crawling up into his stomach. He can see four stories straight down, all the way to the dirt of the construction lot. He tries to imagine—*really* picture—what it would be like to leap, how long the fall would take, what thoughts would go through his head, if he would feel the ground shatter his bones and squash his brain into jelly.

"Don't you even fuckin think about it!" D'libra shouts from behind him, as if reading his mind. Her voice is shrill and terrified.

Kerry slowly shifts on the girder while holding on to D'libra. Now he faces Solomon directly, the two of them separated by that thin ribbon of steel. "What happens to her if I do?"

Solomon's eye remains rooted on Kerry as he steps out onto the girder without so much as a wobble, his right arm tucked in close to his chest. For some reason, Kerry thinks of Captain Hook and Peter Pan, sword-fighting atop a ship mast. "After you are dead, her fate is up to her."

"So you'll let her go? How do I know that for sure?"

The killer sighs. "Will you ever understand my intentions, Mr. Denton? Unlike you, she is an innocent."

"Ha!" D'libra's derisive snort is muffled by the pillar. "You don't know me worth shit if you think that, asshole."

Solomon's jaw clenches in a rare show of annoyance. He's inching forward, narrowing the distance between them. "Be that as it may, I have no desire to kill anyone. Not ever."

A sudden gust of wind causes Kerry to teeter on the steel beam. He presses back into D'libra to steady himself, heart thundering in his chest. He doesn't want to die, certainly not like this, but to save D'libra, to save his parents, he thinks he could do it.

The problem, however...the one thing that makes him hesitate...is the knowledge that, even if this psychopath keeps his word, he will *still be out there*, going through this same horrible routine with someone else, and telling himself that he's doing it for the children.

Kerry decides, here and now, that he cannot allow that to happen.

Even if it's his last act on this earth.

"Yeah, you're a real saint," he says, pouring on the sarcasm. "You tore through all of my roommates, but you didn't *want* to do it, right? They were just collateral damage from your little crusade."

Solomon has crossed half the distance to him. Now he stops and holds up the knife, his hand curling around the handle until the knuckles go white. "Their deaths are on your head, not mine."

"Oh, of course, all my fault. I'm sure you didn't get off on it even the tiniest bit. Like watching me rub one out wouldn't've gotten you hard either."

Beneath his blistered lips, Solomon's teeth clench. "I am merely an instrument of punishment. I presented you with a choice, the same way I am now. The same way I did the others. But I'm beginning to think you're more of a monster than any of them."

Kerry laughs. He can't help it. "You know what I realized while MacCallum beat the shit out of me in there? You went about this the wrong way. Tried to push the wrong buttons in me. I don't feel guilty for sleeping with her. I feel guilty because I wasn't there to protect her from *him*. If you'd worked that angle, you probably could've convinced me to put a rope around my neck a long time ago. But that would've required you to admit that we were in love, wouldn't it?"

"*LOVE IS NOT AN EXCUSE FOR THE THINGS WE DO TO EACH OTHER!*" Solomon roars. He tilts his burned face back and gnashes his teeth at the moon like a werewolf. "*My father told me he loved me EVERY night before he pulled down my pants and forced his way inside me! My mother said the same thing while she recorded it!*" He breaks off abruptly and looks around, as though suddenly confused about where he is. He takes a deep breath and whispers, barely loud enough to be heard, "Love doesn't protect you from the darkness."

"So that's what this is." Kerry shakes his head. "You're no *instrument of punishment*. You're just a fucked-up guy trying to work out your daddy issues. Taking revenge wherever you can."

Solomon's nostrils flare. "My reasons are irrelevant. But you...you may not know it yet, but you need this. I assure you, the others all found their decency—their *humanity*—when they accepted responsibility."

"You know what I think? I think they accepted your offer because you threatened their families, like you did mine." Something happens in the killer's wrecked face at this accusation, a muscle tic or eye movement, something so minute that Kerry can't point it out, but his subconscious recognizes it all the same: acknowledgment. "But you already know that, don't you? That's how come they never talk after you torture them, never try to get help. Why they kill themselves. So you won't hurt the people they love. That's why you research them; you're making sure they'll fit into the little story you're writing." He laughs again, even though he finds nothing about this amusing. "Jesus, what did you hold over Ray, his paper animals? The voices in his head?"

"No. Just his one friend in the entire world." A small, satisfied grin touches Solomon's mouth. "He would've gone to any lengths to protect you."

Kerry at first thinks someone dumped a bucket of boiling water over his head, before realizing that it's fury heating him from the inside like a microwave, flowing down into all his extremities. The fire in his hand races upward to meet it, igniting him in one big inferno of guilt and anger, the only emotions he's truly felt since walking into Wayne Clifford, the two most dangerous sentiments in the human emotional spectrum. His vision narrows until all he can see is the man in front of him, who he hates as much as himself.

He's in motion before he even fully comprehends what he means to do, charging back across the girder. From the way Solomon's remaining eye widens in shock, it's the last thing he expected as well.

Kerry grabs at him, claws at his ruined face. He wants to

destroy this man, for Ray, for Les, for Scott and Lorie, for every sex offender who served their time and then found this monster, this predator, waiting for them. His fingers rake bloody furrows through the blackened, raw skin. The gauze over the killer's eye tears away, revealing the oozing crater beneath.

Solomon lets go of the knife and tries to use his good arm to defend himself. Both of them are off balance, wobbling on the beam. Kerry stops trying to shred his face, wraps both arms around the killer's torso, and throws them both to the side far enough for gravity to take over.

The world blurs past. Wind tears at him. He squeezes his eyes shut and holds on to Solomon, intending to ride the man all the way down, but something slams into his side that brings them both to an abrupt halt. Kerry tries to move, but grinding pain shoots through his chest. He looks around, trying to understand how he's still alive, and sees that they've only fallen one floor, onto the metal deck below. The edge is pressed into his stomach as he lays with his lower half hanging over the brink. He's peripherally aware that D'libra is screaming his name; the impact seems to have shattered a number of his ribs, and each breath he draws is agony. Solomon clings to the ledge beside him, his legs kicking in midair as he struggles to keep his grip with one arm.

Kerry tries to pull himself up. There's nothing to grab, nothing to hold on to except slick steel. He slides backward, helpless to stop himself, and slips off the edge.

His wrist is grabbed as a pain-filled cry comes above him. Kerry dangles three stories above the ground. He fights to take a wet, gurgly breath as he looks up.

Solomon has him, using his injured right arm to keep Kerry aloft while he holds onto the edge with his left. He's shaking with the effort, teeth bared in a straining grimace.

"Tell me…you want it," he growls. It sounds like he's pleading. "Say it…and I'll let you go."

Kerry smiles as blood dribbles from the corner of his mouth. "You choose," he rasps. "Take some…responsibility."

"Goddamn you," Solomon snarls.

He pulls, screaming in pain, lifting Kerry an inch at a time. The killer gets Kerry far enough up for his hands to reach the edge of the metal floor before his strength gives. It's not enough though, Kerry is too weak, and drowning as his lungs fill with blood. But, when he lets go, his arms are grabbed yet again, and then D'libra is squatting above him. The girl plants her feet and screams as she uses the muscles in her legs to haul him upward, like an Olympic weightlifter. With her help, he's able to get a knee onto the ledge and then collapses on top of her as they tumble backward.

"You son of a bitch," she gasps, clutching his head to her breast. "Oh, you stupid bastard."

"You'll do it again," Solomon proclaims. The killer is scrabbling at the edge, trying to claw his way up beside them. "You'll see. You're no different. If you don't seek forgiveness, you'll always be a predator."

"Forgiveness…is a waste of breath," Kerry wheezes. He rears back with one leg and kicks the man in his putrid face.

Solomon plunges backward off the deck.

Kerry is unconscious long before he smashes into the bottom.

THIRTY NINE

His real name is Jacob Baldwin.

The police are unable to identify the corpse from finger-prints or DNA, but as soon as Solomon's picture is broadcast on the news—reconstructed digitally from the unburned side of his face—a slew of calls from former coworkers come in. Up until four years ago, he did low-level IT work for a car insurance company, where he was described as 'quiet, intense, but generally well-liked.' Then, from out of the blue, he receives a generous inheritance from the death of his estranged parents—who, by all accounts, he hadn't seen since leaving home at the age of seventeen. The cause of their death was ruled as a car accident…although, even at the time, the incident is investigated as a possible suicide since his father sent them both crashing into a bridge support at eighty miles an hour. It takes a minimal amount of digging by the FBI to discover that said inheritance was most likely garnered in an extensive child pornography ring that the elder Mr. and Mrs. Baldwin were at the center of. With the money in hand, Solomon quit his job and went completely off the radar while he began stalking sex offenders on the registry. During the investigation, Officer Prentiss is never found, but Ray's van is discovered on a plot of rural land left to Solomon by his parents, next to the entrance of 'an underground dungeon,' as police reports put it. The prevailing theory states that this is a space where many children were once molested and abused, before Solomon used it to torture their abusers.

When this information becomes public, it takes only a few hours before social media begins hailing Jacob Baldwin as a hero.

In fact, one Twitter user calls him the real-life Batman, using the money from his dead parents to fight scum while wearing a mask.

Then he suggests that Kerry should be castrated by live rats.

FORTY

Four months after leaving the hospital, Kerry hears the foreman calling him over the drone of the concrete saw.

He raises his head to look across the warehouse floor. His boss—a hefty little beach-ball-of-a-man with fat wrinkles where his eyelids should be—is hurrying toward him down the long row of workstations. Kerry shuts off the equipment, tucks his safety glasses into his pocket, and goes to meet him.

"Denton," the foreman barks, when he gets close enough to speak without yelling. He jerks a thumb over his shoulder at the front office. "You got a visitor."

Kerry gapes at him. The sense of déjà vu is so strong, he expects to find that his clothes have changed into his orange jumpsuit from Wayne Clifford. "Who…who is it?" he stammers.

"Am I your secretary? I don't know, some guy in a suit! But if you go down there, you're on break! I ain't payin you to stand around and gab!"

Kerry thanks the man and walks toward the office on legs that are suddenly numb. All around him, work continues unabated at Concrete Partners Unlimited. His new parole officer might be impatient and perpetually angry, but the man did help him get this job, which is tedious, so loud that his ears ring for hours, and pays enough for him to afford a one bedroom unit at a run down, roach infested, sex-offender-friendly apartment complex. The other employees have also made it clear how they feel about the pedophile in their midst (he doesn't keep his lunch in the break room fridge anymore, that's for sure), but none of that matters to him.

Because next month, after D'libra's petition to the leave the group home is approved, they plan to find a place together.

If they can stop fucking each other's brains out long enough to do so. Kerry has decided that he doesn't care where his new life tracks lead, as long as they get there via D'libra Barnes' vagina.

By the time he reaches the office door, Kerry is shaking. *It's MacCallum in there*, a hysterical part of his brain insists. *He didn't die, and neither did Solomon, and this is all going to start over.*

But, when Kerry looks through the tiny window in the door, he doesn't recognize the officious man standing in front of the reception desk, inspecting the business permits mounted on the wall. His dark gray suit and briefcase scream lawyer though, an idea which makes Kerry's stomach clench. Between Charles Brimhauer and Gerry Stevens, Esq, representatives of the legal profession have a habit of bringing him bad news.

Kerry steps through the door. The man opens his mouth, glances at the glass front doors of the building that lead onto the street as though he wants to bolt through them, then approaches with his hand out. "Mr. Denton, I'm...my name is Daniel Crawley, and..." He glances around the reception area nervously as Kerry takes his hand. At the moment,

they're the only two here. He lowers his voice to finish introducing himself. "You see…I'm one of the lawyers handling
the MacCallum estate."

Kerry halts the handshake mid-pump.

Crawley retrieves his hand and fiddles with his watch while
speaking. "I'm very sorry to approach you at work like this, but
I couldn't find a home address for you. One of the articles in the
paper mentioned that you'd found employment here."

"Should've checked the sex offender registry. It's all on
there, trust me."

Kerry means it as a joke, but Crawley gives a pained grimace and then nods. "Right, of course."

"So…what can I do for you, Mr. Crawley? Don't tell me
good ol' Rob Mac left me something in his will."

"Ah, no. Lord no. He made no secret of the fact that
he had…well, let's say a deep and abiding hatred for you. I
mean, even before he…"

"Had my parole officer murdered, kidnapped two people, and beat the shit out of me? Yeah, I'm well aware of his
affection for me."

The lawyer grows even more uncomfortable at the mention of his deceased client's crimes. He sets his briefcase on
top of the reception desk, undoes the latches, and pauses.
"Mr. Denton, this is highly unethical for me to be here. Bor-
derline illegal. Can I trust that you'll be discreet?"

"Uh…sure."

Crawley doesn't seem convinced, but he opens his briefcase and reaches for a sheet of paper inside. "I came across a
document in the review of Mr. MacCallum's personal effects.
Since he has no valid heirs, the original is likely to be incin-
erated or wind up forgotten in a legal file somewhere, but I
made a photocopy because, well…it's addressed to you."

Kerry accepts the sheet of paper, glances over it...and feels his jaw drop at the sight of his own name in Kayla's handwriting at the top. That familiar fire in his severed finger rekindles as neatly as a struck match.

It hasn't bothered him much since that night at the construction yard. He'd dared to hope that the ghost had been exorcised, but no such luck, apparently.

"You can keep that." Crawley is hurrying to latch his briefcase. He picks it up and heads for the door, saying over his shoulder, "But again, please don't let anyone know where you got it."

"Mr. Crawley?" Kerry calls out as he steps outside on the sidewalk. "Robert MacCallum...your client...he tried to kill me. So why would you...?"

The lawyer grins for the first time. "I wouldn't be an estate lawyer if I didn't believe in honoring the wishes of the dead," he says, and lets the door close.

Kerry stumbles over to the seats in front of the reception desk. His finger is throbbing, the tingling fire working its way up his wrist. He kneads the stump as he sits down, lays the photocopied page across his lap, and begins to read the scrawled cursive.

Dear Kerry,

This is probably a huge waste of my last minutes on earth, considering this letter will never reach you. I know, in my heart, that it'll be thrown in the garbage five minutes after my body is found, but I keep having this daydream that somewhere, somehow, it still ends up in your hands, years from now maybe, like some kind of message-in-a-bottle type situation. Too many movies in my head, I guess. I would've mailed it, like I did all the others, but besides the fact that doing so would give me time to talk myself out of this, last week the great and powerful Rob Mac found one of the letters I was getting ready to send you and put me on extreme house arrest. Looks like you and I are both serving time now. My sentence, which lasts through the rest of the summer (and possibly longer, since he keeps threatening to get private tutors for my senior year), includes no phone, no internet, no friends, no carrier pigeons, absolutely no way that I could possibly get a message to you until he believes that I've 'gotten you out of my system.' Like you're a flu germ or something. He even sets the house alarm 24/7 in case I try to sneak out. The asshole did leave me candles though, so smoke signals aren't entirely out of the question.

I'm stretching this out, aren't I? Trying to put off saying what needs to be said, which is this: I'm so sorry, Kerry. I can imagine what this will do to you. I try to picture you, sitting in your cell, when you find out that I'm dead. I wonder who will tell you. Your mom, I'm betting. I never got to meet her, but from everything you told me, she sounds like a queen.

I know this is the coward's way out. And that's what I am, a coward. Hell, in a few months, I'll be eighteen, and he won't have any power over me anymore. I'll be free to walk out the door…but that scares me as much as staying here for even another day.

Things got worse with him. Before school let out, I wore long sleeves and makeup as thick as pancake batter to hide the bruises. I kept telling myself to hold on a little longer, that eventually you would get out.

I expected you to ride in here on a white horse and take me away from all of it, from him, that we would go far away and start over somewhere like you keep telling me in your letters.

But…it won't be like that. If you truly believe it will, you've watched even more sappy, romantic movies than I have. It could never be the same between us. We lived in a single moment in time, a perfect fairy tale bubble that the real world burst, and look where we ended up.

None of this is an excuse for what I plan to do, and I'm not saying it's your fault. I know you, I know what this will do to you, but please believe me when I tell you that you can't save me. No one can. The fact is, this was probably always going to happen, even if you'd been here. It's stayed with me as long as I can remember, in the back of my mind, an escape hatch from all his bullshit that he could never take away no matter how mad he got.

And the time has come to use it.

I love you, Kerry Denton. You were the one good thing in my life since my mom died. Please don't blame yourself. If I had one wish for you, it would be that you never stop looking for happiness.

Yours until the end of time,

Kayla

P.S. If I had two wishes for you, the second would be that you stop being so clumsy, you fuckface.

Kerry reads the letter, again and again, the words searing into his memory. When he stops, there are tears streaming down his face, and a bittersweet ache in his heart.

Asking for forgiveness might be a waste of breath, but *receiving* it?

That's worth a million days without sunshine.

The ghost of his ring finger agrees as it goes back to sleep.

AFTERWORD

I'm afraid that many people will take this novel as some sort of defense or endorsement of sexual predators. That isn't the case at all. My intent was to write about a group that we have all decided, as a society, that it is all right to demonize. We don't care what they did, we just want to line up and spit on them. But the laws governing sex offenders are so uniform that rarely is any case viewed on an individual basis. You frequently have people whose entire lives are ruined because of one drunken mistake, such as public urination. This is especially relevant in today's MeToo movement, where all it takes is a single accusation to end someone's career.

But suppose they're all guilty. Then the question becomes this: how long do we hold someone accountable for their mistakes? If a person molested a child at the age of 18, served a prison sentence, and is now in their mid-forties and has never committed another such offense, is it fair for them to still be labeled a sexual predator? I'm not saying that we should trust such a person with babysitting our children, but shouldn't they have the ability to walk into a grocery store with their heads held high? Many people—including, I suspect, many of you reading this right now—would say no. You would say they should be shoved down in a hole and left there for the rest of their natural lives. And yet, research shows that such continual ostracizing of offenders is often what causes them to commit such deeds again.

Judgement of another human being should never be taken lightly. That's something we all need to remember, in these divisive times.

As an additional note, I've taken many liberties with how the sex offender registry and ankle monitors work for the purposes of this story. Blame me for the inaccuracies.

Like this novel?

YOUR REVIEWS HELP!

In the modern world, customer reviews are essential for any product. The artists who create the work you enjoy need your help growing their audience. Please visit Goodreads or the website of the company that sold you this novel to leave a review, or even just a star rating. Posting about the book on social media is also appreciated.

About the Author

Russell C. Connor started writing horror at the age of five, and is the author of two short story collections, four eNovellas, and fourteen novels. His work has won two Independent Publisher Awards and a Readers' Favorite Award. He has been a member of the DFW Writers' Workshop since 2006, and served as president for two years. He lives in Fort Worth, Texas with his rabid dog, demented film collection, mistress of the dark, and demonspawn daughter.

His next novel—*The Halls of Moambati*, Volume IV of *The Dark Filament Ephemeris*—will be available in 2021.

www.ingramcontent.com/pod-product-compliance
Lightning Source LLC
Chambersburg PA
CBHW030829110726
47900CB00006B/1807